Jen Holling

My Devilish Scotsman

The MacDonell Brides Trilogy

Pocket Books

New York   London   Toronto   Sydney

This book is a work of fiction. Names, characters, places and incidents are products of the author's imagination or are used fictitiously. Any resemblance to actual events or locales or persons, living or dead, is entirely coincidental.

An *Original* Publication of POCKET BOOKS

 POCKET BOOKS, a division of Simon & Schuster, Inc.
1230 Avenue of the Americas, New York, NY 10020

ISBN-13: 978-0-7434-7107-7
ISBN-10:   0-7434-7107-5

First Pocket Books printing July 2005

10 9 8 7 6 5 4 3 2 1

POCKET and colophon are registered trademarks of Simon & Schuster, Inc.

Interior design by Davina Mock
Cover design by Min Choi; cover art by Alan Ayers; lettering by David Gatti

Manufactured in the United States of America

For information regarding special discounts for bulk purchases, please contact Simon & Schuster Special Sales at 1-800-456-6798 or business@simonandschuster.com.

"If you marry me, you do so understanding that you are *mine*."

His hands tightened on her arms and he stared down at her, eyes hard. "I will not share you."

Gillian tried to twist away from him. He was a fool if he thought he could be rid of her so easily, and since he would not release her, she stopped struggling and met his gaze. "You're not getting rid of me."

A hiss of frustration passed through white teeth as he glared down at her. "You're such a little fool."

Before she could respond to that, his mouth covered hers in a hard kiss of possession that sent her senses reeling. She surrendered immediately, her body softening, melting into his. He released his hold on her arms to wrap his own around her, drawing her against him. Her hands had just come up to touch his face when he shoved her away, holding her at arm's length and staring at her, disconcerted, brows drawn together in a troubled frown.

"I won't share either," Gillian finally said. "Do *you* understand *me*?"

My Devilish Scotsman **is also available as an eBook**

ACCLAIM FOR JEN HOLLING'S BRIDES OF THE BLOODSTONE TRILOGY

Captured by Your Kiss

"Passionate, engrossing. . . . *Captured by Your Kiss* is a book to lose yourself in, falling into the intense emotions of the characters and the harshness of the setting and time period, and letting the complex threads of the plot hold your attention until the last page."
—The RomanceReader.com

"Great depth, drama, and action. . . . A very strong novel that will satisfy readers of the series. You'll be captivated and completely engaged with the myth, the magic, and the romance Ms. Holling has so beautifully created."
—*Romantic Times*

"Sure to captivate. . . . A trilogy full of love and adventure. All three [are] sure to thrill those who enjoy a medieval tale."
—*Romance Reviews Today*

"Ms. Holling creates a romantic tale with characters who stay in your heart long after their story is over. *Captured by Your Kiss* is a gem of a book, and not to be missed. Get your copy today."
—TheWordonRomance.com

"It was hard to catch my breath as I galloped through the pages of *Captured by Your Kiss*. Ms. Holling's plots are so skillfully written that each book of the trilogy seems to melt into the other. The readers feel right at home in the period, enjoying the company of friends, some old, some new."

—*Rendezvous*

"*Captured by Your Kiss* is a fantastic conclusion of this fascinating trilogy. There is adventure, danger, and a beautiful love story."

—ReadertoReader.com

Tamed by Your Desire

"Time stands still as the reader is caught up in the conflict and experiences the excitement of this romantic tale."

—*Rendezvous*

"The clash of wills and biting and dynamic repartee are reminiscent of Shannon Drake's Scottish romances."

—*Romantic Times*

Tempted by Your Touch

"A tender triumph that tempted me to keep reading all night long."

—Teresa Medeiros, author of *A Kiss to Remember*

For Beth, the other sister of my heart
With much love and a special thanks
This one's for you

Prologue

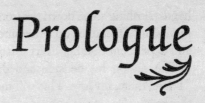

The woman hummed a tune she had heard recently and fancied, as she prepared the final fatal dose of poison for her current husband. Excitement gripped her, anticipation of the long-awaited denouement. She liked to draw it out, to watch them suffer and decline as they looked to her to care for their needs. And she did. Sympathetically. Lovingly.

They deserved her special treatment. Most of them had been very good to her. She worked hard to make their short time together full of happiness.

She brought the steaming cup, poison masked in rich broth, to her husband. He was older than the others, but wealthy and kind. Handsome in a distinguished way, with graying black hair and dark eyes, and a finely muscled form before the poison had wasted the muscle from his bones. He'd reminded her of another man.

The memory soured her pleasure, so she was rather brusque when pressing the broth into her husband's hands, sloshing some down the front of his snowy white nightshirt. He looked up at her uncertainly. So worried and dependent that her heart softened to him.

She sat on his bedside and dabbed up the spill. "There, there, my love. This will make it all better, methinks."

He drank it down. When he was finished, she took the cup from his palsied hands and set it aside.

And then she watched him, waiting. Soon the first signs of the poison began. The skin around his mouth and eyes drew tight. His hands clutched his belly. His gaze jerked to her, eyes bulging with fright.

"That's it," she cooed and slid beneath the blankets, putting her arms around him. "It will only hurt a moment."

His mouth opened and he gasped her name, his body drawing rigid in her arms. His throat worked, expelling garbled words. He fought her embrace, but he was weak and she was strong. Excitement flowed through her, gathering deep in her belly, sending heat and tingling down her thighs. She held her lover tight in her arms as he convulsed, her own pleasure contracting her body in perfect harmony with his. It was beautiful. It always was. But when it was over, she did not feel sated.

It was not enough anymore. There had been a time when she could live happily with a man for years. Sometimes she would take lovers and seek her pleasure there before ending her union. But of late, her marriages grew shorter and shorter. This one had barely lasted a month. She would have to move on; people would suspect.

As she looked down at the still face of her husband, his mouth contorted in pain, eyes wide and staring, she knew it was not her failing, or even her dear husband's. It was the one that got away. He haunted her, still living. She'd failed him and so failed herself.

She pressed a soft kiss to her husband's still-warm lips and decided it was time to set things right.

1

Nicholas Lyon, twelfth earl of Kincreag, raced across the heather, his horse foaming in a flat-out run. He never mistreated his animals, but then never before had he received such a missive as he had on this night. Alan MacDonell of Glen Laire was dying.

This was not exactly startling news. Alan's health had been failing for some time—all knew death would soon take him. Even so, he continued to linger, giving Nicholas hope that his friend would beat the mysterious illness that gripped him. Tonight that hope had been shattered.

He arrived at the loch that surrounded Lochlaire. After handing off their horses to the stable hands, Nicholas and his men clambered into three skiffs and rowed to the castle. The entrance glowed softly from the torches within. The creaking of the rising portcullis echoed in the distance. The night was dark. Quiet. Ominous.

Inside the bowels of Lochlaire, Nicholas leapt onto the stairs that disappeared into the water. The castle was subdued, fires dampened, hall deserted. As if already in mourning. Was he too late? He strode straight to Alan's chambers, misery constricting his chest. Before he could knock, it opened, and Hagan slipped out, shutting the door behind him.

"You came," the big, black-haired Irishman said. Barrel-chested and harsh featured, Hagan cut an imposing figure and was a bulwark shielding Alan from the world.

"You knew I would."

"Aye."

Hagan hesitated, which was odd. Nicholas had never known Hagan to be unsure of himself. But then Alan's illness had taken its toll on everyone, most especially Hagan, who had become nursemaid to Alan.

"I must see him," Nicholas said and pushed past, opening the door.

A candle flickered on a table near the bed. A woman sat at the table, a book open before her. Her voice, soft and feminine as a dove's wings, glided softly over him, easing the crushing fear in his chest. Candlelight bathed the delicate line of her jaw, but the rest of her was in shadows. Alan's deerhound lay at her feet, its nose between its paws. It did not lift its head; it merely shifted its strange, cloudy eyes to look at Nicholas.

She stopped her reading and raised her head. Her eyes and hair appeared black in the gloom, but Nicholas remembered them well. Eyes the soft gray of a Highland sky after a storm. Hair a rich sable, thick with curls. The candlelight was full on her face now, illuminating the alabaster texture of her skin, so fine that it shone with a radiance he'd only seen before in paintings of the Madonna.

Another of Alan's duplicitous daughters. Gillian was her name. The meekest of the three. He should have insisted on her from the beginning—then maybe he and Alan would not be estranged.

"You came," she said, fine brows arched in surprise.

As if he wouldn't have. He ignored her and went straight to the bed. He couldn't bring himself to look at Alan—not just yet—and so he busied himself with lighting the candelabra beside the bed. He felt Gillian's gaze on him, searching, questioning. It was this one that Alan had tried to foist on him after his oldest daughter had run off with some renegade knight, practically leaving Nicholas at the altar. It was a woman who had caused this rift between Nicholas and his best friend. Women were the authors of all his problems. He was finished with them—especially with the MacDonell sisters.

He took a deep breath, then finally allowed his gaze to rest on Alan, bracing himself to see gaunt cheeks and a deathly gray pallor. His brow lowered in surprise.

Alan was sleeping—quite peacefully, it seemed. He'd clearly gained weight in the past month, and there was a healthy pink tinge to his cheeks above his white-streaked auburn beard.

Nicholas stared at him a long moment, his eyes moving to Alan's chest, where he watched the gentle rise and fall for several moments before turning abruptly to Gillian.

"What is this? I was told he was dying."

Gillian seemed frozen in her chair, hands folded primly in her lap. A slow blush climbed from her neck, staining her cheeks. Too terrified of him to speak? He had that effect on many people. The devil earl, they called him—murderer of wives and children.

"He is." Her answer came out in a rush of breath just as he turned away. He turned back quizzically.

"He has been dying for months. You know that."

"Aye, but that's not what the letter I received said."

Her lashes fluttered nervously, hands gripped tightly in her lap. "What did it say?"

She was lying. She knew what it said. He gave her a narrow look before returning his attention to the bed. Her skirts rustled as she came to the bedside.

"What did it say?" she repeated, her voice strong and steady.

"As if you don't know."

She let out a small breath. "I do not!"

His mouth twisted with disbelief, but he said, "The letter claimed he was at death's door. That this is it—he's to die before first light."

"Oh." She looked at her father askance.

Nicholas snorted softly and glanced away dismissively. "Wake up, old man."

Before he could shake Alan awake, a small, pale hand touched his sleeve. "Wait." Though she looked meek, a thread of command ran through her voice. She met his gaze. "Why did you make that noise?"

"What noise?"

Color slowly filled her cheeks again, and she dropped her gaze. Her chin immediately popped up, as though she forced herself to be bold. "You think I am lying."

Nicholas's mouth curved. "I know you are."

She blinked at him, her mouth slightly ajar, exposing a line of small, white teeth. "But I am not! I knew nothing of a letter, only that you were summoned. I did not know why. Father has been trying to bring you here for months!"

Summoned. He should be insulted. A mere chieftain did not summon an earl, but then nothing about his relationship with Alan had ever been normal.

"Aye, letters and letters in which he tried to foist you off on me. I've had a taste of the MacDonell idea of fidelity, and that was quite enough, thank you. Your father is fortunate we are friends. I could have forced the betrothal, or demanded restitution for his default. But I did not."

"He offered restitution." She drew herself up taller and squared her shoulders, though her chin trembled and she nervously twirled a silver ring on her finger. "Me."

Nicholas looked her up and down. She was a beauty, all soft curves, but he did not exaggerate when he said he'd had his fill of duplicitous women. He wanted nothing more to do with MacDonell women.

"I'm not interested. I never was."

Her throat tightened, and her strong stance slowly sagged. She looked away from him, to her father.

He felt a small stab of remorse until she said, "My

sister is not as horrible as you believe. She did not even know you. Did not know anything about you but the rumors. She entered the betrothal in good faith, not expecting to fall in love with the knight who delivered her."

"Aye, it was quite inconvenient for all parties."

Gillian nodded quickly. "I respect your own . . . disappointment, my lord, but—"

"You are mistaken if you think me disappointed. Indeed, I am overjoyed to have discovered her true nature before being tied to her for life."

The corners of Gillian's mouth tightened, and she darted him an irritated look. She returned her gaze to her father and took a deep breath. "It is unfair of you to judge me by my sister's actions. I am not like her . . . we weren't even raised together."

That was true. After their mother was burned for witchcraft, Alan sent his daughters away for their safety, each hidden from the world and from each other. For twelve years.

Gillian raised her chin again, fixing him with a determined, gray stare. "I would be a good countess."

He rubbed his chin with his thumb and studied her, amused and intrigued by her false bravado. "And this has nothing to do with your betrothal to the Frenchman?"

Her expressive skin flushed. "Well. Aye. Of course."

"My heart palpitates. I am the lesser of two dreadful fates. I am thus wooed."

Her brows drew together. "Wooed? I am not wooing you!"

"Obviously."

"My lord!" she said, a shrill edge to her voice. "You never speak, and when you do, you make no sense. Women do not woo."

"We don't know the same women."

She seemed completely bewildered. In truth, in his amusement at teasing her, he'd forgotten for a moment the deceit that had brought him here. Her eyes widened with comprehension, and she took a deep, shaky breath, her ample bosom rising.

"I understand. You have many other opportunities. I have been impertinent. Forgive me."

He raised a hand to stop her, but it was too late—she'd scurried to the door and was gone. He stared at the closed door several seconds, discomfited. He had not intended to upset her. He shook his head at himself. He didn't want to marry her anyway, so what did he care?

He returned his attention to the bed and found Alan watching him. How long had the old fool been awake?

Nicholas moved closer to the bed. "I nearly killed my horse to get here. Yet you look quite well . . . considering." He did not look well now that Nicholas examined him closer without the distraction of Gillian. He looked nothing like the good friend Nicholas had known most of his life. The man in bed was a pale shade of his former self. But still, it was an improvement over the last time Nicholas had been here.

"Really?" Alan said, pleased. "Nearly killed your horse? Well, and here I didn't think you'd even come."

"Clearly you'll live to see the daylight. So why am I here?"

Alan looked a bit abashed, but he met Nicholas's eyes directly. "I knew of no other way to bring you back here. Your replies to my letters were distant . . . and I could not come to you."

A heavy cloud of dread enveloped Nicholas. He'd been afraid of this. He owed Alan his life—a debt the chieftain had never called—and yet Nicholas felt the weight of it, knowing Alan's time was short.

The deerhound pushed past, laying its snout on the bed as if to solicit affection, watching Nicholas with those strange eyes.

"Now that I'm here," Nicholas said carefully, "I'm glad I came. I have much to say . . . but on the matter of marriage, I've not changed my mind."

Alan stroked the hound's wiry fur. "But if you'd just get to know her. Spend some time—"

"No." Nicholas's voice was forceful, but he felt himself faltering.

Damnation. Nicholas would not be forced into marriage. He'd given in to Alan grudgingly the first time because of the life debt—protecting Alan's daughters had seemed fair payment of it. Scotland was a dangerous place these days, with women burning for witchcraft nearly every other day. Alan's first wife, Lillian, had been burned for witchcraft, and it was said that his daughters were fey, too. There were few prospects for women carrying the taint of sorcery. Alan had asked Nicholas if he would marry his eldest daughter, Isobel, knowing Nicholas's title and honor would protect Isobel and her sisters. Nicholas had needed a wife, but the suitable women in Scotland, though eager enough to become countesses, had not appealed to him. He'd accepted that he might never marry again. There had been relief in acceptance, partnered with loneliness, but he could have lived with that.

And then Alan had offered him Isobel.

She was the oldest and practically an heiress. Should Alan's half brother, Roderick, die without issue, as it seemed he would despite years of plowing the barren fields of three wives, Glen Laire would pass to Isobel's husband. And so they had been betrothed . . . until she'd run off with some Highland knight.

Alan sighed deeply. "I'm sorry I deceived you. But it wasn't a complete untruth. I don't know how it is I live still. Most days I cannot even eat. Rose forces water down my throat with her disgusting concoctions. I haven't walked on my own legs in three months. I tried, yesterday, and fell. Hagan scolded me, then turned Rose loose on me." Alan shuddered. His eyes turned up to Nicholas's, mournful in the folds of loose skin. "I don't know how I can go on like this . . . I can't see it getting any better. I'm still here because of Rose and her healing, but even she cannot fathom what is wrong or how to end it. And this . . . this existence . . ." He closed his eyes and swallowed. "Well, it's unacceptable. I want to see Gillian well married. Then I can go in peace."

Nicholas stared down at his friend, vague alarm quickening his pulse. "It's a sin, what you speak of."

Alan's gaze stabbed him. "You're one to speak of sins. Besides, is it not a mercy to end a beast's suffering? Why is a man any different?"

There was a stool nearby. Nicholas hooked his foot

around the leg and drew it near, lowering himself onto it so he was closer to Alan's level.

"What of Rose? You've said she's the most willful of the lot and she's determined to heal you."

"Rose fancies herself in love with her betrothed, Jamie MacPherson. But she refuses to marry him so long as I am ill. She has committed herself to nursing me to the end. My death will free her to be happy."

"How selfless of you." Nicholas shook his head in mock amazement. "I never thought I'd say this, but you're a coward."

Alan's green eyes fired at the insult, and he seemed ready to leap out of bed to challenge Nicholas. But then the fire died, and he laughed softly.

"You think to shame me from my path? Fine, then. I can use shame, too. You owe me a life. Let it be my daughter's."

Nicholas closed his eyes and lowered his head to his hands. The dread that had pressed at his chest since he'd arrived settled in his gut. He couldn't bear to hear these things. He did not want his friend to die. Did not want to do what Alan asked of him—and yet he was bound by their friendship and by the debt. He'd known he would be when he'd answered the missive by racing here. Had known, though he'd not admitted it to himself until this moment, that he would agree to whatever Alan asked. He had no choice.

Gillian paused outside her father's chambers, her hand still on the door latch, ears straining, but with the door closed, she could hear nothing. She pressed her ear to the wood.

"What do you think you're doing, Miss Gillian?"

She gave a little yelp of surprise and turned to look guiltily at Hagan. The enormous Irishman stood nearby, waiting patiently.

"What does it look like I'm doing?"

She glanced around the hall but saw no one except two small children playing in a far corner. A vague headache throbbed sullenly in her temples. She rubbed absently at it, then turned back to the door, pressing her ear close again.

"Now stop that, Miss Gillian," Hagan said, a frown in his voice, but he made no move to stop her.

"I must hear what happens!"

Hagan caught her arm and pulled her away from the door. "You've been away too long, lass. You should know better than to eavesdrop. I'll be telling your uncle if you don't behave yourself."

Gillian sighed. Hagan was right. She *had* been away too long. The only reason Alan had brought them home now was to see them married before he died. It had been a shock for all of them, as they'd not even known their father was ill. She'd lived in the Lowlands for the past twelve years. Glen Laire did not feel like home. Home was somewhere else, with other people. She'd have known if her foster father was dying, or even if he'd had a touch of ague. She'd lived more than half her life with the Hepburns. She knew nothing of Glen Laire and the MacDonells anymore. And yet her sisters had slid back into it so easily, as if they'd been born to it, and she hadn't.

"Now be gone until your father sends for you," Hagan said sternly.

Gillian went in search of her remaining sister. Isobel was in the west, living with her new husband, Sir Philip Kilpatrick. Only Rose and Gillian were left, and not for much longer. Kincreag had been Gillian's last hope. If he didn't marry her, it was the old Frenchman. Her father insisted. And besides, no one else would have her. It was laughable, really, though she couldn't muster the will to laugh at it. She was the only one of the three sisters who had not inherited their mother and father's magic. Alan was not a powerful witch, but he had a shine. Lillian had been a great witch, and Isobel and Rose were both gifted witches. Gillian was nothing. She didn't even look like a MacDonell, with her brown hair and gray eyes. And yet she still carried the MacDonell taint. No one would touch her except the Frenchman.

Isobel and Rose were so fortunate. Isobel had married for love, and Rose would wed a man she'd known since they were children. There was fondness there, potential for deep love and contentment. Gillian knew nothing of her suitors except one was old and spoke no Scots, and the other, though relatively young and handsome, was supposed to be a murderer. But he didn't want her anyway.

She found Rose in their chambers, mashing something in a small stone bowl. Her slender back was to Gillian, her white sleeves rolled up so the taut muscles of her forearms were visible. Thick, shimmering auburn hair hung sleekly down her back to her waist and trembled with her efforts.

"He's here," Gillian announced, throwing herself on the bed.

The grinding and mashing stopped. "So he came. I didn't think he would—not after what Isobel did. Will he marry you?"

Gillian sat up and stared at her sister gloomily. Rose was not exactly beautiful, but she was striking. She had the fierce features of a Viking, broad forehead and narrow nose. A wide mouth and catlike dark blue eyes. Her body was lean and strong. Gillian had not yet seen her on horseback but deduced she was probably a skilled horsewoman. Men's eyes followed her—several MacDonell lads seemed quite taken with her, though Rose was oblivious to anything but her healing.

"No. I put forth my case just as you instructed. I was strong and confident. I looked him in the eyes, just like you told me to. He was unmoved. He finds me ugly. And fat. And stupid. He looked at me like I was an unexpected worm in his apple." Gillian sighed and dropped her head to her hands. "It's to France with me."

"You are not fat nor ugly nor stupid, and you know it. If he is blind enough to think so, then I say good riddance to the earl of Kincreag."

Gillian wanted to agree, wanted to reject him as he'd so clearly rejected her. But she couldn't. She wanted to be a countess. Wanted it more than she'd known. The disappointment weighed her down. If she were a countess, she'd finally be somebody. Countesses had duties.

Countesses were respected. Countesses mattered. She felt certain that when she became one, she would be transformed into someone strong and brilliant, just like her sisters. She might not have magic, but she could have that.

And Kincreag was no old Frenchman. He was young and virile and handsome. Her insides tightened at the memory of his smile when he'd teased her. She pressed her fingers into her eyes. He'd not smiled at her or teased her. He'd smirked at her and mocked her. Her shoulders drooped further.

Rose's hand touched Gillian's shoulder, and she looked up. "Don't despair. I'll think of something."

Rose's words filled Gillian with more unhappiness. It was *her* life. She wanted to be master of it, but she didn't know how. If only she could be a countess. . . . She wished she could think of some way to win Kincreag. But she was out of ideas.

Rose dropped onto the bed beside Gillian and took her hand. There was nothing left to say. Gillian knew her sister was thinking furiously, auburn brows drawn together, blue eyes narrowed and distant. Rose was quick and clever. If she had no schemes, all truly was lost.

There was a sharp knock on the door. Gillian stood wearily and answered it. A man stood in the hall toying nervously with a loose thread in the crest upon his shoulder. The earl of Kincreag's crest.

He dropped his hand and straightened importantly. "Lord Kincreag wishes a word with Gillian MacDonell."

2

Gillian's palms were damp as she stood outside the door of Lord Kincreag's chambers at Lochlaire. He was a frequent visitor and had his own apartments, though he'd only been here once since Gillian had returned home. What could he possibly want to speak with her about? Perhaps he wanted to apologize for being so snide earlier. But that made no sense. He was an earl. It was unlikely he even realized how rude he'd sounded.

She took several deep breaths and raised her fist, but she did not knock—only held it suspended, thinking. Rose had coached her some more before she'd come, reminding her that this was her opportunity to somehow win him over. She must charm him. Her stomach lurched with fear and something else, something foolish and exciting. She pressed her other hand against her belly, struggling for calm. *Charming. Be charming.*

As she considered her most charming smile and stance, the door opened. Kincreag stood in the doorway

staring down at her, black brows drawn into a severe
frown. He was dressed entirely in black. Black breeches
and a black leather doublet. Black boots. The only color
was the white of his shirt, open at the throat, a bright
beacon against his dark skin. Gillian stared at the shadowy hollow where his collar parted, absurdly afraid to
meet his gaze.

"Mistress MacDonell? Are you unwell?"

She forced herself to look up, to meet the black eyes
that both frightened and fascinated. He was coldly handsome, his features at once savage and refined in their
beauty. His skin was so dark that Gillian and her sisters
had speculated about his heritage—could there be Spanish Moor in his family? Or perhaps something even more
exotic—a Turk? His face lacked the narrow, angular lines
of the aristocracy. He looked more the warrior, with an
unrelenting jaw and a strong, slightly crooked nose. Thick
black brows shadowed eyes even darker than his hair,
which was devil-black and rich as silk. It was tied at his
nape, but an errant lock fell across his high, clear brow.

Gillian swallowed and forced herself to smile. "I'm
quite well, my lord. You sent for me?"

His freezing gaze passed over her, then behind her to
the empty corridor. "You came alone?"

"Aye."

He sighed and shook his head slightly.

"Was I to bring someone?"

"You and your sisters have no sense of what is proper
for a woman. Well, at least we're betrothed." And he
turned away, his tall figure disappearing into the room,
merging with the darkness.

Gillian's heart thundered in her throat. *Betrothed.* She felt nailed to the threshold, unable to move forward. He was inside, part of the darkness. Had he been sitting alone in the dark? Seconds later, the glow of candlelight grew stronger so that she could see.

She'd never been in these rooms. They were nearly as large as her father's chambers and just as finely furnished. Tapestries decorated the walls and soft Turkish carpets covered the floor.

She took a hesitant step forward, then another, until she was just inside the doorway. He stood at the cold fireplace, his back to her. He was so very big. She'd noted his great height when he'd been in her father's room, looming over the bed. It wasn't just his length but the breadth of his shoulders, too. Even without the remote sternness of his features, he intimidated. And she was betrothed to him.

Her heart leapt with alarm. They were to be married. Why was she suddenly terrified? It was what she wanted!

He did not speak, and the silence in the room grew heavy. Gillian twisted her ring. "Betrothed, my lord?" Though she'd spoken softly, her voice seemed to crash through the room. When he made no indication that he'd heard her, she moved closer. "My lord? Why?"

"Does it matter?"

"Aye, of course it matters."

He turned then, his gaze touching her, but with no more interest than he displayed as he surveyed the rest of the room. "Alan knew that if he could just get me here, I would give in to him. So his plan worked."

She frowned, not quite liking the resignation in his voice. But what else had she expected? "You're an earl. You can do whatever you want."

His brow twitched, his face settling into condescending lines. "Is that what you think?"

Gillian just stared at him, wide-eyed. He did not seem angry . . . exactly. He thought she was silly, childish. She swallowed and determined to appear more mature.

"My thanks, my lord, for agreeing to marry me."

He gave her an odd look, as if he didn't believe she was truly grateful. "You should have married your Frenchman, at least he'd be dead soon."

He turned away, leaving her blinking and contemplating his obliquely threatening statement. He went to a table and sat down, smoothing a parchment in front of him. Gillian had not been dismissed, and so she lingered, unsure of herself. There was no candle on the table where he sat, so she fetched one, lit it at the candelabra, then set it on the table beside him. He did not thank her or even acknowledge her.

His quill scratched across the parchment. Gillian stared at his hands as he wrote. They were strong hands, dark and lean. She imagined them touching her in affection, and she wondered if they ever would. The last time she'd seen him he'd been very neat and well groomed. Tonight he was a bit disheveled, his thick black hair escaping from the thong at his nape. She wished to repair it, to tenderly smooth back the lock that surely impaired his vision, though he did not seem to notice. Although she wished this, she didn't dare touch him; the very thought caused her to blush with mortification as she imagined his response. How strange to marry a man she feared touching.

He put down the quill and stood. "Sign it."

Gillian moved to the table and sat on the stool he'd just vacated. His handwriting was bold, with long, lush strokes. She read the document he'd prepared, heart pounding.

She looked up at him, confused. "I've never read a betrothal contract before, but surely this cannot be correct."

"It's not common, but it is correct."

Gillian held his gaze, waiting for him to say more, but he just stared down at her with those black eyes, arms crossed over his wide chest, waiting.

Gillian licked her lips and looked down at the contract. Her belly churned. She toyed with the quill but did not sign. "This is unnecessary, my lord. I will not elope as my sister did, you have my word."

"Nevertheless, I'll not marry you unless you sign it."

Gillian contemplated ripping his contract in half and just walking away. But she didn't, of course. She never did things like that, things Rose or Isobel would do. Fury clenched her belly tight as she stared blindly at the words. The contract specified a nonconsummation clause, as well as the distribution of her dowry if she ever tried to terminate the union (she would be penniless). But the worst was the stipulation that if she was ever unfaithful, she faced imprisonment, the forfeiture of ever seeing any children they produced, and the possibility of other punishments, depending on the circumstances.

She would never do such a thing, so she was not worried about the sentence ever being carried out. But it was galling to have her integrity questioned because of something her sister or his late wife had done. She shouldn't submit to such terms. Rose wouldn't. Gillian dipped the quill in ink a few times but still did not sign.

"Is it . . . legal?" she asked, annoyed at the uncertainty in her voice.

"It will be when you sign it."

Her lips thinned. "I'm under duress."

He let out a short, sarcastic laugh. "I'm not forcing you to wed me. If it's what you wish, those are my terms." He nodded to the contract.

Gillian exhaled loudly through her nose and glared at him. "It is bad luck to start the marriage on so little trust."

"Bad luck is the only luck I have with women, Mistress MacDonell. Now sign the damn contract or don't. Either way, let's be through with this. I have other business to attend."

"You don't have to swear at me," she muttered through clenched teeth. So she was inconveniencing him now. For a red, fuzzy moment she couldn't remember why it was she'd wanted to marry him. Then it flooded back to her, diffusing some of her anger. Frenchman. Countess. Her quill moved to the bottom of the parchment and hovered there.

"You *can* write?" he asked.

Gillian looked up at him, her face taut with suppressed fury. "I can write, my lord. My mother taught me when I was—"

"Fine. Then sign."

Gillian's mouth snapped shut. She took a deep breath and started to sign the blasted betrothal contract. But the tip of the quill barely touched the parchment before she withdrew it again, leaving a tiny black dot behind. She couldn't bring herself to do it.

"You'll not have bad luck this time, my lord. I vow it."

His gaze moved slowly from the parchment to her face, his brow twitching slightly. "Let us hope not." When she only stared back at him, trying very hard to look trustworthy, he gestured impatiently at the contract.

Gillian twirled the quill, pressing onward. She had nothing to lose now, since she did not intend to sign the contract. "But wouldn't it be better to know your wife remained faithful out of love and loyalty to you, rather than fear of dire punishment?"

"That doesn't concern me. What concerns me is your behavior."

Gillian shook her head and set the quill down, defeated. He really was a devil earl. Perhaps he had planned this all along so he could tell Alan that at least he'd tried—she was the one who'd refused to sign the contract.

"I won't sign this. It's not fair."

"Life is not fair, Mistress MacDonell."

"What if you are the unfaithful one? Shouldn't you be subject to the same penalties? Once you tire of me, you could claim I did all sorts of things and lock me away. Who would believe me? It's only fair I have a modicum of protection."

He crossed his arms over his chest and stared through her, eyes narrowed. There was no sense in reasoning with him. He didn't care.

She sighed and stood. "Forgive me for wasting more of your time." She couldn't keep the bitterness from her voice and didn't try.

She was almost to the door when he called out, "Wait." Something different colored his voice, something relenting and perhaps even regretful. She felt it from her neck to her heels, a tingling of hope.

He sat at the table again, taking another parchment from the small stack on the table. "Burn this." He handed her the contract she'd just refused to sign and began writing again. His brow was smooth, but it was clear he was in deep concentration.

Gillian started a fire in the fireplace and used the horrid contract as kindling. Her hands shook, amazed she'd been so bold—and that it had somehow worked! The new contract took longer to write than the first, and he paused often, staring meditatively at the parchment before writing furiously again.

After nearly an hour of silence except for the scratching of the quill, he sat back, squaring his shoulders and tilting his neck, stretching. He set down the quill with a hint of satisfaction.

"There," he said. "That should satisfy your sense of justice."

Gillian moved behind him to read it over his shoulder. It was quite a bit longer than the last and included some things he'd apparently forgotten to put in the first one. But the most significant difference was the terminology. Everything applied to both of them equally.

She looked down at him, pleased. He sat very still, and she realized she'd leaned against his back at some point in her reading. Her hand rested on his shoulder. She could feel the warmth of his body through his clothing and was surprised by it. She'd imagined him to be cold, like marble. He stared hard across the room, at the fireplace, deep in thought.

"Thank you, my lord," she said softly.

His head turned a fraction toward her voice, black lashes lowering as he looked toward her, but not at her. Her heart's tempo increased as she studied his profile, the faint shadow of black whiskers hugging his jaw. How would it feel? Scratchy? Smooth? Her fingers twitched against his shoulder. He did not move or speak, and a sense of awkwardness descended.

"Shall I sign it?" she asked, moving away from him so he could stand.

And he did, the moment she removed her hand from him, as if her touch had held him captive. She sat down and quickly signed beside his signature. She shook sand over the entire document, pouring the excess back into the bowl.

"You're dismissed," he said, his back to her.

The spark of warmth she'd begun to feel toward him sputtered out. But she didn't leave. He was an earl. She must become accustomed to his brusque manner if they were to live together.

"When is the wedding?"

He turned, frowning his displeasure. "I know not."

"Should we not set a date? My father wishes to see us wed before he . . . before he . . ." She couldn't finish. Couldn't force the words through her constricted throat. Couldn't speak about her father dying, though it was a reality they'd all come to accept.

The look he gave her was very odd, enigmatic and thoughtful. "I know. That's why I think we should draw this out indefinitely."

Gillian blinked. "To what purpose?"

After a lengthy pause, he said, "To know one another better."

If Gillian had believed him, such an answer would have pleased her. However, the way he said it made her believe he was formulating an excuse, rather than giving a legitimate reason.

She looked back down at the contract before her. There was something new he'd added in this version. If either of them came to find the other unsuitable before consummation, they could part ways with no consequences. Gillian had thought it odd, considering all the other penalties for even the suggestion of disloyalty, but now she saw it for what it was. He meant to drag this betrothal out as long as possible—past her father's death. And when her father finally passed away, he would declare her unsuitable and be done with the whole affair.

She stood abruptly. "I know what you're doing."

A black brow arched. "Do you now?"

Her palms were sweaty and her heart raced, but she would say this. "You truly are as soulless as everyone says if you believe you're somehow outwitting a dying man. Do you think he'll not know, just because he's dead? If you don't want to marry me, then just say so."

"I don't want to marry you."

Gillian could think of no response; she just stood there, hands fisted at her sides, speechless by his admission and furious with herself for goading him into admitting it.

He walked slowly toward her, his black eyes taking in every nuance of her expression. "But I have every intention of following through."

"Then why the lengthy betrothal? I'm not a child that needs to reach maturity. I'm two and twenty."

"And eager to get on with it, aye?"

She ignored the suggestive sneer in his voice. "Aye— I am. For my father's sake."

"You're too selfless," he said, a sardonic tilt to his mouth. She inhaled sharply as his finger trailed along her jaw, the warmth nearly singeing her with surprise. "Sacrificing so much to make your father happy."

With some effort, Gillian jerked her face away and stepped back. He dropped his hand, watching her with what appeared to be mild amusement, though she couldn't be certain. It chafed that he was right. He knew she wanted to marry him—and how selfish her reasons were.

"You're right, of course. I want this marriage more than you do." When he turned away from her, practically smirking, she grabbed his arm. He stared down at her hand on his sleeve, clearly unused to being handled by anyone. "But it's not about you. It's about my family. I want to be here in Scotland rather than far away, across a sea." Her declaration was met with cold silence. She pressed on, frustrated. "It's clear from your contract you expect the worst from me, to be rid of me soon enough." She shook her head gravely. "But I will not find you unsuitable, nor will I ever be unfaithful. I will be so bloody loyal you'll *never* be rid of me."

There was a bored glaze to his eyes when he said, "Are you finished?" He glanced at his sleeve again where she gripped it, his brows raising patiently.

She squeezed his arm harder for a moment before releasing it. "Am I not even allowed to touch you? Mayhap you should add that to the contract, too—severe penalties for touching without permission."

He stared down at her, hands on his narrow hips, his eyes shadowed. "You are welcome to touch me at will, mistress."

His suggestive tone sent shivers racing down her spine. It came to her of a sudden—how she had spoken to him. The rush of anger faded, and in its place was only confusion. What did the infernal man want? He seemed far more interested in her when she was as rude as he was, and somehow that just seemed wrong to her.

He continued to watch her through dark, heavy-lidded eyes, as if he expected her to do something more. Touch him, perhaps?

"Uhm . . . that's good, then," she said and quickly took her leave before he noticed the hot flush suffusing her skin.

3

Over the next several days Gillian saw the earl only twice. She suspected this was intentional and that the earl was purposely avoiding her. She wondered if she should attempt to spend time with him, since that *was* his excuse for drawing out the betrothal. But the thought of forcing her company on him made her cringe. Besides, her father's health had deteriorated again, and Kincreag's company cheered him.

Rose kept Gillian busy reading from her library of crumbling books, searching for some clue to their father's illness. Gillian's help was limited, as her education was not as thorough as Rose's had been. Many of the manuscripts were written in French and Latin, languages Gillian couldn't even speak, let alone read. She knew her Scots and Gaelic, and could write them, too, but that was all.

They sat in their father's study, a small, book-lined room adjacent to his bedchamber, poring over hand-sewn books. Gillian had a small stack beside her, while Rose's stack towered. Their father's deerhound, Broc, lay at Gillian's feet, sleeping.

An entire candelabra blazed beside her, but still her eyes watered and stung as she peered at the handwritten manuscripts.

"What about this?" she said, her finger trailing down the page. "The author writes about a man with 'extreme lethargy' and 'strange skin discolorations.'"

Rose got up from her stool opposite to stand behind Gillian, reading silently over her shoulder. She shoved Broc with her foot, and the dog whined but refused to move.

"Good work," Rose said, taking the volume and returning to her seat.

Gillian straightened. "That's it? Does it have a cure?"

Rose shook her head. "No, the patient died."

Gillian's shoulders slumped as she reached for another manuscript. "Why are all these handwritten? Have the authors never heard of a printing press?"

Rose glanced up and smiled. "There was no printing press when many of these were written—and even if there was, most of these are the personal diaries of healers and witches. Why would they have them printed?"

"How did you get them?"

"Many were Mother's. She left them to me, of course. Others I've collected over the years. And the rest were given to me by the healer on Skye I trained with."

Gillian surveyed the scores of books stacked on the table and floor around them, impressed. Surely in all of these healers' experiences someone had encountered their father's illness.

She spied a letter sticking out of a book. "Has Jamie written you again?" Rose's betrothed was forever writing her letters.

Rose fingered the edge of the letter. "No. This is a letter I'm writing to the Wizard of the North. Have you heard of him?"

"Aye, I've heard some things. Strathwick, aye? Didn't the Sinclairs try to hunt him down a few months ago to try him for witchcraft, but he disappeared?"

Rose nodded, eyes shining as she stared across the table at Gillian. "They say he turned himself into a wolf. He is a powerful witch. More powerful than Mother was. It's said he can heal by merely putting his hands on you." Rose looked down at her own hands, her face tight with suppressed frustration. "Not like mine. Mine only tell me what's wrong but guarantee no cures. I must find the right remedy. Luckily I've a head for such things. But with Father, they tell me nothing." Rose frowned, her eyes far away, hands fisted on the table.

"What are you thinking?" Gillian asked warily.

Rose looked around the room, as if afraid they had an eavesdropper, then leaned forward conspiratorially. "I've asked him to come to Lochlaire."

Gillian looked at her in astonishment. "And do you really think he'll come? He's safer in the north—further south more witches are burned."

Rose sat back, her shoulders slumping. "I know. He hasn't written me back, anyway."

Gillian reached across the table and covered her sister's hand. "I'm sorry, Rose. I know how hard you work to heal father . . . but . . . if you cannot . . . you mustn't blame yourself. You've done more than anyone—"

"No!" Rose jerked her hand away and stood. "There has to be something more. There's no sense to this . . . this malady. It responds to nothing. When he improves, I don't know why! When he fails—I canna understand it, either. It's *never* like this. Never am I so completely impotent . . . even when I lose a patient—"

Rose stopped abruptly, staring at the door. Gillian had been watching her sister sympathetically, wishing there were some way to ease this burden she carried. She followed her sister's distracted gaze until it rested on their uncle Roderick.

He stood in the open door, his muscular frame filling the width of it. His long red hair was pulled back and secured at his nape. He wore Lowland riding clothes—leather breeks and a fine leather mantle.

"Uncle Roderick!" Gillian cried, jumping up and running to the door. "When did you return?" He'd been on some errand in the east.

He gave her a quick hug and peck on the cheek before turning his censorious gaze back to Rose. "Could you be a bit quieter? Your da and I can hear every word you say."

Color flamed in Rose's cheeks as she turned away, muttering something beneath her breath. She shot Gillian a look before sitting back down to her books.

Roderick gazed at Rose's rigid back, his ruddy brow

creased with worry. "Your sister is right. You're being too hard on yourself. The best physicians in Scotland have seen your father, and none of them know what to do. As for the Northern Wizard, we don't want him here. He'll bring naught but trouble." He paused, as if waiting for a response, but Rose feigned interest in her books, ignoring Roderick completely. He sighed and shook his head, giving Gillian a raised-brow look.

He smiled suddenly, his blue eyes crinkling at the corners. "I've some good news, though. I've brought back the healer Lord Kincreag sent for several months ago—the one from Spain. He's an infidel, mind you, but we've tried everything else, aye? What have we to lose?"

"Indeed!" Gillian said, pleased that Lord Kincreag had done such a thing.

"Come, he's examining your father now." To Rose he said, "Maybe he'll teach you something new, aye?"

When Roderick was gone, Gillian scowled at her sister. "What is the matter with you? You were very rude to Uncle Roderick."

Rose waved this away impatiently. "We've been fighting about the Wizard of the North for weeks now. He thinks it's too dangerous. I don't."

"He's probably right. Maybe you should forget about this wizard. I have a bad feeling about it."

"Well, if you were Isobel I might heed your bad feelings, but since you're not, I think I'll be writing the wizard another letter."

If Rose had slapped her, it couldn't have hurt worse. Isobel was a seer. She could foretell the future or see the past by touching things. Rose's reminder that Gillian was an outsider in her own family stung.

"I'm sorry," Rose said, immediately abashed and looking at Gillian anxiously. "I shouldn't have said that." She sighed, covering her face with her hands. "I know Uncle Roderick means well, but he doesn't understand, and neither do you. I think this man can help Da."

"Then write him," Gillian said coolly, still wounded from Rose's remark. "I'll not stop you, or inform on you."

Before Rose could say anything else, Gillian left the study and entered her father's bedchamber.

Several people crowded around the bed. Gillian's eyes were drawn first to Lord Kincreag. He stood back from the rest, arms crossed over his chest, watching the proceedings with his customary frown in place. He nodded to Gillian in greeting. His enigmatic eyes lingered on her a moment before returning to the bed.

Hagan and Roderick were both there, warily watching the strange little man who leaned over Alan. Encouraged by Kincreag's greeting, Gillian hesitantly moved to stand beside him.

The healer was an Arab—Gillian had seen paintings and woodcuts of them in histories of the Crusades. A cloth was wrapped around his head, so that his hair was completely covered. He wore colorful robes and pointed shoes, and his beard was long and black. He was smaller than she was. His dark hands, sure and quick, passed over Alan, pulling down the bedcovers and checking her father's eyes and mouth.

After a moment, his black eyes scanned the room,

taking in the audience that had formed, but fixing on Gillian, and then Rose, who'd come out of the study to watch.

He said something in heavily accented English. Gillian did not understand him, but Kincreag took her arm to lead her from the room. Rose came closer to the bed and glared back into the large jet eyes.

"I've been treating him for nearly two moons. I'm not going anywhere."

The man protested, scandalized, but Alan put a hand on the healer's arm. "I wish her to stay."

The healer looked most displeased, but he nodded shortly and returned to his work. Gillian saw no more, because Kincreag pushed her through the door and closed it behind them.

"What's his name?" Gillian asked when Kincreag led her across the hall.

"Hekim Mahir Ibn Zafir."

"How is an infidel addressed? Hekim? Or Mr. Zafir? Or maybe just Lord Physician?"

"You will not speak to him."

Gillian stopped abruptly, dumbfounded. "What? Why not?"

He grasped her elbow firmly. There was an attendant outside the kitchens, a young boy. Kincreag directed him to pack some food and meet them in the quay.

"Where are we going?" Gillian asked as he propelled her through the keep. "And why can't I speak to the healer? Is he a Moor? How did you find him?"

They stopped outside the door of the room Gillian and Rose shared.

"You talk too much," he said.

Gillian did not open the door but turned instead to face him, her elbow still in his grip. "Surely it's considered normal to inquire after the healer who is examining my father."

Nicholas looked down at her, frowning, then opened the door and stepped inside her chambers, pulling her along after him.

"Where are we going? Why do we need food?"

"Your father pointed out that delaying the wedding in order to acquaint myself with you was useless if I made no effort to remedy that defect. So we are spending the afternoon together. You'll need a wrap." He went to a hook on the wall and removed her gray velvet mantle. She went to him when he held it out expectantly, letting him settle it on her shoulders. He laced it at the throat for her, as if she were a child.

"What about the healer?" she asked. "Where did you find him?"

He glanced up from the laces, meeting her gaze. His hands stilled. He seemed strangely entranced, or perhaps thinking intently. She searched his gaze, her pulse quickening.

"My lord?" Her voice came out soft and uncertain.

He dropped his hands and strode to the door. "Need you anything else?"

Gillian sighed and finished lacing the mantle herself. "No, my lord, only answers."

He ignored this, leading her out of her chambers and back to the hall. Several of Kincreag's men came forward, ready to accompany them, but the earl waved them away. As they descended the steps to the quay, Gillian mustered the courage to ask, "How are we to ever know one another if you refuse to speak to me?"

The lad was waiting below with the sack of food. Kincreag took it from him and sent him away, tossing the bag in the bottom of a boat. Gillian began to despair that she would be the only one who knew nothing about the mysterious healer when he said, "I met him in Algiers. He was the bey's physician until he was exiled."

"Exiled," Gillian breathed as Kincreag helped her into the boat. How intriguing. She sat on a cross plank, nestling the bag of food securely between her feet. "For what? And how did you meet him? Were you ill? Why were you in Algiers?"

Kincreag settled on the plank across from her and just stared at her, his mouth slightly open, his brows furrowed. "Which am I to answer first?"

Gillian smiled sheepishly. "How did you meet him?"

"I'd been stabbed. I have my own leech, who sometimes travels with me. This one was useless and did naught but staunch the wound. It became festered, so I sent for another. I got Hekim. He put maggots on it and various other things . . . and well, I'm still here, aye? Most men would not have lived through a festering wound such as I had, but Hekim knew what to do."

"Maggots?" Gillian exclaimed as Kincreag rowed them out of the castle and onto the loch.

He nodded. "Aye, maggots. And I've seen him work various other miracles since."

"Miracles? Is he a wizard, then?"

He looked at her as if she were a simpleton. "Ah, no. Just a gifted leech."

Gillian bristled at his tone but tried not to take offense. Kincreag seemed to be serious about becoming acquainted with her, and she was not about to ruin it. "Why were you in Algiers?"

He shook his head slowly. "Next question."

She was curious about the foreign healer but didn't want to waste her questions, in case he tired of them. The earl was where her true interest lay.

"How old are you?"

"Five and thirty."

"How long have you been earl of Kincreag?"

"My father died when I was two and twenty."

"How long were you married before your wife died?"

He had been answering readily enough, if shortly, as if he'd wanted to get this over with, but now he paused, his mouth flattening, considering his answer carefully—or perhaps considering whether or not to answer at all.

"Five years."

Gillian opened her mouth to ask another question about the late countess and, as if reading her mind, he shook his head firmly.

"No more questions about Catriona. I'll not speak of her."

"What? Why?"

"Because it is of no concern to you."

"But it does concern me. She was your first wife; I should like to know more about her."

"She's dead now. I don't want to discuss it—least of all with you."

Gillian fell into injured silence. It wasn't just that he didn't want to talk about his late wife—he didn't want to talk to *Gillian* about her. She turned the ring on her finger. It had been her mother's wedding ring. She thought of her mother and father's marriage, full of love and happiness, and her heart sank lower, the outing soured. She did not speak to him again the rest of their trip, nursing her disappointment and wounded feelings. He didn't seem to notice.

He held out his hand to help her from the boat, but Gillian scrambled out on her own and walked stiffly behind him. He made no mention of her silence. He was probably relieved. This was supposed to have been an outing to get acquainted, and he hadn't asked her a single question about herself. The more Gillian thought on these things, the angrier she became, so that by the time the stable lad led her gray stallion out to her, she was practically fuming.

Kincreag caught Morfran's bridle to hold him steady so she could mount. Morfran was having none of it and twisted his head around, velvet lips peeled back from his teeth. He snapped viciously at Kincreag. The earl jerked his hand away but not in time. The large white teeth grazed his knuckles. Rather than backing away cautiously, like most prudent souls would, the earl pushed his other hand against the nose that jerked forward to take another bite.

The stallion did not like this at all and started to rear upward. Gillian caught his bridle. "Morfran, no!"

The horse dropped his forehooves but pawed at the ground, snorting and shaking his head, his large black eyes glaring maliciously at the earl.

"A fitting name," Kincreag said, inspecting his knuckles before viewing the horse again, this time at a more respectful distance. "He is as ugly as a demon."

"He is *not* ugly. And I didn't name him," Gillian said, mounting the now-docile horse without aid. It turned and lipped gently at her skirts. "But I am thinking of renaming him. He's such a sweet boy, aren't you, my laddy?" She stroked his neck and crooned at him. Morfran shook his mane and whickered.

Kincreag stared at them a moment before turning away, muttering about gelding shears. Gillian smiled, mollified now that Morfran had taken the earl down a peg, and followed his large white horse around the loch. Even as a child Gillian had not explored the glen extensively, and so she was pleased when Kincreag entered the north wood. The glen was a peaceful place to live and free from most of the raiding and feuding that plagued the Highlands, thanks to being situated in a remote and naturally defensive valley, but it still had its dangers. Children were kept far from the wood with stories of ghosts and dragons—but in truth, the real danger was wolves and other nasty creatures.

They followed a faint trail for a bit, but soon even that disappeared, and the thick underbrush forced them to dismount.

Kincreag made no attempt to hobble Morfran, so Gillian led him a safe distance from the earl's mount and secured his reins to a tree trunk. She and Morfran were still getting acquainted, though they'd taken to each other nicely. He was very aggressive to most people—and very intelligent, too. She rubbed his nose and followed Kincreag, who'd already disappeared into the trees.

The terrain was much more difficult than she'd expected. She'd known, of course, that the glen was nearly impregnable, with the mountains rising all around it, but in truth, she'd never bothered with anything but the single southern pass. They were at the far north of the glen where a thick wood climbed the mountainside. The ground had grown rocky, with great jagged black crags jutting out of the ground. Those weren't so much the problem. It was the smaller ones, camouflaged with pine needles and birch leaves, so that they seemed to pierce her feet right through the soles of her shoes when she stepped on them unexpectedly.

She was about to call out to Kincreag to wait for her when she saw him, leaning against a tree, his back to her. The forest had grown so quiet that the sound of her stumbling after him seemed magnified. When she was close, Kincreag's hand snaked out, pulling her around in front of him. She managed not to yelp in surprise.

He pressed her back against his chest, his head lowered near her ear, his warm breath tickling the hair at her temple. Gillian shivered. His hands rested on her shoulders, holding her motionless—a useless gesture, as she was frozen, unable to believe he'd touched her at all.

"Look. There," he whispered. His voice was soft and deep. Gillian searched the thick trees and bushes, the steeply inclined ground, but saw nothing, just foliage and shadowed rocky ridges. One of his hands moved from her shoulder and came slowly around in front of her, pointing upward. "There, watch carefully."

Gillian's gaze climbed upward in the direction he pointed. High above them, a wolf lounged under a large gray outcropping. Its gray and brown fur blended into its surroundings. It was not asleep but seemed sleepy and content, its eyes half closed. Fear jolted through her as an unpleasant thought followed on the heels of her wonder.

"Don't they live in packs?" she breathed, backing into the earl. He'd dropped the hand that had been pointing. It reappeared at her waist, holding her still.

"Aye."

She turned her head toward him. "What about the horses?"

He said nothing. She turned more fully toward him, to see what made him so still and quiet. She found him gazing down at her. His face was taut, intent, his thick black lashes obscuring his eyes.

"The horses will be fine." His hands, one firm on her shoulder, the other on her waist, turned her away from him again, but he did not move her from her position nestled against him. Though the weather was chill, the exercise of climbing the mountain had left Gillian warm and winded. Her temperature rose another notch at the warmth emanating from his body and hands, heating her so that perspiration dewed her forehead and dampened her palms. She still felt winded, too, though she'd had plenty of time to catch her breath.

"There's more, if you look hard." He pointed again,

and she located several more wolves, reclining lazily. "The pack is small. The MacDonells have been trying to kill them for dozens of years."

As she watched, one of the wolves, a large male, rose and moved closer to the first wolf they'd seen. He lay partly on her, his head rolling with entreaty, and after a moment she groomed him, licking his ears and head thoroughly. The male's eyes closed in slits of ecstasy. Gillian smiled, surprised at how adorable they were. She'd seen few wolves in her life, and the ones she had seen had all been fleeing from a rain of arrows and bullets.

"That must be his mate," Kincreag whispered. "They mate for life, you ken. The most loyal of beasts."

He shifted behind her, and she thought he reached for his dag. Her hand moved back, catching his. "You're not going to kill one now, are you? Please don't. They're so beautiful and peaceful . . . right now, that is. And they're so far away—surely they won't sense us if we're quiet."

A breeze swept through the forest, ruffling the wolves' fur and showing the lighter bands of ticked hair. The male's large head lifted; he sniffed casually, then went still, his head turned in their direction, yellow eyes locked on them.

Gillian inhaled softly but didn't move or speak. Kincreag's hands tightened on her.

"Fear not," he whispered, his voice so low that it was a mere breath against her ear. The hair on her neck tingled and her knees wobbled. "They're afraid of man and will only run if we make ourselves known." When he spoke to her like that, warm breath on her ear and temple, voice low and rumbling, she turned to soft wax and longed to turn her head so his lips made full contact with her skin. She wouldn't dream of acting on these wanton urges, but just thinking of them made her weak and strange to herself.

They stood that way for what seemed an eternity, even after the wolf looked away in disinterest. The wood had been quiet except for them and the wind stirring through the trees, but now other sounds started up again—the whirring of insects, the twitters and calls of birds, the scritching of mice in the underbrush. Gillian could feel Kincreag's heartbeat against her back, fast and strong. Their fingers were still tangled and pressed between their bodies. She had the oddest sensation of being watched—not by any beast in the forest, but by the man standing so close behind her. Her skin warmed at this thought, and she could no longer focus on the wolves but on the way his hands felt, gripping her fingers and her waist, the way his breath felt against her temple, the faint, pleasant scent of his sandalwood soap. She nearly gave in to the urge to turn to him.

His hand slid more fully around her waist. Her heart skipped with anticipation, but he only eased back, pulling her along with him. She took small, silent steps but was still far noisier than he was. It was her skirts and cloak, disturbing the leaves and bracken around them. He released her fingers and gathered her skirts and cloak in one hand, pulling it up and tight against her legs. That's what he'd been about to do before, not draw a gun and shoot the beasts. Now that she thought of it, she recalled that he did not even carry a dag—only a long dirk in his boot.

When they were far enough away, he released her. Gillian turned quickly, her face blazing and her breathing still uneven, as if she'd been running.

He stood with hands on hips, gazing around the forest thoughtfully. He nodded to the west. "There's another way, I think, but it's a bit rougher. Can you make it?"

Gillian nodded, gathering her skirts in her hand and trudging after him. It was some time before she discovered their destination. She saw it before they reached it—a bright light filtering through the trees. She stepped into the sunny clearing. It was very small—a cliff, really, where no trees could grow. Sunlight filled the clearing, blinding her after the dimness of the forest.

Kincreag stood at the edge of the cliff, looking down. Gillian moved beside him. The entire glen of Glen Laire spread out before them. She'd never seen it from this perspective, and she let out a long breath of appreciation. It was lush and green, black crofts dotting the glen, with small smudges that were sheep and shaggy red kine. Lochlaire sat in the center of the calm gray loch, an enormous edifice jutting from the steely waters. The silver snake of the burn that emptied into the loch appeared from the trees somewhere below them.

"Thank you for showing me this."

"This is not what I want to show you."

He took her hand and led her back into the forest. A distant sound emerged, a low roar Gillian could not identify. Soon it grew louder, resonating through her chest, and just before they reached it, she realized it was a waterfall.

The trees parted for it, and it tumbled down the rocks between them. It emptied into a large pool just below them, then spilled out to continue its journey through the forest and eventually to the loch.

"I didn't know this was here!"

He led her down to the pool and crouched before it, scooping water and splashing it over his face, then drinking from his cupped hands. Gillian knelt beside him to do the same, wetting her handkerchief and mopping her face, watching him surreptitiously. He was so tall that he gave the impression of leanness when standing, but crouching as he was, the leather of his breeks strained against the thick muscles of his thighs. His elbows rested on his knees, dripping hands dangling between his legs. Gillian noted how very large his arms were as well, as big as one of her thighs. His size and strength made her fluttery and weak again.

"We'd come here sometimes, your father and I, when he was well." He turned to her. Gillian quickly averted her gaze, embarrassed to have been examining him so intently. "Your mother is buried here."

Gillian's eyes widened, and she looked around. Just past the long, curved slab of rock they crouched on, the trees crowded in again, but just beyond the trees her gaze snagged on it. A stone cross. She rose slowly and entered the trees. The cross was carved in the old Irish style, with a circle where the arms crossed the body. She passed her fingers over the raised spiral and knotwork patterns, her throat tight.

Memories flooded her, memories she'd purposely refused to dwell on—nay, to even *think* on—in a dozen years. Fear and dread descended like a rancid cloud, enveloping her, gagging her. She was the only one who'd seen her mother die. Her sisters had been at the castle with their father, but Gillian and her mother had been out gathering herbs. Some plant her mother had needed grew only in rock crevices, high on the mountain. So they'd ridden to the pass and had been wandering about with their baskets when Lillian had been lynched.

It had been a group of men. Gillian had recognized none of them. They'd struck Lillian and dragged her away. Gillian had cowered behind a boulder, and they'd not seen her at first. She'd stumbled down the mountain to get help but hadn't gotten far before they'd caught her.

A throbbing clawed Gillian's temples, and she struggled for air, horror crushing her chest as the long-suppressed memories consumed her. The men had talked about burning two witches. Gillian had been terrified, sobbing and carrying on so that they'd gagged her. When Lillian had woken, she'd begged them to release Gillian, pleading that she was only a child and not a witch. But they'd ignored her. Mother and daughter had been taken to a village not far from their glen. A mob had greeted them—people had screamed at them and thrown rotting vegetables, accusing them of all sorts of horrors. They'd meant to burn Gillian, too, but they hadn't. Someone had made them let her go. She'd run all the way back to the mountain pass, and when she'd turned to look back, she'd seen the smoke . . . then she'd seen . . .

Pain exploded in Gillian's temples. She cried out, her hands flailing blindly before her, catching the cross and falling to her knees with her arms around it. The pain receded almost immediately.

She blinked slowly, alarmed to find her face pressed against the rough-cut stone.

"Mistress MacDonell?" the earl asked. He crouched beside her, peering worriedly into her face. "I should not have brought you here. I didn't realize it would affect you so."

Gillian sat back on her heels and shook her head. "No, no, that's not it. I got a sudden pain in my head . . . it was so strong I couldn't see." She still felt queasy and weak.

He continued to peer at her, as if expecting her to topple over. "You still get the pain? After all these years?"

Gillian looked at him sharply. "What?"

"Your father told me you were with Lillian when it happened. And afterward, when they tried to get information from you so they might discover who was behind the burning, you were struck with such severe pain that sometimes you'd faint. They thought someone was poisoning you at first, but so long as no one mentioned your mother, you were fine . . . almost as if it had never happened."

Gillian stared at him, frowning—not just because what he said made no sense but because the pain crept back, a mist in front of her eyes, blinding her, choking her. She covered her eyes. "I don't . . . remember this—I don't think I do. . . ." But she wasn't so certain. There was a ring of familiarity to his words, but her head ached dreadfully. She turned away from him abruptly and heaved up her breakfast. She leaned over the ground, panting, the back of her hand pressed to her trembling lips.

"I don't understand this," she said, suddenly frightened.

And then his hands were on her shoulders, turning her, pressing her face against his shoulder.

"Dinna think of it," he whispered, his Scots—usually nearly imperceptible—growing broad.

Gillian closed her eyes and tried, but she saw her mother's frightened face in her mind, and the pain hammered at her again. She groaned, pressing her forehead into his shoulder and gripping his doublet in her fists. She made a fantastic effort to think of nothing but the man crouched on the ground before her, his arms hard around her, stroking her hair and making crooning noises as if to a child.

As the pain receded, her body grew limp and she molded to him, the beat of his heart setting a cadence for hers. His deep voice urged her not to think on it, so she thought instead of their wedding night. He would be gentle with her, she believed that now. There was more to him than arrogance and coldness. She felt safe and comforted, engulfed in his strong arms.

It ended too soon when he stood, pulling her up with him. "Can you walk?"

Gillian nodded. She felt drained and shaky and desperately wanted to leave. Waves of pain washed over her when she even looked at the cross. He led her back to the cliff clearing. They sat on the sunny rock, and he pulled the bag of food from his belt. He handed her a chunk of bread and cheese, watching her carefully as she ate it.

When Gillian's nerves had steadied, she said, "I knew you and my father were very good friends . . . but I hadn't realized, until just now, how very close you are."

He said nothing, looking away from her, to the view below them.

"He would not have told you that, or showed you where my mother was buried, if you weren't very important to him."

He still said nothing. She gazed at his hawklike profile, in sharp relief against the brightness of the sun. He seemed so dark and remote, apart from everything. And she supposed he was. It was said he was reclusive and rarely left Castle Kincreag, though he had many other houses scattered across his lands.

Gillian frowned at the bread in her hands, frustrated with his silence. "You seem to find me so . . . distasteful. Most of the time," she added, thinking of how kind he'd just been. "I couldn't understand why an earl would wed someone he doesn't like. You could marry anyone you wanted . . . why bother with me? Especially after what Isobel did. But I understand now. You'd do anything for him, wouldn't you?"

"Aye," he answered readily enough, still not looking at her.

"Including marrying someone you hate."

He had been looking out over the glen, but when she said that his lashes lowered as he looked at his hand propped on his knee. His mouth compressed. After a moment, he said, "I don't hate you, Gillian." It seemed a great effort for him to force the words out. But he'd made the effort.

Gillian studied his profile. Once she had wished for great love and passion when she married. Then everything had changed, and all she'd hoped for was to be saved from the French fate. But now, sitting here with this cruel, powerful earl—a man hated by many, loved by few, a man who had shown her wolves and held her when she was crippled with pain—she found that "I don't hate you," was enough. For now.

As if sensing her scrutiny, he glanced at her and arched a cynical brow.

"I don't hate you, either," she said. "Perhaps there's hope for us after all."

He grunted skeptically and turned back to the view, but Gillian was certain the corner of his mouth twitched the slightest bit in a smile.

4

Nicholas stood outside the door to Alan's chambers for several pensive minutes before finally knocking. Hagan showed him in, giving him anxious looks as he followed him to Alan's bedside. The woman perched on the bed drew his gaze. Her soft voice flowed over him, calming him when whisky and great effort had not. Gillian looked up from her book, then closed it when she saw him. Large gray eyes studied his face, unsmiling, before returning to her book.

Rose stood at the head of the bed, looking as if she hadn't slept in a week, and stirring something in a pewter cup. She also turned, fixing Nicholas with a slightly accusatory look. "Well?"

Nicholas didn't know why he felt guilty—he'd done nothing wrong. But the news he bore was grim. Hekim had just left Lochlaire. After several days spent examining Alan, he could not determine what was wrong, but

his conclusion had been the same as everyone else's—
Alan was dying.

Alan was still asleep. His skin had taken on a grayish
tinge in the few days Nicholas had been here. Nicholas
stared down at his friend, unwilling to wake him.

"What did the Turk say?" Rose asked.

"That if you were his woman, he'd have you beat—"

"Not that!" Rose said, exasperated. "About father."

Nicholas heard a soft breath of laughter from Gillian
and ignored the prick of pleasure he felt at having
amused her.

Nicholas sighed. "The same as all the others have
said."

Rose stared at him, the high, flat cheekbones stark,
pale skin stretched taut across them. "It's not hopeless,"
she said forcefully. "Stop acting as if it is, else he'll begin
to believe it and give up. Once the soul gives up . . .
there's nothing I can do."

Nicholas looked away from her and, against his will,
his gaze returned to Alan's other daughter. She stared at
her father, tears standing in her beautiful gray eyes. His
stomach bottomed out, and he forced his gaze to the
fur-covered bed, angry with himself for not being able
to do more. All the money and power and lands he had
could not save his friend. He pulled up his customary
stool beside Alan's bed and watched his friend sleep.
The deerhound lay nearby, drowsing. Rose returned to
her work, and after a moment, Gillian read softly again.

Nicholas closed his eyes, listening more to her voice
than the story she read—the tale of the Green Knight.

He'd spent no more time alone with her after their forest outing. He'd considered it several times, perhaps inviting her to join him for a meal, or a game of draughts, before realizing that such things would not do. It had been an understatement when he'd admitted to not hating her. In the scheme of things, one would suppose liking one's betrothed to be a positive development. But Nicholas didn't particularly want to like Gillian. He didn't want to be amused by her curiosity, didn't want to admire her courage, or feel the uncomfortable tugging in his chest when she was so hesitant and uncertain. He would not make the same mistakes with this wife. He would remain vigilant to deception. A husband was lord and master, not friend. He would protect her with his life, take pleasure in her body—but she would be nothing more to him than a vessel for his children.

Gillian stopped reading abruptly and closed her book. Nicholas opened his eyes to find Alan awake. It was clear he'd not woken from a peaceful sleep—his eyes were wild, his mouth open in a silent scream. Something jerked against Nicholas's feet. The deerhound twitched madly, in the midst of its own nightmare.

Nicholas was on his feet beside the bed. "Alan—what is it?"

Hagan loomed behind him, reaching for the fur coverlet, but before he touched it, Rose gripped the edge and flung it back.

Alan gasped a few times before his breathing calmed. His eyes drifted shut, but he did not sleep.

Gillian made a strangled sound.

Nicholas glanced at her. She stared at her father's uncovered body, eyes wide and white, fingers pressed hard against her lips. Nicholas had seen it before, and he forced himself to look again, to see what new horror had sprung up on his dearest friend's helpless body.

Alan wore his shirt tied up to his throat, but his legs from the knees down were exposed. Nicholas remembered seeing him but a few short months ago in his plaid, his legs bare. They'd been thick, muscular legs, covered with auburn hair. They looked like wizened twigs now, the skin hanging off the bones and milky white except for the bruises.

The bruises were but one of the many mysteries of Alan's illness, but they were the most disturbing one. His sleep was frequently troubled, and when he would wake, sometimes he would be covered with marks, as if he'd been in battle, though he remembered nothing of his dreams. Hagan was always present with Alan and could attest that no one had touched his master. And though Alan sometimes thrashed about, never so much to cause himself such damage.

But even if he *had,* it would not explain these marks. The newest one, verily glowing on his calf, was in the shape of a half moon. Not so curved that it looked like a horse's hoof had struck him, though he had a few of those, which were fading and a sickly yellowish color on his other calf. No, this was precise, with a fine point at either end of the bruise, as if he'd been branded with a crescent. Except it wasn't a burn.

Rose pulled his shirt up further, and there were more

on his thighs—one in the shape of a star. Hagan untied Alan's shirt. When he spread it, yet more marks colored his sunken chest.

Alan waved his arms irritably. "Enough! We all know what they look like. Let me be."

"Da?" Gillian asked softly, almost timidly, from behind them. "Do they hurt?"

Nicholas allowed himself to glance back at her, but he turned away quickly at the stricken look on her face as she stared at her father's ravaged body. She hadn't seen them before. Rose should have been more thoughtful. He scowled at the redhead, but she was intent on Alan.

"Och, my love, no." Alan sighed, pulling the fur close around himself. "Gilly, my sweet, do me a favor?"

Gillian came forward, sitting on the edge of the bed. "Yes, Da, anything."

"Write to Isobel and Sir Philip. Tell them to come. And to bring Stephen, aye?"

Gillian's face froze. She did not answer. Alan gave Nicholas a *Help me* look and lifted his chin toward his daughter. Nicholas touched Gillian's shoulder.

She didn't look at him. She was stiff and pale—an image stricken in marble.

"Gillian," Nicholas said in a low voice, slipping his hand under her elbow and lifting her forcibly off the bed. "Come. You can use my messenger."

He led her to her chambers. She did not speak, only stared straight ahead, eyes blank. He took her to her writing desk, and she sank onto the stool but did nothing, staring vacantly ahead. Nicholas pulled a piece of parchment out from under a large glassy rock and placed it in front of her.

She looked down at the parchment. A tear splashed onto it.

Nicholas did not know what to do. Instinct told him to hold her again, as he had in the forest, but the memory of her body pressed against his was too fresh, even two days past, and he found himself frequently preoccupied with carnal thoughts, as if he were a green lad again—even when he wasn't near her.

He pushed the inkwell and quill toward her and said gruffly, "Write the letter, and I'll have it sent."

She wiped at her eyes and sniffed delicately. "You know why he's sending for them, don't you?"

"Aye."

Gillian picked up the quill. "I don't know what to write. 'Father is dying and has asked for you. Time is short. Make haste'?"

"Aye, that would work."

Gillian bit her lip uncertainly, then began to write. When she finished, Nicholas called for Evan, who waited outside the door, having followed them when they'd left the hall.

"Have this delivered to Sir Philip at Sgor Dubh."

"Aye, my lord," Evan said, but before Nicholas could turn away, the knight added, "there's news from Kincreag." When Nicholas raised inquiring brows, Evan rushed on, "Campbells are feuding with the Gregors again. They lifted a score of kine—sheep, too, and a few goats when passing through your lands."

Nicholas clenched his teeth in frustration. The

Campbells and Gregors—as well as the MacNabs and Colquhouns—were always at one another's throats. Since the king had outlawed the Gregors, it had gone from bad to worse, since the other clans believed they could persecute them with impunity—and for the most part, they could. Nicholas had recently found himself in the unlikely position of defending the Gregors, and he was paying the price. He only hoped the king didn't hear of it. The king had no fondness for Highlanders and considered the Gregors the most distasteful of the lot.

Nicholas looked back at Gillian. She'd risen from the stool and approached Nicholas cautiously.

"Is aught amiss?" she asked.

Nicholas considered sending Evan to deal with the situation, but he knew that would be futile. The Campbells would deal with no one but himself, and if he sent Evan, he might find himself paying a hefty ransom to get his man back.

"I have to go."

He started out the door, but Gillian caught his arm. "Where are you going?"

"I have business to attend."

"What business?" she cried, her fingers tightening. "What about Father? What if you don't return . . . in time. . . ." Tears shimmered in her gray eyes again as she gazed up at him, pleading.

Nicholas felt himself faltering in the face of her tears. His knight was watching avidly, so he shut the door and took her firmly by the shoulders. "I'll only be gone a few days."

"Can we not marry before you go? Something quick, but in Da's presence, so he knows, in case . . ." The tears spilled down her face freely, dripping from her delicate chin.

There had been a time in Nicholas's life when he'd openly given and received affection. A time before Catriona. Since then he'd hardened his heart—and at times, it seemed he truly was made of stone, as few could elicit sympathy from him. Perhaps it was their shared concern for the chieftain of Glen Laire. Or maybe it was just because she was his best friend's daughter. He didn't know what made him soft to her, but her tears hollowed out his chest.

She gazed up at him, large gray eyes studying his face, and then her expression crumpled and she moved toward him, pressing her face against his plaid. Nicholas put his arms around her without thinking.

He held her for several minutes, patting her back awkwardly, her face pressed into his shoulder. She was small, yet beautifully well rounded. Heavy breasts pressed into him, and his hands drifted over a narrow back and tiny waist to the wide flare of hips. She was made to bear children. He should not be thinking of such things now, with Alan dying and her tears of grief drenching him, but he could not wait to bed her.

She moved back slightly, staying within the circle of his arms when he would have let her go. "It could be quick. Father keeps a pastor here . . . for when it's time."

Marriage. She wanted to have a quick ceremony before he left. But Alan had indicated that once Gillian and Nicholas married, he would take his own life.

"No."

She tilted her head back to frown at him. "I don't understand . . . it's what he wishes."

He could not tell her what Alan planned. It had been told to him in confidence, and besides, it would only upset her more.

"But it's not what I wish."

Her mouth dropped open, and she huffed an incredulous breath. When she tried to pull away from him, he held her shoulders.

"You don't ever intend to go through with this, do you? If you will not do it now, when? Why wait until he's dead?"

She had a point, and he felt himself caving in. Perhaps it *was* inevitable, if Alan had sent for Isobel and Sir Philip. Surely Alan knew the end was near, and he did look awful. But then he'd looked this awful before—worse even—and rallied back.

When he didn't answer, she asked, "What *do* you wish?"

He stared down at her flushed cheeks and soft eyes, long lashes still damp from her tears. Before he even knew what he intended, he found his mouth on hers. She stiffened, her hands against his chest. Her lips were soft, though, and bore the salty tang of her tears. He took her face in his hands and kissed her deeply. She responded immediately, her lips parting, fingers digging into his arms. It was a brief kiss, but it roused a hunger in him for more. He raised his head slightly, still holding her face between his hands.

She was very still, her gaze holding him prisoner. He

did not know why he'd kissed her, other than sheer instinct from holding a beautiful woman, but he generally had more control than to act on errant impulses. Damn troubling that he was tempted to kiss her again. But that's all it was, really. Lust. She was fragrant and soft—what man wouldn't be sore tempted by such a woman? Her skin was silken and warm beneath his hands. His heart beat loudly. Her lashes were impossibly long, and he watched them as they lowered, her own gaze dropping to his mouth, as if she expected him to kiss her again. With a terrific effort, he dropped his hands and stepped away from her.

She watched him with a dazed expression. "Why did you do that?"

Various responses, all inappropriate, flitted through his mind. He finally settled on, "A promise."

A look of almost comic surprise crossed her face as her fingers touched her lips lightly. "A promise?"

He couldn't suppress the smile tugging at his mouth from her bewilderment. "Aye. I'll be back and we'll be wed. Until then I leave Sir Evan at your disposal."

He quickly took his leave before he spouted any more foolishness.

Gillian was still standing in the center of the room, fingers still pressed to her mouth, when Rose slipped into their chambers. She closed the door, jabbing a thumb over her shoulder.

"Why is Kincreag's man standing outside our room? Lord Kincreag is with Father."

"Oh!" Gillian cried, hands fluttering. "I have a knight!"

Rose's brows shot up, duly impressed, as Gillian hurried to the door to inspect her knight. Sir Evan leaned against the wall opposite the door. He was an attractive man with close-cropped, dark brown hair and sun-bronzed skin. His sword belt was strapped over his chest, the hilt visible over his shoulder, and he was fairly bristling with other weapons—several dirks and two guns.

As soon as he saw her, he straightened. "My lady."

Gillian laughed nervously and glanced at Rose, who'd joined her at the door. "I'm not 'my lady' yet." She quickly composed herself, straightening and donning a serious expression worthy of a countess. "Well met, Sir Evan."

He inclined his head solemnly. His pale blue eyes looked right through her, lifeless. "Will you be needing me tonight?"

"Uh . . . no, thank you. You may go about your business. I'll summon you if I need you."

He bowed smartly and marched down the hall, weapons clanking.

Gillian closed the door and turned to her sister. "Isn't he marvelous?"

Rose's lips drew down in a grimace. "A bit peculiar, don't you think?"

"Not him! Lord Kincreag!"

Rose eyed her curiously. "Something happened."

Gillian's fingers touched her lips again as she remembered the feel of his mouth on hers. Her blood raced, the fluttering in her belly returning. "Kincreag kissed me."

Gillian didn't think it was possible for Rose to look astounded, but her jaw dropped in shock, and her midnight eyes, usually catlike in appearance, were as round as an owl's. "For no reason?"

Gillian had not told her sister about the contract—in truth, it was rather embarrassing, but she told her now, as well as her suspicions that Kincreag meant to evade ever marrying her by waiting until their father died, and then deeming her unsuitable. "I wanted to get married before he left in case aught happened to Da. When he refused, I accused him of planning to never marry me. He kissed me then. He said it was a promise."

Rose tapped at her teeth thoughtfully. "You might be right. He probably thinks he can charm you along, then drop you when Father dies."

Gillian shook her head in disbelief. "You weren't kissed by him . . . it didn't *feel* false. It felt . . ." She paused, biting her bottom lip as she remembered. "It felt like a promise of . . . of . . ." Well, she didn't know quite what. But something warm and wonderful that made her quiver in anticipation of more such kisses, and the eventual fulfillment of what they promised.

"Oh dear." Rose shook her head sympathetically, auburn brows arched. "It never does *feel* false. Did he put his tongue in your mouth?"

Gillian blinked. "No . . ."

"Well then!" Rose said, as if that explained everything. When Gillian just stared blankly at her, she elaborated. "When a man really wants a woman, he puts his tongue in her mouth."

"What? Where do you learn these things? Has a man ever put his tongue in *your* mouth?

Rose smiled wisely. "A few have tried."

Rose *did* seem very knowledgeable about relations between men and women. Gillian frowned, her heart sinking. The earl was remote and cool, but she'd not thought him false. But what about the contract? He'd told her he didn't want to marry her, but she'd believed him when he'd said he meant to anyway. Was it just to appease her so she didn't complain to her father?

Gillian plopped down in a chair near the fire and buried her face in her hands. "I'm so confused!"

Rose was beside her immediately. "What is it? Is your headache back?"

Gillian straightened. "No. It came back earlier today but then was gone again seconds later." She'd told Rose about what had happened at their mother's grave. Rose had been puzzled, and when she'd passed her hands over Gillian's head, she'd found nothing amiss.

"What were you doing when the headache struck?"

Gillian thought about it for several minutes. "I don't think it has anything to do with that. I've been doing all sorts of things."

Rose scowled thoughtfully. "Most vexing. I can't do much if I can't touch you when the pain is present. Next time you get a headache, you must find me posthaste, aye?" Rose stood suddenly. "I must go—Uncle Roderick says Aunt Tira is having cramps." She shook her head, looking heavenward. "She's probably just full of wind. The baby hasn't even dropped yet."

She left, muttering, leaving Gillian alone to think about her future husband. *She hoped he was her future husband.* She thought of the kiss and how it had sent her heart racing. She'd never been kissed like that before. But, according to Rose, it hadn't meant a thing to him.

5

After a night spent thrashing against the bed-clothes, worrying for her father and the fate of her betrothal, Gillian formulated a plan to secure Kincreag for good. Early the next morning Sir Evan accompanied her to the little hamlet across the loch. Her attempts to make polite conversation with the knight were met with monosyllabic replies or silence, so she quit trying, thinking instead of her task. To visit Old Hazel.

She vaguely remembered Hazel from when she was a child. Hazel had been a great friend of her mother's, and some relation to them as well. Some of the Mac-Donells of Glen Laire were relations to the chieftain's family. Others had just adopted the MacDonell name to live under Glen Laire's protection.

More importantly, Old Hazel was a witch, and gifted with potions. It was not spoken of now, and when Gillian had tried to ask around about it, folks had made the sign of the horns and shaken their heads fearfully. Gillian knew it was the state of the country that caused such fear. No one wanted it known they'd associated with a witch—mere association was cause enough for burning these days. But they'd also wanted to protect one of their own. For now at least. And so no one mentioned Hazel and her doings aloud. Glen Laire had been blessed with good luck these past years—no failed crops, no plagues, no rash of dying animals—and so no scapegoat was yet needed. But a time could yet come when Hazel and other fey members of the Mac-Donells would be forced to serve as sacrifices to ease folks' fears.

Gillian hoped that day would never come. The witch hunt had spread throughout Scotland, even to the remotest parts of the Highlands, and it showed no signs yet of dying down. And so her excuse for visiting Old Hazel this morning was to ask about an herb Rose had no time to fetch herself.

Gillian waved greetings to the cottars they passed as she and Sir Evan strolled down the single hard-packed dirt lane that constituted the hamlet of Glen Laire. All the while she thought furiously of some means to rid herself of her escort.

She paused in front of the alehouse and gestured to it. "Perhaps you'd like to wait within. I'll be visiting with an old friend and may be a while."

Sir Evan shook his head firmly, staring at some point above and beyond her right shoulder, his pale eyes remote. "Nay, I'll come with you."

Gillian smiled weakly and continued on her way. Having her own personal knight was not nearly as amusing as she'd thought it would be. She'd tried to leave the castle without him, but he'd been keeping track of her and had insisted on accompanying her for her protection. Nothing she'd said had dissuaded him. Though her visit to the village was a sensitive one, she didn't want to rouse his suspicion by making an issue of it, so she'd relented, hoping she could somehow lose him in Glen Laire. Unfortunately, he was sticking like a barnacle.

Hazel's cottage was at the end of the lane. Mud and heather protruded from the cracks in the black stone house, and peat smoke blackened the thatched roof. The door opened before Gillian could knock.

Hazel had been uncommonly old when Gillian was a child; now she was positively ancient. Paper-thin skin stretched over her narrow skull, sagging in soft folds beneath her eyes and chin. A red and green plaid shrouded her from forehead to toes.

"Mistress MacDonell, I've been expecting ye."

Gillian stepped forward uncertainly. "You have?"

She smiled, displaying a row of stained and missing teeth, rickety as an old fence. "Aye, I have." Old Hazel disappeared inside, crooning, "Come in, come in."

Gillian turned to Sir Evan. "I would like to visit with Hazel alone. Prithee wait outside."

He stepped to the doorway and quickly scanned the interior of the cottage before giving her a curt nod and taking up his position beside the door.

Gillian hesitated, wondering if he would be able to overhear their conversation from his post, but she finally decided it would be suspicious to ask him to move.

She entered the cottage and shut the door behind her. The interior was dim and dusty, motes swirling around before her eyes. The small windows let in little light. It smelled of must and mildew, wrenching a sneeze from her. Once her eyes stopped watering and adjusted to the gloom, she surveyed the little cottage with interest. It was spartan—only a table, a bench, a single chair, and a cabinet against the wall. A profusion of glass bottles and clay bowls of various sizes and shapes cluttered the cabinet and tabletop. Gillian peered at a dingy jar that appeared to be filled with scores of dried frogs.

"Come, come," Hazel urged. "A spot of trouble wi' the lad?" She nodded to the door.

Gillian frowned absently. "Oh . . . him. Aye, I don't know how to make him go away." She was to be a countess, and she supposed countesses needed guards and attendants. She hadn't thought such a thing would be so inconvenient.

"Ye'll be wantin' to curse him?"

Gillian laughed ruefully. "I'd better not."

Hazel gestured to a bench. "Gude, because I dinna do that. White magic only."

Gillian sat and looked up at the old woman. "You're free with your speech. Have you no fear of the witch hunters?"

"Nay, the MacDonells will protect me."

"For now . . . but what if things go poorly? They'll blame you."

Hazel just smiled her rickety smile. "I'm auld, lass, and past caring. I mun go sometime, aye?"

Gillian smiled weakly, recalling her mother. She

thought there were better ways to go. Her temples throbbed sullenly, and she closed her eyes, blanking her mind until the pain receded.

When she opened her eyes, Hazel peered at her with a narrowed green gaze. "It still hurts, aye?"

"No, it's gone now."

Hazel said nothing, though the folds in her skin deepened as she stared at Gillian.

"What?"

"That's no what I meant, lassie, but ye've confirmed my suspicions."

"What did you mean, then? What suspicions?"

"Ye've been cursed since ye've been a child."

Gillian blinked. She opened her mouth to speak, then closed it in consternation. Cursed? She didn't feel particularly cursed. She'd suffered hardships, but she'd had her share of goodness, too. Unlike her sisters' foster families, hers had been warm and loving. True, she'd lost her mother in a most horrible manner, and her father was dying, but with the witch hunts, many others had lost mothers, wives, daughters—even some husbands, fathers, and sons—to the fires. No, she was no more cursed than many others.

"I don't understand," Gillian finally said.

Hazel smiled at her rather sadly. "Ye would if ye could, my lass—oh, ye would."

"What does *that* mean?"

Hazel reached out a long, thin finger and tapped Gillian's forehead. "It's yer head. The pain is meant to hide something from ye, but I fear trying to determine what may kill ye."

Gillian shook her head to deny such a thing was possible, but she trailed off, staring blankly into the cottage. The headaches *were* fleeting, and she often *was* forced to think of other things—or of nothing at all—to make them recede. She turned the silver ring on her finger, trying hard to remember what she'd been thinking when the pain had assaulted her. Her mother, or more specifically, her mother's lynching, and—

Gillian clutched her head as pain ripped through her temples, blinding her with a searing flash of white light. She had the sensation of falling, and when sense returned to her, she lay on the dirt floor of the cottage, blinking up at the ceiling, motes drifting about in front of her. She sneezed.

Hazel's face appeared over her. "Dinna think of it, lass! Not here!" She looked fearfully at the door.

Gillian sat up gingerly. The pain had receded but her temples felt bruised. How could such a thing be? Why would someone curse her? The pain encroached again, like a sharp silver mist, and she quickly cleared her mind.

The thought that she was cursed terrified her, but Hazel was right—this was not the place to investigate it further. She would need Isobel's and Rose's help. She settled back on the bench, achy and weak.

"Is there some way to remove the curse?"

Hazel shook her head. "It would take powerful magic and knowledge of the curse in order to counter it. I'm but a wise woman, child. Yer mother, God rest her soul, could have saved ye, but I fear, unless yer sisters are as skilled as she, there's no hope."

Gillian sat very still, fighting against the pain again. *Think of something else. Think of something else.* She hadn't realized how difficult it was to clear her mind of these painful thoughts. In fact, it hadn't been before. But now her fear made it difficult.

Hazel seemed to sense the difficulty she was having and said, "But this is no why ye're here, is it? Tell me why ye came to see Old Hazel."

Grateful for the distraction, Gillian pounced on the subject. "A philter—a love philter."

Hazel's beetled brows raised. "Well now . . . I can do that. But it's no a simple thing, ye ken?"

Gillian leaned forward eagerly. "Tell me what I must do."

Hazel considered Gillian silently for a long moment, her brows knit together in a frown. "What would such a bonny lassie need wi' a love philter?"

"Surely you've heard I'm to wed the earl of Kincreag?"

"Och, I have. And it's him it's for?" Hazel looked wary, her frown deepening.

"Aye, but I vow to you, I will never reveal from whence it came."

Hazel waved at the door. "Ye wilna have to. Yon knight will do it for ye."

Gillian hadn't thought of that. But she couldn't let that stop her—Hazel had said she could give her a love philter. Gillian's pulse skipped excitedly. It *was* possible. "No, he thinks I'm here for another reason. And if I am caught with the philter, I'll lie."

Hazel still looked uncertain.

Gillian clasped her hands together in a pleading manner. "I pray you, I *need* this."

Hazel shook her head, clearly perplexed. "But why, my dear? Ye're to marry him, what need ye of a philter?"

"I don't think he means to marry me at all. I think the betrothal is to make my father happy, and then when he dies"—she stumbled over this, but then rushed on—"then he will break the betrothal. If he does, my uncle will send me to France."

Hazel considered her for a long time, clearly uneasy about it, but finally she nodded. "Verra well. Here's what ye mun do. . . ."

Gillian left Hazel's cottage nearly an hour later, with a packet of herbs tucked into her bodice and a set of instructions committed to memory. She felt better than she had in days, as if a great weight had finally eased from her heart. She had a plan, a good one, and she'd thought of it on her own. If the earl believed himself in love with her, he would go through with the wedding, and the sooner the better. Her belly tightened in anxious anticipation. The moment he returned, she would slip him the philter.

6

It was several anxious days before Kincreag returned, and when he finally did, he surprised Gillian by inviting her to join him for dinner. It was the perfect opportunity to administer the philter. She'd gone over and over her plan, but still found herself queasy with fear when he finally sent for her. A servant escorted her into his chambers, then discreetly left, shutting the door quietly behind him. Gillian glanced around the room, at the fire roaring in the fireplace, and the table, covered with a modest feast.

She was alone. Her eyes were immediately drawn to the closed door of his bedchamber. She tiptoed closer and heard muffled voices on the other side—Kincreag and Sir Evan. She hurried to the table and snatched up the earl's goblet of wine. It was empty. She carried it to the decanter resting on the cabinet near the table. She darted a glance at his bedchamber door, then removed a small packet from her sleeve. It contained the philter

Hazel had given her, plus the burned ashes from a lock of her own hair. She must also find a way to steal some of his hair, as she had to burn it on the full moon, chanting an incantation over it to bind the spell.

She shook the packet into the empty goblet and quickly crammed the packet back up her sleeve. Her heart hammered in her throat, and there was a strange buzzing in her ears. Being devious was not fun. With trembling hands she poured wine into the goblet, spilling it on the cabinet. She raced to the table, stirred the wine with his knife, grabbed a linen napkin, and mopped up her mess.

Moments later, as she loitered by the table with false idleness, she realized he might be suspicious if wine had only been poured for him. The table was clearly set for two. She poured wine for herself and was replacing her goblet on the table when the door to his bedchamber opened.

She jumped guiltily and almost spilled her goblet of wine. After a moment's hesitation, she brought the wine to her lips and took a sip, so she at least had a reason to be hovering over the table.

The easy part was over. After he drank the philter, she must somehow get him to kiss her—a feat equal to the twelve labors of Heracles, she feared. True, he had kissed her once before, but that had been a shock, and she had no notion how to induce him to do it again.

She turned, a smile of greeting on her face. "Good evening, my lord. I trust your business was concluded to your satisfaction?"

He wore his customary black—black breeks and

black doublet. His neck was dark and corded with muscle. Though he wore his usual severe attire, he looked more comfortable this evening than he'd ever appeared before. He'd bathed recently. His damp hair hung sleek past his wide shoulders, gleaming like black ink.

"As well as can be expected."

He came to the table and looked it over curiously. Gillian noticed the linen napkin then, stained with wine. She reined in the urge to snatch it up and try to explain it away. That would only make her look guilty. He noted it immediately, picking it up and frowning at it. No servant at Lochlaire would leave a stained napkin crumpled on the earl's table, but Kincreag was a guest and a good friend of Gillian's father, so, however uncouth it was, she doubted that he would bring up the breech of courtesy given the condition her father was in. He might, however, bring it up with Uncle Roderick. In that case, Gillian said a silent prayer of apology to the poor servants who would suffer for her foolishness.

When they were seated, the earl heaped food on Gillian's plate, which surprised her. He'd not shown himself to be particularly solicitous. She found his quiet courtesy unnerving and so rushed to cover her discomfort with meaningless chatter.

"Whatever do you mean, as well as can be expected?"

He shrugged, peering at his wine but not drinking. "It is the way of the Highlanders to fight among themselves. I try to stay out of it, but sometimes they make it difficult."

"*You* are a Highlander."

"I'm an earl. Not quite the same thing."

"Really?"

He leaned one elbow on the table, between the basket of bread and the plate bearing a whole smoked salmon. "Most chieftains have never met the king, let alone spent time at court. Their whole lives are contained within their own lands—and the neighbors they choose to feud with. My course was plotted the day I was born and has not varied since. I've served the king, traveled abroad, schooled in Paris, and though I've tried very hard to stay at Kincreag these past ten years, I find myself endlessly summoned to court."

Gillian was impressed and even more intimidated by him than before. She felt very simple and provincial in comparison. "A mark of the king's favor."

"I wish sometimes that I could live as your father does and rarely leave my home except for a good raid or a MacDonell gathering."

Gillian sipped her wine. "And why not? I've heard of many noblemen running raids. I've lived near the border the past twelve years. The noblemen there are as cutthroat as the outlaws . . . many of them were outlaws at one time or another."

"They are unwise. I aim to stay in the king's favor."

Gillian looked down at her plate. "What of our marriage? Will that not put you in disfavor?"

"I petitioned the king for your sister, and he did not refuse me. He'll not refuse this either. He knows my need for an heir. My first wife was a noblewoman, whom I married at the king's insistence. Our only child died."

Gillian nearly dropped her knife. "You had a child? I didn't know."

He raised a dubious brow. "I'm surprised. Most believe I killed him, too."

Shivers chased down her spine. She didn't like thinking about the rumors. She returned her attention to her meal and hastily picked up the thread of their conversation.

"Are you certain the king is not displeased? I am a Highlander . . . and, well, many people think the Mac-Donells of Glen Laire are witches. The king hates nothing more than Highanders and witches."

"You do not have the reputation of being a witch or healer or aught else, and you spent more than half your life in the Lowlands. You have much to recommend you, to His Majesty's way of thinking."

Gillian toyed with her spoon. "And have I anything to recommend me to *you?*" She glanced at him beneath her lashes.

He had lifted his goblet to his mouth, but he lowered it, his gaze fixed on her. "Aye, your chastity. You've the hips for bearing braw lads, as well—less likely you'll die in childbirth. I know the stock you come from, and it pleases me. You'll do."

Gillian's face flamed at being referred to like a good breeding mare, but she suppressed her indignation, feeling perverse pleasure that he was about to fall hopelessly in love with her against his will. *Hips for bearing braw lads, indeed.* She smiled and raised her goblet. "Shall we drink then to the offspring you shall sire on me?"

He raised a brow, the corner of his mouth twitching slightly, but he lifted his goblet readily enough. Gillian drained hers, needing to fortify herself for the task to come—inducing him to kiss her. The task grew more difficult by the moment. When she set her goblet on the table, she noticed his was back in place, too. She could not see the contents without being obvious. They ate in silence for a moment, Gillian doing little more than picking at her food.

She stood suddenly. "Would you like more wine?" She crossed to the decanter.

When she turned back, he was replacing the lid on a crock, but he held his goblet out to her, watching her closely as she poured. His goblet was empty. She let out the breath she hadn't realized she'd been holding. So that was done. She left the decanter on the table and took her seat. As he lifted the goblet to his lips, her heart skipped in sudden fear he would note a difference in taste, but he said nothing, merely resumed eating.

After a long time, he asked, "Are you not hungry?"

Gillian had done little more than push her food around on her plate, though she'd consumed several goblets of wine. Her head swam, and she decided she'd had enough. Any more and she might make a fool of herself.

"I find myself preoccupied."

"Aye?"

"I'm wondering why I'm here. Did my father force you to dine with me?"

He wiped his hands methodically on the stained napkin. "Do you think your father could force me?"

"Aye. He forced you to take me to the woods."

"Ah, no. He only suggested that I make good on my reason for prolonging the betrothal. I chose to take you there because I like the wood and it occurred to me that you never saw your mother's grave. If I truly didn't want to be with you, even your father, friend that he is, couldn't make me."

Gillian stared at him, not quite sure what to make of his little speech. Was he saying he *did* want to be with her? The very thought made her heart stutter, until she remembered that he'd consumed the love philter. *Of course.* She must be certain to seal the effects by kissing him.

"But you're correct that I didn't invite you simply to share a meal with me tonight."

Her heart sank, though she endeavored to look merely curious, rather than discouraged. "Why did you invite me, then?"

He sighed, looking down at his plate. "Your father . . ." He paused, as if trying to collect his thoughts. His unaccustomed uncertainty made her uneasy about what he would say.

He raised his head, regarding her seriously. "When I asked you to join me, I did so with the intention of telling you several things. I've since reconsidered. But there is still one thing you must know. I've set a date. We're to be married in three days."

Gillian gasped, her hand involuntarily clasping her throat. "Three days?"

"Aye. Your father's condition is not worsening, and I have business to attend at Kincreag. You're welcome to stay with your father after the ceremony. I will return frequently, of course, as I have these past months."

Gillian thought of her father's long illness. He'd been lingering for months already. There was little she could do to aid him except read to him. Rose and Hagan handled everything. She knocked around Lochlaire most days, not knowing how to fill her time. And then there were the headaches. She'd had some headaches when she'd lived with the Hepburns, but nothing of the intensity of the ones she'd had recently. She'd told Rose what Old Hazel had said, and though it had baffled her sister, she'd promised to help Gillian investigate it. Even so, the headaches were getting worse. She would welcome a respite from Lochlaire. Maybe at Kincreag she could determine who had cursed her and why. Just the thought of it made her temples throb.

She rubbed at them absently and said, "I would like to go with you . . . so long as I can return with you, as well. Kincreag is not far. Should something happen, we can be here quickly."

The earl studied her, frowning vaguely. "Your head aches again?"

Gillian shook her head. "Not anymore. It did for a moment, but it feels fine now."

His eyes lowered to her goblet meaningfully. "Perhaps you've had enough wine?"

Gillian's cheeks flamed. "I am not soused."

"Of course not. Shall I help you back to your chambers?"

"Aye, I'd like that." She did not need help to her chambers—and was more than a little irritated that he was ready to be rid of her now that he'd said his piece—but she had yet to kiss him. And what a good excuse excess drink was! Why hadn't she thought of it before? She might lose some dignity tomorrow, but at least he wouldn't assume anything but drunkenness.

She stood, making a show of being unsteady. He came around the table and caught her elbow.

"Come now, let's get you into bed before you fall down." He spoke as if she were a slow-witted child.

She gritted her teeth and smiled up at him gratefully, clasping his arm. He led her out of his chambers, down the corridor, and up the stairs. Gillian had a moment of panic, remembering Rose, but the room was dark and empty.

He peeled her off his arm, pushing her lightly into the black room. "Good e'en." He started to turn away.

"Uhm, my lord? Could you help me locate the flint? Rose never puts it back in the same place . . . and it's so dark." Before he could refuse, she disappeared into darkness, scrambling for a scheme to win a kiss. She'd never had to do such things before! In the past she'd spent more time rapping groping knuckles and dodging ardent lips.

The faint light from the door illuminated his dark shape moving surely through the gloom, as if he could see perfectly. If she didn't do something quick, he'd have the candles lit and be gone.

She moved closer to him on the pretense of searching for the flint. Unfortunately, her night vision was not nearly as sharp as the earl's, for she tripped over something and ended up sprawled inelegantly on the floor. A scrape and flicker informed her that the earl had located the flint. Seconds later, he stared down at her in the candlelight, frowning with irritation.

Gillian started to scramble to her feet when an idea struck. "My ankle," she gasped, gazing up at him in distress. "I hurt it."

His chest and brows rose simultaneously as he took a deep breath. He seemed to be praying for patience, but he said nothing. He strode over to her and slid his hands under her arms, lifting her to her feet. Gillian put weight on her right ankle, then let herself crumple, confident he would support her. He did better, sliding his arm beneath her knees and swinging her into his arms.

Gillian caught her breath and slid her arms around his neck, feeling faint at the sheer thickness of his neck and the brush of his silky hair, dry now, against her fingers. She rested her head against his chest. He placed her on the bed and straightened. Gillian released his neck reluctantly, annoyed that she had not used that opportunity to kiss him.

He moved to her feet. "Which ankle is it?"

Gillian couldn't remember now which one she'd let crumple under her, and after a moment of frantic thought, she pointed vaguely toward her feet. "That one."

He stared at her a moment, then wrapped his large hand gently around her left ankle. "This one?"

"Ow! Aye—that's the one."

His head tilted toward her leg, black hair sliding down to hide his face. He slipped her shoe off. His fingers moved over her ankle, and Gillian made appropriate noises of discomfort. The breath left her when his hand slid up past her ankle, to her calf, then to her knee.

"My lord?" she gasped. "What are you doing?"

His hand burrowed under her skirts, to her thigh. Gillian trembled with trepidation, an odd quiver in her belly, but she didn't move. His fingers found the tie to her garter and made quick work of it.

"I need to remove your hose to get a good look at the ankle."

He pulled her hose off slowly. Gillian bit her bottom lip. Her chest fluttered strangely, like a tiny bird trying to escape. She couldn't catch her breath. However, she sensed panting would not be appropriate, so she strove to breathe normally.

When her hose was off, he tossed it aside, then straightened, garter in hand, and used it to tie his hair back. He looked a proper pagan god, dark and strong, and so huge, looming over her. He leaned back over her legs, and when his hands touched the bare skin of her ankle, a strange sound escaped her. He looked up, fathomless obsidian eyes holding hers.

"Did I hurt you?"

Gillian couldn't tell him the truth, that his touch had been so unexpectedly hot that she'd felt certain for a brief moment he'd burned her.

"Aye," she said feebly, regretting this foolish plan.

He sat on the bed, cradling her ankle on his thigh and rubbing it gently. Gillian suppressed a moan and closed her eyes to hide the fact that they were rolling into the back of her head. She'd never felt anything quite so wonderful as his fingers moving purposefully over her skin. His thumbs firmly massaged the bottom of her foot, from heel to toes.

Then his hands moved upward, massaging her calf. Gillian cracked an eye nervously and found his gaze on her face. He watched her with a dark intensity that made it impossible for her to form speech, but when his fingers began working their magic on her knee, she said, "M-my lord? It is my ankle that is wounded."

He rose onto his knees, placing a hand on either side of her legs, and leaned toward her. Gillian pressed back into the headboard, heart rising.

"Are you certain?" he said. "Because when you fell, it was your right leg you favored."

The heat of mortification pricked her scalp as she stared back at him, speechless. He'd known all along she'd faked it, and still he'd touched her with unseemly familiarity. And she knew why, too. To punish her—because he was a black-hearted knave!

He leaned closer so his face was mere inches from hers. "We're to be wed in three days, Gillian. If you want something from me, this subterfuge is not necessary."

"Want something?" she squeaked indignantly, trying to roll off the bed, but he caught her, pushing her back against the headboard, a frighteningly wicked gleam in his eye. "Whatever could I want from you? I hurt *both* ankles!"

"Oh?" His brow creased with mock concern. But it was enough to make him sit back, taking up her other ankle. "Well, let me see to that one as well."

Gillian could have bitten her tongue off as his hands

slid up her skirts, past her knee, to remove the other garter. He knew she wasn't hurt. Why was she allowing him to continue this charade? She wasn't at all certain, but for some reason, she was. She should have kissed him a moment ago, when he'd called her on her ridiculous scheme, but she'd been too mortified to admit to such machinations.

His hands spun the same sorcery they had on her other foot. But this time she stayed tense and alert, aware that he was watching her the whole while, gauging her reactions. She had a sneaking suspicion she'd get her kiss tonight—and likely more than she'd bargained for, which brought a sheen of perspiration to her temples. She tried not to squirm, wanting this torture to end and yet longing for him to touch her more, to slide his fingers higher. . . .

He raised one of her feet, bent his head, and kissed her ankle. Gillian stopped breathing. She stared down at the black head bent over her foot, shocked and scandalized—and unspeakably aroused.

"Such a pretty ankle," he murmured against her skin. "A shame for it to be bruised." His breath was warm, and his other hand slid further up her calf. When his mouth touched her ankle again, she felt his tongue.

She jerked her leg away, tucking both ankles safely beneath her skirts. "My lord!" was all she could think to say. Her voice was breathy and thin.

He sat on her bed, one long, muscular leg bent in front of him, the other hanging off her bed. "I don't like games, Gillian, and I thought you better than that. Be direct with me and we'll get on fine."

He shamed her. She looked away, embarrassed she'd made such a fool of herself. How could she think him stupid enough to fall for her silly virginal schemes? She was tempted to inform him that she wanted nothing from him and send him away so she could wallow in her shame. But the philter. He'd drunk it. Perhaps that's what had prompted him to kiss her so improperly. Somewhat emboldened by that thought, she said, still staring down at her skirts, "I was hoping you would kiss me again."

She didn't hear him move, so she was startled when his finger tilted her chin up to look at him. She met his black gaze, waiting, pulse throbbing erratically in her throat. He studied her face.

"All this for a mere kiss?" he said doubtfully.

Gillian nodded.

"I'm flattered," he murmured, leaning toward her. She watched him, fascinated, as his long black lashes lowered, seconds before his mouth covered hers. Then Gillian's own eyes fluttered shut, lips tingling from the contact. His hand slid beneath her hair, cupping the back of her head as he pulled her forward and tipped her head back.

This kiss was nothing like the last one—which had been a perfectly lovely kiss. There was no softness in him as he parted her lips to kiss her deeply. Gillian's hand flailed out to grab onto something, and he caught her wrist, bringing her hand to his chest and holding it there. Her head spun, and when she parted her lips to suck in more air, he pushed his tongue into her mouth.

Gillian melted, vaguely aware that his hand no

longer held hers trapped against his chest. Her arms had slid around his neck to draw him closer, and his hand was full over her breast, the palm open, stroking and shaping it, while his other hand turned her head to taste her mouth deeper yet.

His kiss laid her bare. Despite everything, she wanted *him*, not just rescue from France, not just elevation to a countess; she wanted the man. She'd not realized how much until he'd kissed her. It bloomed inside her, pulsing in time with the wild beating of her heart. She pressed closer, kissing him back, relishing in the slow and purposeful slide of his tongue against hers.

She did not know how long they kissed, or what would have happened—their marriage would have been a sure thing, she suspected—but she was not to find out.

Rose's voice roused Gillian from her stupor. "Er—should I come back?"

Gillian tore her mouth away and strained away from Kincreag, but he held her fast, his dark eyes burning down at her. "Next time," he said in a low voice, his breath warm on her upturned face, "just ask me, and I'll be happy to oblige." Then louder, he said, "I was just leaving." He did not take his eyes from Gillian.

"I see that," Rose replied dryly.

He appeared unashamed of the situation they'd been caught in and not nearly as affected as Gillian was, evidenced by his regular, calm breathing. He straightened slowly and bid them both a good evening. When the door closed behind him, Gillian chanced a look at her sister, whose eyes were practically popping out.

"Was that a garter in his hair?"

"Uhm . . . aye. He seems to like me better now," Gillian offered, her cheeks flaming.

"I noticed."

Rose strolled over to the bed and stared down at Gillian's bodice. Gillian glanced down at herself and saw that several of the hooks had been undone. It gaped at her side—that explained why she'd been able to breathe deeper. Her breasts felt heavy and fuller than usual, the nipples excruciatingly sensitive. She quickly rehooked her bodice, binding her breasts up tightly.

Rose bent to pick something up and straightened with one of Gillian's hose dangling from her fingertips, brows arched nearly to her hairline.

Gillian snatched it away and gathered the rest of her things. "Don't look at me like that. We *are* to be married. In three days."

"He seems to have resigned himself to the drudgery of marriage, aye?" Rose grinned. "This is cause for celebration! He's set a date—*and,* if not a love match, it is surely a lust match."

Gillian sighed, despondent suddenly. "No, not really." She filled her sister in on her acquisition of the love philter. "So you see, he doesn't really want *me*, it's the love philter."

Rose frowned thoughtfully. "That was unwise."

"Why? If he thinks he's in love with me, he'll not back out of the betrothal."

"If he doesn't even like you, there's not much chance he'll kill you in a fit of jealous rage, is there?"

"What?" Gillian said, perplexed, as she sometimes was by her sister's logic.

"The late countess?" Rose said, exasperated. "He *murdered* her—threw her from a cliff for cuckolding him. I've heard he once loved her before she became loose of morals."

"He pleaded innocent and the king found him so," Gillian said tartly. "Besides, I don't think a man has to love his wife to become wroth with her infidelity . . . in fact, I would think that if he thought himself in love with me, he'd be more inclined to believe my lies." She looked heavenward and took a deep breath. "*Not* that I have any plans to either lie or cuckold him, but you see my meaning."

Rose nodded sagely. "You're right. Wives are chattel, and regardless of what a man feels, he doesn't like others to touch his possessions. Well, then! Good show, Gilly! A love philter is just the thing."

Gillian sighed, wondering why she no longer felt so excited about her brilliant idea. If that kiss was any indication, it was clearly working.

She lay back on the bed, hand to her forehead. She had another headache, though this one—a dull throbbing at the back of her skull, accompanied by mild queasiness—was different from her others.

"More headaches?" Rose asked, passing her hands over Gillian's head, then lower, over her torso. "Och, well, that one's simple. You've had too much wine. Not much I can do for that, but I do have an infusion that will help you sleep and keep ye from bocking."

She turned away to fetch her wee wooden box of remedies.

Gillian sat up abruptly and cringed as her head

spun. "The headaches," she moaned. "Did you learn aught about the curse?" She'd told Rose about Hazel's suspicions right after her visit to the village, though she'd left out the part about the love philter until tonight.

Rose set the box on the bed beside Gillian. "No, but I did discover something interesting. Lochlaire has not a single servant that was here twelve years ago. Everyone is either dead or gone, though no one seems to know where."

Gillian could see the wheels turning in Rose's head. "Really? What could it mean?"

"I don't know. Maybe you saw who was responsible for Mother's murder? So a curse was placed on you. And that same person made certain no one was left at Lochlaire to remember anything."

"But who had the power to do such a thing?"

"I dinna know. Can you stand the pain enough to try to think through the memories?"

Gillian shook her head. "If I dig at it, it becomes so fierce I faint."

Rose chewed her bottom lip, hands now moving automatically through her box. "We need Isobel. She should be here any day. My magic is healing, but Isobel has Mother's magic. Perhaps she can divine something."

Rose handed Gillian a cup full of foul, thick liquid. Gillian swallowed the contents, grimacing at the taste, then lay back at her sister's insistence.

She closed her eyes and tried to clear her mind for sleep, but found she couldn't stop thinking about Kincreag and the way he'd kissed her. Would he have ever kissed her in such a manner if not for the love philter?

Back in his chambers, Nicholas cursed his bad luck with women. He removed the lid of the crock. It held a slab of butter swimming in wine. It was not some rare delicacy served at Lochlaire: Nicholas had poured his wine in it when Gillian's back had been turned. He studied the butter closely but saw no evidence that the wine had harmed it.

Could the wench actually mean to poison him? He could hardly believe it, and yet it was clear this wine was tainted. He'd been suspicious when he'd seen her hovering about the table, but he'd not expected this. Then he'd noted that his knife was damp, and the linen stained, so he'd sniffed the wine carefully. He did not take medicinal wine, yet this was rife with herbs and the faint odor of ash.

He'd been deeply disappointed, more so than he'd thought possible, but he'd said nothing to her. After three days in the saddle and dealing with the Campbells, he'd found that when he returned to Glen Laire he was not only anxious to see Alan and assure himself that his friend still lived but also preoccupied with thoughts of Gillian. He'd come to some conclusions on his little trip, the most important one being that Gillian was not Catriona, nor any of the other women he'd had relations with, and it was unfair to expect her to be. The least he could do was give her a fair chance. He truly did not wish for a cold marriage. And so he'd decided to give this union between them the opportunity to be something more than a contract to be fulfilled.

He shook his head, disgusted with himself. It seemed that even after all these years, he'd learned nothing. He'd been the same way with Catriona at first, wanting to believe her and trust her. He would not be Gillian's fool.

It troubled him that he'd begun to weaken without even realizing it. He would have to be more vigilant—*if* he married her at all. He'd intended to, prior to this evening, and not just because he'd promised her father. After all, even the Lord counseled that it was better to marry than to burn, and she'd nearly turned him to ash tonight. But now . . .

Three days. That's how long he had to discover what she was up to. He'd been forced to set a date. Not that he'd truly minded at the time. In fact, it had worked out quite well.

He'd gone to see Alan before leaving for Campbell lands. Alan had signed the marriage contract the same day Nicholas and Gillian had, but he'd been so weak that he'd been unable to read it carefully. But in the days following, he'd managed to go over it meticulously, and he'd accused Nicholas of the same thing Gillian had.

When Nicholas had assured him he had every intention of wedding Gillian, Alan had challenged him to prove it by setting a date. That's when Nicholas had told him why he was prolonging it. He would not set a date unless Alan promised not to take his own life. Grim and resigned, Alan had promised, and so Nicholas had set the date.

And now she was trying to poison him.

Even more perplexing was her behavior. She hadn't behaved like a person waiting for her victim to fall to the ground gasping and twitching. He knew the look of a predator toying with her prey. Perhaps it was a slow-working poison? Catriona had favored those.

He considered the crock for several more minutes, then decided he couldn't rest until he knew what it was. He replaced the lid and carried it through the castle to the great hall. Several hounds and a mastiff lolled near the fireplaces. Broc, the wiry gray deerhound, waited patiently outside his master's chambers. The deerhound raised his head from his paws and stared at Nicholas with his strange, cloudy eyes.

A rat was what he needed. Nicholas took the crock into the kitchen. It was empty except for a single scullery maid. She quickly averted her eyes when he entered. He set the crock on a low table and asked her, "Do you have a rat problem?"

She seemed struck with terror that he'd addressed her, and he had to repeat himself before she could formulate a reply. "Oh, no, my lord. The cats kill them all."

"All of them?"

"Most. We still get them in the larder." She cowered slightly, as if she expected punishment for this transgression.

The larder was unlocked, a sign of the trust Alan had in the MacDonells. Nicholas opened the door and peered inside. It was dark, so he fetched a candelabra. The flickering flames shone yellow in the eyes of several cats. They greeted him with soft meows, and a silky black one leapt from its perch on a barrel to rub against his ankles.

The rats weren't likely to come out as long as the cats were here, so Nicholas removed them, two at a time, closing the door behind him each trip so they couldn't slip back in, as they clearly wanted to do.

He poked around the foodstuffs a bit until he was satisfied he'd not missed any cats. He started for the door when the flame caught a red shine of small eyes. A rat, hiding behind several barrels.

He returned to the kitchen to fetch his crock of butter and poisoned wine and was stunned to find the crock empty. The scullery maid was gone, too, but she wouldn't have left the crock there if she'd cleaned it. He scanned the kitchen, his gaze finally resting on the gray deerhound sitting in the doorway, tongue lolling out of its mouth. When Nicholas looked at it, it became momentarily excited, licking its chops, tail swishing across the floor.

An unaccustomed feeling of dread descended on Nicholas, sinking like a stone in his belly. Broc. Alan's favorite dog. Nicholas dropped to his knees and called the dog. Broc came to him, tail wagging. Nicholas smelled his breath, praying it just smelled doggy, but he was further sickened by the scent of herbed wine.

"Stupid, stupid dog," he said, staring into Broc's dark eyes. The dog seemed to be smiling at him. Nicholas's mind raced, desperate to find a way out of this horrible predicament. He tried to force the dog to drink fouled water so it would vomit, but Broc refused. When Nicholas tried to gag the deerhound with his fingers, the usually docile dog nearly took his hand off. All that was left was to wait.

Nicholas had no idea how long he knelt on the floor, scratching Broc's ears, waiting for the dog to convulse or vomit or whatnot, wondering what he would say to Alan, and cataloging his own dogs. He had a fine deer-hound back at Kincreag. It was one of his favorites, but he would gladly give it up to make amends for this stupid mistake.

After a bit, Broc yawned and lay down.

"Oh God." Nicholas sat beside the dog, wondering if he was dying now. He didn't seem to be in any pain—in fact, he seemed to be in ecstasy from all the attention Nicholas lavished on him. He lifted his front leg and cocked his head, inviting Nicholas to scratch his belly. Nicholas obliged. It was the least he could do.

"Broc?" someone called from the hall.

Broc's ears pricked, but he didn't move. The voice came closer and took on a puzzled tone. It was Hagan. Alan must be asking for his dog. Broc was never far from his master. Nicholas felt like a wee lad again, caught sneaking his father's whisky and waiting to get his arse strapped.

Hagan filled the doorway to the kitchen. His gaze went from Nicholas, sitting cross-legged on the floor, to Broc, lying beside him, neck craning to look at the Irishman.

"My lord?" Hagan said, perplexed.

Before Nicholas could formulate a response, Broc got to his feet and trotted to Hagan's side. Nicholas stared at the dog, then looked back at the empty crock on the table. Perhaps it had not been poison? But then what could it be? He was utterly confused. He got to his feet, brushing his breeks off.

"My lord?" Hagan said again. "Is aught amiss?"

"No . . . I'm just . . ." He became aware of the chorus of meows and looked back at the larder. Half a dozen cats crouched outside the door, meowing and looking at the men expectantly.

"Who let the cats out?" Hagan asked, frowning deeply. He glanced suspiciously at Nicholas as he crossed to the larder and let the cats back in. Nicholas took the opportunity to examine Broc again. He took the dog's face in his hands and gazed carefully into the dog's eyes. Broc panted happily, then licked him. Unless it was an extremely slow-working poison, he couldn't fathom what Gillian had slipped into his wine.

He straightened when Hagan returned, eyeing him with wary concern.

"If you're hungry, my lord, I'll have something sent to your chambers. Just let me fetch Cook—"

"No, no," Nicholas said, hand still on Broc's head.

Hagan looked from the dog to Nicholas again, brow furrowed.

"He's a good dog," Nicholas said in explanation, giving Broc a final scratch before exiting the kitchen and returning to his chambers.

He slept little that night, worried he'd wake to find his best friend's beloved pet dead and wondering—with an unpleasant mixture of dread and intense curiosity—what mischief his bride-to-be plotted.

7

Gillian?" Alan said, his irritation tinged with affection. "What happened next?"

Gillian started from a daze of daydreams and looked down at the open book on her lap, searching for her place. It was the third time she'd trailed off in her reading, leaving her father to stare at her in amused exasperation. She couldn't stop thinking about Lord Kincreag. *Nicholas.* She loved the sound of his name in her mind. She dared not speak it aloud, but as she'd lain in bed last night, she'd imagined calling him by his given name as he kissed her again and held her. In fact, she couldn't seem to concentrate on anything this morning, her mind forever drifting back to her betrothed.

Alan sighed. "Let's leave off the reading for now."

Gillian closed the book and set it aside. He'd had a good night. No nightmares. Healthy color replaced the pallor of his cheeks above his beard, though they were still gaunt and rawboned. At times like this, it seemed there really was hope for the chieftain of the Glen Laire MacDonells.

"You're certain you don't mind me leaving?" she asked again. She'd told him of her conversation with Nicholas and that she wished to accompany him to Kincreag. But she felt a pang of guilt for leaving her father, whom she'd been separated from for so long.

"Why should I? I'm the one that wished to see you wed before I died. It's what I want. Your place is with your husband. Isobel lives at Sgor Dubh with Philip. It does my heart good to know she has a good man to protect her in these times." He took Gillian's hand. "As it does my heart good to see you with Kincreag."

Gillian squeezed her father's hand.

"Besides, Kincreag is not far—closer than Isobel at Sgor Dubh."

Isobel and Sir Philip's party had been sighted from the walls nearly an hour ago. They would be here soon, so Uncle Roderick had crossed the loch to wait for them. Gillian had missed her sister this past month. She hoped they would visit often in spite of the awkwardness the broken betrothal caused.

Alan studied her closely. "Are you happy with him, sweeting?"

Gillian had gotten her wish—to marry a Scotsman and remain in Scotland, close to her family. And besides that, she was intrigued and drawn to the brooding earl. Perhaps it wasn't deep love, like her sisters had for their men, but it was the best Gillian could hope for.

"Aye, Da. I'm satisfied."

His green eyes narrowed as he studied her critically.

"Now, ye dinna have to lie to me. I ken he . . . seems unpleasant and perhaps a trifle cold, but in truth, he's a good man. His first wife . . ."

"Aye?" Gillian leaned forward eagerly. She hadn't thought to ask her father about Kincreag's first wife, but now it seemed a thoughtless oversight. Of course Alan would be biased, but still, he'd known Nicholas when he'd been married to Catriona. Her father should have much to tell.

But before he could say anything more, the door opened and Broc trotted in, followed by Hagan, then the earl himself.

Gillian sighed, curiosity unsatisfied. She was determined to finish this conversation before she left for Kincreag. She was developing a rather morbid curiosity about the late countess.

She avoided looking at the earl, as his presence did more than remind her of the night before; it sent her pulse galloping and made her feel flushed and awkward. She was so involved in trying to behave normally and hide her suddenly trembling hands that she was startled when Broc bounded over and jumped on her, planting his large, hairy paws on her chest and licking her face enthusiastically.

"Down, Broc!" Alan laughed. "I've never seen him like this. Oh, Hagan, get him!"

Hagan grabbed the dog's collar before he knocked Gillian out of her chair.

"Good morn—" Alan started to greet the earl, but he was cut off by Gillian's shriek as Broc flew at her again.

"Confounded dog!" Alan sat up in the bed, scowling fiercely.

Hagan wrestled with the ardent deerhound, finally shoving him out the door. Broc scratched and whined at the door for several minutes before finally falling silent.

Alan shook his head, bewildered. "I've never seen him behave so."

Gillian hadn't either. The deerhound usually lay at her father's bedside like an old rug, barely rousing himself to eat.

She chanced a glance up at Kincreag and found him staring darkly at her. She quickly looked away, her cheeks burning in embarrassment. Perhaps the love philter had worn off and he regretted kissing her the night before? But that couldn't be. Hazel had told her it would last for some time, a month at least. But then she remembered she'd not completed the spell. She still needed his hair.

She gathered her courage and turned to Kincreag, smiling cheerfully. "I was talking to Father about preparations for the wedding—"

"My people have prepared everything," he said, his enigmatic stare still fixed on her.

Gillian blinked. "Oh."

He moved to the other side of the bed and began to chat with her father about the Campbells. For some reason Gillian felt as if he purposely ignored her, though in truth he acted no different than he always did. Had last night meant nothing to him?

Gillian's shoulders slumped. She excused herself and slipped out of the room. She stood outside the door, thinking. Perhaps this was a good time to go to Kincreag's chambers to steal hair from his comb. She started out of the hall but was distracted by two little girls playing by themselves near the largest fireplace. Gillian watched them for several minutes. They were remarkably familiar, reminding her of children she'd played with when she was a child, right down to their stained smocks and the flowers—wilting daisies—stuck jauntily in their curls. This last detail caused Gillian's heart to leap in a sickening manner. This was more than mere similarities—they were identical.

She started toward the girls but was waylaid by Broc, bouncing joyfully around her legs, tongue lolling out of the side of his mouth.

Gillian scratched his head absently, continuing across the hall, dog on her heels. She searched her mind for the girls' names. Pain throbbed momentarily in her temples, but she pressed on, a worm of fear wiggling in her belly. Why did her head ache when she thought of these girls or of her mother's death?

The girls did not seem to notice her until she was beside them. Her head screamed, but she would not let that stop her. "Good morn," she said.

They turned toward her, poppets clutched to their chests, and Gillian saw their faces clearly. They were the *same* children. But that was impossible . . . and yet as she stared into the girls' eyes—blue and brown—they were the same eyes, the same welcoming smiles, the same childish voices. The blood drained from Gillian's face. Her mouth gaped in horrified surprise.

"Gilly! We've missed you!" one said. Cinnie was her

name. It came back to Gillian all at once. Cinnie and Rowena. She gasped, the pain squeezing her head like a vise, blinding her.

She clutched her head, fighting against it. "How can this be . . . ?" she heard herself ask from a distance. The pain was too great, crowding everything out. Yawning blackness opened before her, promising a refuge from the crippling pain.

The next thing she knew she couldn't breathe—something crushed her chest and smelled of sweaty dog. Someone yelled her name.

"Bloody Christ!" A man. "Get Rose!" Her uncle Roderick.

"Gilly! Oh my God, Gilly!" A woman—her sister, Isobel.

"Get off," Uncle Roderick said. A fierce growl rumbled through Gillian's chest, resonating into her spine. She cracked an eye and saw wiry gray fur. Broc had stationed himself on her chest. No wonder she couldn't breathe—the deerhound weighed at least seven stone.

Uncle Roderick reached for the dog again and it snapped at him, snarling viciously. Gillian couldn't see her uncle, but she heard his sharp intake of breath. Then he whispered in Gaelic, his voice low and angry. "I command you—stand down, Beast!"

The growling died, replaced by a whine.

Gillian pushed at Broc and the dog moved off her, hovering over her face and licking her ear. The slurping was like a cannon, splitting her head. She groaned and feebly tried to move her head away.

Her uncle pushed the dog away; then his face was

over hers, frowning worriedly. "Can you speak, Gilly?"

She peered upward, catching sight of a crowd forming around her. She had to close her eyes, as moving them sent excruciating pain radiating through her skull.

"I think she fainted again," Roderick murmured.

"No," Gillian managed to force out between stiff lips. "I'm awake."

Someone took her hand. It was cool and soft. "What happened, Gilly?" Isobel asked.

"I was trying to talk to Cinnie—" The pain stabbed her again. She cried out, trying to curl into herself, clutching her head.

"Move aside," Rose said. Gillian heard the shift in the crowd around her, but she was afraid to move. Her head ached horribly, and she feared any movement would cause her to vomit.

Rose's hands touched hers, moving them gently away from her head. "Let me see, darling," she murmured. A cool hand pressed against her forehead.

An anxious voice from her other side asked, "What happened?" Kincreag. Gillian's heart did a little leap, but she couldn't move, afraid her head would split open.

Rose was silent. She knew what was wrong but was unwilling to speak of it among so many people. There was silence as Rose passed her hands over Gillian, trying to discover the cause of her pain.

"Gillian? Can you hear me?" The earl again.

Gillian tried to nod her head, but a wave of nausea rolled through her, and she moaned instead.

"Pick her up," Rose ordered.

Strong hands were on her, and a moment later she was pressed into the warmth of Kincreag's chest, his arms tight around her. As he carried her through the castle, she felt better by increments. He laid her gently on her bed, and she squinted up at him. He had turned away already to face Rose.

"What the bloody hell is wrong with her?" There was a strange edge to his voice she didn't understand.

The door closed, and Rose said, her voice low, "We believe a curse has been placed on her."

The silence drew out, thick and heavy. Finally Kincreag swore violently. "I'll send for my own physician." He strode away, then turned back to point a finger at Rose. "Do nothing to her while I'm gone."

"What?" Rose said indignantly, hands on hips. "That charlatan you call a healer *will not* touch my sister."

He returned to the bed. "She is my wife, and *you* will not touch her while babbling about curses."

"She's not your wife yet."

Gillian craned her neck gingerly to watch Rose and Kincreag glare at each other. He turned decisively and scooped Gillian up into his arms, wrenching a muffled gasp from her as her head bumped against his chest.

He murmured an apology as he continued across the room, stopping at the door. "Move, Sir Philip."

Gillian turned her head, wincing at the pain that gripped her from the slight movement. Isobel's husband blocked the door, arms folded over his plaid-covered chest.

"Peace, my lord," Sir Philip said, his voice soothing. "Rose means her no harm. She's a fine healer and would never hurt her own sister, you must know that. You're distraught."

"Move. Now." Kincreag's voice was low and threatening.

Gillian curled her fingers into Nicholas's doublet and forced herself to speak. "My lord, I pray you. Let Rose tend me. I trust no one more."

He frowned down at her, muscles working in his jaw. After a moment he returned her to the bed. He pulled up a chair and positioned himself on the other side of the bed, staring at Rose challengingly. "Fine. Heal her. I'll watch."

"Very well," Rose said. "First, I'll give her something to help her rest." Rose dug about in her wee wooden box.

Gillian's stomach felt wambly again, so she closed her eyes and leaned her head back, willing it to calm.

"What's in that?" Nicholas asked when Rose apparently mixed together some concoction for Gillian to take.

"Willow bark and betony to soothe her pain, chamomile and valerian to help her sleep, and a bit of fenugreek to settle her stomach."

"Very well," Nicholas said reluctantly. A long silence followed in which Rose brewed the concoction.

"Help me lift her head," Rose said.

Nicholas's large, warm hand cupped the back of Gillian's skull, and she let him raise her slightly, tilting her head so Rose could press the small wooden cup against her bottom lip. She swallowed the liquid and was gently lowered back to the pillow. When she opened her eyes, everyone crowded around the bed, watching her expectantly.

With great effort, she forced herself into a sitting position, though it caused her head to ache again. "It's just a headache. I'm not near death. Someone really should tell Father I'm fine." She looked pointedly at Isobel and Sir Philip. "Surely Da is waiting to see you."

When they were gone, only Rose and Nicholas remained. Rose flipped through her stack of sewn manuscripts, and Nicholas stared down at his hands, clasped loosely between his knees. A lock of black hair had escaped from the thong at his nape, and it hung down to feather against his jaw. His presence comforted Gillian.

The tight pain in her temples eased as Rose's medicine took effect, and a warm drowsiness settled over her.

There was a quick knock on the door; then Roderick entered. Broc slipped past his legs, nearly tripping him, and leapt onto the bed. Nicholas was on his feet, holding the dog back when it would have sat on Gillian again.

"What is the matter with him?" Nicholas demanded. He grasped the dog's snout and stared into its eyes. "Is this the same dog?"

"Aye! It is, I'm sure of it." Roderick shook his head, glaring at Broc. "I know not what's wrong with him. I didna even know he followed me up here. I had closed him up with Alan. He must've escaped." He let out an angry breath. "I'll take him back and tie him up this time."

"It's all right," Gillian said. "Lay down, Broc."

The dog obeyed immediately, eyeing her with soft,

adoring eyes. Gillian smiled and scratched the wiry hair sticking up between his ears.

Roderick appeared upset. "He shouldn't be in here troubling you when ye're ill. He's yer da's dog." He made a grab at the dog, but Broc strained away, crawling on his belly until his head lay on Gillian's thigh.

"It's fine, Uncle. I want him to stay."

Roderick's mouth flattened. He looked as if he wanted to protest further; instead he blew out a breath. "Fine." He glanced over his shoulder at Rose and asked, "What's she looking for? Does she ken what ails ye, lass?"

Gillian nodded. "Aye, she does. But we don't know what to do about it."

"Well?" he asked, when Gillian was not forthcoming.

Nicholas leaned back in his chair, face leaning on his fist so that his mouth was hidden. His eyes revealed nothing of his thoughts.

Gillian glanced at Rose. Her sister nodded encouragingly.

"We believe I've been cursed."

Her uncle said nothing. His normally ruddy skin paled.

"Uncle Roderick?"

"Cursed?" he sputtered. "Who would do such a thing, and why?"

Gillian shook her head. "I don't know."

Roderick sat beside her on the bed and took her hand. "This is terrible tidings. If there is aught I can do to help, pray tell me."

Gillian squeezed her uncle's hand in appreciation. It was unsettling to think she held the key to punishing the person responsible for her mother's murder but could not recall it without nearly killing herself. The witch who'd done this to her must be very powerful, for this was no simple spell. Gillian was not a witch herself, but she remembered her mother performing complex spells and still being skeptical that they would work as she'd hoped. Lillian MacDonell had counseled that magic was dangerous and should never be dabbled with, for many spells had unintended effects, and even the most conscientious witch couldn't predict all of them. That was another very important reason to stay away from the dark arts. Curses and black spells let loose evil in the world and were just as unpredictable.

Roderick leaned forward, his dark blue eyes intense. "In the hall you said a name—Cinnie. You said you were talking to her. I know of no Cinnie at Lochlaire. Could that have aught to do with the curse?"

Gillian shrugged, her mind shying away from the name. "I-I know not."

Roderick rubbed his lips thoughtfully. "Rose, is there something you can give her to suppress the pain so she can think of it?"

"No," Rose said shortly.

Roderick glanced back at Rose. "What are you looking for in those?"

Rose let the manuscript she leafed through flutter shut. "Mother had a grimoire . . . it was also a sort of diary. She left it to me with all the rest, but as she did no healing, I rarely look at it. She worked in charms and spells, so perhaps there's something in it about breaking curses."

Roderick mulled this over for several minutes before standing. "I'm not a witch, but if you find a task for me, let me know." He leaned over to buss Gillian's cheek. "Rest, love."

When he was gone, Gillian looked shyly at her betrothed. He'd been very protective of her, as if she already belonged to him. As if he truly cared. It did strange things to her belly.

He still leaned on his fist, but he looked troubled, frowning meditatively at Broc.

"What are you thinking?" she asked.

"I'm thinking . . . *this* is the reason so many innocent people burn." He dropped his fist to his thigh and straightened, turning his hard black gaze on her. "People like your mother."

Gillian's brows drew together in confusion. Had Rose's medicine muddled her head? "What do you mean?"

"Just because we don't understand something, doesn't mean it's witchcraft."

He didn't believe. And so he thought this was a bunch of foolishness. A flush stole up Gillian's throat, from both anger and embarrassment. Rose shook her head condescendingly but remained uncharacteristically quiet.

"How else can you explain what is happening to me?" Gillian demanded. "Surely a real ailment wouldn't strike only when I think of certain things?"

He nodded slowly. "You're right—if this were a sickness of the body. But what about a sickness of the mind?"

Gillian wilted against the pillow. Such a thing had not occurred to her, but hearing him say it, as well as the resigned way he looked at her, made her pray it *was* a curse and that she was not going mad.

"I'm not insane," she said, but her voice was strained and unsure.

He considered her quietly, then asked, "Without causing yourself any undue pain, do you recall what you thought of—perhaps not the exact thought, but what it was about? Who is Cinnie?"

Gillian's head ached sharply, but she pursued the thought, fingers rubbing her temples. "The girls I saw . . . they'd not changed at all, not since I was a child . . . Cinnie . . . and Rowena . . . even the flowers . . . but how could that be?"

She closed her eyes, pressing her fingers against her lids, unable to go on. Pain clawed at her, leaving her weak. She slid down the bed so she was lying again, waiting for the knives stabbing her brain to abate. When it had receded enough for her to open her eyes, she looked at the earl, hopeful.

He stared back at her with a disturbed expression. "There were no little girls in the hall. Sir Philip asked if anyone had seen what happened. One of my men was there. He said you were alone."

"Maybe they ran away when I fainted," she said desperately. But she knew that was not so. She wanted to think of it but couldn't, or she would be ill.

"Why would they do that? Would they not go for help?"

Gillian pushed herself up with a burst of strength. "I'm not mad!"

He said nothing.

"They were there."

"And they caused you to collapse in pain, these children?"

Gillian's anger dissolved into despair. *She was not insane.* She wasn't. "Leave me alone." She curled into herself on the bed. When he didn't obey, she said, a note of hysteria in her voice that surely made her sound like a madwoman, "Leave me!"

He straightened, his handsome face grim. "Very well. But my physician will be in to examine you later."

"Why? To be sure you're not getting a tainted mare?"

He looked as if he might say more, then sighed heavily and left.

Gillian covered her face, wanting to weep, but afraid to pain her head anymore. Maybe she was insane. She must be delusional, for what she thought she'd seen was impossible. And she was the only one who'd seen it. She must be mad.

"Gillian," Rose said, excited, gripping Gillian's wrists and pulling them away from her face. Slanting midnight eyes peered at her mischievously. "You're not mad."

"I'm not?"

Rose shook her head, smiling as though she might burst. "And you *are* a witch, Gilly. Just like Isobel and me."

Gillian frowned, unable to see the connection. "What do you mean?"

"No one else can see the wee lassies in the hall but you . . . because they're dead. They've been dead some twoscore years."

Gillian just blinked at her, horrified wonder filling her.

Rose gripped Gillian's hands tightly. "You're a necromancer, Gillian. You can speak with the dead."

8

Gillian reclined in shocked silence as her sister paced the floor, thinking aloud. The concoction Rose had given her had taken full effect, and she fought to keep her eyes open and follow her sister's mutterings.

"It's all beginning to make sense. Whoever cursed you did so because they didn't want you to speak with the dead. They *knew*. Who else but Mum and Da would have known you had this gift? I didn't know, neither did Isobel. Da doesn't know, or he'd have said something. Whoever cursed you knew that no one else knew—or at least no one *alive* knew—and that they could curse you without suspicion. And you say you've had the headaches afore?"

Gillian nodded groggily. "Occasionally, but never like this."

Rose's mouth flattened in thought. "Hm. There are ghosts everywhere. I'm sure even the Hepburns have some somewhere. That was likely the source of your headaches, but you never forced yourself to think on it until recently. Which is why they've now grown worse."

Gillian thought back and did seem to recall that her notice of something or someone unusual had preceded her headaches, but the vague aching always distracted her and made her forget.

"In order for the spell to work," Rose went on, "you must know on some level that what you're seeing is dead."

Joy swelled inside Gillian. She was a witch. All these years, she'd felt she was some kind of mistake, the only MacDonell to possess no magic. She'd tried for years to discover how the MacDonell legacy had manifested in her, before finally giving up in despair, unhappily resigned to the fact that she was not special. And all along it had been inside her, lying dormant and suppressed.

Broc whined softly and wiggled closer. Gillian put her arm around the dog and laid her head on his, her eyelids heavy. *She was a witch.*

Rose's pacing stopped. "Oh, Gilly, I forgot I'd given you the infusion. You sleep. We'll talk more later."

She pulled the bedclothes around Gillian and Broc, and Gillian drifted to sleep, her last conscious thought that she was not mad but a witch. What would Nicholas think? She feared he'd prefer madness.

When she finally woke, the sun had set. The room was bathed in purple hues, and a single candle flickered on the nearby table. Gillian stretched luxuriously. Her headache was gone. Something very warm pressed against her side, and when she pulled back the covers, she was amused to find Broc had not left her. The dog lifted his head and panted, so that he looked as if he were smiling.

She slipped on her shoes and went to her father's chambers, Broc at her heels. Hagan ushered them in, grinning cheerfully. Gillian smiled back at the enormous Irishman, his rare good spirits lightening hers. Isobel sat beside their father's bed, Sir Philip and Stephen Ross were at a table nearby, playing cards. Rose was across the room, in front of the fire, reading one of her manuscripts. Everyone was together again. Gillian savored the moment, knowing how ephemeral it was and how quickly things change, always with such finality.

"You look much better," Isobel said. She rose and embraced Gillian. Sir Philip came to greet her as well, pecking her on the cheek. Stephen stumped over, leaning heavily on his ebony cane, and gave her a heartier greeting, embracing her tightly. "Glad to see ye well."

Stephen was friend and companion to Sir Philip. Several months ago he'd been beaten and shot in the back, and Gillian had been pressed into nursing him. In that time they'd become fast friends.

"Stephen," Gillian cried, clasping his shoulder and staring down at his legs. "You're walking!"

He looked exceptionally well, considering the severity of his injury and the fever that had followed. He'd lost weight due to the fever, but already the thickness of his shoulders had returned, and the hollows of his cheeks did not seem so pronounced. His long, golden hair had been cut so the deep gash in his head could be stitched and tended, but he'd apparently chosen to keep it shorn, as it was still cropped close to his head.

"I wouldna call it walking, exactly."

"I would." Gillian smiled warmly at him before settling herself on her father's bed.

"How are ye, lass?" Alan asked, gripping her hand and studying her face.

"I feel better, thanks to Rose."

Alan scratched his dog's head but frowned when Broc moved away to position himself next to Gillian. "Methinks he likes you better."

Gillian shrugged helplessly. "It's the oddest thing. He won't leave my side since this morning."

"Huh." Alan eyed his dog. "Then he's yours. If you want him, that is. He obviously wants you."

"Thank you, Da," Gillian said, pleased with the gift.

Alan smiled benevolently, quickly reconciled to his dog's abandonment. "Now, to more important matters. Rose told me everything." He shook his head slowly, brows raised. "I never knew, love. Your mother never told me you spoke with the dead. Useful magic, that."

"Perhaps she didn't know either?" Gillian wanted to think back but was afraid to. She would let it be for now, but eventually she would have to force the memories, regardless of the consequences.

"That's what we're going to find out tonight." Alan gestured to Isobel's husband. Sir Philip fetched a wooden casket, about two feet long and a foot deep. He laid it across Alan's legs. Alan opened the lid and removed a child's striped smock.

"Your mother kept certain things that belonged to

you lassies. She'd put them away and not let anyone touch them." He gazed at the garment sadly. "You ken she was like Isobel, she could divine things from touching an object. She always made sure she had objects belonging to all of you, so she could watch over you in her own way."

Alan handed the smock to Isobel, who'd removed her kidskin gloves moments before. Looking at her older sister, Gillian's chest hollowed. She'd been ten when Lillian MacDonell had died, but her image was burned in Gillian's memory. Isobel looked just like Lillian. Fine, fair skin, curly, copper-blond hair, silver green eyes, delicate and ethereal as a fairy.

Isobel took the smock and rubbed it between her palms, eyes closed. Sir Philip had risen from the table to stand at his wife's shoulder, watching her anxiously. He was an exceedingly comely man, with longish, chestnut hair and whisky-brown eyes. Gillian knew from Isobel's letters that though Philip accepted his wife's magic and her need to exercise it, he was uneasy about it, always fearing she would harm herself or get caught by someone bent on burning witches. To ease his mind, she only did it in secret, helping people surreptitiously.

Isobel frowned and rubbed at the cloth vigorously. Her fingers skated along it until she touched the large horn buttons. She gripped these in her fingers, but her frown only deepened.

She opened her eyes. "What else is in there?"

"You saw nothing?" their father asked.

Isobel shook her head, perplexed. "Well, I wouldn't say nothing . . . it's as if there's a mist . . . it has color, silvery gray. And I can't see through it. Very odd. The only other time I've seen such a thing was the letter you sent me, Da, the charmed one, in which you tried to hide your illness from me."

Alan frowned at the smock uneasily, then removed another item from the box, a piece of parchment covered with childish scrawl. "A letter you wrote me once, Gilly."

Isobel passed her palms over the slightly discolored surface, eyes closed again, coppery-blond lashes fanned against her pale cheeks. The small vertical line appeared again between her brows, and she opened her eyes.

"The same."

There were several more items in the box, but everything Isobel touched gave her the same image, that of a thick, silvery mist, resisting her efforts to strip it away.

"I'm sorry," Isobel said. "I don't understand it . . . I rarely have this much trouble." She laid a hand on her flat stomach. "Perhaps it's because I'm with child? I have noticed some difficulties recently . . . but nothing like this."

"It's not the baby." Rose had been watching from the end of the bed, silent until now. "Someone with knowledge of all our gifts has gone to great effort to hide something."

"You think these garments are cursed, too?" Sir Philip asked, a note of skepticism in his voice.

"Not a curse . . . just a spell. One we might be able to unravel a lot easier than Gillian's curse. Mother wrote some about countering spells, though not a concealing spell such as these, but I think, if I study it more, I might be able to counter it."

Alan combed his fingers through his gray beard, his mouth pursed thoughtfully. "You're a healer. You don't do spells."

"Aye, but you do, Da. So I'll need your help."

Their father wasn't a powerful wizard, but he did have some skill, as well as the uncanny ability to know before a child was born whether it was a lad or a lassie.

Alan sat up straighter against his pillows, his face glowing with purpose. "Aye, let's do it."

As disappointed as Gillian was that Isobel's effort had proved fruitless, she couldn't help but be pleased that unraveling the spells gave her father a sense of purpose he'd lacked for many months now. His determination to see his daughters married to men of his choosing was nearly accomplished and no longer required any effort from him. He'd turned over the entire running of Glen Laire and his other estates to Uncle Roderick, and now he did little but answer correspondence and lay in bed, wasting away as he waited to die.

Rose settled herself on Alan's bed, spreading her books out around them.

"Is there something I could do?" Gillian asked.

Rose shook her head. "No. We don't know if something we say or do will trigger your pain. You just stay well and keep your mind free of it for now." She gave Gillian a grim look. "The day may come when you'll be forced to think on it. I want you strong for that day."

Gillian nodded, subtly frightened by her sister's words but unwilling to show it. She crossed the room, drawn by the silvery glow and cool breeze spilling through the open window. She stood at the window, staring at the nearly full moon, her mind filled with fear and wonder. There *must* be a method to break a curse. *There must.* She was afraid, yet it vexed her that whoever had cursed her had achieved their ends. This was what they wanted, her fear and reluctance. She resolved to be strong and brave and do her part. After all, she was a real MacDonell now.

Stephen's cane echoed hollowly on the wooden floor, drawing nearer. Gillian turned with a welcoming smile. Stone benches were built into the wall on either side of the deeply recessed window, creating a small alcove. Stephen lowered himself onto one of the benches to catch his breath.

His mouth curved self-consciously. "Sorry. It tires me just to cross a room. But Rose says if I do her wee exercises I'll be better in a few months, though I'll never lose the limp."

"Many men limp, and it hinders them not."

"Aye. Sometimes the pain is unbearable." He stared down at his hands folded over the top of his cane, golden lashes hiding his eyes. "And I take poppy juice. Rose gave me some, after, but told me I mustna keep using it, else I'd go mad from it."

Gillian sat beside him. "Are you still using it?"

He shrugged, his charming grin back in place as he slid her a look. "Och, no. Never mind me, babbling on, I am. The reason I mention the poppy juice is because when I take it not only does it ease my pain greatly, but I'm not myself. At times I feel . . . detached from my body."

Gillian sensed he was doing more than sharing his experience with poppy juice, and she didn't like this description. Other than for the surcease of pain Stephen required, she couldn't understand why anyone would want to feel that way.

"I was thinking," Stephen went on, "that if you took some, mayhap you'd not only be able to bear the pain . . . but be able to step away from it."

"My thanks," Gillian said softly. "That's a fine idea." Though she really didn't think so. She'd been given poppy juice once years ago and had no desire to repeat the experience. She'd had horrible nightmares.

"You'll need someone there, of course," Stephen continued. "Once you take it, you may find you dinna care much about magic and curses . . . or anything much anymore."

He stared hard out the window, his jaw set, blue eyes icy hard.

Gillian put a hesitant hand over his, folded on the cane. She sensed that his injury caused him far more than physical pain.

He looked down at their hands for a moment, then grinned at her, shaking off whatever dark emotion had momentarily possessed him. His eyes shifted to look past her. He nodded to something behind her.

"Yer man is here."

Gillian turned to see that Lord Kincreag had entered the room. He stood near her father's bed, but he watched her and Stephen with a narrow, assessing gaze. Gillian removed her hand from Stephen's.

"You look recovered," he said when she joined him, his impassive black gaze passing over her. He was as darkly handsome and subdued as always in his black attire, unrelieved by a ruff or bit of lace. Gillian wanted to undo the silver buttons of his doublet and loosen the small collar of his white linen shirt so he did not seem so hard and implacable. She couldn't now, but one day she would be able to touch him without fearing rejection.

"Aye, my lord. Rose relieved my headache well." She clasped her hands behind her and tilted her head. "Do you still believe me mad?"

"I never said you were mad."

"You implied that my sickness was of the mind, rather than the body."

He lifted one shoulder in an eloquent shrug of dismissal. "I merely made the suggestion."

"Is there any merit to the suggestion, think you?"

His brows raised thoughtfully. "That remains to be seen."

"And when it is seen, what then? Will you find me *unsuitable?*"

His gaze raised slightly to look over her head at the window, where Stephen still sat. When he looked back at her, his face was severe. "Or perhaps your own resolve falters?"

Was he jealous? The thought pleased her. She glanced back at the window, at the shaved moon. She must burn his hair tomorrow night. And since he had just arrived to visit with her father, this was the perfect opportunity to take her leave and slip into his chambers.

"I assure you, my lord, nothing has changed." She smiled. "In fact, I must be sure I have a dress suitable for the wedding."

She bid good night to everyone and left, hurrying down the corridors, looking over her shoulder repeatedly for fear of being followed. She paused in front of his door, looking up and down the hall before entering. Once inside, her heart thumped erratically in her throat, in terror of being caught. *Hurry, hurry, hurry.* She ran to the bedchamber and fumbled with the latch, her hands trembling violently. She searched frantically through his cabinet, but his comb was immaculate and free of hairs. She found several of the thongs he used to tie his hair back, but they were also hair-free.

She muttered darkly to herself about fastidious men as she snuck back to her own chambers. What to do now? It seemed she had little choice but to rip it from his scalp. Her stomach flopped at the very idea. How could she possibly contrive such a situation? A sharp rap startled her out of her ruminations. She flung the door open, surprised and somewhat unsettled to find the object of her scheming on the other side.

"My lord?"

"You left your dog."

Broc sat obediently at Nicholas's feet. When she called the dog, he trotted into the room and situated himself in the center of her bed.

"My thanks," she said.

They stared at each other for a long, awkward moment. Gillian's gaze darted repeatedly from his eyes to his hair, her fingers itching to yank some out. How to go about it?

"May I come in?" He didn't wait for her to invite him. He strode past her, pushing the door closed after him. Gillian's heart raced as she remembered the evening before. More kisses? She hoped so.

He crossed to the hearth and poked at the fire with the iron. She had the impression he stalled, reluctant to speak.

"Are you troubled, my lord?"

After a few more unnecessary pokes at the coals, he set the iron aside and turned to her. "I'm beginning to have some reservations."

Gillian didn't immediately understand. Reservations? And then it came to her like a slap. Reservations about marrying her. After all she'd gone through, now he had reservations? She would not give up so easily. She stormed across the room.

"Reservations? Why? Do you honestly think I'm mad? Do I look like a madwoman?"

He smiled slightly, brows raised. "Well . . ."

"Because of the curse?"

He looked heavenward before giving her a look of long-suffering patience. "Ah, no, though all this talk of curses has become tiresome."

"What then?"

He inhaled deeply, eyes fixed on her, and exhaled slowly through his nose. Gillian raised her brows in expectation. He seemed to be preparing himself to say something unpleasant, though she'd not have thought a man such as himself would be reluctant to say anything. Her gut churned in anticipation, hands fisted at her sides.

"I have thought long about this . . . well, not really long, a few minutes, but I've thought *hard* on it." He steepled his fingers and paced past her. "I know I may be . . . well . . . I *may* be wrong."

When he turned toward her again, he only stared at her, lips parted. But no words passed his lips. He seemed at a complete loss.

"Just say it, my lord, for I am bursting with curiosity."

"That man, the cripple. I know about you and he."

She blinked, taken aback by his unexpected statement. "Aye? What do you know?"

"I know you spent time alone with him in an inn."

"If I hadn't, he would likely be dead. Believe me, he was barely conscious most of the time and unable to move at all. Seduction was the last thing on either of our minds." He didn't say anything but continued to study her, as if trying to determine if she was being truthful. She couldn't help it. She laughed. "Are you *jealous?*"

"No," he said quickly.

"Because you have nothing to fear, my lord. He is a friend, nothing more. He's never been anything more than a friend."

He waved this away impatiently and advanced on her. "Jealousy has nothing to do with it. After the debacle with your sister, I find myself cautious. I will not have my earldom passed to some bastard you try to foist upon me as my own."

Her jaw dropped, and her breath left her in an indignant rush. How dare he. She'd done nothing to deserve such questioning of her virtue. Her eyes narrowed as she suddenly understood him. This wasn't about jealousy or his earldom—it was about the infernal contract.

"I am so blind." Her body trembled, the heat of anger flushing her. She shook her head, lips twisting bitterly. "Am I unsuitable now, my lord? That's what this is really about, isn't it? You're really scrambling for reasons if this is the best you can manage. Why not pick someone capable of cuckolding you, like my brother-in-law? Or what about Hagan? We've been carrying on secretly since I returned from the Lowlands." Gillian laughed harshly. "Oh, or what about Old Greer in the village? Even at five and seventy he makes me shiver—and he doesn't even need a cane."

He closed the distance between them in two steps, grabbing her arms. He gave her a hard shake. "This is not a jest, Gillian. I won't do it again. Do you hear me? I *will not* do it again."

Gillian strained away from him, unsettled by his vehemence. "Do what again? I don't understand you."

"I'm sick of women who dissemble, and I'll not stand for it. If you marry me, you do so understanding that you are *mine.*"

She glared back at him. "You think if you bully me and falsely accuse me that I'll break the betrothal? You will not rid yourself of me so easily." She threaded her fingers in his hair and yanked.

A hiss of pain passed through white teeth, fury and surprise erupting in his eyes. Gillian's hand was still tangled in his hair. He grabbed her wrist before she could yank again.

"You are a little fool."

She opened her mouth to call him worse, but he silenced her with his mouth, a hard kiss of possession that scattered her thoughts. She sagged against him, her hand clenching in his hair. He released her wrist and wrapped his arms around her, drawing her against him. A sigh shivered through her body. Then as quickly as the kiss began, he shoved her away. He held her at arm's length and stared at her, breathing hard, his brows drawn together in consternation.

Her heart, already beating wildly, jumped and stumbled in her breast. He suspected something. She didn't know what, as he gave no credence to witchcraft and so likely wouldn't believe in a love philter, but he knew something was amiss. Perhaps he sensed a dissonance between his will and his actions. She could see it in his eyes, the bewilderment. He didn't understand why he'd felt compelled to kiss her. He clearly wished he hadn't kissed her, but he'd been unable to stop himself.

Desperate to distract him before his skeptical mind actually began to grasp at witchcraft, she said, "I won't share either."

Her words broke his intensity. "What?"

"I'll not be worrying every time you lay with me that I'll catch the pox from one of your whores. Do *you* understand *me*?"

He dropped his hands from her arms and turned away, one hand spanning his temples, as if forcing away a headache.

He gave her a wary sideways look. "I'm going to bed."

When the door closed behind him, Gillian opened her fist. Three black hairs lay across her palm. She glanced at the open window, at the moon, not quite full. She couldn't wait until tomorrow night. He was having second thoughts. The moon might not be full, but as far as Gillian was concerned, it was close enough.

9

*W*ake up!"

Gillian jerked awake from a rather unpleasant dream in which she stumbled endlessly along a cliff, pursued by an enormous dark figure. She blinked up at the red blur slowly coming into focus.

Rose stood over her, dressed in fine velvet skirts but no bodice. Her silk-embroidered shift strained across her breasts. Rose saw where Gillian stared and glanced down at her chest.

"Do you think they're getting bigger?" Rose had smallish breasts and had expressed concern that Jamie MacPherson would not find them to his liking. She'd told Gillian she'd even placed an "enhancing" spell on her bosom, but it had proved futile.

Gillian frowned at her sister, shading her eyes to block out the blaze of candles illuminating the room. "You woke me for that?"

"No! Your love philter worked perfectly!" Rose spun away and returned, slipping into a crimson velvet bodice with gathered and pleated shoulders, trimmed with gold thread and silk roses. She struggled to hook the front of it. "Jesu! I'm just getting fat!"

Rose was anything but fat—she was lean and muscular—but perhaps she'd been a bit thin a month ago. Her face, previously angular and as sharp as a wolf's, had filled out, giving her a softer appearance, belying the hard-edged cynic beneath.

Gillian tried to shake off the sleep fogging her brain. "What are you talking about? My love philter worked? How do you know?"

"Because he can't wait until tomorrow to wed you. He wants to marry you today. This morning." Rose beamed down at her. "He's completely smitten."

Gillian fell back on the pillow, hands over her mouth. She'd been afraid that burning the hair when the moon had not been quite full would render the philter useless. But apparently it had been full enough. A surge of excited anticipation shot through her, and she threw back the covers, jumped out of bed, and embraced her sister.

"Come on," Rose said. "Our hair will take forever, so let's get you dressed."

Gillian perched on her father's bed in her finest gown, one he'd had made especially for this occasion. It was the most beautiful thing she'd ever seen—a froth of pale pink caffa, silver embroidery, and gossamer white lawn puffed out through slits in the sleeves and bodice. Her braided hair was coiled at her nape and encased in a silver mesh caul.

Her father had just informed her there would be no wedding celebration. There was trouble at Kincreag, and Nicholas had to return posthaste. After the wedding they would depart. Gillian had been a bit chagrined that it wasn't his great passion for her that made him rush the nuptials, but it was for the best. Once it was done, it was not so easily undone. Rose also assured her it was a good thing. Away from Glen Laire, her headaches would likely ease. As soon as Rose discovered a means to break the curse, she would come to Kincreag. All would be well.

"Yesterday you began to tell me about Lord Kincreag's late wife," Gillian reminded her father.

Alan frowned, scratching the head of his newest pet, a silver-gray Skye terrier. Long, thick hair fell over its face, parting at the snout and hiding its eyes. Another gift from Uncle Roderick. Gillian thought it was very sweet. Uncle Roderick took a great deal on his shoulders, yet he always had time to fash on his poor pregnant wife and make sure Alan had a special pet. Like Broc, this dog seemed satisfied to lie on his master's bed, panting contentedly. Not that Broc was content to lay around anymore—something odd had happened to the dog. Now that he belonged to Gillian, he was a ball of energy. Stephen currently had him in the courtyard letting him run before putting him in the kennels so he didn't ruin the ceremony.

"What was I saying about her?" Alan asked. He was

a bit wan today, which made Gillian's heart heavy after the burst of health he'd experienced the day before. She supposed all the searching for a counter-curse with Rose had overtired him.

"You were telling me that the earl only *seems* unpleasant, and then you brought up the late countess, as if she had something to do with it."

"Ah. I remember." He patted Gillian's gloved hands. "I've been meaning to tell you this, and I'd better now, since it's certain he will not. The king arranged Kincreag's first marriage. Catriona Campbell was a very rich widow. She'd been married young to an old man, and he'd died a few years later. He'd had one son and a daughter—not from her, mind you—and they both died shortly before he did. So it all went to Catriona. The king did not like such power in the hands of a woman and so married her off to Nicholas, one of his favorites. Nicholas was very pleased with the match. Catriona was a great beauty in addition to being a financial windfall."

Seeing the sour look on Gillian's face, Alan laughed, giving her hand a weak squeeze. "She was not nearly so bonny as you, my love, dinna fash. Besides, there is a big difference between the two of you that Nicholas will no doubt cherish."

"What's that?" Gillian asked doubtfully.

"Let me finish. Though Kincreag is a very good friend, he does not speak of his marriage to Catriona. Here is what I know. She was unfaithful to him, but he did not set her aside, because they had a son. When both wife and son died within days of each other, much suspicion was aroused."

Already Gillian didn't like this story. It made her belly clench uneasily.

Alan smoothed his hand over the dog's silky fur. "Then there was the matter of several of her lovers dying mysteriously. And a few of her servants. Afore you know it, the rumors were thriving and the king himself was investigating. Nasty business."

Gillian's brows drew together and up with concern. "But it does sound awfully suspicious, don't you think? What with him being so jealous, everyone associated with her dying, and finally she dies in a convenient accident."

Alan's expression grew implacable. "Listen to me, Gilly. I don't believe Nicholas killed his wife. He told me he didn't, and I trust him. But if he *had* murdered her, he would have been justified. She was unfaithful. And evil. There was something . . . wrong with her. Something missing in her eyes, from her heart."

When Gillian said nothing, only stared at her father wide-eyed, he said, "But he didn't, understand? Just before their son died he'd begun searching for a legal means to rid himself of her. Why murder her and cast suspicion on himself? He's smarter than that. Besides all that, the king found him innocent."

"But if he *had* killed her, you believe he would have been justified?" Gillian asked, stunned and uneasy at her father's sentiments.

Alan nodded. "Aye. She tried to poison him once that I know of."

Gillian gaped.

"I drank wine meant for him, wine that she'd served

him. Thank God I didn't drink all of it—it nearly killed me."

Gillian covered her mouth, sickened with disbelief. She dropped her hands and said, "How could he keep her after that?"

"She had a way about her . . . a way many men could not resist. Nicholas was quite immune to her by the end, but early on, well . . ." He shrugged. "She was very convincing. She told him it was a remedy to help him sleep. She carried on and on about her concern for him, because he paced the floors at night. It's no wonder, his son was so ill, he rarely left the bairn's side. Anyway, she claimed she'd gone to the local healer for a physick. The healer confirmed this but swore she gave the countess exactly what she asked for. In the end Nicholas ruled it a mistake."

"But it wasn't?"

Alan shook his head. "Nay, I'm sure of it. There's more he has never told me, but she was a wicked woman, mark me." Alan studied Gillian's horrified expression carefully. "Isobel's recent actions, bless her, haven't helped. I think he's quite convinced that all women are full of wickedness. But once he sees your loyal heart, Gillian, he will not remain so. He is a good friend to me—a very good friend. And I believe he will be a very good husband."

Gillian fell silent, digesting her father's story. Even if Nicholas had murdered his wife, she'd deserved it, according to her father. The things he'd said to her last night began to make more sense. Her heart ached dully for the earl, guarding himself diligently against being deceived again. Gillian would never do such a thing. Even if she found marriage to him misery, she would never break her wedding vows and would certainly never try to kill him. Her father was right—she'd always been intensely loyal to those who deserved it. And as her husband, Nicholas did better than deserve it; she owed it to him.

The door opened, and Isobel entered with her husband. Hagan intercepted them, and they stayed near the door. But others soon arrived, and finally Alan said, "Do you feel better now, knowing the story?"

"I worry that he will never become fond of me . . . that he feels forced into this because of your illness."

Her father made a rude sound. "If he doesn't ken what a fine lassie ye are by now, he's surely drawn to your other, more obvious, attributes."

Gillian blushed and felt conspicuous in her low-cut bodice.

"Fash not, lass. He'll come around." Her father's gaze moved to something behind her. "It's time."

Gillian turned and froze, suddenly breathless. Lord Kincreag stood at the door. He had forgone the severe black attire he usually wore for something more fitting to the occasion. His coat was still black silk, but over it he wore a scarlet-and-black plaid, secured with a blood-red ruby. His hair, devil-black and rich as silk, was tied at his nape with a scarlet ribbon, an errant lock touching his brow.

But it wasn't his clothes or hair that arrested Gillian. It was his fathomless black eyes, intent on her. His face was carefully expressionless, yet savage in its dark beauty. But his eyes—they burned over her possessively. Gillian's heart beat a rapid tattoo, so loud in her ears that she was certain everyone could hear.

The next few minutes passed in a daze. Her father called the room to order. The pastor came forward. Isobel and Rose practically lifted Gillian off the bed and positioned her beside Nicholas. She placed her hand in his, startled by the heat from his skin, penetrating the thin lace of her glove. She glanced up at him and was caught again in his black gaze, riveted on her. She barely heard the pastor's words, though she was vaguely aware she repeated her part on cue. Nicholas finally looked away to pass the ring over each of her fingers in turn—to protect her from evil—before coming to rest on her fourth. His lashes, so long and black, shadowed his sharp cheekbones. She never looked away from him through it all. Her husband. To love and cherish.

When his gaze captured hers again, she wondered if she'd somehow drunk the love philter by mistake, for she felt warm and fluttery and slightly giddy. She had no time to consider it further; his mouth was on hers in the kiss to seal their union. She squeezed his hand reflexively, her mouth pliant, giving him whatever he wanted. It was a brief kiss, but when he broke away, he stared down at her for several heartbeats, eyes narrowed. Though his expression remained impassive, a war raged behind those shadowy eyes. She hoped one day he would share it with her.

Then people surrounded them, offering congratulations. Gillian was urged to say good-bye to her father, then was bustled through the castle, a sister on either side of her, gripping her arms.

Back in their chambers, they helped her change into something suitable for travel.

"Did you see the way he looked at you?" Isobel said, silver-green eyes wide with amazement. "Perhaps Da *is* right and this is a good match."

Rose smiled secretly at Gillian. "Aye, he looked like a ravenous wolf and you but a juicy wee lamb."

"He never looked at *me* in such a manner," Isobel said. "He looked at me like I was a piece of rotten meat someone was trying to force him to eat!"

Gillian tried to smile at their jests, but she felt inexplicably melancholy. She told herself it was because she was leaving her family, but she knew that was only part of it. Her husband's desire for her was a sham, induced by a love philter. That made her deceitful. After hearing about his late wife, she felt particularly uncomfortable about what she'd done. When the effects of the philter faded, she would not repeat it. She would take what fate meted out and not seek to cloud his mind with untruths.

She had not anticipated the regret she would feel at deceiving him. At the time, it had seemed the only thing she could do to ensure he would follow through with the betrothal. But now it felt insidious. Her mind briefly touched on the idea of telling him the truth, but she shied away from it. They hadn't yet consummated the marriage. She couldn't predict how he would react to such a confession. So perhaps she wasn't *really* sorry for what she'd done. Just sorry she'd been forced to resort to such tactics.

But what couldn't be changed, must be endured. She could not change what she'd done, and so she must endure the consequences. She would make up for it by being a most loyal wife. No one would ever question her devotion to her husband. And maybe, when the philter faded, his affection for her would remain.

10

They rode for several hours in silence, excepting the occasional shouted order, the clank and jangle of harness and bridle, and the creak of saddle leather. Nicholas and his men seemed extremely watchful to Gillian. He'd hardly spoken to her since they'd set out. He'd said more to her horse, Morfran, than to her, admonishing the beast when it tried to bite his men. But still, it seemed Morfran had resigned himself to the earl's continued presence in his life and tolerated him well enough, merely baring his teeth and glaring nefariously. Gillian's belongings and Broc were to follow, arriving at Kincreag a few days after them.

Gillian slid another look at her husband from beneath her lashes. He sat tall and straight on the enormous white horse beside her. He squinted slightly into the sun, thick black lashes shadowing his eyes.

Her husband. It was done now. There was only one thing left to bind them together. With nervous anticipation Gillian wondered when and where. Kincreag was not far from Glen Laire, but they'd started late, and unless he planned to travel at night, they would have to camp. She surveyed the score of men in their party and didn't relish laying with her husband for the first time among so many strangers. But then again, they were witnesses. No one could claim nonconsummation later if they heard it all.

Gillian glanced over to find her husband watching her like a sleepy wolf.

"My lord?" she said, cheeks warm from the direction of her thoughts.

"My lady." He inclined his head to her.

Gillian's mouth curved into a secret smile of pleasure. She was no longer Gillian MacDonell. She was now the countess of Kincreag, Lady Glenesk, and an assortment of other titles he held, including the sheriffdoms of a dozen shires. Kincreag's men treated her with great respect and deference. She found herself a bit nonplussed by it all and uncertain how she was expected to behave.

She studied Nicholas's expression—obscure, as always. "Do you still have reservations?"

"Oh, aye," he said readily, still watching her with that curve to his lips that wasn't quite a smile.

Her lips thinned in irritation. When would she learn that if she didn't want to hear the truth, she shouldn't ask the question? For Nicholas was always brutally honest.

"Then why did you rush forward with the wedding?"

"I promised to wed you. I keep my promises."

"So do I," Gillian said meaningfully.

He raised a skeptical brow but didn't respond. She wondered how long it would take for him to trust her. She understood his distrust now, but she still didn't like it, and wished they could just get past it and on with their lives.

"Tell me about Kincreag."

"You'll see it for yourself soon enough."

Gillian smiled patiently. "You are going to make this difficult, aren't you?"

"No."

"Really? Why won't you tell me something about my new home, then?"

He lifted one shoulder. "Because my poor words cannot do it justice. You must see it."

"When will that be?"

Nicholas looked at the sky thoughtfully. "Tomorrow—by midday, I should think."

They traveled that way for several more hours—Nicholas never leaving her side, Gillian making a valiant effort to uphold a conversation with her taciturn companion. After a time she just enjoyed the countryside in silence. Coarse moor grass spread around them in dips and swells, freckled with colorful wildflowers. Rough, lichened rocks jutted from the ground, lush ferns sprouting from crevices. There were few trees here, but they frequently passed thick stands of birch and juniper.

As twilight neared, the sky darkened and a thick fog rolled over the ground, obscuring the riders a horse length away. Nicholas called a halt. His dark eyes scanned the wall of fog as he gave orders to set up camp. Everyone was subdued and watchful. They were probably on Kincreag lands now or on some of his clan-held lands. With a twinge of uneasiness Gillian remembered the reason for the rushed wedding and departure: feuding clans under Nicholas's jurisdiction. Men had died. Living near the border for twelve years, Gillian was no stranger to feuds and lawlessness. Memories of life on the borders, the blood feuds—racing to the tower house and bolting themselves in while English Foresters tried to burn them out—came back to her with sickening clarity. The Highlands were no different. Blood feuds abounded, carried down generation after generation, the hate and remembered slights more precious than any valuable heirloom. And they were still far from Kincreag, with no tower house or other protection in sight.

Gillian peered into the swirling mist. The shadowy figures of Kincreag's men milled around her, some starting fires, others pitching the earl's tent, but she couldn't identify any of them. Sir Evan emerged from the fog directly in front of her. Gillian took a surprised step back, glancing around for her husband, but she could not identify him through the rapidly thickening mist.

Sir Evan stared down at her with his pale, empty eyes. "I'm to take you someplace private."

"Why?" Gillian wrapped her mantle more closely around her.

"So you can do your womanly thing without anyone tripping over you in this fog."

"Oh," Gillian said sheepishly. "My thanks."

He took her elbow and led her through the soupy fog. She kept an eye out for a tree or bush she could hide behind to do her business, but there was nothing. Just heather and mist.

After what seemed a rather long walk, Sir Evan stopped and stood very still. Gillian stood beside him, waiting. She couldn't hear the camp anymore, just the lone call of a raven.

"Go on." Sir Evan pushed her.

"I need a bush or something."

He let out an impatient breath. "Just walk about ten paces and I'll not be able to see you at all, aye? When you're ready to come back, call to me, so I can call back and you dinna lose your way."

The fog had rapidly grown so thick that she thought five paces would likely put her well out of sight, but she went the recommended ten, just to be safe. She glanced furtively around her, preparing to raise her skirts, when a hand snaked around her waist and another clamped over her mouth. A scream burst in her throat, muffled to a squawk behind the hard hand. Panic streaked through her. She struggled wildly as her captor dragged her quickly and silently away.

He made not a single sound and smelled faintly of earth and damp wool. She threw her weight toward the ground, but he only hefted her into the air and carried her, legs flailing. She tried prying at the hand over her mouth and managed to peel one finger back. A screech got through. She kept bending his finger, hoping to break it. He grunted and jerked his hand away.

"Help!" Gillian cried. "I'm—"

Her kidnapper jammed a wad of wool into her mouth and wrenched her arms behind her back. He whispered low in her ear, "Sámhach!" Gaelic. *Quiet.*

The wool was crammed too far into her throat. She gagged and moaned, but he only jerked her arms higher. Tears pricked her eyes, and she stumbled. She retched in earnest, fighting to pull in enough air through her nose, terrified she would choke to death on her own vomit.

The wool was quickly yanked from her mouth. Gillian dropped to her knees and lost her last meal. Leather boots, laced to the knees with a crisscross of fabric, paced around her, waiting for her to finish. The air, cold and damp and smelling of decay, pressed in on her, dampening her hair and clothes, filling her nose so that she couldn't stop heaving.

When her stomach was hollow and aching, she sat back and wiped her mouth with a shaking hand. Her throat hurt. Through blurred vision she finally saw her captor—a young man with silver-blond hair and pale eyes. He looked from her to the mist around them. After a minute he put his hands to his mouth and made the same harsh raven call she'd heard earlier.

"You must return me," she rasped, her throat raw.

He came at her the moment she opened her mouth. She tried to scramble away, feet slipping on damp heather. "Listen to me! I am the countess of Kincreag! You've obviously made a terrible mistake, but if you return me now, I'm sure my husband will be lenient."

The young man hauled her off the ground. "I've

made no mistake," he said, speaking Scots now. "It's you we want."

Gillian started to scream, but he waved the wool threateningly at her. "I'll let ye choke on it this time."

Gillian's mouth snapped shut.

"She'll not be much use to you dead," a disembodied voice rumbled from the haze of fog.

Her captor seized her, hauling her hard against his chest. He produced a dirk and pressed it to her ribs. "Who's there?" he called, his head whipping about wildly.

Gillian searched the mist, desperately trying to locate the source of the voice. A dark shape appeared, moving toward them, materializing out of the murk. It stopped just far enough away so only the great height and breadth were clear, the features obscured. But Gillian knew exactly who it was, and her heart did a painful leap of joy. *Nicholas.*

She bit her bottom lip until she tasted blood, wondering what she could do to aid him. Her bodice, arisaid, and stays were thick enough that the dirk's blade was only a threatening pressure. He'd have to exert great force to penetrate the stiffened leather of her stays—at the angle he held her, it would be a mean feat even for a man of his obvious strength.

"Kincreag!" the man said. "Come no closer or I'll kill her."

"You won't do that, Scott," Kincreag drawled. "You want something from me, and ye'll never get it if you kill her. You'll only share her fate. So tell me now and let's end this, aye." While talking he'd moved closer, circling them.

The man's breathing quickened. He shifted, turning with jerky movements to keep his eyes on Kincreag. The pressure at her side increased.

"You dinna ken what I want. I swear I'll kill her!"

With a surge of pure terror Gillian believed he meant to do it. It was unusual for a hostage to be killed outright—they had more important uses, such as ransom—but perhaps it was different in the Highlands.

Kincreag was close enough now that his face was visible. His expression was hard, uncompromising, black eyes burning in a composed and determined face. Her captor's muscles tensed as he stepped back. Gillian's blood rushed, gripped with a sudden fearful excitement. She took advantage of Scott's uneasiness and jerked away from him. He cursed, grappling with her. The dirk came at her, jabbing hard beneath her breast while she twisted violently from his hold.

Kincreag was there, forcing himself between them. He had her kidnapper's knife arm, and he turned it hard. Gillian heard a sickening crack. Kincreag backhanded him, and there was another moist, splintering sound. The blond man stumbled away and fell to his knees, his mouth open on a silent cry of agony, blood streaming from his nose.

"Evan!" Kincreag barked, shoving the man onto the ground with a boot and pinning him there. Scott lay still, clutching his useless arm and panting. The dark-haired knight appeared. He looked from Scott to Gillian with furrowed brow, baffled—and afraid, too, his skin paling. But Nicholas made no mention of his mistake. Gillian was certain he'd take it up with the knight in private, later.

"Make our guest comfortable," Nicholas said, smiling darkly at his prisoner. "We'll visit soon, Scott." To Sir Evan he said, "Bind his arm. Keep a guard on him."

Sir Evan helped the Highlander to his feet and led him away.

Gillian rubbed at her ribs, trying to catch her breath. It had all happened so fast. Her hands encountered torn fabric. Relief swamped her, weakening her. One of her fingers poked through a hole in her arisaid. Her hands were pushed aside.

She raised her head and looked into Nicholas's eyes, intent on her ribs as he moved her arisaid, folding it over her shoulder. His warm fingers slid through a hole in her bodice to her stays, probing beneath. Gillian winced. He pulled his fingers away and looked at them, but there was no blood.

"It's just a bruise, my lord. Leather stays are as good as armor, methinks." Even as she said it, her body quivered with delayed fear. Had she really actively aided in her own rescue?

He still stared at his fingers. He dropped his hand slowly and raised his gaze to hers. He said nothing for a long moment. Her belly fluttered sickeningly from vomiting and fear, and she swayed, overcome.

He reached for her, steadying hands grasping her elbows. She leaned into him, her hands curling into his plaid. He remained still and silent, allowing her to regain her composure. He was so strong and steady; she didn't want to move away from him, but his grip on her elbows slowly tightened.

She tilted her head back to see his face. He gazed down at her, black lashes partially obscuring obsidian eyes, their expression inscrutable. What was he thinking? Was he angry with her for causing so much trouble? She wished he'd say something. His heavy silence made her anxious.

He set her away from him. "That was thoughtless. A countess cannot be so thoughtless with her life."

"It was not thoughtless. I considered my chances of coming out of the encounter unstabbed. I calculated correctly." The high-pitched break in her voice belied her flippant words.

He closed his eyes and his jaw shifted slightly, as if he searched for patience.

Was he truly upset? Or had he actually feared for her? Pleasure shivered through her. She lifted her hand to touch his sleeve, but when he opened his eyes and fixed them almost angrily on her hand, she only fluttered it about near him.

"I did not mean to vex you, my lord. Only to aid you. He had the dirk, after all."

He looked into her face, his gaze no longer harsh or cold—though not exactly warm either. It was as if he considered her for the first time. "We are alone, Gillian. I pray you, address me familiar. We are married."

A lump rose in her throat, rendering her unable to comply with his request. Instead, she nodded.

He took her arm. "Come. Until we arrive at Kincreag stay close to me." He led her through the soupy fog as if he could see clearly. They stopped in front of a large tent, and he nodded to it. "There's food inside, and then you can sleep."

"Where will you be?"

"Near. The Campbells are still here and might decide to come for their man." His brow lowered thoughtfully. "They may come for you again as well. Do not stray from me again. There's nothing that can't wait until we're at Kincreag."

She shifted uncomfortably, reminded painfully of just why she had strayed. "Actually, there is something. . . ."

His mouth tilted so slightly that she wondered if she imagined it. "There's a chamber pot inside the tent."

Gillian sighed thankfully. He started to turn away, but she caught his sleeve.

He turned back to her, a sleek, black brow raised in question.

"Be careful . . . Nicholas."

His gaze traveled over her face. He nodded thoughtfully, then left her.

Shortly after he left, the shaking set in. It was odd. Though she'd been frightened, certain the Highlander had meant to kill her, she'd been exhilarated immediately afterward. Now she felt ill. She'd removed her arisaid and wrapped it around her. She lay on the ground and stared at the glowing coals of the brazier, trembling violently. It was beginning to irritate her. She clenched her hands into fists and willed it to stop, but she only shook harder, her teeth chattering together.

The sounds of men settling down to sleep outside

the tent comforted her. Nicholas was near, and she was safe. So why did she still shake?

One wall of the tent shuddered as someone untied the doorway. A moment later Nicholas slipped in. He unpinned his plaid and looked down at her. He paused when he saw she was still awake.

"It's all right," he said, his voice low and soothing.

Gillian tried to nod brightly but feared it was more of a shuddering jerk.

He wore his plaid like a mantle rather than kilted about his waist and knees as many Highlanders did. He dropped it near her and unhooked his leather doublet, still watching her curiously.

Heat crept up Gillian's neck. He was coming to bed. With her. She averted her eyes, exhorting herself to have courage, then abandoning it as her shaking increased.

He knelt behind her and removed his boots. When his hand touched her arm, Gillian started and nearly screamed.

"Are you afraid?" he asked.

Gillian shook her head, still not looking at him, willing her body to stop shaking. "I was fine . . . after. Then I started shaking and I can't stop."

He made a soft noise of understanding, as if comforting a distraught child, then lay beside her and gathered her close against his chest. His arm was heavy and warm around her. She stiffened, then slowly relaxed when he did nothing more.

"I always feel so after doing battle," he said. "You feel as if you could climb a great mountain, lift a horse, right after. But then, a short time later, the shaking sets in, and I must be alone."

"Did you shake tonight?" Gillian asked, assuaged by his words and no longer trying to hide the chattering of her teeth.

"No . . . tonight was nothing." He'd broken a man's arm. She'd nearly died. And he called it nothing? She couldn't stop shaking from it.

"You know that man?" she asked.

"Aye, Scott MacGregor, a broken man, clanless. No doubt he hoped to win a rich ransom from the earl's bonny new bride."

"What will happen to him?" She did not miss his subtle compliment, and a smile pressed at the corners of her mouth.

"That's his decision. He claims he works alone, which I do not believe. When we arrive at Kincreag I'll break him. A holiday in my dungeons will loosen his tongue."

His ominous words sent a more violent shiver through her.

He gathered her in closer and whispered, "Fash not, it will stop eventually."

They lay quiet for several minutes, his arms strong around her, containing the odd rhythmic quality of her tremors. Warm and protected, she snuggled deeper into his embrace. After a time she slept.

It was dark as pitch when she woke. The coals in the brazier had burned out. She felt him, his arms snug around her, his body pressed warm all along her back. But he no longer administered comfort. He sensed her wakefulness and rubbed his jaw gently against her hair. His biceps flexed beneath her cheek.

Gillian tensed, comprehending what he was about. She could feel his arousal behind her, pressed into her bottom. Fear of the unknown nearly paralyzed her, and for a brief moment she hoped he would think she still slept. But that was cowardly. This must happen if their marriage was to be a true one. Before she could think any more about it, she turned her face toward him, her skin brushing the shadow of whiskers on his chin. The hand that clasped her waist came up, cupping the side of her face as he set his mouth on hers. The kiss was long, and slow, and lascivious—with firm intent that had been absent from his previous kisses. His fingers trailed over her temple, cheek, and jaw. He stopped kissing her, his thumb on her bottom lip, the backs of his fingers beneath her chin, resting against the wild pulse beating in her neck.

His absolute stillness disquieted her. "My lord?" she whispered, her voice muffled against his thumb. Then, "Nicholas?"

His thumb moved away and his mouth was there again, at the corner of hers with kisses soft as butterfly wings, murmuring her name. His hand slid under her, lifting her so he could move his other arm from beneath her, then she was on her back. His hands slid up her waist to her ribs, pausing when it encountered the knife hole from earlier.

Instantly his kiss grew forceful, his fingers making short work of the hooks at the side of her gown. This particular bodice was a bit complicated to remove, as the sleeves laced on at the shoulder and it hooked down the side, but he managed it and her stays with unnerving skill, leaving her in naught but her shift and skirts.

One hand closed over her linen-covered breast. Gillian drew in a ragged breath. Though he'd touched her breast, she'd felt it elsewhere, lower. He made a deep sound in his chest, breaking their kiss to trail his lips, feather soft, down her neck. Gillian's lashes fluttered shut. Fear and excitement filled her, making it impossible for her to breathe evenly. She gripped his shoulders, thick and solid beneath his shirt.

The tip of his tongue touched her breast through the linen of her shift, and his breath, warm and urgent, blew against the dampness. Gillian writhed, the sensation gripping her low, deep in her belly. He moved to her other breast, one hand shaping and kneading while the other slid beneath her skirts, his palm open and hot. Wicked fingers stroked her thighs until she whimpered. Coherent thought dissolved as her world shrunk to his hands and mouth and the furious thrumming of her heart. Then he touched her center, pushing deeply until she raised her hips to beg for more.

He moved over her, one knee pushing her thighs wide. She wished it weren't so dark, that she could see his face, know his thoughts. But it was all blackness and quiet, except for their ragged breathing. Gillian reached for him, finding the silken fall of his hair. She took his face in her hands and brought him close. His mouth took hers again, and down below, he pushed into her.

Gillian gripped his arms in shock. Rose had warned her it would hurt, but this was not at all what she'd expected. Intense pressure skated the border of pain. He stretched her too much—he was too big—it wouldn't work. Her teeth sunk into her lower lip to contain her moans of distress. His muscles quivered beneath her hands. He pushed harder, until it hurt and she cried out and then he was in so far and deep she couldn't catch her breath. His body pressed hard against hers, enveloping her. Gillian sucked in air, her fingers digging into him with such rigid tension that they began to ache.

He held very still, buried deep inside her body. His muscles still quivered slightly, as if it were an effort not to move. He brushed at the stray hairs clinging to her forehead and pressed his lips there.

"I know, I know," he murmured against her skin.

Tears squeezed from the corners of her eyes, more from his show of tenderness than from the pain.

"It's fine," she said, but her voice was thin and weak. It wasn't fine. It hurt and burned, but she'd been prepared for pain and could bear it.

His mouth moved lower, pressing tiny kisses to her eyelids and nose, soothing the pain. Until he moved again. Gillian inhaled harshly. His fingers quickly manipulated the lacing of her shift, baring her breasts. Then his mouth was there, hot and urgent against her skin, tugging deep at the nipple, causing that profound pleasure in her loins to mingle with the pain so that she arched against him, moaning, hands flexing in his hair. She gasped his name. He answered with a deep muffled sound. His hands slid beneath her, lifting her to his thrusts, pushing so deeply that he touched something inside. The pain transformed with every stroke, drowning her in mindless bliss. It splintered, and her body bowed hard against him, her breathing arrested.

He drove hard into her, his body shuddering and an agonized groan resonating through her. He clutched her tightly, his shuddering bone-deep, his face buried in her neck. Gillian held him, faintly surprised to hear him cursing as if in pain. Her body was heavy-limbed and liquid, a rather pleasant sensation, as if she'd just imbibed of strong spirits.

They lay quiescent for a long while, until their breathing returned to normal and the new aches in her body made themselves known. She blinked into the darkness, wishing again she could see his face.

When he rose off of her, she asked, "Did it hurt you, too?"

He lay beside her, his hand on her waist. "I'm sorry it hurt you. It usually does, the first time. And no, it didn't hurt me."

"Oh," she said, thinking about that. Her own cries might have sounded as if she'd still been in pain, when what he'd been doing had felt unspeakably wonderful. And at times the pleasure had been so intense she thought she might break from it. But she burned now, deep between her legs, and she only wanted to curl into herself.

She turned away from him, pushing her skirts down and pulling her shift closed. She heard him relace his breeks. It would have been unwise to remove much clothing, with the danger of further attacks imminent. For some reason Gillian's eyes burned and her nose went stuffy. She fought the tears, curling herself up tightly. A blanket was draped over her. It smelled of wool and Nicholas—his plaid. He lay behind her again.

"Lay your head, lass," he said softly.

She lifted her head and rested it on his biceps again. His other arm slid under the plaid, gathering her close, and then covering her hands. She closed her eyes, trying hard not to cry. She sniffled quietly.

"I'm sorry, Gillian." There was real regret in his voice.

"No, I pray you, do not apologize. I'm glad it's done. Rose said it would not hurt again . . . unless we go a long time between couplings."

A thoughtful pause. "How does Rose know so much about it?"

Gillian lifted one shoulder in a shrug, wiping her face with the corner of his plaid. "She's a healer. She knows a lot of things." Talking to him in the dark eased her and kept the tears at bay.

He sighed, deep and heartfelt. "I should have waited. I meant to. I didn't want our first time to be on the ground, fully dressed with men all around us . . . but . . ." He didn't say anything for a long time.

"Aye?" Gillian prompted.

"Well . . . I wanted to, and you're my wife now . . . and, well . . . I suppose I just didn't think." Despite his justifications, he sounded troubled by his own behavior. And likely he was. The love philter was hard at work.

His arms tightened around her. "You were very brave today, Gillian."

The pride in his soft-spoken compliment washed away the last of her melancholy, and Gillian smiled into the darkness.

11

Gillian got her first sight of her new home before noon the next day. Kincreag Castle was visible from miles away, an enormous, sprawling stronghold, perched atop a craggy mountain. The thick outer walls wound around it for miles it seemed, as big as a city.

"Sakes me," she murmured. And Kincreag was just one of his castles. She had married well. Her gaze turned to her husband, riding beside her, tall and straight, his subdued plaid mantle flapping out behind him. This place fit him, she thought: harsh, uncompromising, unforgiving—and impossibly beautiful. She remembered how he'd loomed out of the fog to rescue her, then held her in the dark until her shaking stopped, and later, shown her passion she'd never imagined. She *had* married well.

The road to the castle was narrow and treacherous, winding steeply up the mountainside. Nicholas reined in, placing a hand on Morfran's bridle. The horse

jerked his gray head, then submitted and stood docile-
ly. Gillian had barely spoken to Nicholas since the
night before. She'd woken alone, too shy to approach
him. He'd been busy, anyway. The prisoner had escaped
in the night. She'd watched from the safety of the
tent as he'd paced up and down the ranks of men-at-
arms, Sir Evan standing off to the side, glowering
menacingly at the men. He'd sent a handful of men to
pursue the outlaw and had been in a foul mood all
morning.

"I'll ride before you," he instructed. "Keep a firm
hold on the reins. In some places the rocks are loose.
Stay close to the side."

He spurred ahead of her, his enormous horse picking
its way up the sloping path. He did not jest—the road
was treacherous, at times dropping off a sheer cliff that
ended in nothing but sharp boulders and dry scrub.
Gillian peered down, remembering the rumors of the
late countess's death. She'd plunged from these cliffs.
Gillian's stomach plummeted at the thought, and for
the remainder of the climb she kept her eyes fastened
on Nicholas's back.

The pace was slow, and it took them several hours to
reach the great gatehouse. The metal teeth of the raised
portcullis framed the open gate like the yawning mouth
of a dragon. Sun glinted off the helms of the guards lin-
ing the walls. They stared down stoically. When Kincreag and his entourage entered the courtyard, the
servants were lined up in clean livery, waiting.

Gillian scanned the household, modest for a castle of
this size. Two dozen men, women, and boys—the boys

unnaturally clean. Gillian smiled, imagining the baths forced on them for the occasion.

Nicholas helped her down from her horse and led her past the line of servants. She'd taken his arm and now held it tightly, intimidated by the demeanor of her new charges. She supposed living atop a windswept mountain might make anyone a bit dour.

The thick doors opened directly into the great hall, which was three times as long and twice as high as Lochlaire's. Deep fireplaces lined the walls. Gillian counted eight of them. Enormous wooden candelabras hung from the ceiling by chains, their candles not yet lit.

Nicholas made no comment to Gillian's gasps of astonishment, leading her across the hall and out, and through a bewildering series of corridors and rooms before finally coming to a stop before an open door.

"Your chambers," he said, gently pulling his arm away from her grasping fingers.

She dropped her hands self-consciously. "My chambers?" She frowned up at him. "Where are your chambers?"

He waved his hand vaguely to the left. "They adjoin yours." He stepped over the threshold and indicated a door. "I'm through there if you need me. Wash up, rest, have a bite, and I'll show you around. Aye?"

The door closed behind her, and she was alone. Her chamber was enormous, far finer than anywhere she'd ever lived. A huge canopied bed perched upon a dais. Heavy crimson velvet curtains draped it, secured to the carved posts by silk ropes. She wandered through the room, inspecting the fine tapestries, opening doors and peering inside. An engraved silver tray set on a cabinet bearing an enameled decanter and matching goblets. She found the ewer and basin in a cupboard and poured out the scented water, washing off road dust and travel.

A fire roared in the fireplace near the bed, so Gillian sat beside it, waiting. She poured herself some wine but was too nervous to drink, so she set the goblet on the floor beside her. It would be some time before her chests were brought up, or she would have changed into clean clothes. The weight of her new role as countess already chafed more than she'd anticipated. Separate chambers. Lillian and Alan MacDonell had shared a bedchamber, though her mother'd had other rooms for her personal use. The family had eaten together, there'd been no question of it, though things had changed now that Uncle Roderick was in charge. But then her father was only a Highland laird, not an earl. Gillian had learned much about running a household from her foster mother, but nothing of this size. She shrank smaller in her chair, gazing about the vast, immaculate room.

There was a knock on her door, too soft to be the earl, but she still stood anxiously and called, "Come in?"

A woman entered bearing a tray laden with cheese, oatcakes, and small bowls of dried fruit. She placed it on a sideboard and curtsied. She started to leave, but Gillian called after her, "Wait!"

"My lady?"

"What is your name?"

"Aileen." The woman was in her mid-twenties, her

skin sun darkened, and her pale blond hair pulled back at her nape.

"Are you my maid?"

"Aye, my lady. What be ye needing?"

"Oh, nothing."

"Verra good, then."

She was gone before Gillian could respond, leaving her impatient with herself. She should have interviewed the maid, asked questions about the running of the castle.

The next knock on her door was strong and solid, and Gillian nearly tripped in her haste to answer it.

Nicholas stood outside the door, his black doublet partially unfastened and the neck of his crisp white shirt untied.

"I want to show you some of the castle, at least enough that you can find your way should you become lost."

He led her back to the hall, pointing out various landmarks to help her remember the way. "At the tapestry of Robert Bruce and the Battle of Stirling, go left." "That strange sconce, that looks like a gargoyle? Pass through the doorway next to it. . . ." "There's three doors in the red room, take the middle one. . . ."

Gillian was thoroughly confused by the time they arrived back in the great hall, and she vowed to make him or her maid walk her through it several more times before she attempted it alone. The hall was a bustle of activity. Servants brought their baggage in and stacked it against a wall, and trestle tables were being set up for the evening meal. Much talk and laughter filled the air, but it became subdued the moment Lord Kincreag stepped into the hall. Everyone bent to their tasks with new industry. The earl did not seem to notice.

Gillian looked up at him expectantly.

He gazed around the hall, as if seeing it anew as her guide, then led her back the way they'd come, this time making different turns and using different doors, up and down staircases, some grand, some small and little used. All the while he pointed out various rooms: the gallery, solar, study, library, guest lodgings, and great chambers. Then they moved into an older section of the castle, hung with sheets and covered in a thick layer of dust and cobwebs. The windows were all closed up tight, so there was no light save the candle Nicholas had appropriated as they'd moved deeper into the castle.

He had been brisk in his tour, not stopping to linger over anything, answering her questions in monosyllables. Gillian was beginning to feel as if she kept him from something important. He paused in the middle of a large, dark chamber, the candlelight a dim halo surrounding him.

"We don't use this part of the castle anymore . . . it's likely not safe. I think it best you stay in the east wing."

He started to leave, but Gillian wandered across the dark room. Indistinct white shapes lined the walls. His footsteps paused when he realized she wasn't following him.

"Why?" she asked, running her finger over a sheet-covered structure that came nearly to her chest. It was very big and oddly shaped, but it was difficult to see much without a candle of her own.

"Because no one comes here anymore. It's not safe."

"No, I mean, why doesn't anyone come here anymore?"

He fell silent, and she turned to find he'd moved closer, bringing the faint light with him. The air tasted musty and old, forgotten.

"When . . . Catriona was alive we had a bigger staff. I no longer find it necessary to keep so many servants. My needs are few. I'm sure you've heard of nobles with various castles moving among their residences, giving the unoccupied ones an opportunity to be cleaned." He paused, gazing around the room meditatively. "I prefer Kincreag and rarely reside elsewhere. Before, we would move from one wing to the other, so the unoccupied wing could be cleaned."

"And now?"

"Now we do not even fill one wing, so we move about within the east wing. Things manage to stay relatively livable." After a moment, he added, "If you find this unsatisfactory, I could hire more servants to clean."

"I'm sure I cannot find fault with your ways, my lord—I mean, Nicholas. The east wing seems quite vast." She touched the structure before her again. "But do you not worry that the rest of the castle will fall into disrepair?"

"No."

His voice sounded strange, and she looked up. He stared at the same structure on which her hand rested, his brow furrowed, jaw set.

Gillian turned to face it. "May I remove the sheet?" When he didn't answer she dragged it off anyway, sending up a cloud of dust. She sneezed violently several times. It was the largest dollhouse Gillian had ever seen, and as she studied it, a gasp of wonder escaped her. It was not just any house, but Kincreag in miniature, right down to the very furnishings. She quickly located her own chambers and saw the bed she would sleep on tonight, small enough for a mouse to snuggle in. It sat upon a dais, with curtains and all. The bedding was a different color, but just as fine, silk ropes tying back the bed curtains. The posts appeared to be carved with the same detail as her own bedposts, but it was difficult to discern in the dim light. The room's other furnishings also appeared the same, and the candelabra on the cupboard was fitted with tiny wax candles.

"It's splendid! We must move this—"

"No," he said so forcefully that Gillian flinched and took a step back.

He circled the miniature castle, holding the candle high. Gillian followed. The right side of the dollhouse had been smashed but not beyond repair.

"Nicholas, let me fix it. I'd love to have it in my chambers. Our children could play—"

"I said no." A brittle mask had fallen over his face, drawing his skin taut and shadowing his eyes.

"What is it? Why does it upset you?"

"I thought it had been destroyed. I'd *ordered* it to be destroyed." He looked away from it now, eyes narrowed, the wheels turning in his head, recalling who'd defied him.

Gillian laid a hand on his sleeve, fearful he meant to rectify the oversight and destroy the house himself. "I pray you, Nicholas, do not destroy it. I'm charmed by it. I would very much like to have it. I'll visit it here if you don't want it brought to the east wing."

He looked at her fingers on his sleeve, then into her eyes. His face relaxed, and he sighed deeply. "Very well. Leave it here. But I don't want to see it."

He turned abruptly and strode from the chamber, not even looking back to see if she followed. He stopped at the doorway, however, and waited for her.

In the shadowy light, Gillian retrieved the sheet, shook it out, and draped it back over the house, since she didn't know how soon she'd be able to return. As she straightened the sheet, she heard the deep rumble of a man clearing his throat. She turned to Nicholas, but he wasn't even looking at her; besides, it had come from her left, and Nicholas was on her right.

She turned toward the darkness beyond her and stared hard, wondering if she'd imagined it. She started to turn away when a whisper reached out to her. Something pale moved in the corner of her vision, and she whirled, eyes wide, breath short.

Nothing but darkness and the indistinct white shapes. Her scalp tightened.

"Who's there?" she called, her voice strained and cracking with fear.

Nicholas joined her. "What is it?" He peered into the darkness.

"I heard something. First, a man clearing his throat . . . and then whispers . . . I thought I saw something, too."

"Where?"

Gillian pointed into the darkness. Nicholas strode forward, candle aloft. He wandered about, pushing at sheet-covered structures, finally rejoining her.

"There's no one here but you and me."

Gillian frowned, but shrugged. "I suppose I might have imagined it . . . the dark, I guess . . . it's making me fanciful." But somehow she didn't think so. She'd definitely heard the man, though perhaps the whispers had been nothing more than the wind rustling the sheets— and that could have been what she'd seen, the billowing of a sheet. However, there was no wind in this room, not a breath of fresh air to be had; the candle's flame never flickered.

A ghost? Her heart tripped, and instantly pain stabbed behind her eyes.

Nicholas seemed amused. There was a definite tilt to his mouth that couldn't quite be called a smile, and his eyes crinkled slightly at the corners—a most becoming expression for him. "There have been some complaints that this wing is haunted, but I assure you, I've never seen a ghost."

"I want to go now." She rubbed hard at her temples, miserable the curse had followed her to her new home. She wanted to leave the room posthaste. She would not collapse again in front of Nicholas and endure his treating her like a madwoman.

One side of his mouth curved higher. "Of course." He took her arm and led her from the room.

They were almost out the door when Gillian heard the whispers again, chasing her on a gust of frigid air. The pain in her head intensified. She gripped

Nicholas's arm tightly, glancing behind her, urging him along faster.

"The wind," she said. "Did you feel that? Where did it come from?"

"I felt nothing."

Gillian said no more, unsettled and a bit annoyed this curse would make living in her new home a chore. They were soon back in the east wing. Rather than returning her to her chambers, he led her to his own. Gillian's heart still raced, but now with an odd, fluttery anticipation. According to Rose, when they came together again, it would not hurt.

A meal had been laid out on a small trestle table. Candles lit the room, and a fire blazed. Gillian moved near the fire to warm herself.

"Are you hungry?" Nicholas asked, removing his clean, fresh doublet so he was in shirtsleeves.

Gillian's hands spread over her skirts self-consciously. "Perhaps I should change . . . my clothes are filthy."

"You'll not be wearing them much longer." His black gaze was intense, pinning her so she could barely think or move. Heat flooded her, making her legs tremble as she slowly approached the table. The way he looked at her made her weak, brought forth memories of last night with such force that she could almost feel it all over again. She averted her eyes, cheeks hot, but felt the weight of his stare on her just the same.

She slid into a chair, and he sat opposite her. He filled a plate, then passed it to her. Gillian took it with mumbled thanks, still unable to look at him. As she picked at her food, he set a silver goblet in front of her.

She lifted it, gazing at the dark contents. It smelled strongly of herbs and spices, quite medicinal. She gave him a narrow look over the rim.

"What is it? It smells . . . odd."

His black gaze was on her, both lazy and watchful, a drowsy wolf toying with its prey.

"It's mulled."

Gillian frowned into her goblet, then up at him. Mulled wine had a sweeter, spicier scent, as of nutmeg. The smell of this cleared her head, as if it contained camphor. It was on the tip of her tongue to accuse him of tainting the wine, but how could she, when she'd done the same but a few nights prior? His wine had been poured from the same flagon as hers, and she watched as he raised his goblet to his lips and drank deeply of it.

Gillian's mouth tightened, and she looked back at the goblet. "This doesn't *smell* mulled."

"Suspicious, aren't we? Do you think I'm trying to poison you?"

She looked at him sharply, but he just watched her with an indolent look.

"Of course not." She lifted the goblet to her lips and took a dainty sip. It was quite good—sweet and spicy, and thick like nectar. She licked her lips and took another drink, then set the goblet resolutely on the table. The drink warmed her, spreading outward from her belly, tingling through her limbs.

Her appetite disappeared completely with the "mulled" drink. She was content to just watch Nicholas, and he didn't seem to mind. He ate with surprising enthusiasm for one so laconic. He was a very large man; of course he needed to eat a good deal, but somehow she'd envisioned him not succumbing to normal human frailties such as hunger.

He did not speak to her throughout, though he did occasionally glance pensively at her. Gillian wondered if the mulled wine he'd given her had other properties he'd not shared. She *was* feeling relaxed, luxuriously heavy limbed and slightly drowsy.

She was on her second goblet when she asked, "Why did you order the dollhouse destroyed?"

"I didn't. I said you could have it."

She gave him a reproachful look as he chewed placidly. He was being purposely obtuse. "Before . . . years ago, is what I mean."

He set his knife down. Then picked it up. Never looking at her. Finally he said, "It's damaged."

Gillian tilted her head incredulously. "I'm sure that it was no small investment of money and labor. Surely it makes sense to repair it."

"Not to me."

Before she could ask another question, he said, "You really should eat something . . . that's not wine, and it's very strong."

Gillian raised her brows, surprised. "You said it was mulled wine."

"No, I said it was mulled. It's actually an Italian drink, made by their monks originally, but now I believe every Italian goodwife makes it." He gazed into his goblet. "It's spirits, like whisky, but mixed with various herbs and spices from the East. The papists think it's good medicine." He drained his goblet, his throat working as he swallowed. "It will certainly get you sotted if you drink too much."

Gillian set her goblet back on the table gingerly and began to eat a piece of bread. "Have you been to Italy?"

"Aye."

"What's it like?"

He shook his head, sighing. "Words are too poor, Gillian. I will take you there one day."

Gillian leaned forward, bread forgotten. "Really?"

He nodded, smiling slightly, his gaze intent on her. Then the sensual line of his lips curved down moodily, his black brows lowering. He stood abruptly.

"I want to show you something."

He came around the table and took her hand, enfolding it warmly. She rose and let him pull her along. They passed through several doors before stopping in a long, dark gallery. He had taken her through this room on their tour earlier, but they'd not lingered. He released her hand and moved away from her to light a candelabra. Paintings were arranged in sets of four the length of the gallery. He gestured for her to join him in front of a quartet of portraits.

Gillian studied the faces, three men and one woman. "They're very nice," she said politely.

He waved a hand at the portraits, encompassing them with his gesture. "This is my family, my ancestors." He pointed to a man wrapped in a crimson-and-black plaid, a dog beside him. His reddish blond hair was cropped close to his head and topped with a cap set at a rakish angle. His eyes were a pale, pale blue.

"That is my father, the earl before me."

"Really?" Gillian said, looking from the portrait to Nicholas with more interest. There was no resemblance. His father's nose was straight and pinched, whereas Nicholas's was larger and aquiline, the nostrils slightly flared. His father's skin was pale—and probably freckled, too—though the artist had been kind enough to leave that out. Nicholas's skin was very dark, and other than the shadow of whiskers on his jaw and upper lip, there was not a single freckle or mark on his fine-grained skin. And his eyes . . . quite unlike his father's. Nicholas's were larger and deep set, shadowed and mysterious.

"That's my mother." He pointed to the pale blond woman, with pale eyes to match her husband's. Though his mother and father could have been siblings, so similar did they look, they bore no resemblance to their son.

Gillian wasn't certain how she was expected to respond. He was obviously making a point, but questioning someone's—especially an *earl's*—legitimacy was not something one did lightly. Not even his wife. *Especially* not his wife, if one considered his first wife's rumored end.

Gillian turned the ring on her finger, searching her mind for an appropriate response.

"Don't you see the family resemblance?" He tilted his head, as if to give her a better view of him. There was an odd note to his voice, a razor's edge that made her uneasy. He was being facetious, she understood that, but there was an unpleasantness in the twist of his lips and the glint of his black eyes that made her tense.

Gillian still could not formulate a proper reply. The mulled beverage seemed to have dulled her wits. So she said nothing, turning her ring, staring up at him silently, and wishing they could just leave the gallery.

He turned to face her when she didn't answer. "What? You cannot see it?"

She shook her head. "You know I cannot, my lord."

"My lord?" he mocked, his dark brows arched high. He reached a hand out and traced her jaw softly. She shivered in response, her eyelids lowering. The merest touch from him set her body humming.

He dropped his hand. "That's because he was not my father."

Gillian blinked at this astounding news. If the previous earl of Kincreag was not Nicholas's father, then how was it possible he was the earl?

He smiled, thin and humorless. "I see you understand the implications—but fear not. We'll not be stripped of lands and titles, and left to starve." He turned back to the portraits. "My father claimed me until the very end. Swore on several statements that I was his true and natural son."

Gillian touched his sleeve hesitantly. "I don't understand. If he swore to it, then it must be true?"

He folded his hands behind his back. "Thirty-six years ago my father took my mother to Rome. She wanted to see all of Italy. She was quite pious. There was some kirk or relic on an island several miles off the coast. My mother had to see it, and my father refused her nothing. The ship they took was attacked by pirates." He glanced at her, a brow arched slightly. "They're called corsairs on the Mediterranean—and they're often Turks, or Moors."

Gillian's hand covered her mouth as she began to understand the direction of this story.

"My mother was taken to be sold as a slave, and my father was wounded. He began searching for her as soon as he was able. She was found a few weeks later— alive but weak and ill-treated. They returned to Scotland immediately." He turned to her, black eyes intent. "Nine months later, I was born."

Gillian shook her head, eyes wide. "But no one can know for certain—"

"My parents were married for ten years before I was born. My mother never became pregnant. Not once. Nor did she get with child again after I was born. And when she died, my father remarried. My stepmother did not bear him a child. No miscarriages, either. She did not become pregnant. But after my father died, she remarried and now has four sons and two daughters."

"But your father swore—"

He stuck his hand in her face, right beneath her nose. "Look at this, Gillian. What more proof do you need? This is not the skin of a Scot."

She bit her lip, looking down at the dark skin before her. His hand was strong and well made, dusted with black hair. She lifted her hand and placed it in his, lowering it so it was between their bodies. He did not grip her hand back. He stared down at her hand, resting against his open palm, her skin pale and fragile against his.

Then his hand curled closed over hers.

"Why did you show me this?" she asked.

"You're my wife. I thought you should know."

"Did you think it would change anything?"

He did not look at her but at the picture of his mother. He did not reply.

"Does anyone else know?"

"Not . . . anymore."

"Your first wife knew?"

He nodded.

Something powerful shifted in her chest, at once painful and sweet. He'd trusted her with a very sensitive secret, making himself vulnerable to her. And she fell in love with him for it.

Emboldened, she stepped closer, so their bodies almost touched, their joined hands pressed against her belly. His head tipped down, smoldering eyes on her.

This whole evening seemed unreal, a dream—his warm hand holding hers, his thumb moving now, slowly, softly across her skin. Her heart quickened, and her thoughts flowed thick and languorous. It *was* a dream, she supposed, given to her by Old Hazel.

"Did you think I would care?" she whispered.

"I thought it better that you know in the beginning, rather than find out later and feel . . . disillusioned."

She thought it rather ironic that she had speculated with her sisters on his heritage, wondering with fascination if he had Spanish Moor in him. She had found it rather exciting to think about then. But regardless of his father's heritage, his mother had been a Scot. He'd been raised in Scotland, as a Scot—his Scots burr was proof of that, as well as his command of Gaelic. Surely he was more Scottish than aught else, despite his paternity or the color of his skin.

"I'm sorry for what your mother suffered. But as it resulted in you, I cannot be truly sorry it happened."

He said nothing, only continued to stare down at her, his gaze hot and black.

He'd shared something so personal with her that she felt compelled to do the same. "Nicholas," she said, her voice wavering. "There's something you should know about me. I'm a witch . . . except my magic is useless to me. That's the source of the headaches, a curse placed on me so I can't use my magic—necromancy."

As she spoke, the heat cooled from his eyes and he arched a quizzical brow, listening to her hurried speech.

After a thick moment of silence, he said, "I see."

Damn that mulled drink. She felt foolish now and wished she'd kept her mouth shut. "I just thought you should know," she murmured, looking away from him, cheeks hot.

His finger tipped up her chin, forcing her to look into his eyes. "Your secret is safe with me, Gillian. But let's keep it a secret, aye? No summoning ghosts, or the servants will talk."

"You don't believe me."

He opened his mouth, brows raised earnestly, as if to deny it, then his mouth snapped shut. He exhaled through his nose. Finally he said, "I believe that you be-lieve. But more importantly, I *know* the great majority of Scotland believes and would love to burn you for it." He chucked her chin lightly. "Necromancy is not a necessary skill for a countess anyway, mind, so let's not speak on it again."

His tone was even, but there was a slight crinkling to the corners of his eyes. He was amused. There was also a thread of steel in his voice. He expected her to obey.

Gillian gazed up at him, sullen, her bottom lip heavy. "Are you forbidding me, my lord?"

"Aye. I am."

He was not accustomed to anyone questioning his edicts, nor would he tolerate disobedience. Gillian really wished she'd kept her mouth shut now. If Rose discovered how to break the curse, Gillian would have to defy him and be secretive about it. She'd not wanted to do that.

She stepped away from him and tried to pull her hand from his. "I told you. It's of no use to me, anyway."

He held her fast and with a quick tug brought her up against him again. His other hand slid around behind her back.

"In the event your headaches disappear and you're able to converse freely with the dead"—this was said with dry mockery—"then I want you to ignore them. Understand?"

Gillian would not lie to him, so she stared off to the side stubbornly.

He sighed. "I see you are going to be a trial."

Her cheeks burned hotter. "I apologize for being such an inconvenience."

His body molded to the length of hers, hot and hard. She tried to ignore her response to him, but it was difficult. Her heart raced, her palms damp with anticipation. She could smell him, feel the heat of him.

"You're forgiven," he said dryly.

She looked at him from beneath her lashes and saw the wry twist of his mouth.

"You're teasing me."

His palm on her back—hot even through layers of clothes—pressed her closer. He lowered his head, his mouth near her ear. "It's you that teases me. Let's return to my chambers."

Gillian nodded, his edict forgotten in the shivers that raced over her from his warm breath blowing softly against her ear. He started to raise his head. Gillian turned hers so that her mouth brushed his lips. He froze, and Gillian drew back a fraction to see his expression.

Candlelight flickered across his face, reflected in his black eyes. She'd been bold, but she could not help herself with him. He was her husband now, after all, and she wanted to touch and kiss him. She leaned into him, kissing his mouth, darting her tongue to taste his lips. He was firm and cool, flavored faintly of his mulled drink.

He made a rough sound, then pressed his mouth to hers, roughly at first, then gently, as if restraining himself. Gillian's free hand clutched at his shoulder, her other hand squeezing his. Already she felt the dampness between her thighs, the excitement of what was to come. His mouth was soft, the faint bristle of beard beneath his bottom lip scraping her skin. His tongue teased her, touching her lips briefly, sending a tingling of sensation from her mouth to her belly.

His hand untangled from hers, sliding into her hair and cupping the base of her head. He deepened the kiss then, his tongue pushing into her mouth, joining with hers. Gillian lost track of how long they stood there, their mouths mating, her hands clinging to his shoulders as if she were falling—and was falling, carried away by a raging storm, helpless to resist it.

When he took his mouth away, she whimpered, turning her face to follow, and he groaned, kissing her again. She could taste his hunger, and her body answered it, hips shifting closer. He broke away again, catching her face between his hands.

Gillian could barely open her eyes, but when she did, her heart snagged. Had he looked at her so last night, as he'd made love to her? As if she were the only woman in the world, and the only one he wanted. She whispered his name, her hands sliding up his chest restlessly, her eyes drifting shut again as she leaned heavily against him.

"Not here," he said, his voice rough. He kissed her again, a hard, possessive kiss, his fingers curling hard in her hair. Then he took her hand and led her back to his chambers.

12

Nicholas led Gillian back to his chambers, her small, pale hand engulfed in his. He did not know why he'd shown her the portraits. She'd have seen them eventually and would have noted the difference. He supposed he couldn't stand the idea of her looking at him and wondering. As for her reaction, it had been most unexpected. He'd expected horror, revulsion, even resigned acceptance, but not her sweetness. His parents had kept his mother's misadventure with the corsairs a secret and had severely punished any servant caught gossiping about it, or about Nicholas's presumed parentage.

Alasdair Lyon, Nicholas's father, had loved him anyway, had always been good and fair, had never blamed any of his boyhood escapades on the heathen side of his nature. The late earl had, in fact, behaved as though Nicholas had been no different from anyone else. His mother, however, had been distant. She'd died when Nicholas was a child, so he only had misty memories of her, but he imagined he'd been an unsavory reminder of the nightmare she'd lived through.

Now, in the privacy of his chambers, Nicholas gazed down at his bride and began to hope. The fire burned low, and only the candles from their abandoned dinner illuminated the room. Desire flushed the velvet skin of her neck and chest. Her lashes fluttered open and closed, watching him dazedly as he undressed her, and resting like dark fans against her cheeks. He adored her eyes, large and dove-gray, and so expressive, showing everything she thought and felt, even when she thought she hid it.

He moved behind her. She tried to turn with him, but his hands on her shoulders kept her still. Her hair was pulled away from her face, plaited and packed into a silk-lined mesh caul. He pulled the ribbon that ran through the top of the caul and removed it. Two thick braids tumbled out. He took his time unbraiding her hair, running his hands through the sable silk, watching in fascination as it curled and waved over his fingers.

"So much hair," he murmured, leaning down to kiss her neck through the thick curtain, breathing in the scent of her. He could still smell the rose water she'd rinsed it with, overlaid with heather and the faint sultry scent of woman. It fired him, set his blood simmering.

She stood motionless, letting him do what he wished. She was a contradiction, and it twisted him in knots. He might have been trusting and comparatively inexperienced when he'd married Catriona, but he was something of a cynic in the bedchamber now. He knew when a woman was eager and when she was going through the motions. Gillian was neither. She emanated innocent excitement. Her breath came in short gasps, as if suspended in the moment, savoring each new experience as it came, and breathlessly anticipating the next.

It made him hot and hard to know he did this to her, to watch her flutter with passion beneath his hands. He reached around her, his hands sliding into the top of her skirts. The muscles of her belly tensed and quivered beneath his hands. He found the points and hooks that secured her skirt and made short work of them. Her skirts puddled around her feet.

He smoothed his hands over the swell of her hips, her skin beneath warming and perfuming the linen, and the excitement nearly overwhelmed him. He was torn between a primitive urge to ravish her, claiming her as his, and wanting to worship her for her unbearable sweetness. Since he'd already done the former the night before, she deserved the latter, however difficult it might prove. He turned her to face him. Her eyes were closed, her hands clenching and unclenching in her shift. Her breasts strained against the thin material as she breathed. He would not be able to keep this up much longer. Already the thrumming pressure built inside him, begging for release, but he would see his bride.

"Look at me," he ordered, gathering her shift in his hands and pulling it up and over her head. She raised her arms for him, and then lowered them, trying to cover herself self-consciously, gazing at him beneath the veil of dark lashes. Her hair tumbled over her shoulders, partially obscuring her body. Narrow white shoulders shone through the parted sable. It hung in thick waves down her back, brushing the curve of her bottom. She tried to maneuver her hair so it covered her breasts, but the rosy nipples peeked through. She still wore her hose, gartered at the knee, and her slippers.

She charmed him, so prim and luscious, trying to modestly hide her voluptuous figure behind her hair and stance. He sat back on the bed and gazed at her.

"Nicholas!" she pleaded, moving restlessly, arms crossed over her breasts, but unable to hide their luxuriant weight.

"Are you embarrassed?" he asked.

"Aye." She moved closer to the bed, white teeth worrying her bottom lip, cheeks stained pink.

"You're my wife. I want to look at you." His gaze traveled slowly over her. He wanted to drag her down on the bed with him, but he restrained himself, wanting to look a bit longer.

"You're my husband," she said, her voice soft. "I want to look at you." She closed the small distance between them and reached toward him hesitantly. "If I may, my lord?"

Nicholas froze, his mouth dry. He managed a nod, never tearing his gaze from her as she pulled at the ties on his shirt, then, with his help, drew it over his head. She studied him for a long moment, her lips curved in a half smile. Then she touched him, trailing her fingers from the base of his neck, over his shoulder and down his arm. Bone-deep tremors wrenched through him.

"You are beautiful," she whispered, her hand retracing its journey, bolder now, fingers drifting lower to tangle through the hair on his chest.

Nicholas seized her wrist and pulled her between his thighs. She made a soft sound of surprise but offered no resistance. Her hands rested lightly on his shoulders, and her hair fell all around him. He rubbed his face against the firm skin of her breasts, filling his senses with the scent of her. His blood rushed, hot and thick. He thought he might die if he didn't take her now. He tried to think of other things, mundane things, to prolong the moment, but she still touched him, making thought impossible. Her hands sifted through the hair at his temples, brushing it back, tentative at first, then with sensuous purpose, so that shudders of want rendered him weak.

He anchored himself by grabbing handfuls of her bottom and pulling her close, nuzzling her breasts through her softly scented hair. She squeaked and wriggled against his erection, and that was enough for him. He quickly divested them both of their remaining garments, then tumbled her back onto the bed, his thigh pushing between hers. He set his mouth on hers. She arched up into his kiss, already an expert at driving him mad, licking and sucking eagerly at his mouth and tongue.

Nothing separated them now. Her bare skin pressed against his. The hair on his chest brushed her breasts, and lower down, he pressed inexorably against her damp curls. Her languid passion vanished instantly, and she stiffened in his arms.

He remembered her tears the night before and regretted his urgency. "I'll not hurt you, Gillian."

She nodded, trying to look brave for him, his sweet little countess. He brushed her cheek with the backs of his fingers, a surge of affection setting him momentarily off balance. He drew back from her. She blinked up at him, flushed and beautiful with her hair fanned around her, waiting for him. Lust possessed him again.

He kissed her and whispered against her lips, "Fash not another moment, love. It'll not hurt at all. I promise."

She nodded, swallowing nervously. He sat back between her thighs, hands trailing over her breasts and hips. Her body was gilded in candlelight, the soft light turning her skin dusky rose. The skin beneath one breast was stained an ugly purple from Scott MacGregor. He leaned forward, kissing the bruise, open-mouthed, his heart in his throat again as he relived those terrible moments on the foggy moor. His hand slid down her belly, open palmed, stopping as he covered her thatch of dark hair. She bit her lip and made a soft, agitated sound, her hips pressing upward.

Her sweet eagerness drove him insane. He reined in the urge to fold her legs over his shoulders and just take her. *Slow.* He rubbed his thumb through her damp hair, teasing the sensitive nub within and causing her to gasp reflexively. He lowered his head, his hands sliding under her hips, lifting her to his mouth.

She cried out in surprise and alarm and tried to squirm away, legs kicking. He laughed softly and got a better grip on her thighs. Once he got started, she quit fighting him and writhed, pressing herself fretfully against his mouth, twisting her fists in the bedsheets. He slid his finger inside her, and her gasps and moans escalated, her body contracting around his finger. She cried out as her release seized her, her body twisting beautifully in the candlelight. He released her and leaned over her. She lay boneless beneath him, gazing up at him through sultry, half-lidded eyes. He smiled as he pressed inside her. He did it slowly, carefully, watching her face for signs of discomfort.

She arched against him, her body tight and hot and perfect. She whispered his name and he moved inside her, arms braced on the bed. He went slowly at first, but she kissed him, licking his ears and neck, spurring him faster and harder, until he was mindless, lost in her body. Her thighs tightened, her body squeezing his, wringing the pleasure from him, drawing it out until he was weak from it. His crushed her in his arms. The air left him in an explosion, and he swore, clasping her tightly.

He pressed his forehead to hers, waiting for his thundering heart to calm, wrung out and infinitely satisfied. She pushed the damp hair back from his face, stroked his shoulders and back. He basked in the attention she lavished. He kissed her again, then moved off her and lay beside her, one leg still hooked over her thighs, one arm draped around her waist.

He closed his eyes but didn't sleep. After a time he sensed her watching him, and he opened his eyes. She leaned on an elbow, hair artfully arranged to hide her breasts again. His mouth curled lazily, endlessly charmed by her. She returned his smile, then bit her lip shyly and toyed with the ends of her hair. Marriage to her would be sheer bliss, if only . . .

If only he knew what she'd slipped in his wine and why. The longer he knew her, the less sense it made. But whether or not he understood it didn't change the facts. She'd tried to impair him somehow. His pleasure in her and the moment faded. The sinking uneasiness returned.

She looked up at him, her large eyes searching his face. Her expression grew confused and uneasy. "Why do you look at me so?" She tried to move away, to pull the sheet over her, but he held her fast with his leg.

"Is there anything I should know? Anything you haven't told me?"

Her brows drew together. "What do you mean?"

"Is there something you wish to tell me? Anything you haven't yet?" *Please tell me.*

There was fear in her eyes as she lowered them, unable to hold his gaze. She was a terrible liar. She swallowed and shook her head against the pillow. His hope bottomed out. He couldn't look at her anymore; the disappointment was too intense. He wanted to rage at her for ruining the night, but he couldn't let her know he was on to her. It would only make her sneakier, make her a more creative liar. He rolled away from her and pulled at the furs and sheets so he could slide beneath them.

"I'll be leaving tomorrow," he said. "I don't know how long I'll be gone. A day or two, I imagine. You're safe here. I'm leaving you Sir Evan."

He settled onto his side with his back to her. She did not move for a long time, and though he tried valiantly, he could not sleep knowing she was there. Lying to him. He fought to put her from his mind but instead found himself dwelling on all that had transpired tonight, and growing angrier by the moment.

She slid out of his bed. He heard her scurry about, gathering her clothes. Feet padded softly across the floor, and their adjoining door opened and closed. She was gone.

That was not what he'd wanted. He wanted her in his bed. He wanted to shake the truth out of her. He didn't know what he wanted anymore. When sleep finally came, he dreamed of his son, as he often did when he was troubled, standing beside his bed, watching over him.

Gillian lay in bed the next morning, the curtains closed around her, hiding her from the servants who bustled about her room. A bath was being brought up, bucket after steaming bucket carried from the kitchens to fill her big brass tub. Food was on her table; she'd smelled it when she'd woken—hot mulled wine, warm bread, sausage, and likely other delicacies suited to a countess. Precious jams and sweetmeats. Perhaps even an orange. She hoped so. She'd had one once and thought it the most wonderful thing she'd ever eaten.

As she waited for her bath to be ready, she thought about the night before. She was dreadfully confused. It had been a beautiful evening, altogether. He'd talked to her, made love to her . . . then dismissed her. What had she done wrong? He'd seemed to enjoy their love-making. She certainly had. He thought she was hiding something from him. But she'd told him she was a witch, and he hadn't wanted to speak of it. Maybe he wasn't angry at all. Maybe that was just the way of things. After all, she had her own chambers and her own bed—a fine, huge bed it was. Perhaps this was her *place*. Perhaps he did not wish to sleep with her. She recalled how he'd held her in the tent. Her body ached to be sheltered in his again. But perhaps he'd only done it because they'd been traveling and she'd been in danger.

Gillian covered her face with her hands, her stomach so knotted and miserable that she didn't think she could eat anything, not even an orange. She flung back the covers and sat up, peeking through the curtains. A heavyset maid with dark hair sat serenely on the hearth, watching two lads pour water into the tub and then depart.

"They're finished, my lady," the woman said, standing. "Do ye wish a bite afore ye bathe?"

"No." Gillian pulled her shift over her head and sank into the steaming tub of water. Blue petals floated on the water's surface, surrounding her with an intoxicating fragrance. Gillian scooped up a handful of water and let it drain until a petal lay in her palm. She inhaled the soft scent.

"What is this?"

"It's a lilac petal. My lord brought them from his travels in heathen lands. There are many bushes in the garden." After a moment the maid added with a knowing smile, "He thought you might like them in your bath."

Gillian hadn't ordered a bath this morning, so apparently the earl had. "He told you to add lilac petals to my water?"

"Aye."

Gillian smiled to herself and sank lower into the tub. The maid busied herself making Gillian's bed. She was an older woman, with a kind, broad face and a few missing teeth.

"What's your name?" Gillian asked.

"Earie."

"Where is Aileen this morning?"

Earie faltered as she shook out the velvet coverlet. "Oh, my lady . . . I'm not supposed to trouble you with this, but since you're asking . . ." Earie's voice dropped to a whisper. "She killed herself."

Gillian sat up so quickly that water sloshed onto the floor. "Killed herself!"

"Aye, she was found dead in her own bed this morning." Earie smoothed the coverlet over the bed and straightened the corners. "Drunk some poison, she did."

"How do you know she killed herself?"

Earie cocked her head in confusion. "Why else would she drink poison?"

"Maybe someone made her drink it."

"Who would do that? She got on well enough with everyone."

After her bath Earie combed Gillian's hair dry before the fire and plaited it, wrapping the coils around her head. All the while Gillian thought of the young maid she'd met the night before, taking her own life. What had been so horrible that death was preferable?

When Gillian was dressed and coiffured, Earie directed her to the great hall. The enormous hall had been transformed from the night before. The trestle tables were gone, and the hall milled with people. From the quality of the attire it was clear these were not servants—many not even villagers—but lairds and merchants.

Gillian hung back near the wall, uncertain what to do. Several men gave her appraising looks, but she ignored them, searching for her knight. She peered past the clusters of people to a table set upon the dais. Sir Evan sat behind it, and beside him sat another man, small and balding. Beside him was yet another man, this one young and thin, and writing furiously on a long piece of parchment.

Sir Evan spotted her and stood, motioning to someone behind him. To Gillian's utter horror, yet another man stepped forward—a herald—and bellowed, "The countess of Kincreag!"

A hush fell over the hall. Every face turned toward her. Gillian froze, staring back into their faces with blank terror. Then Sir Evan was beside her, taking her arm and leading her through the crowd. Slowly her wits returned, and her cheeks burned brighter as she imagined herself paralyzed at the back of the room. What a poor countess she was turning out to be.

At the dais Sir Evan seated her in an elaborate high-backed chair, then took the chair beside her. He leaned close and said, "This won't last long, my lady, then I'm at your disposal."

Gillian nodded numbly. She had no idea what was transpiring in the hall, or what might be expected of her, seated at the high table. But soon it all became clear, and she relaxed. This was Kincreag's court session for settling grievances and hearing petitions, except Sir Evan administered what justice he could in Nicholas's absence. Gillian's foster father had been a March Warden, so she was familiar with courts of law. Nicholas was sheriff of many shires, so his reach was great.

Gillian listened avidly to pleas for mercy from mothers and fathers for their children, requests for loans, and accusations against others. The young man on the dais was a scribe, and he recorded each request for Nicholas to review later, along with any decisions made. Most were set aside for the earl to review later, but some Sir Evan ruled on, with the advice of the bald man, who, it turned out, was Nicholas's solicitor.

A burly, red-faced man came forward with an accusation of witchcraft. Two men dragged an old woman forward, thrusting her in front of Sir Evan. She was haggard and filthy, dressed in rags. Sir Evan's nose wrinkled at her stench, but otherwise he appeared immune to the woman's distress.

Her accuser recited a list of grievances, among them drying up his cow's milk, causing his young child to die of pox by giving him the evil eye, and necromancy. The last charge caused Gillian's heart to skitter uncomfortably.

Sir Evan leaned toward the solicitor, and they conversed quietly. Finally Sir Evan straightened. "Your grievances are noted. Lord Kincreag tries all cases of witchcraft."

Gillian looked at Sir Evan in surprise. That was most unusual. Previously, only the king could try a witch, but a law had been passed several years ago giving power to villages to form committees to try, sentence, and execute witches. As long as the witch was a commoner, most nobles were happy to leave the trying and burning to the committees.

The man turned away, but the woman resisted attempts to remove her. Her watery brown eyes fixed pleadingly on Gillian.

Gillian hesitated, fidgeting in her seat and glancing anxiously at Sir Evan, but he'd already forgotten the old woman and motioned the next petitioner forward.

The old woman called out, "Help me, my lady, I am innocent of these charges. I beg yer sweet mercy. I did none of these things—I only saw the ghost, my lady. I didna summon her, I vow it!"

Sir Evan jerked his arm toward the men-at-arms stationed on either side of their table. "Get her out of here."

Gillian stood abruptly. "Wait!"

The men-at-arms froze, looking from Gillian to Sir Evan. Sir Evan turned in his chair to look up at Gillian expectantly.

Gillian sat down and licked her lips. She gave the old woman a kind smile. "Tell me of this ghost."

The old woman's arms were released. She came back to stand before Gillian. "The late countess, my lady. She walks the cliffs, restless in her death. I was frightened, my lady! I did not summon her or try to speak with her—I just ran!"

Gillian's eyes felt stretched wide with horror. Sir Evan stared at the woman, his jaw rigid. He motioned to the guards again to remove her, but this time the guards hesitated, looking to Gillian for confirmation.

"Where will they take this woman?" she asked the knight.

"She'll be stuck in the thieves' hole until Lord Kincreag returns."

"What?" Gillian cried. Knowing what she did about Nicholas, she felt certain he would not charge this woman with witchcraft. And it was wrong to shove an old, feeble woman in a dank hole when she was innocent. And even if she wasn't . . . Gillian couldn't help thinking of her mother, certainly a witch, but a white one, being mistreated and burned.

"I forbid it."

The first real emotion passed over Sir Evan's face—surprise, and something else, something cagey. He inclined his head deferentially. "My lady? Your ruling?"

Sudden panic choked Gillian. Ruling? What ruling? She held a life in her hands, and she couldn't think of what to do. "I . . . I . . ."

After what seemed an eternity of her stuttering, Sir Evan turned back to the men-at-arms. "Confine the witch to suitable chambers within the keep and set a guard on her."

"And give her hot food," Gillian chimed in, powers

of speech returned. She slid Sir Evan a grateful look for his fast thinking. "And a warm blanket," she added.

Sir Evan nodded to the men-at-arms to make it happen, and they led the old woman away.

Gillian sank back into her chair, shaken by the confrontation. Would Nicholas be displeased with her for interfering? She feared she'd handled the whole thing poorly and had made a bad impression on Nicholas's people. That's what happened when earls married so far beneath them.

When court finally adjourned for the day, Sir Evan led her from the hall into a solar. Servants bustled in serving her wine and cakes.

Gillian toyed with her little iced cakes, still a bit queasy from her outburst. Sir Evan stood near the door like a sentry while she sat eating. It felt ridiculous.

"Sir Evan? Would you join me?"

He came forward but didn't sit down. He positioned himself in front of her, hands behind his back. And just stood there, staring blankly at something above and behind her head. His square-jawed face was granite, as if carved from the cliff Kincreag sat upon.

"Prithee, sit with me." She motioned to the chair opposite her. "Have some wine and cakes."

"I cannot."

She considered him, lips compressed thoughtfully. "I order you to."

He sat.

She smiled, then immediately felt silly and mean-spirited.

"I want to thank you for aiding me out there . . . I

was lost . . . I *am* hopelessly lost. I don't know how to be a countess. I feel terrible ordering you around."

His bland stare became interested. "I'm here to serve you, my lady. There's no need to feel terrible. And you did well out there."

Gillian sat up straighter, pleased by his praise. "Do you think Lord Kincreag will be angry with me?"

"No."

A great weight lifted from Gillian's chest until he added, "This time. In the future, ruling when he's absent could put him in a very difficult situation. Have a care."

"But I didn't rule."

"That was for the best, but I thought for a moment that you meant to."

He was right. She might be a countess, but that gave her no authority in Kincreag's courts. A flush stole into her cheeks as she nodded vigorously, wanting him to see she understood and took his advice seriously.

"Have you any more advice for me? Anything else a countess should know?"

"Lord Kincreag could give you better counsel than I, my lady."

"Of course." She ate a cake. Sipped some wine.

The silence between them drew out. He sat stone-faced across from her, not drinking or eating or looking at her. She peered closer to be sure he was breathing. What a bore. Maybe she should command him to sing for her. And dance a jig.

"There is something else I'd like to ask you."

His empty gaze fixed on her. "My lady?"

"Did you know my maid, Aileen?"

"The suicide?"

Gillian leaned forward. "Are you certain it was a suicide?"

"Aye, I am."

"Why? What is the evidence?"

He paused, his brows lowering, then said, "The poison was in her possession."

"Perhaps someone murdered her and made it look like a suicide."

"Who would want to murder a maid?"

"Maybe a jilted lover."

"She had no lover."

"A *secret* lover."

Sir Evan regarded her silently, as if she were a conundrum he had no idea how to approach. He shifted slightly in his chair, then said, "It's fine to amuse yourself with such fancies, my lady, but these are not things a countess concerns herself with. Lord Kincreag and myself have experience in these matters. You must trust that we know what we're doing."

Gillian leaned back in her chair and picked the icing off her cake, properly chastised. "Forgive me. It's just . . . I'd only just met her, and she seemed so nice."

"She was a strange lass—or so the other servants say. Kept to herself, was a bit too fond of the bottle. It's a miserable life most commoners lead, especially unmarried women. It's not surprising many of them take their lives to end the drudgery."

"No, I suppose not. Forgive me for my ignorance."

He inclined his head. "Forgiven."

Gillian gave him a tight smile and vowed to never need his help again.

Gillian woke the next morning ready to explore Kincreag. She decided to start with a visit to her dollhouse. She fetched a candelabra and a tinderbox, and made her way through the mazelike rooms and corridors of the castle. She lost her way a few times and had to backtrack, but eventually she found it.

She paused at the entrance to the darkened room, her heart thumping. Memories of her first night here, of the strange whispers and the cold draft, assailed her. She scanned the room hesitantly. Thin streams of sunlight filtered through the edges of the shutters, casting the white lumps that filled the room in hues of dark gray. It was just a room, Gillian told herself firmly, and if she wanted to repair the dollhouse, she would have to brave it. If she got any headaches, she would have the men-at-arms move it to another room in the east wing and tell Nicholas later. With any luck, he would never know.

The room was very large, a sort of small hall, or meeting room. She removed the sheet from the nearest flat surface, a wooden sideboard, and set her candelabra down. She opened all the shutters and lit more candles. Her fear dissolved as the dark shadows disappeared. By the time she finished, the room was alight and she'd not had a single pang in her temples. When all the sheets were removed, she realized this was some sort of solar. Four chairs sat in a semicircle in one corner. On the seat of each chair was a musical instrument—a lute, a fiddle, a flute, and a harp. The instruments rested on the chairs as if their musicians had only left them there a moment ago.

Gillian wondered if this was the late countess's solar. Had she listened to music while she'd embroidered? Did her ghost really walk the cliffs? Gillian longed to see for herself. It infuriated her that it would be possible if not for this curse.

She yanked the sheet off the dollhouse and gazed at the work of art before her, wondering who had actually built it. Had Nicholas's son been old enough to play with it? Had Nicholas sat with his son and watched him explore the dollhouse's many wonders? Was that why he now hated the sight of it?

Gillian bent to explore it herself. It was truly exquisite. Kincreag in miniature, right down to the dragon's teeth portcullis. Gillian touched the gate wonderingly. It was cleverly stained to look discolored and well used. The top of the gatehouse could be removed, and inside, the tiny clockworks opened the gate. She turned the handle, and the gate rose. She laughed and imagined her own children playing with the dollhouse. Nicholas's children. She placed her hand over her belly, recalling last night's lovemaking. Even now a child might be growing inside her.

She sighed and circled the dollhouse. The table was split and hinged so it could be parted and the house could be opened with little effort. It was already partially open. Gillian pushed it wider. Several cushioned stools were situated beneath the table. Gillian pulled one out and seated herself in the table opening. From this vantage she could see all the levels of the keep. In the kitchen, fireplaces lined the walls. Black pots hung on working iron swing arms, and working spits sat in the fireplace. In the larder, tiny ale casks and bags of grain lined the walls. Circles of cheese made from small yellow rounds of wax tied with string rested on the wooden shelves. Gillian moved on through the castle, pausing in the armory and exclaiming over tiny swords and working crossbows.

Then she came to the room she'd seen on her last visit here with Nicholas—her room. With the sun's light, she could see that the wood was intricately carved with the same swirling pattern as the furniture in her real room. The bed had different hangings, but it was indeed her bed. There was a lump beneath the covers that she didn't recall. Of course, it *had* been dark that night. She pulled back the covers with her fingertips and found a small doll, swathed in velvet trimmed with gold. Its hair was made from fine, pale flax and its features were painted delicately on its wooden face. Tiny jewels adorned its hair. Was it supposed to be the late countess? Gillian frowned down at the doll, inexplicably disturbed by it. She did a quick study of the rest of the dollhouse but saw no other dolls. She stared back down at the blond doll, wondering where it had come from.

A cold draft blew through the room, disturbing some of the tiny furnishings. A miniature candelabra tipped over. Gillian set the doll aside and took the delicate candelabra between her fingertips, examining it with amazement. Such skilled workmanship. She'd never dreamed such things could be made. She stood and went to the large candelabra, lighting each tiny wick. She would not let it burn for long, but she had a childish urge to see it burning in the replica of her bed-chamber.

She returned to the dollhouse and set it on the side-board. She leaned back, examining the little room. The smile froze on her face as her gaze passed the bed. The lump was back. She looked quickly to where she had set the doll down, but it was gone. Gillian stood abruptly, her heart hammering in her throat. She started to back away, then stopped. *Courage!* She pulled back the covers of the tiny bed and found the blond doll.

Gillian stared at it a long time before glancing fear-fully around the room. Nicholas had said the servants believed the west wing was haunted, and she'd had pain in her head last night. But she didn't today. She sat back down, unable to look away from the doll. Something very odd was happening, but Gillian could not com-prehend what. She decided to leave the doll in the bed for now. She blew out the tiny candles and turned her attention to the west wing.

She cocked her head, examining the damaged sec-tion of the miniature Kincreag. Someone had appar-ently hit it with something. One of the walls had splintered and caved in, buckling the top floor, but that was the only damage. Surely a good carpenter could re-pair that.

Something rustled. Gillian turned sharply, her gaze snapping to the doll. It was still where she'd placed it. She scanned the room, eyes narrowed and watchful, body tense. She was alone. Still, the uneasy feeling was with her now, and she decided she'd seen enough of the dollhouse for today. She took the doll and put it in her pocket. She would ask Nicholas about it later.

She was blowing out the candles when a thump startled her. It came from deep in the west wing. She took a candle from the candelabra and walked cautiously through the doorway. Darkness closed around her like a musty cloak, weighing on her. She raised her candle higher. Cobwebs hung from the ceiling, swaying gently in a faint, cool breeze.

She passed several open doors, peering inside each one, but she could see little except shapeless white lumps. She had just decided that it must have been her imagination when the low murmur of voices froze her in her tracks. Her heart throbbed so loudly in her ears that she couldn't make out what the voices were saying. She had no headache, so the voices couldn't be ghosts. That calmed her somewhat. She wove her way through the maze of sheet-covered furniture that filled the room, straining to understand what was being said. It was a man and woman talking, and though she still couldn't understand them, it didn't sound ghostly. She extinguished her candle as she neared the doorway.

It was good that she did, for she soon discerned a soft glow of candlelight coming from the open doorway. Gillian pressed herself against the wall and peered around the frame.

She was barely able to contain her gasp of astonishment. Sir Evan stood in the next room, a small bedchamber. He held a woman in his arms. She wore a long velvet cloak. He kissed her roughly, and it fell back from her head, exposing the gleam of golden hair. Gillian tensed, wondering if he was forcing himself on her, but her arms were around him, and she pressed herself close in a way now familiar to Gillian.

Apparently he wasn't as cold and emotionless as he appeared. Gillian eased out of the room. None of her business. He wasn't married, after all, and she didn't recognize the woman—not that she would in the short time that she'd been here.

Ghosts. Gillian scoffed to herself as she returned to her chambers. She was sure Sir Evan liked everyone to believe the west wing was haunted: It kept them away from his little rendezvous. But by the time she was in her chambers, she felt a sense of amusement about what she'd witnessed. The stone-faced knight had a lover. Perhaps she would tease him about it.

She wondered if she should tell Nicholas, but he probably didn't care about his knight's love affairs. She wandered over to her cabinet. Someone had dumped her untouched wine from yesterday. The goblet was clean and sitting with its mates on the silver tray. Had that been the last thing Aileen had done before she'd decided to take her own life?

Gillian sighed, wondering why it bothered her so much. She didn't know the lass or how things worked at Kincreag. Sir Evan was right, she should stick with what she knew. Her hand slid into her pocket to remove the doll she'd placed there earlier, but it was gone. Her pocket was empty.

13

*S*everal days later Gillian decided it was time to see more of Kincreag, and she asked Sir Evan to escort her to the village. With a handful of men-at-arms they spent hours picking their way down the mountain path, only for Gillian to discover there was little to see. It was bigger than Glen Laire's wee hamlet, but it was still small, like most Highland villages. Gillian had grown spoiled living in the Lowlands, with Edinburgh not far, as well as several other large towns where merchants gathered weekly. Sir Evan informed her that merchants came to Kincreag quarterly and set up a great fair, so she shouldn't fash overmuch. Their visit caused much excitement in the village. Everyone turned out to have a look at the new countess, and she was presented with a basket of fruit and a goat.

On the return journey Gillian casually asked Sir Evan to point out the spot where the late countess had fallen—ostensibly to avoid that spot herself, but in truth, it was just her morbid curiosity, worse now with the possibility of a ghost lingering about.

Sir Evan looked at her sharply, then said, "Not here . . . on the north side of the castle. There the wall is built verra close to the cliff edge, but there's a walking path. You can get to it through a postern door."

"Did she walk there often?"

He shook his head grimly. He'd become even more taciturn with her today. His sharp eyes were watchful as he hurried them along, making certain they passed through the gates of Kincreag before dusk. He dismounted in the courtyard and led Morfran beside the west gatehouse tower. He then sent someone to fetch her a step. Gillian didn't really need the step to dismount but it was a very fine step, made especially for her by the master of horse. It had been presented to her with such pride that she really had no choice now.

A minute or two passed, then Sir Evan sighed. "A moment, my lady, I'll get the step myself."

Gillian watched his retreating back. He was exceedingly impatient today, snapping orders at the men. She wondered if she'd made him late for a tryst in the ghost wing.

The clear warm day was passing into a fine evening. Gillian sat comfortably in her saddle, watching the courtyard activity. Her goat was led around the side of a building, and a young girl lugged the basket of fruit inside. A frigid chill abruptly settled over Gillian, as if she'd just stepped into a dank, close cellar. The air stirred around her, gathering, pressing in so she felt as if her stays were too tight, her face covered with a snug veil. Her gasping breath came out a white plume of frozen air. She gazed at it in astonishment, but no one else noticed as they bustled about their duties. Her hair crackled, and a peculiar energy pressed in on her, humming over her skin. Gillian put her hand to her head and found the loose wisps of her hair standing straight out, as if reaching for something. Before she could study this phenomenon closer, pain stabbed through her temples, blinding her, and a scream rent the air around her.

Gillian squinted her eyes open, the dying light piercing them. She caught sight of several people stopped, transfixed by something above her, mouths open. Her eyes fixed on Earie—the one who'd screamed—pointing above Gillian, fist in mouth. Something slammed into Gillian's back. She sprawled forward over Morfran's withers. He shrieked and bolted. Gillian clung to the horse's mane as he raced around the courtyard, rearing up as people rushed out to stop him. She tried desperately to catch her breath as the pain in her temples faded to a dull throb.

She scrambled for the reins, then pulled back, whispering soothing words to Morfran. The horse's dark eyes rolled as he continued to cry plaintively, jerking his head. She rubbed at his neck and he stopped rearing, though he pawed the ground and snorted threateningly at the servants trying to close in on him.

Gillian straightened. Sir Evan ran to her, wooden step in his hands, his mouth open in horrified amazement.

"I'm fine!" she called. "Just stay back. He's mad and liable to hurt someone."

Sir Evan readily obeyed, backing away. After a moment he yelled at someone to fetch the physician.

Gillian slid from Morfran's back but stayed beside him, stroking his neck. Sir Evan approached cautiously, handing the step off to a passing servant.

"Jesus God," he breathed. "What happened?"

"I'm not certain . . . but I'm unhurt . . . something hit me in the back."

Sir Evan stared at her incredulously. "Unhurt . . . how can that be?"

Gillian rubbed at the back of her neck. She could feel where something had hit her, but the spot was not tender. It probably wouldn't even bruise. The bruise on her side from Scott MacGregor's attempted stabbing hurt worse than this.

"What was it?" Gillian asked, gazing up at the tower, where the men-at-arms wrestled with a man. "A basket someone dropped from the walls? I'm sure it was an accident."

Sir Evan gaped at her as if she'd claimed she could fly. Morfran snapped nastily at him and caught his plaid between large white teeth. Sir Evan jumped back, ripping his plaid.

Gillian shushed the horse, putting a hand over his nose to let him know that was unacceptable. Morfran blew warmly against her palm and lipped her fingers.

"My lady." Sir Evan's voice wavered. She'd never seen him quite so emotional. " 'Twas no basket that fell on you, but ballast—a twenty-pound ball of iron." He pointed to something on the ground not far from the tower. Several people stood over it, looking from the ground to her and back. A cannonball.

"That's impossible. Why, I'd be—"

"Dead," Sir Evan said on a harsh breath. "That should have killed you, but you're not even hurt."

"She might be hurt at that." A large bearded man appeared, examining Gillian critically from afar. "I've seen it before. A person can be so stunned by what's occurred they feel no pain until later. Then they collapse. My lady, please come away from the horse so I can better look at you."

Gillian blinked in amazement. This was no jest. The man patiently gesturing for her to join him was apparently the physician, and he looked very concerned. Morfran had calmed, and when Gillian motioned a servant over, he let the boy take his bridle.

Once Morfran was gone, Sir Evan rushed forward and tried to pick her up, but she pushed him away testily. "I can walk!"

With Sir Evan on one side and the physician on the other, they pushed her along until she was inside the keep, then propelled her to her chambers, a crowd of servants trailing behind them. Once inside Gillian's chambers, the physician shooed everyone except Earie out.

"Tell me what happened." The physician was a barrel-chested old man with a short graying beard and long, silver-gray hair. He wore a fine blue robe over his plaid trews and carried a wooden box. Gillian told him everything she could remember about the incident. The physician—he said his name was Gilchrist—listened closely, scratching absently at his beard.

When she finished he only nodded, frowning wisely.

"It was at least a twenty-pound ballast that fell on her," Earie said, speaking for the first time. She had been silently removing Gillian's arisaid and bodice so Gilchrist could examine her. "I *saw* it hit her."

Gilchrist made Gillian sit on a stool with her back to him. He instructed her to untie the top of her shift, then pulled her shift back so he could examine her back. He grunted a few times and probed at her skin with rough fingers, asking her periodically if it hurt.

"Not at all. I vow I am fine."

He grunted again, then gathered his things together. "I can find nothing at all wrong with you, not a mark or bruise."

Earie goggled at this. She moved around behind Gillian to look for herself. "Yer leave, my lady?"

"Go ahead."

Earie gently touched Gillian's back. "My God," she breathed. "It's a miracle. Yer back should be broken at the very least, and yet there is not a mark on ye."

Gillian rubbed at the dull throbbing that lingered in her temples.

Gilchrist eyed her shrewdly. "Mayhap. Mayhap not. For now she needs rest." He came at her with a vial of dark liquid. "Drink this and take ye to bed."

Gillian drank the thick brew and shuddered with disgust. "What was that?"

"Theriac. Will help ye sleep."

"What's in it?"

"Juice of the poppy, honey, brandywine, and various other ingredients. It's verra good. I make it myself."

Earie tucked Gillian into bed, snuffed all the candles but the fat one near the bed that marked the hours, and eased quietly out of the room. The theriac made Gillian think of Stephen and how he'd said poppy juice made him not care. Already she felt odd, as if she were floating. When she closed her eyes, colors swirled behind her eyelids. When she opened them, the room tilted and with it her stomach, so she closed them again, willing sleep to come.

When it did, it brought dreams, fevered images of a woman gliding along a cliff, fog parting for her. A dark figure loomed behind her, and Gillian knew he meant to push her. When she turned, the hood of the cloak fell back, and Gillian saw her own face. Then she was running, heart in throat, the heat of her pursuer's breath on her neck.

The scene slowly faded and changed. She was in a dark room. It was so cold. She shivered, chill bumps raising on her body. The hour candle gave her enough light to see that her breath was a white mist before her. It was summer, she thought distantly. Why was it so damn cold?

Then she saw him, kneeling beside her bed, his face in his hands. He had a shag of brown hair and wore a dirty and torn plaid. Gillian's arms and legs were leaden. She wanted to speak, to ask what was the matter, but she couldn't move her lips.

He looked up as if she'd spoken. Tears tracked his

dirty face. He was so young, no more than sixteen. His large, dark eyes were as soft and luminous as a doe's. "I'm so sorry, my lady. Forgive me. He made me do it."

He buried his face on the bed and wept brokenly. He lifted his head again and turned, looking at something behind him. The grief that etched his face transformed to exultation. His body began to waver and fade, the furniture behind him faintly visible, then growing sharper until he was gone. *A dream.* Effects of the theriac.

She didn't like this dream, but the room wouldn't go away, and she couldn't leave. Slowly she became aware of movement across the room. Someone worked busily and silently near the fireplace. Gillian tried to call her maid's name, but it was too hard, her lips were too stiff. She tilted her head on the pillow, squinting across the room.

Someone swept out her fireplace . . . through the fire. Gillian blinked, watching as the maid stuck her hand right into the fire, sweeping through it as if it wasn't there. Then the maid turned, picking up a goblet on the floor beside the chair and downing it in one swallow. She stood, rinsed the goblet in the basin, dried it, and returned it to the silver tray. Then disappeared.

Gillian gasped, only to sense the movement again. She forced her head up. The maid was back at the fireplace, sweeping and sweeping, right through the fire. And then she drank the wine again. And washed the goblet again. Then she was at the fireplace again. And again. And again.

Gillian dropped her head back on the pillow and

closed her eyes tightly, willing the nightmarish maid to go away. *Nicholas*. Where was he? She wanted her husband.

When she woke again, she was able to raise her hand to her head. It throbbed sickeningly, and Gillian vowed never again to let anyone give her that nasty medicine. The candle showed she'd only slept two hours. It had seemed much longer. A glance at the shutters showed no light peeping through.

With great effort she dragged herself out of bed. Her body felt as if it had been trampled, every muscle sore and heavy. Her neck ached, too. That's when she remembered what had happened. The cannonball. The cold, the pain in her head. It was all very strange. She wished desperately for her sisters. Had something protected her from harm? A twenty-pound ball of iron should have done her significant damage, dropped from that height. She'd felt something, just before the blow, something cold and strange, wrapping itself around her.

With sudden resolve she went to her desk and lit more candles. She took out her quill and began composing a letter to Rose.

She started violently, as if waking from a falling dream. The room was freezing. Her hand ached. The candles on her desk were gutted. Wax spilled onto the surface, hardening already at the edges. Gillian looked down and saw the top of her desk littered with parchments, words scrawled across them in an unfamiliar hand, written so deep and violently at times that they tore through the parchment. She gripped the quill, white-fingered, hand cramped. Gillian released it as if it were a firebrand, pushing away from the desk and staring at the pile of ruined parchments as if they dripped blood.

It took her a moment to catch her breath, but when she did, she moved hesitantly back to the desk. She couldn't read the words. They were strange, another language that she didn't recognize. Over and over the same words were written—a hundred times or more. Gillian's breath wheezed in her chest. What was happening to her? She snatched all the papers up and threw them in the fireplace. With shaking hands, she started a fire and watched them burn. At the last moment she snatched one out of the fire and slapped at it. She must show it to Rose. Her sister would understand it.

She sat on the hearth, hands over her mouth. Why would she write such things? She'd been writing to her sister, and then she didn't remember anything. The theriac. The cold. The aching throb in her temples, making her stomach churn. What had Stephen said? *If you took some poppy juice, mayhap you'd not only be able to bear the pain . . . but be able to step away from it.*

She lowered her hands and stared at the burning parchment, the edges glowing red and curling. Was it a message? A spirit trying to contact her? She looked down at the partially burned parchment on her lap, willing herself to understand the letters, but they meant nothing to her. Only one word was familiar. *Nave.* But in context with the rest, she could only suppose it meant something else in some strange language. What of her dream? Had it been a dream, or a premonition of things to come? That she might end up haunting the cliffs, just like Catriona?

As Gillian sat there, thinking, she remembered the other dreams she'd had, of the man beside her bed, begging her forgiveness. *He made me do it.* Of the servant, repeating the same actions over and over, as if caught in some horrible loop.

Gillian put the parchment facedown on her writing table and threw on her heavy velvet dressing gown, hooking it as she hurried to the great hall. Several servants turned toward her, startled. It was late, the wee hours of the morning.

"Where is Sir Evan? I must see him at once."

Someone pointed toward the courtyard. The enormous double doors to the great hall stood ajar. Gillian ran to them and slid through the opening. Sir Evan stood just outside the door. He turned toward her and stepped back in surprise.

"My lady! What are you doing out here? You should be in bed."

He grabbed her arm, trying to turn her back toward the doors, but she pushed him off. "I'm fine! I must talk to the man on the gatehouse—the one that dropped the ballast."

Sir Evan's face went slack. "I'm afraid that's impossible—"

"What do you mean, impossible?" Her voice rose in anger and anxiety. She'd not gotten a good look at the man on the tower that the men-at-arms had been fighting with, but as she'd raced through the castle, she'd felt a strong certainty it was the lad who'd come to her bed-side to weep.

Sir Evan opened his mouth, then closed it in a thin, flat line. The muscles of his jaw bulged and hardened. He stepped aside, giving her full view of the courtyard and gates. She heard the slow creaking of the rope before she saw the boy. His limp form hung from the gates, feet swinging lazily in the breeze.

The air rushed out of Gillian, her knees weakening. "You hanged him? Why did you hang him?"

"He tried to kill you, my lady."

"What evidence have you of that? I am unharmed! It could have been an accident!" But she knew it hadn't been. Someone had made him do it.

"It wasn't."

"Did he confess?"

"Aye, he did."

"And did he tell you who made him do it?"

Sir Evan started violently. "What?"

"He told me someone made him do it! Who?"

Sir Evan only stared at her, eyes narrowed. "That's impossible, my lady. You could not have spoken to him. We hanged him immediately after."

Gillian's hand went to her mouth, and she sank to the ground. She sat on her knees, staring at the figure on the gate. The courtyard was silent except for the obscene creaking. Sir Evan's hand was on her arm, lifting her to her feet.

"Come, my lady, you're distraught. I'll fetch Gilchrist."

As he led her through the castle, she noticed several of the servants making the sign of the horns as she passed, warding off evil.

Gilchrist attended her shortly after with his little vial of theriac.

"No," Gillian said, pushing it away. "I need you to do something for me."

"Aye?"

"I'm afraid. . . . I can't write now—please, send word to Glen Laire. I need my sisters. Tell them to come."

His bushy gray brows drew together, clearly worried the ballast had addled her brain, but he nodded. "Aye, my lady, I will."

As he turned to leave, she gripped his hand and whispered, "Tell no one."

Night had just eased into dawn when Nicholas rode into the courtyard in a foul temper. The dead man that greeted him at the gate did nothing for his disposition.

Evan was sleeping when Nicholas burst into his chambers, not bothering to knock. The knight came off the narrow bed, dirk in hand, eyes wild, stark naked.

"What the hell is hanging from my gates?"

Evan exhaled loudly, relieved. He lowered his knife and sat on the bed, scratching at his short brown hair. "Some wee beggar that tried to kill the countess."

"What?" Nicholas's heart stuttered. He put a hand out, touching the wall for support.

"Aye, he dropped ballast on her from the gatehouse tower." Seeing Nicholas's face, Evan stood abruptly, alarmed. "She's fine, my lord. Perhaps you should sit down."

"It missed her?"

"Ah . . . not exactly."

"Then how . . . ?" But he didn't finish. He strode out of his knight's quarters. Evan hopped after him, a plaid flung about his loins, blathering on about questioning the lad and then hanging him. Nicholas paused just outside his wife's chambers.

"And he wouldn't say who he worked for?"

Evan frowned. "No . . . he didn't work for anyone. I told you, my lord, I questioned him carefully."

Nicholas gave his knight a cold stare. "We'll talk about this later." He closed the door firmly in Evan's face.

The room was dark except for the hour candle beside her bed. He removed his mantle and hung it on a peg by the door. *He said she was fine.* But his heart still beat unnaturally hard, and his step was fearful as he approached the bed. He'd ridden all night to get here, fool that he was, thinking of naught but lying with her. Now he wished he'd ridden harder or left sooner.

She slept on her side, legs curled beneath the velvet blankets. Thick sable hair spread over the pillow behind her and fell over her shoulders to tuck under her chin. Her mouth was open slightly. There were no marks on her skin, and when he gently peeled back the bedclothes, he saw no bandages. She wore a velvet dressing gown over her nightshift, secured to her throat.

The fist squeezing his heart eased. He thought he should leave, go back to Evan and get the rest of the story, but he didn't move. He didn't know how long he stood there, his thoughts circling. Someone was trying to kill her. *Why?* He could not understand it. She was no one. A chieftain's daughter. She brought little to their marriage, and besides, it was his if she died. Who could possibly want her dead?

He'd accomplished the purpose of his little expedition, though it had done him no good. He'd found Scott MacGregor. Unfortunately the buzzards had found him first. He'd been dead for days. Nicholas had then gone to the Gregors, but they'd been no help. They'd not seen Scott in a fortnight and had no idea who he might have been working for.

All that paled in significance to what had happened at Kincreag in his absence. First Scott MacGregor, and now the lad swinging from his gates. Nicholas did not know the lad's name, but he'd seen him in the village. He'd brought fish to the castle with his father once a week. Whoever was responsible surely planned another attempt. Nicholas's gloved hand curled into a fist and pressed hard against his thigh, his other hand on his dirk, clenching the hilt. He tried to relax, but the thought of someone trying to kill her made him sick with fury and the need for action.

He started to back away quietly, when she stirred. He stopped, waiting for her to still before he took his leave. Her lashes rose, eyes hazy with sleep. Her gaze fixed on him, and after blinking several times, her eyes widened in fear. She drew in a breath as if to scream, huddling deeper into the bedclothes.

Nicholas was struck dumb with dismay and confusion. She scrambled across the bed as if to escape him. He crawled after her, catching her wrists and pushing her back on the bed.

Her eyes were wide and terror stricken, and she kicked at him, struggling wildly, babbling about a dark man on the cliff. He straddled her body to keep her from hurting herself or him.

"Gillian!" He said her name loudly several times, finally grabbing her shoulders and shaking her. She lay still, her brow marred with sudden confusion, gazing up at him, so close he could see her eyes. They were unfocused, the gray iris a narrow band, circling an enormous black pupil. She blinked dazedly at him.

Opium dreams. Damn Gilchrist. He administered that poison as if it were as harmless as honey.

"Nicholas?" she whispered.

"Aye." He relaxed his grip on her and moved beside her on the bed. "You were dreaming. What did Gilchrist give you?"

She covered her face, rubbing at her eyes. "Theriac, but that was"—she craned her neck to see the hour clock—"hours ago."

"Are you hurt?"

She shook her head and lowered her hands. Her eyelids were red, and her long lashes tangled from scrubbing her eyes. She looked so sweet and trusting as she gazed up at him that he planted a kiss on the smooth skin between her dark brows.

"Where did it hit you?"

She put her hand on her back, just below her neck. He removed his gloves and turned her away from him, moving her hair aside. She loosened her dressing gown so he could see her back. Smooth as alabaster, without a mark on it.

"Evan must be mistaken. It couldn't have hit you."

She turned back toward him, her eyes already clearer, though she looked fatigued. "He must have." She was not good at hiding her thoughts or feelings, and he saw that she did not believe the knight had been mistaken.

Though her eyes remained open and her gaze on him, he could tell by the heavy way she lay on the pillow that she was exhausted. He smoothed the backs of his fingers over her forehead and the tender curve of her cheek.

"Go back to sleep. I'll see you later." He started to ease off the bed.

She caught his hand, gripping it with surprising strength. "Don't leave."

He hesitated. "I'm filthy—I've been riding all night."

Her grip loosened, and she slid her hand up his arm. "Then you must be tired. Lay with me."

He started to protest again, but she gazed at him with such a winsome and hopeful expression that he couldn't refuse her. He lay beside her and gathered her against his chest. She shuddered in his arms, then sighed deep and contentedly, her hands curled into his doublet.

There was an odd tightness in his throat, and he was having trouble swallowing, but soon her contentment transferred to him and he slept, despite the dirk hilt digging painfully into his side.

* * *

Elsewhere in the castle Bradana slept, warm beneath her thick wool blanket, her belly full of hearty stew and ale—all thanks to the new countess. The countess was good and kind and would save Bradana from the stake. She was certain of it. The jangle of keys woke her from her dreams of fire. She sat up on her narrow cot, peering into the darkness.

The door opened and there was light. A beautiful woman entered, bearing a candle and a cup. Golden hair gleamed in the candlelight. She wore it loose, like a maiden, flowing down her back. The woman was hardly a maiden, though. At least in her thirties, but still as breathtaking as an angel.

She smiled at Bradana. "Hello, my friend. I've been wanting to see you again." The door shut behind her.

Bradana studied the woman closer but did not recognize her. "I don't know you."

The woman set the candle on the table beside Bradana's cot. "We haven't actually met, but a very good friend of mine has told me all about you." The woman sat on the cot beside Bradana, still smiling. She had all of her teeth, and they were straight and white. "I brought you something." The woman offered Bradana the cup.

She accepted the cup and sniffed the dark contents. "Who are you?"

"I'm a friend of the countess. She sent me to see to your comfort."

Bradana smiled back, liking this woman. She was no servant. Her clothes were well made and of fine materials, her skin soft and smooth except for faint lines beside her eyes and mouth, well kept and unaccustomed to the harshness of nature. She must be a guest of the countess. Any friend of the countess was a friend of Bradana's.

Bradana sipped the brew and was pleased to find it thick and rich, mulled spirits. She'd never been served such fine fare as she'd had during her brief imprisonment in Kincreag Castle. Except for being confined, she rather enjoyed it. And now she had a visitor.

They talked of Bradana. The woman wanted to know if she had children, and Bradana told her about her daughter and her two grandchildren. By the time Bradana finished the cup of spirits, she wasn't feeling so well. There was a strange taste in her mouth, as if she'd been sucking on a penny, and she couldn't seem to swallow.

The woman gently removed the cup from her fingers and set it aside. "You'd better lay down, my friend."

Bradana did as she bid, her throat working to swallow the excessive amount of spit in her mouth. The woman pulled the blankets up over her and sat by her side, watching her.

"What's wrong with me?" Bradana asked as pain streaked through her abdomen. She pulled her knees up to her belly, groaning. "What did you give me?"

"I had to. You saw me."

Bradana shook her head, confused. "I dinna . . . understand you." She gasped as her belly gripped. Something shredded her from the inside. "I've . . . never seen you . . . afore tonight."

The woman sighed, a long, sensuous sound. She lifted the covers and slid beneath them next to Bradana. Bradana wanted to fight, to force this frightening woman out of her bed, but she was old and frail and in so much pain. Sweat soaked her thin shift. Her body shook.

The woman put her arms around Bradana, her embrace firm. She put her mouth near Bradana's ear. "On the cliff. You saw me."

Bradana did fight then. She was the ghost! It had been wearing a cloak before, the hood dark. Bradana had not seen its face, but it had come for her. She struggled, arms flailing, legs kicking, but the ghost subdued her quickly. Pain wrenched Bradana again, worse this time, bowing her back and sending tears of terror streaming down her face.

"No, no, no, no . . . ," Bradana chanted, writhing and shuddering.

The ghost cooed at her and dried her face. "It'll be over soon. Fash not, you won't die alone. I'll stay with you and hold you until the end." Its voice trembled with excitement, its body pressing closer.

Bradana was past speech, her mind filled only with pain and terror. She shook her head over and over again and finally managed to gasp, "Why?"

The ghost smoothed the hair away from Bradana's face and whispered, "The earl can only have one countess, and I'm not finished with him yet."

14

When Gillian woke, she was alone in her vast bed. She lay very still, holding close the memory of Nicholas climbing into bed with her in the wee hours of the morning. Had that been a dream, too? But the pillow next to her still bore the imprint from his head. She smoothed her hand over it. No warmth of him remained. He had been gone for a while. She rolled over onto the pillow, inhaling deeply. It still smelled of him. She sighed and felt it to her toes.

"Ah, you're awake."

Gillian rolled away from the pillow guiltily, cheeks flaming.

The door between their chambers stood open, and Nicholas leaned against the doorframe, arms crossed over his chest. His damp hair was combed away from his face. He wore close-fitting black breeks and a snowy white shirt, unlaced at the throat.

How long had he been standing there? His expression was inscrutable as he crossed to the bed. Her heart stepped up its tempo.

She glanced at the open shutters and saw it was nearing noon. "You've let me sleep all day." She started to get out of bed, but he motioned for her to lie down again.

"You had a difficult night. You should rest."

She lay back slowly. "I'm fine, my lord."

He sat on the edge of the bed. "I told you before, when we're alone there is no need to 'my lord' me."

Gillian smiled shyly.

"I have a question for you."

"Aye?"

"Does anyone want you dead?"

He said it so matter-of-factly that she blinked, then said, hesitating, "I can't think of anyone."

"Are you certain? Someone you've offended? An angry suitor?"

Gillian's lips curved reproachfully. "You know I had no other suitors but you and Father's Frenchman."

He touched a lock of her hair that fell over the bedclothes, rubbing the ends of it between his fingers. His black lashes shadowed his eyes. "What about in the Lowlands?"

Gillian watched his fingers caress her hair. She could not actually feel his touch, and yet she felt it all over.

"Maybe it's not about me," she said, "but about you. I am your new wife. Maybe one of your lovers didn't want you to wed."

He wrapped the end of her hair around his finger. "I

thought of that. But I can think of no one who would benefit by your death."

Gillian released the breath she'd been holding. He had no recent lovers, at least.

"Maybe it's revenge," she suggested. "What of your enemies?"

"For your death to hurt me, the attacker would have to believe ours was more than a marriage of convenience. That you meant something to me." Her hair was wrapped so tightly about his finger that it pulled at her scalp.

Gillian's gaze dropped to her ring, and she twirled it on her finger. "I'm sure no one thinks that."

Her heart sank when he remained silent. Maybe Hazel had given her a lust philter by accident. She didn't expect him to love her.

But she wished for it.

"Besides," he continued, his grip on her hair loosening, "when one seeks revenge, they usually declare themselves. What good is it if the object of your vengeance doesn't understand why?"

"I hadn't thought of it that way."

He tugged gently on her hair. "You wouldn't." He released her hair and moved his hand away to rest on his bent knee. "I tried to discover more about yesterday's . . . mishap. I've heard some very strange accounts."

When he didn't elaborate, Gillian said, "Aye?"

"The cook swears the ballast *bounded* off of you, as if you were wearing armor. A stable lad claims it changed direction right afore it hit you."

"That *is* very odd."

"Aye. All insist it should have hit you. And yet you are unharmed."

Gillian felt vaguely guilty, as if she'd done something wrong. She tried for her best look of wide-eyed innocence, then remembered the lad hanging from the gates.

"Sir Evan should not have hanged that boy. I am unhurt."

"He tried to kill you, Gillian. If Evan had not hanged him, I would have."

Gillian shook her head, leaning toward him and resting a hand on his arm. "But he was not acting on his own. Someone made him do it. Sir Evan should not have hanged him until we discovered who . . . and then maybe not at all."

"Aye, and I'll talk to Evan, fash not. But likely he acted in passion, furious at the attempt on your life." His face hardened, eyes flat obsidian. "I might have done the same in his place."

She wanted to tell him about the visit from the boy. Had it been a dream or something else? Her fingers tightened unconsciously on Nicholas's arm. The muscles beneath her fingers flexed.

"What is it?" he asked, studying her closely, his expression guarded.

"I had strange dreams last night . . . fantastic dreams."

He patted her hand. "Opium will do that."

Gillian nodded, her lips rolled inward.

He cocked his head and narrowed his eyes. "But you're not sure these were dreams. Tell me."

"The lad that Sir Evan hanged . . . he came to me, here in the bedchamber. He wept and said, 'He made me do it.'"

"And . . . ?"

She shrugged. "And then he left."

One of his black brows twitched. "If this is one of your ghosts, they're not very informative. Did he give you any names?"

She gave him a sour look and shook her head.

"It was a dream, Gillian."

"But it seemed so real."

"Opium-induced dreams do seem real."

She let out a frustrated breath, her eyes narrowing. "Very well. I had another visitation."

He closed his eyes, as if the word *visitation* pained him.

She rushed on before he could stop her, "It was a maid. She cleaned my fireplace over and over again—even though there was a fire burning. And she drank my wine." It sounded ridiculous when she said it out loud. Heat suffused her neck.

Nicholas just looked at her.

She crossed her arms over her chest. "Very well. Maybe that one was an opium dream."

Nicholas scratched behind his ear. "I'd like to remind you of the conversation we had about this—"

Gillian huffed out a breath. "Aye, I remember. I'm forbidden. I didn't summon him, though. He came to me."

Nicholas unfolded her arms and took her hands in his. "Gillian, I pray you. Forget this ghost rubbish. You know what the clergymen say? That there's no such thing as ghosts and that those who claim to see them are communing with demons. What does that make you?"

"A witch." Her voice was stubbornly defiant.

His grip on her hands tightened. "I vowed to your father that I would protect you, but I need you to help me by not begging for trouble. We have enough to worry about, with two attempts on your life, without you announcing to the world that you think you're a witch."

Gillian stared down at the velvet coverlets. He spoke wise words, but she still didn't like them.

"You're angry with me," he said.

She shrugged, her mouth pursing, unhappiness filling her. "It's not you . . . it's just not what I thought it would be."

He sat back. "What's not?"

"Being a countess. Oh, Nicholas, I'm the worst countess ever!" And suddenly the wretchedness and confusion of the past day bubbled up inside and she burst into tears. "I don't know what I'm doing! Sir Evan hates me, and my servants are killing themselves, and now someone wants me dead, and you think I'm crazy."

She covered her face with her hands. Nicholas pulled her into his arms.

"I don't think you're crazy . . . maybe a little dotty. . . ."

Dotty? Despair hit her anew, and she sobbed harder. Maybe she *was* dotty to interpret opium dreams as ghostly visitations—but she didn't want to be dotty. That's not what she wanted him to see when he looked at her.

"I mean that in a good way," he said, his voice strained, hands stroking over her back. "And I'm sure Evan likes you. How could he not? He's that way with everyone. Dull as a stone—that's why I like him. He doesn't annoy me with mindless chatter."

"Like me!"

He groaned. "No, not like you. And what else . . . you're a beautiful countess, a perfect countess."

She sniffled against his shirt. "Liar." But she felt better that he'd said it.

"I mean every word of it." When she had calmed down somewhat, he asked, "What's this about your servants killing themselves?"

She told him about Aileen, growing a bit tearful again and ending with, "Sir Evan said the servants kill themselves because they're so miserable. We must do something to improve their lots, Nicholas, something to make them happy so they want to live."

He let out a breath. "Very well, aye—if it makes you happy, improve the servants' lots, but I vow my servants do not go about killing themselves. I've never mistreated them."

She sniffed and nodded. She hadn't thought he mistreated them, but maybe he didn't pay enough attention to them. She knew some people considered their servants some sort of different form of life, like a talking horse.

"Has anything else happened while I was gone?"

"Sir Evan has a sweetheart. I saw them kissing."

"Sir Evan has many sweethearts, sweetheart."

The endearment broke through her melancholy. She smiled at him.

He tilted her chin up with the edge of his hand and kissed her, his mouth soft and warm. Gillian closed her eyes and sighed, leaning against him. She was glad he was home.

"Are you sorry you wed me yet?" he asked. "Someone has tried to kill you twice in the short time we've been married. Not a very auspicious beginning."

"I'm not sorry." She kept her face buried in his shirt. "I'll never forget how you appeared out of the fog to rescue me. A *very* auspicious beginning, methinks."

He pressed her back on the bed, his hands sliding eagerly into her dressing gown, and he made love to her, bright sunlight streaming through the windows.

They spent the afternoon in bed, talking and making love. She told him about her foster parents and the border feuds, and he observed that borderers didn't sound any different than Highlanders—they both loved to feud. Once while she was talking, he caught her hand in one of his.

"You keep turning this ring." He took it between his fingers and twirled it himself, studying it. "Where did you get it?"

"It was my mother's."

His gaze flicked to hers, then back to the ring, brows arched.

"Afterward . . ." Gillian swallowed, unable to think

about her mother's death for fear of the pain it would cause. "Father tried to find the person responsible for what happened. He was gone for a fortnight. Uncle Roderick collected what things they had of hers in the village where it happened. He brought me this ring. He had picked it out of the ashes. I don't know if my father wanted me to have it, but he's never said anything."

Nicholas turned it on her finger again. "It's too big."

"It hasn't been until recently."

He leaned back a bit to study her sheet-draped body, his black eyes moving over her from head to toe. He placed a hand on her hip and squeezed. "You are getting a bit thin. Are you eating?"

She shrugged.

His gaze rose to her face and narrowed. "Are you happy here, Gillian?"

"Aye, of course I am."

One brow arched skeptically, but he said, "The gold-smith does some work with silver. Perhaps he can make it smaller so you don't lose it."

Before Gillian could thank him, a knock on the door interrupted them.

"Go away," Nicholas bellowed, annoyance making his handsome face severe. Gillian smiled inside, knowing she was the reason he didn't want to be disturbed.

There was a moment of silence, then Sir Evan called through the door, "My lord, the hall is full of petitioners . . . Lord Boath is here to see you as well."

Nicholas sighed, his long fingers curling into Gillian's hip through the sheet.

"Shall I send them away?" Sir Evan asked.

After a long pause Nicholas said, "No . . . I'll be down in a bit." They listened to the clank of Sir Evan's weapons as he left.

Gillian whispered, "We're being slothful. You should go. I'm keeping you from your duties."

He pushed the sheet off her. "We just married. I am allowed some sloth to become better acquainted with my bride. I should not have to listen to people begging for money and favors. Not for a while at least."

Gillian turned toward him, sliding her hands up his hard belly to his chest. The muscle was heavier on his chest, the skin stretched taut and smooth. His pulse throbbed in the hollow of his throat.

"Does this mean you've no more reservations about marrying me?"

He grabbed her bottom and maneuvered her closer. His head bent to lick her shoulder. "Och, I've reservations. For one, I can clearly get nothing done with you here."

"Oh, I think you've been most industrious this morning." Her voice was breathless, her body quivering.

He pulled her tight against him so that she could feel he was prepared to toil some more on her behalf.

"What other reservations do you have?"

"I have to worry about someone hurting you now." His voice was muffled against her throat. "I have not had to worry this way in a very long time."

"Are you really worried about me?" she asked softly.

He pushed her onto her back and rose on his elbows over her, his hands cradling her head. He examined her features slowly before meeting her eyes. "Aye, I am—

not because I'd ever allow such a thing to happen, mind you. But . . . But . . ." A shutter fell over his face and he frowned, eyes averted. His body above hers hummed with tension.

Gillian took his face in her hands, turning him to look at her again. "What is it?"

"My son was just a bairn when he died . . . two years old. Consumption, Gilchrist said. I . . . uh . . ." He took a deep breath and continued in a rough voice, "I was supposed to keep him safe, protect him, as my father protected me. And I failed." His black eyes burned fiercely as they bore into her. "I will not fail you."

Gillian didn't think she could love him more than she did at that moment. She had no words, so she kissed him, touching his mouth with her lips and fingers. He kissed her back, but with restraint. He broke the kiss off, holding her head between his palms.

"I have one more reservation."

His expression was so serious that Gillian's heart stopped. "What is it?"

He said nothing for a long moment. "Before we wed, you put something into my wine."

There was no way for Gillian to master her reaction or lie her way out of this. The blood drained from her face, and her mouth worked soundlessly. His hands tightened on her head, as if he meant to crush her skull between them.

"There can be nothing between us if there's not trust, and I can't trust you if you're trying to poison me."

"No!" Gillian burst out. "Not poison—I would never!"

One brow twitched slightly. "That's good. As I am

not dead, and you don't seem terribly disappointed about that, I surmised that it was not a lethal poison, but several other unpleasant possibilities present themselves."

"I would never cause you harm, Nicholas, I vow it. What I put in your drink . . . it was harmless. Surely you see that, you're healthy and hale as ever."

He released her head and pushed himself higher on his elbows, though he still lay between her sprawled thighs. Sleek black hair spilled over his dark shoulders. "Then what was it?"

Gillian bit her lip, gazing up at him helplessly. She did not want to tell him. Would rather drink poison herself than tell him. She felt trapped beneath him, and she squirmed, pushing her hands against his shoulders. He caught her wrists and pressed them into the pillow on either side of her head.

"I'm not moving until you tell me."

All affection had fled from his countenance. He stared down at her, dark and piratical, and determined to have his way.

Gillian worried her bottom lip and closed her eyes. She couldn't say it.

"The longer you try me, the worse it will be for you when I discover the truth."

"Fine!" Gillian burst out, eyes screwed tightly shut. "This . . . this . . . fondness you have for me . . . it's not real."

He flexed his hips against her, nudging his hardness against her so that she gasped and instinctively arched into him.

"It's not? Feels real," he murmured.

Her body was on fire—a full body blush of complete mortification. "It's not real . . . none of it. It's a love philter. I gave it to you so you would fall in love with me."

Her face was scalding. She wanted to sink into the bed and let it swallow her. He was so still and quiet that she cracked an eye and peered up at him.

He looked as though he wanted to laugh but valiantly fought the urge. "A love philter?"

Gillian nodded and jerked at her wrists. He held them fast.

She turned her head away, staring blankly across the room. "I pray you, let me go."

His breath blew warm across her breasts. "I cannot, my lady, I'm under your spell."

She bucked violently. Now he would humiliate her with it! She caught him in the ribs and he grunted, falling full length on her. His face was buried in her neck, and his shoulders shook with laughter.

Since struggling was useless, Gillian lay limply beneath him, her embarrassment transforming to indignant anger. "Why is this amusing? It has clearly worked!"

"Oh, clearly." This made him laugh harder. Gillian waited him out, temper simmering. It was not remotely amusing to her.

After a time he gained some semblance of control and pushed himself off her. When she tried to escape, he hooked a long, muscled leg over hers and an arm around her waist, dragging her back. He rubbed his face in a pillow to wipe away the tears of mirth. Gillian wanted to cram the pillow down his throat. She lay stiffly on her back, staring at the carved wooden canopy above her.

He hiccupped and laughed again, apparently finding this noise amusing.

"Well, I suppose you thinking I'm an idiot is better than you beating me."

"You thought I'd beat you?" This made him laugh again.

Gillian rolled her eyes. The man rarely cracked a smile, and now he couldn't seem to stop laughing—at *her!*

When she did not answer, he asked, "How do you know it worked?"

"Right after you drank it, you stuck your tongue in my mouth."

"Right after?"

She turned her head to look at him. His brows were drawn together in mock confusion. Amusement still lined his face, as though he might burst out laughing again at any moment. The fact the expression was completely disarming and contagious didn't help. She quickly averted her eyes, her own lips twitching now. She hardened her mouth into an angry line.

"I don't remember that," he said. "Potent stuff."

Gillian expelled an exasperated breath. "I don't mean immediately. In my chambers? On my bed? When Rose walked in on us? Do you recall *that?*" Her face grew fiery again.

He watched her with interest, then finally murmured, "Oh, that. I remember now." From his tone, he'd known all along what she referred to, but drew her humiliation out to amuse himself. "You're pink from your belly to your hair." He traced the path with his fingers from belly button, between her breasts, to the hollow of her throat.

Gillian tried to ignore his observations. "Ever since you drank the philter it's been the same. You've . . . been . . ."

He leaned closer, a wicked light in his eye. "I've been what?"

"Well . . . you've *wanted* me." A quick glance at his lower body confirmed he still did.

"That explains it," he said with mock relief. "This strange lust for my wife has been *so* troubling."

Gillian let out a heavy sigh, her anger dissolving. "I'm glad you know. Now you know everything." A great weight lifted from her chest, and she truly was relieved. It didn't matter that he thought her a lackwit; at least she had no more secrets. "You think it's a great jest now and that I'm a fool for putting any faith in a love philter, but that's because you're under its spell."

He nodded seriously but bit the inside of his lip, as if holding in another torrent of laughter.

"You will see," she said sagely. "It only lasts about a month. In a few weeks, you'll not be moved to come to my bed anymore." She looked away to master the pressure behind her eyes. "And that's fine, my lord. It's only what I deserve for doing such a thing. I am sorry. I should not have . . . but I was so sure you wouldn't marry me. Can you forgive me?"

"I have no choice. I'm under your spell."

She glared at him. "You jape at me, and I like it not. I said I was sorry."

His hand cupped her cheek, turning her to face him when she tried to move away again. He no longer seemed on the verge of hysterical laughter, which was a relief.

"Perhaps there *is* something to what you say."

Gillian's heart sank. "You know it's true, don't you? I saw it on your face once . . . you looked confused, as if you couldn't understand why you wanted to touch me."

"Do you know, I've never lain in bed with a woman all morning, talking and laughing? It must be powerful magic that makes me want to waste the day in sloth with you."

"Aye, it is." She sighed. "And I fear, my lord, the philter has deranged you. You never laugh."

That made him smile. "Then I should thank you for bringing laughter and sloth into my life."

"Oh, Nicholas." Gillian turned into his arms and pressed her face against his warm chest. He held her to him, his cheek lying against her hair.

"Ah, I'm Nicholas again." His hand stroked her hair from her head down to her bottom. "You should have drunk the philter, too, to be fair. Why should I follow you about like a mooncalf and you feel nothing?"

Gillian's arms tightened around him. *No more lies.* "I don't need the philter to . . . feel that way about you."

He rolled her onto her back again, arms braced on either side of her face. He traced her brows and nose with his thumb, following the trail with his gaze. His face was grave now. He seemed pensive, not speaking, just touching her reverently.

"How much longer until it fades?" he asked softly.

Gillian wanted to weep. He believed. She liked it better when he thought her a fool—at least then he thought what he felt for her was real.

"A few weeks." Her voice wavered.

"Then let me love you as long as I may."

Eventually Nicholas did have to leave. After he was gone Gillian dressed slowly, her body still languorous from a day of lovemaking. She had never been so happy. It was a very good love philter Old Hazel had made for her.

Earie brought her dinner, and she ate alone in her chambers. The sun faded, and still Nicholas had not returned. Gillian wandered down to the great hall to find it milling with people again. Torches lined the wall, and ale had been brought out so the people waiting could refresh themselves.

Gillian hung back in the entryway, uncertain she wanted anyone to see her. She did not want to be announced again. She skirted unobtrusively along the wall until she could see the dais. Nicholas sat behind the table listening intently to a man in a filthy plaid who stood before him, wringing his hands. He was so handsome, sitting tall and straight, his dark brow creased with concentration. She smiled and sighed, content just to gaze upon him.

As if sensing the weight of her stare, Nicholas's eyes moved to her. Though he didn't smile, his gaze warmed.

He held up a hand to the man talking, then gestured over his shoulder. Gillian noticed Sir Evan for the first time, standing behind Nicholas's chair, arms crossed over his chest. The knight bent his head near, and Nicholas said something to him. Sir Evan's gaze immediately went to Gillian, and he nodded.

Gillian panicked, sweat breaking out on her scalp as she waited for the herald to announce her. To her relief it never happened. Nicholas returned to his petitioner, and Sir Evan joined Gillian against the wall.

"You've eaten?" he asked.

"Aye," Gillian said, tearing her eyes from her husband to acknowledge the knight.

"Good. My lord asked me to show you the gardens."

He led her out of the hall through a north door. The cool, foggy night wrapped around her. She shivered and hugged her arms to her body. Torches on the castle walls were glowing orbs in the mist. They followed a cobblestone path a short distance to a wrought iron gate. Sir Evan pushed it open.

"They didn't wait long to descend upon him," Gillian observed, feeling slightly offended for her overworked husband. Though Sir Evan had held court the day after they'd arrived at Kincreag, he'd not done it since.

"Aye, they see him pass through the village and follow, like the piper with his rats." He glanced back at her with the closest thing to a smile he'd ever given her, a slight curling of one corner of his hard mouth. "They much prefer for him to hear their grievances."

Though the fog hung thick, the garden still charmed

Gillian. It was lovely, full of exotic flowers she'd never seen before. Sir Evan walked beside her, pointing out various species of flora and explaining where Nicholas had acquired it. The path ended with a barred wooden door.

"Where does this lead?"

"To the cliff path I told you about."

She desperately wanted to know if Catriona's spirit haunted the cliff, but she couldn't risk collapsing on a cliff path. The consequences could be disastrous. Besides, Nicholas had forbid her from seeking out ghosts. She sighed and turned away from the door, wandering back up the path.

Sir Evan followed her. "I saw the ghost once."

Gillian whirled around to face the knight. "What?"

He shrugged sheepishly and glanced around, as if to be certain they were alone. "It was probably nothing, just the fog playing tricks on my eyes. But the time was right."

"What do you mean?"

"Those that see her only do so on foggy nights and always at the same time—the stroke of midnight. The witching hour. Though no one knows what time she fell, it's believed that it must have been at midnight. Why else would she appear only then?"

It was so strange to be standing in the murky garden talking about ghosts with the stalwart knight. He seemed to agree, because he started walking again, a guiding hand at her elbow. "Foolishness and superstition, I'm sure. My lord would not like you going out there alone."

"No, of course not." But the idea had taken root. She knew where and when the late countess haunted the cliffs. The only thing left was how she would manage it without collapsing.

The gate creaked. Gillian peered into the fog. A second later, a massive gray streak launched itself at her. Gillian screamed and tried to duck away.

Broc bounced up and down, pawing at her skirts, licking and sniffing at her enthusiastically. Gillian laughed, trying to hold the dog back. Sir Evan came forward to help, but Broc growled at him, hair bristling on his nape.

Sir Evan backed away, hand on sword hilt.

Gillian frowned at Broc, rubbing his ears vigorously. "Bad dog! Sir Evan is our friend."

Broc whined, tail between his legs.

Nicholas appeared out of the fog. He dismissed Sir Evan with a nod of his head, then stood over Gillian and Broc, watching the reunion with a faint smile.

"He's most fond of you," Nicholas commented, a strange note of amusement in his voice.

"Aye." Gillian sat on a nearby stone bench. She had to repeatedly shove the amorous dog off her lap. "When did he arrive?"

"Just before dark the wagons came with all your luggage. He seemed to know just where you were. He raced around the hall, barking at everything until I followed. He led me right to you." He sat on the bench beside Gillian and scratched the dog between the ears. "Ever since your uncle gave this dog to Alan he just lay around like a miserable rug. Then one day he seemed to wake up from a deep sleep and fall in love with you."

"Odd, isn't it?"

"Most odd."

She gave her husband a narrow look. He seemed to have some deeply amusing secret lurking in his eyes. He was probably still thinking about the love philter. Since she didn't want him to start laughing at her again, she said, "Have you tried the old woman from the village yet? The one accused of witchcraft?"

"Bradana?"

Gillian nodded.

Nicholas's brows lowered as he grew serious. "No . . . it was kind of you to grant her comfortable quarters. Evan told me of that. She was old and sick . . . she died in her sleep last night."

Gillian sighed, then asked, "What would you have done had she lived?"

He looked down at his hands. "I would have listened to the accusations and her defense. Then I would have ruled."

"*How* would you have ruled?"

"Fairly."

She looked at him curiously, wondering what that meant. She wanted to hear that he would have released her, found her innocent, but he seemed unwilling to admit that.

"Would you have burned her?"

"No."

Gillian let out the breath she'd been unconsciously holding.

"But sometimes *fair* is a relative term."

"Relative to what?"

"Crop failure, years of famine. The like." When she just frowned at him, he leaned a hand on the bench behind her and said, "When I was fifteen, my father was placed in such a situation. I don't think he believed the witch was guilty, but it had been a bad year and even the earl's table was wanting. My father knew his people needed something, a scapegoat to blame and punish, to give them hope life would soon improve."

Gillian let out a horrified breath. "But that's not fair! It's not right!"

"Fair. Right. Again, relative terms." He sighed at her deeply troubled expression. "Fash not, he didn't burn her. He gave her a minor punishment, and she worked in his kitchens the rest of her days. To keep her out of trouble and out of the villagers' sight."

"Would you do the same?"

"I don't know. I haven't had to." He put his arm around her and drew her near. "But I have a softhearted countess now. You can beg mercy for the accused, and I can grant it. Then I don't look weak . . . except maybe where you're concerned. But then, that's not my fault. I'm under the influence of a love philter, after all."

Gillian laughed softly and rolled her eyes. "You're not going to let me forget and pretend your affection is true, are you?"

He shook his head ruefully and bent his head to kiss her.

* * *

Later that night Nicholas tracked Evan down, locked in his chambers with a woman. She huddled under the blankets, and Nicholas only caught a glimpse of golden hair before Evan stepped into the corridor, closing his door behind him. His normally pale skin was pallid, and he seemed tense and preoccupied. Apparently this woman was more than bed sport. Nicholas could sympathize with his knight's haggard condition.

"Come with me."

In his privy chambers Nicholas offered the knight whisky. Evan accepted the cup but didn't drink. He stood stiffly before Nicholas's chair.

Nicholas leaned back and regarded his knight pensively. Though Evan had been in his service for several years, Nicholas still knew little about the knight. When Nicholas had first met Evan, he'd been in the earl of Dornock's service. He'd been impressed with the knight's stalwart demeanor. Evan was a good fighter and a natural leader. And so Nicholas had lured him from Dornock with a fat purse and a promise of more, and he'd never been sorry. Evan ran Kincreag with an iron fist when Nicholas was away and kept his men ready for anything. Several lords had tried to lure him from Nicholas over the years, but none had offered a generous enough price.

He knew the value of the man before him, and so it wasn't often or lightly that he questioned Evan's actions. Nicholas set his whisky aside and steepled his fingers. "Now. Explain to me again, in detail, your questioning of the boy you hanged from the gates."

They had been through it all before, and though

Nicholas couldn't truly find fault with the knight's actions, something about the whole situation sat wrong with him. *Gillian.* If it had been anyone else, he would have trusted Evan's judgment, but because it was Nicholas's wife—and one he'd grown damned fond of—he hated the secondhand account. He wanted to have been the one interrogating the boy. He felt certain he could have gotten the truth out of him.

After Evan had gone through it all again, Nicholas said, "What troubles me the most is how quick you were to hang him. Why not let him stew for a while, withholding food and water, then come back and hit him harder? He would have broken then, I wager."

Evan opened his palms in the closest thing to exasperation the knight had ever shown. "Because I didn't think there was anything more to learn from him. I believed him when he said he acted alone."

"But why would the boy want her dead?"

Evan licked his lips, then said, "Because they believe she's a witch. She's a Glen Laire MacDonell, after all, my lord."

Nicholas nodded, exhaling deeply through his nose and taking a deep swallow of his whisky. He had expected this, just not so soon. He frowned meditatively at the amber liquid before returning his gaze to Evan.

"So you believe the two attacks are unrelated?"

"Aye, my lord, I do."

Nicholas nodded. He didn't agree, but he understood why his knight thought differently. "No more summary executions."

"Aye. Is that all, my lord?"

Nicholas nodded absently, but then thought of something else. "Wait."

Evan paused halfway to the door and turned back. "Aye?"

"Have a care what you say to Lady Kincreag. She's . . . very sensitive and softhearted."

Evan hesitated, eyes darting to the side in confusion. "My lord?"

"The thing about the servants being miserable and killing themselves. It upset her. I would have rather her not known about it."

"I instructed the servants not to tell her, but she asked after the maid. Since I didn't give them orders to lie—"

Nicholas waved his explanation away. "No, no, you did fine. But she thinks the whole castle is on the verge of suicide now."

Evan ducked his head. "Forgive me, my lord. I meant to ease her concerns, not trouble her further. I didn't think it wise for her to ask a lot of questions. The answers others give might trouble her more."

"I know. Just have a care, aye?"

Evan opened his mouth, then closed it and nodded. Nicholas knew what he was going to say and answered as if the knight had spoken.

"That was a long time ago."

Evan's throat worked, his gaze fixed on the ground.

"You're dismissed."

When Evan was gone, Nicholas poured more whisky. He wondered if the knight believed there was any connection between the maid's suicide and what had happened several years ago. Obviously many people residing in Kincreag did, or Evan wouldn't have been worried about Gillian's asking questions. Nicholas found that amusing, in a grim way.

He sighed and drained his cup. The recent suicide was inconvenient. He hoped Gillian would not probe into it any further.

15

Gillian had completely forgotten about the message she'd asked Gilchrist to send to Rose until her sister and Stephen Ross showed up at Kincreag a sennight later. After the perfunctory greetings were out of the way, Nicholas left Gillian to visit with her family. She took them to the west wing, confiding to them in a low voice all the odd things that had occurred since she'd left Lochlaire. Though Gillian admitted that she wasn't entirely certain the specters hadn't been opium induced, Rose was convinced she had communed with the dead.

The three of them stood over the dollhouse, inspecting it carefully. Stephen propped his walking stick against the table and circled it, seating himself on the padded stool. He peered into the house thoughtfully. Rose exclaimed over the workmanship just as Gillian had the first time she'd seen it.

"I want one!" Rose said, making the portcullis rise

and lower repeatedly. "I will make Jamie build me one for a wedding gift."

Stephen put his hand over hers to stop her from raising it again, annoyed at the repetitive creaking. "Try something else now, eh?"

Rose cranked it a few more times, smirking defiantly at Stephen the whole while, but she finally tired of irritating him.

Stephen removed the blond doll from Gillian's bed. "This is the one?" He studied the doll carefully, turning it in his fingers.

"Aye . . . it somehow finds its way back into the bed every time I take it out. Once it even disappeared from my pocket. Watch." She took it from Stephen and set it on the table, then started to walk away. He remained on the stool, blue eyes fixed intently on the doll. Gillian came back and pulled on his arm. "No, you can't watch it. Nothing will happen if you sit and look at it."

He rose painfully from the stool. Gillian took his arm to help him, but he pulled irritably from her grasp. "I can walk without aid, Gilly . . . er . . . my lady."

She raised her brows. "You don't have to 'my lady' me, Stephen."

He tugged an obsequious forelock in answer, and Gillian pushed at his shoulder.

Rose had wandered across the room to pluck at the lute's strings. "This needs to be tuned." She moved to the window and began tuning the instrument. Her long auburn braid nearly glowed in the sunlight spilling through the window, a myriad of dazzling colors glistening in the light—copper, gold, and amber.

Stephen gave Gillian a sidelong glance. "Can I look now?"

They returned to the dollhouse. Stephen was in front of her, so at his sudden stop Gillian bumped into him. He caught the edge of the house to steady himself, then sat heavily on the stool.

"Bloody hell," he muttered.

Gillian peered into the house, knowing what she'd see. She took the doll out of the bed almost every day, and it always found its way back.

Stephen looked around the room warily. "Are you getting headaches?"

"A few, but no bad ones like at Lochlaire."

"Maybe it's possessed of a demon?" Stephen's gaze was fixed on the doll, as if afraid to look away.

"Or maybe," Rose said, joining them, "a ghost is moving it about."

"Why would a ghost want to do that?" Gillian asked.

"I know not. Why don't you ask it?"

Gillian frowned at her sister.

Rose smiled secretly, midnight blue eyes shining with excitement. "I think I found a way to break the curse."

Gillian gasped. "Really? Let's do it now. Stephen, you must watch for Nicholas." When Rose raised an inquiring brow, she explained, her cheeks reddening with embarrassment, "He's forbidden me from practicing witchcraft."

Rose grinned. "You're so obedient, Gilly."

Gillian shrugged. Though she'd been quick to defy Nicholas's edict, she did feel a pang of guilt. He'd forced her to be secretive by being so overbearing. Besides, it wasn't as if she'd promised. In fact, she'd made a point not to promise, so she wasn't technically breaking her word.

Rose set the lute aside. "I memorized the counter curse and brought everything we need." She opened a small pouch that hung from her garter and removed a black candle. "Hold this."

Gillian took the candle and held it in both hands. "Why is it black?" Upon closer inspection she saw that it wasn't black at all but a deep, muddy red.

"Because it's not just wax. I had to make it special for this spell. It should smell nice."

Rose lit the wick with a candle from the candelabra, and after a moment a spicy scent filled the air.

Gillian nodded approvingly. "What's in it?"

"Er . . . you don't want to know."

Gillian raised her brows and shifted her hold on the candle so that she gripped it gingerly with her finger-tips.

Rose surveyed her thoughtfully. "Come stand over here." Taking Gillian's elbows, she steered her across the room, then took another minute to position her. She removed a piece of chalk from her wee pouch and drew a circle on the floor around Gillian, then she drew several odd signs around the inside edge of the circle.

She stood, dusting her hands off, and glanced around the room. Spotting the ewer and basin Gillian had brought to the room earlier that week, she poured water into the basin and carried it to where Gillian stood. She removed several small packets from her pouch and sprinkled the contents of one into the water.

"What's that?" Gillian asked.

"Salt."

Rose passed her hand over the water, eyes closed, and said something in a language Gillian did not understand. Gillian glanced nervously at Stephen. He leaned against the wall near the doorway, watching them. He smiled encouragingly.

Rose pushed the water into the circle and positioned it right below the candle Gillian held.

"I purified the water," Rose explained. "Some burning sage would be useful but not necessary."

Rose tossed her braid over her shoulder and scrutinized the scene. "The fire and water purify you and your space within the circle. Mother said curses put bad magic out into the world. So by breaking this curse we will be sending this bad magic back out into the world. We must give it direction."

"I think whoever cursed me should get the curse back at them."

Rose shook her head. "We can't do that unless we know who cursed you, and as we don't . . ." Rose shrugged. "Perhaps there is someone evil you'd like to curse?"

Gillian looked anxiously around the room, as if a candidate would appear. "There's no one."

Rose chewed her lip a moment, then her eyes lit up. "We'll curse an object, then we can bury it." Rose fished around in her pouch until she located a satiny black stone. "This will work."

She set the stone on the floor just outside the circle and made Gillian repeat after her words in a language that resembled Gaelic but made no sense to Gillian.

"What does it mean?"

"I'm not exactly certain," Rose said. "But the important thing is that you understand the intent and put your will behind it. We want to break the curse and send the bad magic to the stone. So long as you keep that to the fore of your mind and infuse your words with that intent, it doesn't really matter, aye?"

Gillian did as her sister instructed. They chanted the words for what seemed a very long time, until the dripping candle wax burned Gillian's fingers and her calves began to ache.

Finally Rose bade her to blow the candle out. She removed a shiny white oblong stone from her pouch. "Lick this in the sign of the cross."

Gillian looked at the stone dubiously. "Why?"

"Just do it!"

Gillian licked the stone across and down, then offered it to her sister.

"Was it salty?" Rose asked hopefully, opening her pouch so Gillian could drop it in herself.

Gillian shrugged. "Aye, a bit."

"Good." Rose beamed. "The curse is broken." She looked down her thin nose at the black stone on the floor. "We'll bury it later."

Stephen limped over to sit in front of the dollhouse again. "Did it work?"

"Rose says it did." Gillian looked around the room but didn't see or hear anything odd. No headaches, either.

"We need a test," Rose said. "Any place that you know is haunted?"

"The cliff path," Gillian said. "But not until midnight. And there has to be fog."

"Look at this," Stephen called from across the room.

They joined him at the dollhouse. His forefinger lay against the paneling of one of the rooms. When he saw that they both were watching, he pressed in on the paneling. It opened; inside was a small lever. He depressed it with his finger, and with a creak, the outer wall of the dollhouse opened a crack.

Gillian gasped. "What is it?"

Stephen pushed it apart. It wasn't much. A series of small wooden corridors and staircases, but as Stephen further manipulated the walls of the dollhouse, it became clear that this hidden hallway opened into most of the rooms, honeycombing the west wing.

"It's a servants' hallway. A lot of large castles have them. My uncle's largest castle is riddled with them." Stephen was the bastard son of a bastard son of the previous earl of Irvine. The current earl, his uncle, had raised him, so he had lived in castles such as this his whole life.

"How did you know it was here?" Gillian asked, gesturing to the house.

"Och, just look at it. It doesna match. The walls are thick, aye? But there's a good bit of room unaccounted for here; it made no sense to me."

"That's very clever, Stephen," Rose said, handing him his walking stick. "But now we must find a ghost."

"We can't go to the cliff path until midnight. Why not look here?" Stephen indicated the secret passageways in the dollhouse. "Gillian said the west wing was closed off and no one goes there. Seems to me the perfect place for ghosts to lurk."

Gillian eyed the chalk markings on the floor nervously. "We should clean this first."

"Not yet," Rose said. "Let's test it first, to be certain. There are a few variations of the counter curse, so if this one doesn't work, we'll try another."

When Gillian still regarded the floor uneasily, Rose took one of the discarded sheets and draped it over the markings.

After a quick inspection of the entrances to the servants' corridor, they set off into the west wing, Gillian and Rose holding candles.

"We have to be careful," Gillian whispered. "Sir Evan meets women here."

"They'll never see us," Stephen said, entering a room, with Rose and Gillian trailing behind. "But we can watch them."

He pushed on a panel, and it swung open, revealing a dark rectangle. He gestured for them to enter first. Gillian stepped in cautiously and held her candle high. There wasn't much to see. It was a rough wooden corridor, just like in the dollhouse. It smelled musty and disused. They wandered through the corridor, popping in and out of rooms. Gillian neither experienced headaches nor saw any specters.

As they wandered, she noticed that every so often a slab of wood at about eye level was mounted on the wall. Thinking this odd, she pointed it out to Stephen.

"Not odd at all." He found the catch to a door and sent Rose into the room. Then he slid the piece of wood aside to reveal two holes in the wall. "Spy holes," he said. "Have a peek."

Gillian pressed her eyes to the wall and watched Rose putter about the room. "Some servants' corridor. They can spy on their masters."

Stephen chuckled. "Well, I daresay they're more for the masters to spy on guests or young ladies."

Gillian's jaw dropped. "That's disgusting!"

Stephen laughed again.

"Come look at this," Rose called.

They joined her. She gestured around the room, eyebrows raised. There wasn't a sheet covering anything in this room. In fact, it looked inhabited.

"This must be Sir Evan's tryst room," Gillian said.

Rose opened the cupboards and wardrobe. "Someone is living here."

Gillian wandered over. A half dozen gowns hung from pegs in the wardrobe, and slippers and shoes lined the bottom. Shifts and stockings were folded neatly in the cupboard.

"These are verra nice," Stephen said, fingering the material of the shifts.

Their discovery made Gillian nervous. She wondered how often Evan and his lover met here. It made her worry that he would move the sheet in the solar and see the markings on the floor. Her stomach clenched tightly, and she wished she'd insisted that they clean the floor before going on this expedition.

"Come, let's go." With some urging Gillian induced Stephen and Rose to leave. On their way back to the

solar, Gillian noted that Stephen's limp was more pronounced and lines of pain bracketed his mouth. She'd
also noted how hard he'd worked all day to hide it, with
his jests and amusing stories.

When they returned to the solar, Nicholas was there
waiting for them. Gillian's heart stuttered, and she
nearly tripped over her own feet. He stood by the window, staring down at the circle drawn on the floor. The
sheet dangled from his fingers.

Gillian gave Rose a look of wide-eyed alarm. She
couldn't think of a single thing to say in her own defense.

Rose blurted out, "I did that. It's mine."

Nicholas looked up from the floor, a black brow
arched.

"Gillian told me not to," she added.

Stephen pulled on Rose's braid to shut her up. "But
Rose listens to no one, does she?"

Nicholas didn't reply to any of this. He dropped the
sheet, obscuring the markings again, and crossed to the
dollhouse. "Been exploring?" he asked, opening the sec-
tion Stephen had discovered that revealed the servants'
corridor.

Gillian felt the tension running through both Rose
and Stephen as they watched him warily. Gillian didn't
know what to make of his calm behavior. Was he angry?
She knew he didn't believe she was ignorant of the
magical circle on the floor. No doubt he was merely
being polite and would treat her to another lecture
when they were alone.

She joined him at the dollhouse, her racing heart finally slowing. "Aye, my lord. It's like a wee map of the castle."

"I told you to stay out of the west wing."

"But . . . we were just looking at this corridor. . . ."

With a quick move he revealed another servants' corridor in the east wing. He raised a brow expectantly.

Gillian swallowed guiltily. She'd not thought there was another one. "I didn't see that," she finished lamely.

"If you'll notice," his voice took on an instructive tone, "the east and west wings are nearly identical, with small variations. Here, you have a great hall. There's not one in the west wing, but there is this room"—he indicated the solar they currently stood in—"which the countesses of Kincreag often used for dancing and music."

Stephen and Rose drifted near. Gillian moved to the other side of the dollhouse to see Nicholas's face better. His expression was implacable, eyes guarded. He was very angry. She was certain of it. Her belly clenched so tight that she became queasy from it.

"The east wing houses the original keep," Nicholas said, indicating a rectangular section of the east wing, encompassing the great hall, kitchens, and several sets of apartments. "It was added onto over the years. The west wing is only about a hundred years old. It was built on the insistence of my great-great-grandmother. She couldn't stand her husband and insisted she have her own space to live in. Most of the countesses since have liked that arrangement."

"What happened here, my lord?" Stephen asked, pointing to the part of the dollhouse that was damaged.

Nicholas ran his finger over the buckled floor. "That's where the carpenter fell when he died."

Gillian started violently, looking from the aghast expressions of her sister and Stephen, back to Nicholas.

"What do you mean?" Gillian asked softly.

He watched her from beneath black lashes. "My late wife brought him with her, her personal carpenter, then gave him enough employment to last him many years. Making this and all the furniture inside. Our son never had a chance to play with it. They were always too busy working on it. All the time. Or so they claimed."

He'd barely mentioned Catriona before, and though part of Gillian was glad he seemed ready to share with her now, she did not like his demeanor, nor the fact that he was sharing this ghastly tidbit in front of Rose and Stephen.

Gillian put a hand on his arm. "Perhaps we should talk of this later, my lord?"

Nicholas looked around at Rose and Stephen—both of whom contrived to look disinterested, though they were clearly anything but—then back to Gillian. "Very well."

"We've missed supper," Gillian said with false brightness. "Shall we dine together?"

Rose and Stephen were quick to agree, and Nicholas came along with them. They ate in Gillian's chambers, and though conversation flowed between Gillian, Rose, and Stephen, Nicholas was not talkative. He reminded her of how he'd been when she'd first met him, taciturn and inscrutable.

Stephen drank a great deal of whisky and Nicholas's

mulled spirits, despite Rose's barbed comments about his consumption and the dark looks Nicholas gave him. Gillian assumed the lad did it to ease his pain, for he was obviously in great discomfort. He'd shifted about throughout the meal, the lines that pain had etched in his face finally relaxing when his speech grew slower and he enunciated his words in an exaggerated fashion. When their supply of spirits ran dry, Stephen discovered Gillian's decanter of wine. He'd only taken a few swallows from the enameled goblet when Rose finally dragged him away and bid them good night.

Nicholas remained at the table, swirling his wine about in his goblet, not looking at her, lips curved moodily. Part of her was angry with him. She'd wanted to prove to Stephen and Rose that he was not the evil brooding earl everyone thought he was, and yet he'd done his utmost to act the part all evening. Another part of her was worried that it wasn't an act. He was furious.

Gillian held out her hand to him. "Come to bed."

He regarded her hand for a long moment, then raised his dark eyes to her face. After what seemed an eternity in which she trembled with uncertainty, he took her hand and let her lead him to the bed. He watched her silently as she removed his boots and unhooked his doublet, without the smile or conversation they usually shared. In the past few weeks, she'd grown accustomed to him and his moods. Although he was often quiet and thoughtful, he'd never been so austere.

Setting his boots aside, she straightened before him, flustered and unhappy. "I'm sorry about the marks on the floor. I will clean them up tomorrow."

He said nothing, his gaze fixed on the floor between his feet. When he finally looked at her, his eyes were on fire.

"Damn it, Gillian."

The air crackled.

She swallowed. "I said I was sorry."

He stood and paced away. "Aye, I heard you. But what does it mean? You'll just do it again the first opportunity you get."

He was right. She should be honest with him. She took a step toward him, her hands twisting in her skirt. "It's what I am, Nicholas. I'm a witch . . . it's in my blood."

He swept his hand across the cabinet before him, sending the silver tray, along with the enameled decanter and goblets, crashing to the floor. "No, it's not!"

Gillian's hands flew to her mouth. She stared at the broken decanter. A puddle of wine seeped rapidly into the fine Turkish carpet.

There was a knock on the door, and Gillian jumped.

Nicholas swung around to the door, hands fisted at his sides, latent violence emanating from him. "Go away!"

Fingernails scratched at the wood. "Uh . . . I left something in there." Rose. "I need it."

Gillian's face flamed. *Why* did her sister have to overhear Nicholas railing at her? Gillian dropped her hands from her face and smoothed them over her skirt.

The door opened and Rose peeked her head in. She gave Gillian an apologetic grimace and hurried to the chair where she'd sat at dinner. Her pouch was on the floor beneath it. "Here it is." She stood and glanced at Nicholas. He glared back at her. He looked demonic, black hair slipping loose to fall around his face, black whiskers stubbling his cheeks, standing barefoot in shirtsleeves before a stain of blood-red wine.

Rose took in the scene before her and said, "Did I mention I did the er . . . spell in the solar? Gillian had nothing to do with it."

Nicholas gave her a tight and completely false close-mouthed smile. "Aye, I believe you did."

"Very well then." She looked at Gillian with raised brows. "Need you anything, Gilly?"

Gillian managed a smile that matched her husband's. "No, I'm fine. Good evening."

When Rose was finally gone, Gillian braced herself for more of Nicholas's rage. He stared down at the mess he'd made, hands on his hips and a rueful curve to his mouth.

"Nicholas?"

"You have a very brave and loyal sister. I think she believes I'm beating you in here."

The tight set of Gillian's shoulders relaxed. "Aye, she's also overbearing and meddling . . . and she's your sister now, too, since you married me."

He crossed the room and put his hands on her shoulders. His grip was firm but not punishing. "No more spells. No more witchcraft. The servants are already whispering about you."

His statement gave her an unpleasant jolt. "They are?"

"Aye, they're saying you're a witch and can't be harmed."

She looked away, a wave of anxiety washing over her.

"I had Evan remove the marks from the solar. No more witchcraft, Gillian. Promise me."

Gillian stared at the rapid pulse in his throat. She couldn't make that promise, especially now, when she was so close, when Rose might have actually broken the curse.

He tilted her chin up with his forefinger. "I don't want anything to happen to you."

She searched his dark eyes and saw that he was earnest. She didn't know what to do. She wanted to please him, so very badly . . . and yet she *needed* to please herself.

She licked her lips. "Very well . . . I can't promise, but I will do my best. And if I must, I will be very careful."

Nicholas dropped his hands from her shoulders in weary disappointment and crossed to the bed. "Let's go to bed."

They both undressed in silence. Nicholas helped her with her stays, then moved away, his fingers not lingering as they usually did.

When she turned back to the bed, he was beneath the bedclothes, candlelight gleaming off his bare chest. He leaned on an arm, watching her, his black eyes shadowed. Gillian blew out the candles and slid into bed with him, but when he made no move to hold her, she turned her back to him, staring blindly into the darkness. She felt sick with unhappiness. She closed her eyes tightly, knowing she would not sleep this night.

Finally, when the tension became nearly unbearable for Gillian, he slid down beside her, his knees behind hers, his arm around her waist so they fit together perfectly. His body warmed the length of her. He idly caressed the arches of her feet with his own. The tension flowed out of her.

After a time he lay still, and she thought that maybe he'd gone to sleep when he asked, "What was the purpose of the circle?"

Gillian's heart began to beat very hard. His hand slid up between her breasts and lay against her chest, so that her heart seemed to hammer against his hand.

"Peace," he whispered soothingly, "I'm just curious."

Gillian let out the breath she'd been holding. "A spell, my lord . . . to remove the curse I told you about."

He sighed deeply, his chest expanding behind her back, but said nothing more.

Gillian stared despondently into the dark and her eyes grew accustomed to the blackness. The faint, mist-shrouded moonlight from the open window showed her the darker shapes of furniture.

"You really don't believe, do you, Nicholas?"

His hand pressed against her breast fractionally. "I have seen some very strange things in my life, so it's not that I don't believe."

"You don't believe *me*. You think I'm dotty."

He chuckled softly behind her, and Gillian's heart lightened. It was the first laugh she'd heard from him since Rose and Stephen had arrived.

"Perhaps."

She pinched the hand that now cupped her breast.

"Ow!" He caught her miscreant hand and brought it firmly against her breast, trapped under his.

"What have you seen?"

She felt him lift a shoulder behind her. "I visited Turkey and Africa when I was young . . . I saw some strange things there. The healers are very skilled. I saw a man eat fire and swallow a sword. Some held deadly snakes and came to no harm. But I'm not certain that is witchcraft, though some would argue it's the devil's work."

Gillian knew many noblemen and knights went to the Continent, but she'd not heard much about them visiting with the Turks. "Why did you go to Africa and Turkey?"

He was silent for a long time. "I thought I would see something in their faces that explained me. I thought that by being among them I would understand things . . . about myself. I understand less now than I did before."

"What was it you hoped to understand?" He seemed disinclined to speak further, so she prompted, "Nicholas?"

His chest rose behind her as he took a deep breath. "I became very ill when I was seven. I nearly died. Before then, and after, the servants had been forbidden to speak of what happened to my mother. So I didn't really know I was different. I wasn't stupid; I saw how people looked at me and saw that my skin was different . . . but I was to be an earl, after all, and a bit spoiled by my father, and so I attributed it to my being *verra special*, as my father always told me I was." He exaggerated his burr in what Gillian imagined was an imitation of his father's voice. "But when everyone thought I was going to die . . . their tongues became loose. I heard all manner of things while in a fevered state . . . servants recounting the story of my mother's rape—embellished, I'm sure. I had nightmares about it for a long time. I also heard my mother tell her sister I was being punished by God because of the heathen in me—"

"You know that's not true," Gillian said quickly.

"Aye, I ken," he said softly, a smile in his voice. His fingers stroked hers, finding her mother's ring and turning it on her finger just as she sometimes did. "My father didn't know at the time that these things were said, or there'd have been some floggings. But later, when I recovered, I asked him about it. He said there was no shame in my heritage. He told me stories then about the Vikings invading Scotland and raping the women—and though it was very bad for the women, it brought strength to the people. He said the same of the Normans." He was silent for a moment, and she thought he was finished, but then he continued very softly, "He said my blood would make the Lyons' strong and that I was his son no matter what anyone said. That's why it was so important to deny the truth—because Kincreag would be mine no matter what."

"I would have liked your father very much," Gillian whispered into the ensuing silence.

Nicholas let out a soft breath. "Aye, I miss him."

He still toyed idly with her ring. He slid it from her finger onto his pinky. "So I remember to fix it tomorrow."

Gillian snuggled deeper into his arms and fell into a contented sleep.

It was dark when Broc's cold nose and soft whine woke Gillian from a sound sleep. Nicholas slept on behind her, his chest rising and falling against her back, his arm heavy on her waist. Someone moved silently in the darkness of her bedchamber, barely discernable, a shifting of shadows. Gillian choked on her fear, too paralyzed to cry out.

She lay motionless, heart beating into the darkness. Her eyes quickly adjusted to the dark, and she recognized the pattern of movement. She let out her pent-up breath, her pulse slowing. She shushed Broc and carefully lifted Nicholas's arm from her waist. He muttered something incoherent, then rolled over and continued sleeping soundly.

She scooted off the bed and quietly lit a candle. When she turned to the fireplace, it was exactly what she thought: the maid endlessly cleaning the fireplace and drinking the wine. Rose's spell had worked.

Gillian moved closer to the specter, holding the candle high to see her face. It was Aileen. The suicide. She looked just as she had the last time Gillian had seen her, pale blond hair pulled back tight, wearing a dun brown gown. She bent over the fireplace, sweeping ashes with an invisible brush into an invisible ash pan, her hand passing though the glowing embers. Then she stopped, glanced surreptitiously around the room, picked up the goblet beside the chair, and drained it.

Gillian followed her to the basin, where she washed the goblet. Aileen was oblivious to her, doomed to repeat the same actions over and over and over again.

"What are you trying to tell me?" Gillian whispered.

But the ghost did not answer.

Nicholas did, however. "Gillian?" His voice was muzzy with sleep.

"I'm just adding wood to the fire." She hurried back to the fireplace and tossed on a log.

"Who are you talking to?"

"No one. Broc. His nose is cold."

Hearing his master's voice, Broc bounded onto the bed. He stood over Nicholas, snuffling at his face.

"Bloody dog." Nicholas pushed halfheartedly at the determined dog.

When Gillian returned to bed, Broc had taken her place, lying with his back against Nicholas, who had fallen back to sleep with his arm draped over the dog.

Gillian smiled and crawled beneath the covers on the opposite side of her vast bed, curling up against Nicholas's back. But sleep did not come to her. Much had changed now that the curse was broken, and she couldn't help wondering, as she pressed against the warmth of her husband's skin, if she'd been better off cursed.

16

The next morning when Gillian woke, Nicholas was gone. So was the phantom Aileen. On the table, Gillian's ring rested atop a folded napkin with her breakfast. She slipped it on, and it fit perfectly.

She had much to tell Rose. After eating and dressing, she went to her sister's chamber but found it empty. Sir Evan passed as Gillian emerged from her sister's chamber.

"Have you seen my sister?"

"Aye. She was going to the cripple's chambers. I think something's wrong with him."

Gillian hurried to Stephen's chamber. Her knock met with silence, so she knocked harder. "Stephen? Rose?"

She heard a muffled noise inside and pressed her ear to the door. Someone was moaning within.

She pushed the door open. The dim room stank of sickness. It had only one window, and though it was open, it was but a narrow arrow slit and let in little light. She could barely make out the form huddled in the bed, moaning miserably.

She hurried to the bed. "Stephen? What ails you?"

He curled on his side, eyes closed tight, body shaking. Gillian pushed sweat-soaked hair off his forehead. His skin was clammy. "Stephen, tell me what's wrong?"

"Rose," he gasped, not even opening his eyes.

Panic thrummed through her. Where was Rose? "No, it's Gillian. Has she been here?"

His mouth grew pinched, and he doubled over. "Oh God."

She searched frantically around the room until she located the chamber pot, already half full of vomit, and brought it to him.

He was violently ill. Gillian held him up while he vomited, terrified. The only people she'd ever seen so ill had all died. He collapsed against her, his breath heaving in his chest. Gillian set the chamber pot aside. Tremors shook his body. His face was a ghastly color, like sour custard, the night's growth of blond whiskers vivid against his pale skin.

She placed a hand on his forehead, then his cheeks. He was not feverish. She heard rapid footsteps approaching the open door and looked up quickly.

Rose rushed in, muttering under her breath, shaking a bottle, her thumb over the mouth to keep it stoppered.

"She's here, Stephen," Gillian whispered, relief flooding her. But he was oblivious, trembling violently against Gillian's side.

"Rose, oh my God, what's—"

Rose cut her off with a look. "Has he vomited recently?" Her tone was brisk, efficient. She still vigorously shook the bottle in her hand.

Gillian nodded.

"Good." She poured the liquid from the bottle into a cup. "Sit him up."

Gillian slid her arm behind his back and tried to maneuver him into an upright position. "He's too big!"

"That's good enough." Rose's hand bracketed Stephen's mouth, and she forced the beverage down his throat with the other hand. He tried to pull away, coughing and sputtering, but Rose held his face in a solid grip. "Drink it Stephen or you'll die."

Gillian's eyes widened. *Die?*

His lids raised halfway to regard Rose warily. "I'm not already dead?" His voice was a weak croak.

"Drink it."

Stephen's eyes drifted shut again, and he swallowed everything in the cup before sliding down onto his side and folding into a shivering ball.

Rose stood over the bed, breathing hard, hands on hips. Then she sighed heavily and rubbed the side of her hand across her forehead. Her hand shook.

"I put a bit of laudanum in it. He should sleep a while."

"Will he live now?" Gillian leaned over to peer anxiously at his face. His closed eyelids moved rapidly.

"I know not. Gillian, someone poisoned him."

Gillian jerked back around to her sister. "What? Who? How?"

Rose shook her head wearily. "It's hard to know. He's such a God damned sot, you cannot ken. He'll drink anything—privy water, if he's far enough gone. I don't know how much poison he ingested, so I may be chasing my tail. He could die no matter what I do."

Gillian looked back at the huddled figure on the bed. Her throat tightened. "Why is he like this? Is it the pain?"

Rose shrugged. "Aye, the pain. The cane. The fact he can barely sit a horse. He insisted on coming with me, and the journey took twice as long because of it. He was sore vexed with himself." Rose glanced cautiously at the bed, then motioned with her chin for Gillian to follow her a few paces away. When she spoke again her voice was low. "My mind's not set that he didn't do this to himself."

Gillian's jaw dropped. "What?"

Rose nodded. "Sometimes when he's really sotted, he says things—"

"What things?"

Rose sighed. "That we should have let him die. When I found him this morning, he swore he didn't do this to himself. I don't know. Maybe he didn't. Or maybe he just doesn't want to spend his last moments getting his ears blistered by me."

Gillian pressed her palm to her forehead, struck by the coincidence of this situation. She glanced back at Stephen, then to Rose, who watched her with interest.

"What is it, Gilly? You've thought of something."

"This is what she was trying to tell me," Gillian murmured.

Rose raised her brows expectantly.

"Remember I told you about the woman I saw cleaning my fireplace and drinking my wine—"

"Aye, the phantom maid. I remember."

"Your counter curse worked, Rose. I saw her last night with no pain."

"That's good." Rose smiled faintly.

Neither of them could muster much enthusiasm for the success of the counter curse, with Stephen dying across the room.

"I recognized her last night. She was my first maid, Aileen. She killed herself. With poison."

Rose raised an auburn brow, unsurprised by this information, and nodded for Gillian to continue.

"The wine she keeps drinking over and over again is the same wine Stephen drank last night."

Rose's eyes closed and her lashes fluttered. Her hand covered her mouth. "Thank God, thank God. He only took a few drinks. He might live yet." Her eyes snapped open. "Gillian. That wine was meant for you."

Gillian's shoulders slumped. "I know. This makes three attempts on my life. I must tell Nicholas."

"No!" Rose shook her head vigorously, eyes intense. "You cannot."

Gillian was taken aback by her sister's vehemence. She frowned in annoyance. "Of course I can. He's my husband. He'll find out who's doing this and protect me."

Rose gripped Gillian's hands tightly. "Listen to me for a moment. When I was in the kitchens I overheard the servants talking about Aileen. This has happened before."

"What?"

"When Kincreag's first wife was alive, several servants committed suicide with poison. So did a few of her alleged lovers. Then she falls from the cliff and the suicides stop. Kincreag marries, and they start up again."

"And what do the servants think is going on?" Gillian asked incredulously. "What does marriage have to do with poisonings?"

"They say he's madly jealous—that he's jealous of anyone who even speaks to his wives, so he kills them."

"If that's true, then why isn't my other maid dead? What about Sir Evan?"

Rose nodded wisely. "They probably realize. They're probably very careful about anything they eat or drink."

Gillian let out an exasperated breath. "Da said something about this before I left Lochlaire. He thinks the countess did it."

Rose put her hands on her hips and raised her brows. "Aye? Well if that's true, who's doing it now?"

What Rose thought was impossible. Rose couldn't know that, because all she knew of Nicholas were the rumors and his unpleasant behavior since her arrival. But Gillian knew him. He would never do anything like this. She didn't know who was responsible, but she had an idea how she might find out.

Nicholas and Gillian dined alone that night. Stephen Ross was still very ill, and Rose continued to tend him. Nicholas was in a state of shock from what Gillian had told him. The wine in her room had been poisoned?

There was no way to verify that, of course, since he'd spilled the remainder of it last night. Nevertheless, he'd had a servant taste every plate and beverage before either of them consumed a single bite.

He watched her now in the candlelight. She was a world away from him, deep in her thoughts, large gray eyes gazing off into the distance. It still didn't quite make sense to Nicholas. How did she know her late maid had drunk the wine? When Aileen's body was discovered, there had been poison beside her cot in plain sight. He wasn't discounting murder; then it would make sense for someone to plant poison to make it appear as a suicide. But if the maid drank the poison accidentally and then died . . . why the poison beside her bed? It didn't add up. As for Stephen . . . the lad was a drunkard. Nicholas had seen more than a few men succumb to their love for drink, and as much as the lad had consumed last night, it was no wonder he'd vomited up his innards.

He set down his knife and frowned at his wife. "Gillian."

She blinked, and the clouds cleared from her eyes as she focused on him.

"I still don't understand how you know Aileen drank the wine."

She directed her attention to her dinner and commenced pushing her food around. "I just do."

"Did you see her?"

Gillian thought for a moment, then nodded, shredding a piece of roast chicken with her fingers.

"So one of my servants was imbibing the countess's

wine right in front of her." It was too fantastic to contemplate.

Again Gillian pondered this and nodded.

Nicholas leaned forward. "Then I'm more certain than ever it was a suicide. What deranged servant would steal wine right in front of their employer? She must have been insane."

Gillian didn't reply. She pushed her food around on her plate, gaze fixed on the mess she'd made of her dinner. As he watched her his frustration increased. She was never this uncommunicative. Something was amiss.

"What is wrong with you?"

She met his gaze. "Why didn't you tell me about the servants who were poisoned when your wife was alive?"

Ah. Resignation settled over Nicholas. He set his napkin over his plate and leaned back in his chair. "It's not a very interesting story."

Her mouth curved in a smile that didn't reach her eyes. "I'm interested."

"You are a morbid woman."

She did not reply, watching him patiently. Waiting.

Nicholas sighed. "After I married Catriona and brought her here, there were a few deaths. I don't know that all of them can be attributed to poison or to Catriona, but certainly several of them were her doing."

Gillian's eyes widened. She set her knife down and leaned forward, resting her chin on her hand. She nodded for him to continue.

"I didn't suspect her at first . . . if you'd known her, you would understand. She seemed so kind, so eager to please. But when I discovered she'd cuckolded me and that the man she'd done it with died rather mysteriously, things began to look a bit grim. She, of course, denied it, and I believed her. The first time. It just seemed too fantastic. Why would she murder servants? Why murder her lover if I already knew?"

"Didn't she try to poison you?"

Nicholas nodded. "Aye. My son Malcolm's health was already fading, so when she tried to poison me and poisoned your father inadvertently, I locked her up."

"Aye, my father told me."

He looked down at his napkin, his jaw tight with regret. He often wondered how things would have turned out if he'd handled it differently. "I didn't expose her because I thought I was protecting my son's future. And then Malcolm died."

His hand fisted on his thigh. Grief and fury trembled fresh in his heart, as if it had just happened. "At the time I was certain she did it. Now, I'm not so sure. Catriona loved no one and nothing, but she'd loved that baby." He sighed. "I still don't know."

He swallowed hard, then looked up. "I went to the room where I'd kept her prisoner to . . . to . . . well, I still don't know what I meant to do when I went to her. There was no reason for me to protect her anymore. Kill her? Maybe. But I didn't. We argued. She continued her lies. I grew angrier. She ran. She fell."

He watched Gillian in the ensuing silence, gauging her reaction. The story troubled her, that was evident in the line between her brows, but she didn't look at him with fear or disbelief.

He gave her a hard smile. "The entire castle had

heard us screaming, had heard my death threats—and they weren't the first I'd made within another's hearing. I put the nails in my own coffin, to be sure. I'm intelligent enough to understand that changing my story and pinning all the deaths on Catriona after she 'accidentally' fell to her death would be incredibly suspicious."

"But the king acquitted you." Her voice was quiet, gray eyes steady.

"Aye, God smiled on me that day." He rubbed a finger across his mouth thoughtfully. "I still don't believe Cat's death was an accident. She'd known what was coming. She knew she could no longer hide behind Malcolm. So she killed herself, knowing exactly how it would reflect on me." He laughed, and it sounded rusty, bitter. "It's almost poetic that I am still blamed for all her crimes. After all, I protected a murderess. I am as guilty as she."

Gillian rose from the table and came around to stand behind him. She slid her hands around his neck and embraced him from behind, her face pressed against his. He closed his eyes, stroking her arms and losing himself in the comfort she offered.

"You loved your son and protected him, just like your father protected you. When you realized she was responsible, you stopped her. You cannot blame yourself, Nicholas. All the important people know that you did the right thing. The king knows. God knows. I know. That's all that matters." She kissed his jaw.

He turned his face and caught her lips in a lingering kiss. His fingers slid over her neck, soft as down. He exerted subtle pressure, and she circled his chair, moving around to straddle him. He pulled her hair down. Sable curls flowed around them like a silken mantle. He removed her bodice and pushed her shift off her shoulders so he could touch her, stroke his fingers up the soft skin of her back and feel the muscles contract with pleasure, kiss her breasts and hear the soft sounds she made as she ground her hips into his. She was beautiful. She was his. He couldn't lose her.

She was eager and ready, pulling at the laces of his breeks and settling herself on him with a gasp and sigh. He slid his hands beneath her skirts, over soft thighs, to grip her bottom as she rode him. She gripped the back of the chair, leaning over him to lick and suck his lips until he exploded, violent, mindless, clutching her to his chest as if she might slip away when it was over, like some succubus, come to steal his soul.

She laid her head upon his shoulder, her breath soughing soft and warm in his ear. God, he'd fallen hard. He loved her. She was his whole life now, just as Malcolm had once been, and he would not lose her, too.

Gillian heaved the heavy bar from the postern door with a grunt, getting splinters in her fingers in the process. It fell to the ground with a thump. She pushed the door open and stared at the wall of fog before her. She eased forward a few steps, then stopped abruptly. The ground fell away three feet past the door. Gillian's stomach dropped and she backed up, pressing herself against the wall. She must have a care. She'd hate to fall and have her death blamed on Nicholas, too. Just thinking of that evil woman galvanized Gillian with anger.

Catriona was dead now and couldn't be responsible for the recent poisonings. Could she? Gillian wasn't so certain. If a ghost could move a doll, surely it could move poison.

She edged along the narrow path, keeping one hand firmly on the stone wall to her right. At least she didn't have to worry about collapsing anymore, thanks to Rose's spell. Wind swirled the fog, and at times she could see several yards before her. The path was overgrown, but the tall grasses had recently been trampled flat in places. She didn't chance getting too close to the edge; the sheer drop was enough to make her stomach plummet when she chanced peering over the side.

She didn't know how far she'd gone when she finally encountered the cloaked and hooded figure in the fog. It stood at the cliff edge, as if looking out at the mountains, though it couldn't possibly see anything in the soupy fog. Gillian's mouth opened and closed, but no words issued forth, just a rough croak.

The ghost of Catriona. And Gillian had no headache, not even a twinge in her temples. Now that it was finally possible, she found herself too terrified to speak. She had so much to ask her. And if it turned out she was an evil ghost, then Gillian must find a way to exorcise her. Gillian bolstered herself, struggling to master her erratic heartbeat. Deep breaths. She could do this! But she must hurry so she could return to bed before Nicholas discovered she was gone. That spurred her more efficiently than any mantra—the thought of Nicholas's disappointment.

"My lady," she finally gasped. She took a few tentative steps forward. When the figure didn't turn, Gillian wondered if it was like Aileen, oblivious to the living.

Gillian repeated herself, her voice stronger, and approached the specter. And then she felt it again, as she had in the courtyard when the ballast had hit her, a sudden drop in temperature, as if she'd walked into a pocket of winter. Gillian stopped, heart rising in panic. A glacial wind enveloped her, pressing in on her like a storm. Pain pierced through her temples. She doubled over, groaning, hands to her head. *No! This wasn't supposed to happen. The curse was broken!*

The woman turned toward Gillian, her fine, slender hand reaching up to pull back her hood. And then something shoved Gillian hard from behind. The air left her as she surged forward, toward the cliff edge, but the cold pressed against her chest, held her suspended, stopping her from toppling over. The frigid air suffocated her, smothered her. Her hair stood out all about her head.

Gillian found her voice as the shove came again, hard enough this time to dislodge whatever force strove to hold her back. She screamed with all the fear and horror in her heart. "Nicholas!"

It was late when the knock came. Nicholas had been unable to sleep, so he had left Gillian and Broc snuggled together in bed to sit in his privy chamber and pore over court documents. It was the perfect antidote to sleeplessness, and he was nearly ready to turn in for the night.

"Aye?" he called.

The door opened and a servant stepped in. "My lord, I was sent to tell you about the countess."

Nicholas dropped the parchment he held and glanced at the clock on his desk. It was nearly midnight. She'd been sound asleep when he'd left her over an hour ago. "What about her?"

"She was seen heading for the gardens."

Nicholas frowned, standing. "Well . . . mayhap she had trouble sleeping and went for a walk." He should go after her anyway. With all the attempts on her life he didn't like her wandering around in the dark alone.

He strode briskly to the gardens. "Gillian?" The gate creaked as he pushed it open. He gazed about the foggy gardens but saw no sign of her. "Gillian?" When she didn't answer, he followed the path, his step quickening with the new tempo of his heart. Why wasn't she answering? Then he saw the postern door standing open, and his heart thudded to a halt.

The cliff path. Images of Gillian plunging to her death gripped him. He ran to the door, then stood on the path for a moment, looking right and left, wondering which direction she'd taken. Her scream shattered the night, ripping through every muscle in his body. "Nicholas!"

17

Nicholas broke into a run, heedless of the cliff's edge. "Gillian!" *Please let her be fine.* The thickening fog obscured his vision, but the path before him was empty. He raced along it, shouting her name over and over, fingers trailing the wall beside him. The trail began to descend, moving away from the castle walls to the rocks and river below. He stopped, chest heaving. *This couldn't be happening.*

"Gillian!" His bellow scraped his throat raw. *"Gillian!"* There was no answer.

He turned and started back up the path, feeling as if he were trapped in a nightmare. Why had she come here, the little fool? *Why?*

Nicholas kept walking, yelling himself hoarse, refusing to consider the obvious. She'd come out here for the ghost. He knew it. When he found her, he would shake her and shake her and put his fist through a wall because he might lose her. *Please God, let her be fine.*

He was back at the postern door. Several men-at-arms stood there, staring at him as if he had horns sprouting from his forehead.

"Did she come back this way?"

They shook their heads.

"Why are you just standing there? Get torches—I want the entire path searched. Now!"

They scattered like roaches from light. He swung back around, staring wildly out into the foggy night, at the cliff falling off sharply a few feet away. He could hear her last scream echoing in his ears. The beginnings of a black, irrational rage clawed at him. *Why?* There was no such thing as ghosts and magic. Why couldn't she accept that? Why would she get herself killed over it? He couldn't stand it.

He staggered to the edge of the cliff and yelled her name into the night.

A man-at-arms cleared his throat behind Nicholas. "My lord?"

Nicholas turned toward him, not really seeing him, his eyes searching for some sign of her everywhere he looked. Maybe she'd returned to the castle. Maybe he'd somehow missed her? Walked right past her? On a path that was three feet in width. Not likely.

"Should we send some men below . . . to search the river and rocks?"

"No!" Nicholas roared. "She didn't fall. Search the castle. Maybe she went back inside." Then why had he heard her scream his name?

The man quickly backed away. Rose appeared from

the fog, eyes wild, auburn hair flying around her like a fury. Her dark eyes narrowed in on him.

"You killed her!" she screeched and came at him.

"Rose—" He caught her shoulders as she flew at him, nails raking him across the cheek. He shoved her away, and she fell onto the path. She flung her hair back and glared up at him. "I'll see you dead for this!"

"I didn't kill her!" He raked a shaking hand through his hair. He couldn't think properly. Something very bad was happening. Rose thought he'd killed Gillian. A tight, icy ball of dread formed in his gut, and it worked its way upward, constricting his chest and throat. "Bloody Christ, Rose—I did not murder my wife!"

"Liar," she hissed. "You think because you're an earl you can get away with this? You can't just collect murdered wives and servants. Why, I'll—"

"Rose, listen to me." Nicholas thought for certain that he was going mad. He'd walked into some horrible nightmare that kept getting more and more macabre. Rose opened her mouth to spit more venom at him. He grabbed her arm and shook her. *"Listen to me!"*

Evan's hand fell on his shoulder. "Leave off, my lord. She's distraught."

She's distraught? Nicholas was distraught. He released her abruptly. She dropped to the cobblestone path, buried her face in her hands, and began to weep.

"Rose." He said her name plaintively, wanting her to stop her weeping because *damn it!* Gillian was not dead. She couldn't be. Slowly, like a cut tree, Rose

tipped forward until her forehead touched the stones, sobbing her sister's name.

Dead, dead. Everyone stared at him as if he were a fiend bent on further mayhem. Even Evan had a wary look in his eyes. They all believed he'd tossed another wife to her death.

He put his hands to his face. "This cannot be happening." He raked his hands savagely through his hair, wanting to rip it out if he thought it would do any good. He backed away, back to the cliff path, and resumed his desperate search.

The sun rose, burning off the fog and clearly illuminating the path. But the light revealed no clues about what had happened to Gillian. Nor could Nicholas find a trace of the servant who'd come to him about Gillian, the one who'd said he'd been *sent*. Sent by whom? When Nicholas had described the servant to Evan and others, everyone had denied seeing him, or even knowing who he was. They'd all looked at Nicholas as if he'd been lying. As if they'd known some truth about him—that there was no servant, that he'd followed his wife into the garden, then thrown her from a cliff.

He loved her! He wanted to rage it at them, beat it into their heads so they stopped staring at him like a dangerous madman. Why would he murder the best thing in his miserable life? It made no sense. Couldn't they see that?

He scoured the entire castle before finally giving the order for the men to go below. To look for her on the ground. It felt like an admission of defeat. His chest was an empty void. Dead.

He walked blindly to his chambers and sank into the chair behind his desk. He stared at the documents that he'd been working his way through before his life unraveled. Again. None of it mattered. He'd vowed to protect her, and she'd not even lasted a month in his care.

He sat that way for a very long time. Unmoving, staring blankly at his desk, a hollow bark echoing in his ears. As if the world had stopped and he did not want it to start again.

Evan appeared in the doorway. "My lord, they didn't find her below . . . but she could have fallen in the river, so there would be no body."

When Catriona had fallen they'd done the same for a time, searching the castle and the base of the mountain, waiting for a body to wash up somewhere. He'd sent men to follow the river, looking, but they'd never found her—only her cloak, caught in the brambles on the cliff path, the clasp broken, ripped from her throat as she'd fallen.

"Send some men downriver," he heard himself say.

Evan gave the order but didn't leave. Nicholas wanted him to go away, but he couldn't find the energy to speak. His throat hurt. Everything hurt. He felt as if someone had rammed a lance into his chest. He could barely breath without pain wrenching through him, and he feared that at any moment he would disintegrate.

"There's a party at the gate," Evan said.

Nicholas dimly remembered one of his men informing him of their approach more than an hour ago. "Who is it?"

"The countess's sister, Isobel Kilpatrick and her husband."

And he'd thought matters couldn't possibly get worse.

"Let them in," he said.

Again Evan gave the order but didn't leave. What else? Nicholas refused to look at the knight.

Evan came into Nicholas's privy chamber and closed the door. He crossed to the whisky decanter on the cabinet. Nicholas watched with a sense of detachment as Evan poured a cup of whisky and brought it to him.

"Here, my lord, methinks you need this."

Nicholas slapped the cup out of Evan's hand. The knight jerked back. The cup clattered to the floor, spraying whisky everywhere.

"You think a drink will make this better?"

"No, my lord." Evan's stone mask was in place.

Nicholas dropped his head into his hands. Nothing would make this better. Nothing.

"Go away."

Sir Evan left.

Broc barked and scratched at the connecting door, reminding Nicholas of the last time he'd seen Gillian. Curled in bed with Broc, sleeping like an angel. He squeezed his eyes shut, pressing his fists into them to gouge out the memory.

Broc's barking grew monotonous, so Nicholas let the dog in. Broc raced past him, sniffing frantically at all the furniture, then bounding to the door leading to the corridor. He scratched at it, whining and barking frantically. The dog was in a frenzy, and Nicholas wondered if he somehow sensed what had happened.

Nicholas sat heavily in his chair and called the dog. Broc came to him, but when Nicholas tried to pet him, he ran back to the door, yipping and turning in circles. He raced back to Nicholas again, repeating the ritual.

Nicholas had a sudden recollection of when Broc had arrived. He had done something similar and had eventually led him straight to Gillian, sitting in the garden. The memory of her, sitting on a stone bench, surrounded by flowers and smiling up at him, knifed through him. He stood with a surge of hope.

"Come on, Broc—you've something you'd like to show me?"

What Gillian couldn't understand was, if she was dead, why did it hurt so much? Her head ached so that she couldn't open her eyes, her hands stung, her face throbbed, her right arm burned like a brand, and the rest of her body was filled with a general pulsing ache.

She couldn't stop shivering either, it was so cold. Wind lifted her hair as it blew across her, the strength of the breeze at times nearly rolling her over. Something squawked loudly in her ear. Where was she? She curled the fingers of her left hand and felt grit beneath them, followed by a harsh sting that shot through her abraded palm.

Memories came to her, disjointed. She'd been on the path . . . she'd seen the ghost . . . pain . . . the pain had come back. The counter curse had failed. She'd been struck with pain and had fallen. No, someone had pushed her. She squeezed her eyes shut, her stomach rebelling, pain splintering through her head until the blackness returned.

When she woke next she was reasonably certain she was alive, which seemed rather unfortunate, as the sunlight tried to burn her eyes out. The squawking had started up again—a cyclic sound, growing louder and then fading, only to come very close moments later. Gillian tried to move, but her right arm was a fiery limb of agony and refused to obey. She pushed up with her left arm.

Distant mountains surrounded her, and below, a sheer drop. Gillian stared downward, her stomach lurching. Something screamed and dove at her, tangling in her hair. She shrieked and tried to scrabble away, falling flat again and wrenching her right arm. Whitehot agony exploded through her.

She was under attack from a very large, very angry bird. It clawed and tore at her hair. A sudden frigid breeze blew as she tried to protect her head with her left hand, only to have it brutally slashed. The bird abruptly left with a squawk of terror. But now Gillian's head throbbed so she could barely see. Ghost birds? Just her luck. She waited for the pain to subside, but it didn't. She moaned, pressing her cheek into the ledge, staring at her ravaged and bloody left hand, half curled beside her face. Her mother's ring glinted in the sunlight.

Her mother's ring. And suddenly she understood. Gillian had never been cursed. But her mother's ring had. Using her teeth and lips, she wrenched the cursed thing off her finger. It tinked onto the ledge. The pain immediately abated.

Gillian peeked back out at the vista before her. Two large birds soared nearby—not vultures but eagles. They circled, calling angrily to each other or at her, she didn't know, but for the moment, they were staying away.

"They'll not harm ye, so long as I'm here."

Gillian screamed again and rolled toward the edge, catching herself before she rolled off into nothing but air.

A man was with her. Gillian had slowly deduced that when she'd fallen, she'd not plunged to the river or rocks below but had landed on a ledge, apparently home to a pair of angry eagles. She had a hazy memory of hitting a bulge in the side of the mountain as she'd fallen and scratching desperately for purchase, only to roll and slide off it before crashing to the ground . . . or to this ledge.

The man sat against the cliff side, a plaid wrapped around him. It was very cold, and a strong breeze blew, yet it didn't ruffle his dark auburn hair or make the ends of his plaid flutter. A ghost.

Gillian struggled to catch her breath as she stared at the man. He seemed a kindly enough ghost, his dark green eyes warm and friendly.

"Who are you?" Her voice was a croak, and her lips cracked painfully when she spoke. Her mouth tasted of grit and dried blood.

"Tomas Campbell, yer servant, my lady."

"Oh, aye?" Gillian said, looking upward. The top of

the cliff was completely hidden from view by the bulging rock she'd hit on her descent. It cast a partial shadow over the ledge.

Tomas Campbell hunkered in the shadows. "I tried to warn ye, but ye wouldna listen. I tried to help, but it's no so easy anymore." He held his hands up and frowned at them. "If I concentrate verra hard, sometimes I can feel ye and know I'm doing some good." He sighed and dropped his hands. "But this time it wasna enough. I havena a body, after all."

"It's been you all this time? The doll . . . the ballast . . . the writing?"

Tomas shook his head. "The ballast and cliff, aye that was me. I know nothing about a doll. The writing was a lad. I saw him briefly, but he didna see me. Most canna see me . . . and to be truthful, I canna always see them, either. It's as if I see them from the corner of my eye, but when I turn, they're gone, or just shadows. I hear their voices clear sometimes, and others it's but whisperings. But you . . . I saw ye clearly from the time ye set foot in the castle. Ye're like a blazing torch. I kent that if I saw you, you must see me . . . but it didna work the way I thought. Till now, that is."

Gillian's sluggish and anguished brain took a long moment to digest this. "What happened?"

Tomas leaned forward, face grim. "You were pushed, my lady. I tried to stop ye from falling as I'd stopped the ballast from causing ye any real harm, but yer attacker was most persistent."

"Who attacked me?"

"I know not, my lady. I told ye—as most canna see

me, neither can I see them. I only know the one who did this is a dark man ... dark skin, dark hair ... that is all I can see, I catch snatches of him from the corner of my eye ... but when I turn, there's naught there. But he watches you, and his intentions are dark."

Gillian glanced back over the side of the cliff, at the soaring eagles, then back at Tomas. She decided he was harmless, so she painfully dragged herself away from the edge of the cliff. She shivered from the bracing wind.

"What am I going to do?" she said, more to herself than to Tomas.

"They're looking for you. Call out to them."

"How do you know if you can't see them?"

"I can hear them sometimes, and there is another, not like you, but I see her—she's like a shade. She mourns you."

"Rose," Gillian whispered.

She filled her lungs and screamed for help. But her screams were useless—the strong wind stole the words from her mouth and sent them away.

Her chest and throat burned with every labored breath. She clutched her arm to her side. It was broken. She must have landed on it. She tried not to panic but couldn't help thinking she would die on this ledge, from starvation and exposure. The eagles would feast on her.

She screamed again, tears making mud of the grit on her cheeks.

Tomas watched her sadly. "I had hoped to save you from this."

"Why do you want to save me?"

"It's been so long since I've had someone to talk to. And if you die . . . you probably won't stay here. Most don't."

"Are there others like you here?"

Tomas nodded. "I canna talk to some of them . . . they dinna see me anymore than the live ones do."

She thought of Aileen in her cleaning and drinking circuit, oblivious to anything but that single moment in time.

She looked upward, straining to hear the voices Tomas claimed he heard calling for her, but all she heard was the rush of wind and call of eagles. She had to keep talking, or she would go mad. Her throat was raw from screaming, and the pain in her arm made her weak and sick.

"I saw another ghost, on the cliff. A woman. I think it was the late countess, Catriona. Can you see her?"

"Not really, my lady, though I felt her and caught brief snatches of her." He sighed. "I wish I could speak to her."

He seemed a very lonely fellow.

"Can you not leave?" Gillian asked. "Can you not go to heaven?"

His eyebrows drooped. "I dinna know how. I dinna know if I'm meant to."

The wind whistled as it gusted over the ledge. An enormous nest was a few feet away. The soft, downy brown feathers lifted on the breeze and spun out into the air.

Gillian's stomach rebelled from the pain in her arm.

Her head whirled, gray crowding the edges of her vision.

"I'm going to lie down a bit," Gillian said, her voice a bare whisper, and she slid down until her cheek pressed into the grit of the ledge.

18

Nicholas's anxiety and frustration mounted as he followed Broc to another dead end. The dog picked up Gillian's scent all over the castle, but it was rapidly becoming clear that he followed old trails. Nicholas tried to get the dog out to the garden, but Broc didn't want to go. Finally he found a length of rope and looped it around Broc's neck. The dog resisted at first, then caught Gillian's scent and dragged Nicholas.

At the open gate to the garden, Sir Philip Kilpatrick and his wife were in conversation with Evan. Annoyance and frustration lowered Nicholas's shoulders; he narrowed his eyes. He did not have time for this. They turned at his approach. God only knew what Evan had told them. Nicholas continued past them until the dog decided it wanted to go back inside and abruptly changed direction. Nicholas leaned over and picked the hound up. It was a large dog, at least seven stone, but it lay in his arms like a puppy, tongue lolling. The Kilpatricks only stared at him, wide-eyed.

Nicholas was almost to the postern door when the tapping of light steps on the flagstone path followed him. "What are you doing with that dog?" Isobel stopped in front of him, blocking his way, her red-gold hair a halo in the bright sunlight.

"Put the dog down," Sir Philip said in a tone meant to soothe a madman. "I'm not sure what he did, but—"

Nicholas whirled around, looking at Philip incredulously. "What do you think I'm going to do? Throw him over the side?"

"Well . . ." Philip's brows drew together in confusion, his gaze darting to his wife. "Isobel, come away from him." When Isobel had moved a safe distance away from Nicholas, he continued, "Why don't you come inside and tell me what happened, aye?"

Nicholas set Broc down and turned his back on the knight. He'd not killed anyone, but he was damn close to doing it now. Broc sniffed around for a moment, then lifted his head, ears pricked and gaze fixed on the open postern door. He trotted through, nose to the ground, tail wagging excitedly.

Nicholas started after the dog when Sir Philip dropped a heavy hand on his shoulder. "I think you should come with me, my lord."

Nicholas shoved him off and went after Broc. The dog was out of sight, already around the curving wall of the castle. Nicholas jogged down the path until a sharp bark from Broc snapped him into a run.

Broc was beside himself, looking over the side of the cliff. He lowered his body gingerly, as if he meant to skitter down the side. Nicholas grabbed the rope leash and wrapped it firmly around his hand.

This part of the path looked no different than any other part, and Broc's frantic barking over the side seemed to indicate the worst. Heart sinking, Nicholas stared over the side. Dark mountains rose all around. Sunlight glinted off the river far below. Fury at fate welled up inside him, ripping painfully through his chest. He wanted to shake his fist at the capriciousness of God, that He should take her, too.

Two eagles circled below, their screaming echoing his fury. He watched them for a time, holding firmly to Broc as the dog tried desperately to leap over the side and share his mistress's fate. Nicholas looked straight down. The cliff bulged out, so he couldn't see the ground directly below. He strolled several paces down the path. The way it curved, he couldn't see the cliff face, but he could see the bottom. If she'd gone over here, her body would have been broken on the sharp rocks below, for the river did not pass near the cliff this way.

He had a sudden memory from his childhood, of his father bringing him to the cliff to show him an eagle's nest on a ledge and telling him how eagles mated for life. They'd sat together on the path and watched them mate, plummeting downward, talons locked, in a beautiful dance. They'd come back frequently to watch the single eaglet grow and finally leave the nest.

There were ledges all over the mountains. Could she have fallen to one and was still alive but unable to call out? As they'd not found her body below, that seemed plausible. Broc's claws dug into the dirt of the path, trying to return to the place where Gillian had apparently fallen.

Nicholas needed help. Pulling the reluctant dog along with him, he hurried back up the path. When he entered the garden, Sir Philip was still there, his face set in severe lines.

"I need some rope . . . about twenty ells. And at least four men."

Nicholas's men-at-arms made to obey, but Philip held out a hand and they stopped, looking anxiously from Philip to Nicholas.

"My lord, if you'll come with me—"

Blood rushed to throb in Nicholas's temples. He advanced on the knight, muscles rigid with fury. "I'll answer to no one but the king, *Knight*. You forget yourself. Now get me the God damned rope!"

His men dispersed.

If Nicholas didn't find her, he would have to answer to the king, no mistake. But that did not concern him. All he cared about was finding his wife.

Sir Philip stepped in front of Nicholas when he tried to pass. His eyes were hard, his face set with purpose. "And so ye shall. The king *will* hear of this, my lord. I'll be taking witnesses with me when I leave. Noble or no, ye cannot murder with impunity."

Rage burst red behind Nicholas's eyes, and his control snapped. He slammed his fist into the knight's face. The next thing he knew they were rolling around on the ground, pummeling each other. Nicholas hammered mindlessly at the knight, venting all his fear and frustration with his fists. Clansmen and men-at-arms dragged them apart. Nicholas's knuckles were skinned raw, and he saw with satisfaction that Sir Philip bled copiously from his mouth and nose. Sir Philip shrugged off the men holding his arms, and he spat, glaring at Nicholas.

Nicholas wasn't completely unscathed. By the time his arms were released, the vision in his right eye blurred from the blood dripping into it. Someone handed him a folded handkerchief, and he pressed it against his split brow. The row had eased some of the tension coiling him tight.

"Where is the rope!" he yelled.

A man came forward with a heavy hemp rope looped over his shoulder. Nicholas looked Sir Philip up and down. He was big—bigger than all the other men currently in the garden.

"I think I know where she is," Nicholas said. "Will you help me, or just let her die out there?"

Isobel dabbed at the blood on her husband's face with the corner of her arisaid, but she stopped at Nicholas's words and turned. Her eyes were full of fear and hope. "Is she alive?"

Nicholas swallowed hard. "God, I hope so."

Philip frowned deeply at Nicholas but said nothing.

Isobel looked up at her husband. "Philip? If it's true, you *must* help him."

Philip sighed and nodded reluctantly. "Aye, what do ye mean to do?"

They deemed Nicholas and Sir Philip too heavy, so they sent a smaller man over the side, rope tied securely about his waist. Nicholas and Philip, along with another large, red-bearded man named Fergus, paid out the rope. The wind blew strong out here, and they didn't know how far down the ledge was—if there even was one—or if they'd be able to hear shouts from below. So they worked out a series of tugs on the rope. One tug meant to pull him back up, he'd found nothing. Two tugs meant he'd found her and was securing the rope to her, followed by a third tug when he was ready for her to be brought up.

When the first tug came, Nicholas's heart stopped until the second one came seconds later. He didn't realize he'd made a noise until Sir Philip gave him an odd look over his shoulder. Nicholas had not wept since he was a bairn, but he was on the verge of tears now. His eyes had been dry and burning ever since she'd disappeared, disbelief and anger his only defense against black despair, but now he didn't know if he could control his emotions any longer. He prayed it was not a body they'd found but Gillian, alive and well.

He waited an eternity for the next tug. When it came, Nicholas had to stop himself from yanking the rope up too quickly. She was probably wounded, so they must be slow and gentle. Another man held Broc as he yipped and barked in anticipation.

He heard her agonized gasp of pain before he saw her, and it cut through him like a sword, clogging his throat with emotion.

"Hold tight," Philip said and released the rope.

Nicholas and Fergus took up Philip's slack, while the knight caught her left arm. Her right arm was tied to her side with the man-at-arm's shirt. She whimpered as Philip pulled her to her feet. Her gown was torn and dirty, her face covered with bruises and scratches. Her left hand had a deep, ragged cut across it, covered with crusted blood. Her hair was wild around her shoulders. She was beautiful. And she was *alive*.

Nicholas took a step toward her. Philip's arm came up, blocking his access. Nicholas's muscles tensed, ready to brawl again with the knight, but Gillian's confused and battered visage stopped him.

She looked from Philip's determined expression to Nicholas's pugnacious one with a worried frown. "Nicholas?" Her voice was soft and hoarse.

"Move." Nicholas grabbed Philip's wrist and squeezed.

"Wait," Philip said, refusing to lower his protective arm. "I want to ask her what happened."

"Look at her! She's been through hell. Let her rest."

"One question," the knight insisted, locking eyes with Nicholas.

"It's fine," Gillian said weakly. "I'll answer."

Nicholas released the knight's wrist.

"My lady, how came you to be on the ledge?"

Gillian shook her head slowly, fearful gaze fixed on Nicholas. "I don't know. Someone pushed me."

Fire sparked in Nicholas's blood. "Who?"

She shook her head again. "I know not."

Nicholas held out his hand to her. "Come here."

She took his hand readily, and Philip dropped his arm so she could pass. Nicholas wanted to crush her against him, bury his face in her wild tangle of sable hair, but she was obviously in pain. With as much gentleness as he could muster, he slipped an arm behind her back and another under knees, and carried her into Kincreag, cradled in his arms.

Though everyone assured Gillian she was lucky to be alive, it didn't feel so. With the danger of death or attack from large birds of prey removed, she had time to ponder other matters. And ponder them she did. Nicholas sat with her, holding her hand while Rose set her arm and cleaned all her cuts and scrapes, wrapping her left hand tightly to stop the fresh bleeding from the eagle talons. Gillian was one pulsing throb of pain.

In addition to Nicholas and Rose, Isobel and Sir Philip remained in her chambers. They watched Nicholas with suspicion, as if they expected him to leap on her at any moment and do her injury. There was one other occupant in Gillian's chambers, one who caused her much consternation. Tomas. He stood in a corner, leaning against the wall, his arms crossed over his chest. He never said a word.

Nicholas seemed disinclined to speak in front of Gillian's family, and they were equally uncommunicative. As Gillian was too busy contemplating all that had happened, the uncomfortable silence drew out interminably until finally Nicholas stood.

He leaned over Gillian and whispered, "I'll be back. Evan is interrogating the servants and men-at-arms. I want to check on his progress." From the hard gleam in his black eyes, she surmised he intended to participate in the interrogations.

Gillian gave him a tight smile. He kissed her bandaged hand, promised to be quick, and left.

When he was gone, Rose and Isobel descended on her.

"Come home with us," Rose urged, fiddling with Gillian's arm sling. "The air of Glen Laire will help you mend."

"I like the air here."

"But you're not safe," Isobel said. "This is the fourth attempt on your life since you've married Lord Kincreag."

"I know, and Nicholas is trying to protect me."

Rose made a rude noise. "He's not doing a very good job of it."

"Is that why everyone is acting so strange toward him? He's doing the best he can, truly. Getting pushed from the cliff is entirely my fault. I snuck out to the cliff path without his knowledge."

Isobel and Rose exchanged a sober look. Isobel took Gillian's hand. "Lord Kincreag was on the cliff path with you."

Gillian shook her head. "No. That's impossible."

"It's true," Rose said. "He claims a servant told him where you were."

"Then that's what happened."

Isobel's lips compressed with worry. "The servant doesn't exist, Gilly."

Gillian looked at her sisters in disbelief. "You think Nicholas pushed me?"

They said nothing, but their eyes said it all.

"That's absurd!" Gillian laughed, then grimaced

when pain stabbed her side and arm. "You're both mad. He's the one who found me! It was his idea to use Broc. He kept searching when everyone else had given me up for dead." Indignant anger rose in her chest as she spoke. "So stop these accusations now. I won't have you treating him like a murderer."

Her sisters were stunned at her outburst. Rose averted her gaze but had that stubborn look about her. Gillian knew she'd not give up her suspicions so easily. Isobel stared down at her folded hands, abashed.

Gillian made herself sit up, clutching her arm to contain the pain. "You can discover the truth, Isobel. Touch his things. Go help him question the servants." Isobel was a seer. When she touched objects, she often experienced visions about the owner.

Isobel licked her lips nervously. "I tried. I see nothing when I touch his things . . . some people are like that, they leave few impressions. And he refused to let me help with the interrogations."

Gillian leaned back and let out a noisy breath. "Well, that doesn't mean anything. He has forbidden me to use witchcraft." When they said nothing to this, Gillian rushed on defensively, "He's right, you know. People are dying for less than what we do. He's only trying to protect all of us."

They remained stubbornly silent.

Gillian's shoulders sagged. "It doesn't matter anyway. I don't think he can protect me from what wants me dead." At her sisters' alarmed expressions, she added, "It's nothing flesh and blood. I think it's the late countess."

A tiny line appeared between Isobel's pale brows. "Can a ghost do that?"

Gillian gestured to Tomas in the corner. "I don't know how, but they can. Remember the doll? Something is moving it. And Tomas has protected me twice now."

Isobel and Rose glanced at the corner uneasily. Rose leaned forward. "Is Tomas here now?"

"Who's Tomas?" Isobel asked.

Gillian told them about meeting Tomas on the ledge.

"We must somehow exorcise Catriona's ghost from Kincreag. Rose, you brought your spell books?"

"I brought a few. They might have something." She frowned at Gillian. "Are you certain about this? Two of the attacks were done by flesh-and-blood men, not a ghost woman."

Gillian's mouth compressed. "I've thought of that, and I don't have an answer yet. Maybe she's aided by a malevolent male spirit."

"Or maybe she can possess others," Isobel suggested.

"Oh, that reminds me! Rose, go to my writing desk." Gillian pointed with her bandaged hand. "Beneath the stone there is a piece of paper with strange writings on it. Do you recognize them?"

Rose returned to the bed, slanting blue eyes narrowed at the charred parchment. She shook her head slowly. "I've never seen this before. Very strange. This is what you wrote when you took the poppy juice?"

"Aye . . . though I don't recall writing it at all. Something inhabited my body and forced me to write it.

Tomas said it was a young lad. Probably the one who dropped the ballast on me. So aye, I suppose possession is possible."

Her sisters' expressions had gone from merely disturbed to frightened.

"What are we going to do?" Isobel asked, hands twisting in her lap. "How can we fight something we can't even see?"

"*I* can see them now," Gillian reminded them, "and with no pain. With a little magic, I'm sure the three of us can discover the truth and set things right."

Rose raised her auburn brows. "What about Kincreag? What if he finds out we're practicing witchcraft?"

"Don't worry about Nicholas. He need never know . . . and if he finds out . . ." Gillian's mouth flattened, her heart weighted with regret. "Well, I'll deal with that if it happens."

It was night when Nicholas returned to her. She awakened to his low voice, sending Isobel away. Gillian watched him in the dying firelight, muttering darkly as he undressed. She admired the hard planes of his back, the way muscle molded over ribs and shoulders, sleek and honey-dark. He slid into bed beside her. She slept on her back, a pillow beneath her broken arm. Nicholas's bare chest warmed the left side of her body. His hand slid over her stomach to hold her, and his head tilted on the pillow beside her, his mouth resting against her shoulder. He lay like that a long while, tension quivering from his body into hers.

"You're vexed," she whispered.

"You're supposed to be resting," he admonished softly.

"That's all I've been doing. I'm tired of resting. Why are you vexed?"

"Your brother-in-law has posted a Colquhoun clansman outside your bedchamber. Methinks he has little faith in my ability to take care of you."

Gillian smiled at the petulance in his voice. "I have great faith in you."

"Do you, Gillian? I seem to be doing a very poor job of it."

"You brought me up from that ledge. You alone didn't accept my death. I'm here now because of you."

His arm tightened on her waist, and his head tilted up. He pressed his mouth against her ear and whispered, "I love you."

Gillian's heart stopped. Then thundered forward in her throat and ears. Sweeter words she'd never heard. "Nicholas . . ." Then she recalled the love philter and sighed, feverish pulse slowing. "That's the love philter talking."

He laughed softly. "It's not."

"It is."

He took her earlobe between his teeth. Gillian instantly went limp, pleasure pricking deep.

"How can it be," he whispered, "when I never drank it?"

Gillian didn't move at all for several seconds; then she turned her head so fast they cracked noses. He jerked back with a grunt.

She rubbed her nose with a bandaged finger. "Why didn't you tell me?"

"Because it amused me that you believed in it with such a whole heart." He chuckled softly. "There might be something to it yet. Broc is the true recipient of the love philter."

Gillian let out a breath of disbelief, and then she laughed, too. "No wonder! But I didn't burn his fur."

"What?" He raised his head to gaze down at her in the shadowy light.

"In order to complete the spell I had to kiss you and burn your hair."

He rubbed his head absently. "That's why you ripped my hair out." As he regarded her, his demeanor changed, grew serious. He propped himself up on an elbow.

Uneasy tension gathered in her middle. She recognized that look. She averted her eyes, staring into the dark above her.

"Why did you go on the cliff path, Gillian?"

She didn't want to tell him, didn't want to talk about it, not now when everything was sweet between them.

"You were hunting ghosts, weren't you?"

Gillian hesitated, then nodded, bracing herself for his displeasure.

"Bloody Christ, Gillian. I almost lost you, and for what? For rustic superstitions. You're a countess now. Act like one and stop playing the village hag."

Gillian stiffened. *Village hag?* "I know you don't believe, but—"

He pushed up on his arm, leaning over her. Black hair slid over muscular shoulders, framing his unshaven face. He looked dark and devilish. "Damned right I don't, and I'm weary of having this same discussion."

"It's never been a discussion, Nicholas. You just lecture and forbid."

"That's because talking to you is like talking to a cow. You just nod placidly, then do whatever the hell you please."

Her eyes narrowed. "I never promised I wouldn't do it."

"Promise me now."

"I can't do that."

His lips drew back in a growl, and his black eyes burned murderously. "So help me, Gillian, if you don't promise me, I'll—"

Though she quailed inside, she knew in her heart he'd never harm her, so she returned his stare, brows raised expectantly. "You'll do what?"

"I'll lock you up like I did my first wife—only this time to protect you from yourself."

Her jaw dropped. "You wouldn't."

He lowered himself so their noses nearly touched, and his eyes narrowed maliciously. "Try me."

He meant it. She could see it in his eyes, hear it in his voice. She glared back at him, angry now, too. "Sir Philip would never lock Isobel up."

"Sir Philip hasn't the bullocks of a sparrow when it comes to your sister. He'll be a widower afore the year is out if he doesn't grow a spine."

If Gillian's arm and hand hadn't been in agony, she would have hit him. "You are a foul man."

His lips curved into a dark smile. "I warned you, love, you should have married the Frenchman." Then he kissed her forehead and settled himself beside her. "You've had your warning, wife. Next time there won't be any lectures."

19

Gillian sat on the window seat with Tomas and Stephen. The latter was much improved, though still weak from the poisoning. According to Rose he'd not ingested enough to cause himself any permanent damage. Today they all gathered in the west solar. Isobel sat before the dollhouse, touching everything in it. Rose was in her chambers, researching exorcisms. Sir Philip and his men loitered about, guarding Gillian and keeping the servants away. Evan was there, too, but he respectfully kept a distance.

It was for this reason that Gillian and her sisters were forced to apply much subterfuge. When Gillian conversed with Tomas, another person was always present so it appeared that Gillian spoke to that person rather than to nothing at all. Stephen served well in this capacity. His garrulous nature made it easy for him to contribute to a conversation even when he was privy to only one side of it. And since Isobel couldn't go about touching things and having visions in front of Sir Evan, they had decided the dollhouse was the perfect place for her to start. When sitting behind it, she was completely hidden from the knight's sight.

"Have you had any luck contacting Catriona?" Gillian asked Tomas.

He shook his head. He looked the same as he had on the ledge, the same as he always did in his green-and-red plaid, his auburn hair a bit too long. "She's here. I feel her, but that is all I ken."

"Where can I find more spirits?" He'd already directed her to two ghosts, but neither of them had proved helpful. Both were like Aileen, oblivious to aught but some endless task that engaged them. Gillian suspected these were not true ghosts, not like Tomas and Catriona. They were shades of their former selves, an imprint left behind. To Gillian, Tomas was as real as she was, able to think and reason and feel. She suspected his was a lost soul, somehow left behind. It pained her that she could do no more for him than ease his loneliness.

Tomas leaned back against the wall thoughtfully, arms crossed over his chest. "There's a man in the gatehouse, but he's utterly mad. He screams at me when I try to talk to him, and sometimes he runs, sometimes he tries to attack me. And then that wee lad, there." He nodded to the dollhouse. "I see him about sometimes."

Gillian startled. A small boy stood behind Isobel, watching her. He couldn't be more than two or three years old. His hair was thick and black, and he wore a white child's gown. Gillian stood, her heart trembling.

Could it be . . . ? She took several hesitant steps forward, and the boy looked at her over his shoulder. Enormous black eyes stared out from a dusky face. He looked just like his father.

"Malcolm?" Gillian said softly. Her heart swelled just looking at the boy, so small, so sweet.

He only stared at her solemnly.

"Good day, Malcolm." Gillian approached the spectral boy slowly. She didn't want to frighten him away. "Do you live here?"

He turned back to the dollhouse and darted to it, moving right through Isobel to climb onto the table. His dark feet were bare, small and rounded with baby fat. He snatched the blond doll from the tiny bed, leapt to the floor, and dashed away.

Sir Evan came forward, eyes narrowed. "Who are you talking to?"

"My sister," Gillian lied smoothly.

"But you said Malcolm."

Isobel stood from her stool and frowned at the knight. "No, she said malcontent. Whoever wants her dead is surely malcontented, and we must find him."

Sir Evan's brows drew together as he stared at the two of them. He opened his mouth as if to ask another question, then just shook his head and returned to his post across the room. No doubt he was in complete agreement with Nicholas on the state of Gillian's mind. Dotty.

She knelt behind Isobel's chair, careful of her broken arm, and whispered, "I saw Nicholas's son just now. He's the one who has been taking the doll."

Isobel's gaze went to the tiny bed, her eyes nearly popping when she saw that the blond doll had vanished.

"But why?"

"Catriona was his mother. I thought the doll was some kind of warning, a spirit trying to tell me Catriona's ghost meant me ill. But it's not at all what I'd thought. He must be playing, putting his mother where he thinks she belongs. Nicholas said he never played with the dollhouse because she and one of her lovers were always working on it. Perhaps it draws him now because it reminds him of her."

Isobel let out a breath. "Well, I've seen a great deal of her in this house. Many vile things are associated with it, but I don't see you, Gilly. Or Lord Kincreag, or anyone else alive now."

Gillian peered up at her sister quizzically. "Why would you be looking for Nicholas?"

Isobel's eyes slid to the side, and her lips parted hesitantly. "I . . . I . . ."

"You still think it was him, don't you?" Gillian stood abruptly, clutching her bad arm with her good to protect it. Her hand tightened to a fist. "He did not push me. Why won't you believe that?"

Isobel wouldn't look at her. "I just think you'd be safer at Lochlaire. For now."

"He loves me, Isobel."

Her sister's sage eyes finally turned to gaze up at her. "But he would lock you up for what you are. You are a witch. If he doesn't love that, he doesn't love you."

Gillian sank back to the ground beside her sister, her

anger deflated by Isobel's honest words. She wanted to discount them, to argue that he didn't believe in such things and so that wasn't the same thing as not loving her. But then, if he didn't believe in her, how could he love her?

The questioning of the servants and men-at-arms proved futile. No one knew anything. Evan was in agreement with Nicholas now that the attempts on Gillian's life were related, but currently their investigation was at a standstill. All he could do was guard her diligently and wait for the next attack. To that end he spent as much time with his wife as possible. When it wasn't possible, Evan was with her. In addition to Nicholas's precautions, Philip and his clansmen were a constant presence, hovering around the edges of Gillian and her sisters.

Nicholas knew they were up to something. Gillian's attitude had grown chill toward him since his threat to lock her up. He didn't regret the threat, only the necessity of it. She could be angry with him as long as she wanted. At least she was alive. Every time he looked at her, his heart relived the nightmare of losing her all over again. He'd rather her stare icicles at him than not have her at all.

He sighed and rubbed the bridge of his nose. His thoughts were often disquieting of late, distracting him from other matters. He set his documents aside and poured himself some whisky. Before he could take a drink, however, he was interrupted by a knock on his door.

"Aye?"

Evan stepped in. His gaze went to the cup in Nicholas's hand, and he hesitated.

"What is it?" Nicholas set the cup aside.

"It's Lady Kincreag, my lord. I think you'd better come with me."

When the knight's steps led to the cliff path, rage began to simmer in Nicholas's veins. His hands clenched into fists. He would throttle her for coming back here. And then he would throttle her sisters and Sir Philip for allowing her to. Dusk had fallen and a light fog swirled, obscuring the objects around them but not hiding them. He saw them on the path ahead, rising out of the fog. Three cloaked women holding hands, forming a circle. Three slender candles intersected their joined hands. They chanted, their voices low, thrumming through him. Sir Philip and his men stood around them, allowing this dangerous absurdity to take place.

The wind picked up, shrieking around them like a lost soul. Nicholas pushed past the men and grabbed Gillian's wrist, breaking the circle. The candle fell to the path and extinguished. She blinked up at him, dazed, as if she'd been in a trance.

He didn't say a word to her. Fury throbbed behind his eyes, nearly blinding him. He was beyond words. He dragged her down the path. She stumbled along after him. In the garden she dug in her heels.

"Stop, Nicholas! You've ruined it. Now we have to start over."

He picked her up around the waist and carried her.

"Nicholas!" She pushed at his arm with her good hand but quickly went limp. He smiled grimly, pleased she understood there was no use in fighting this. He took her back to his privy chambers and shut the door; then he locked it to keep her meddling family out.

He set her on her feet. Red blotched her skin from hairline to chest. "How could you?" she hissed.

Now that he had her alone and safe, some of his blind fury dissipated, and the furious beating of his heart slowed. "I told you what would happen."

"So I'm your prisoner now?" She rushed for the door, but he caught her shoulders.

He gave her a small shake. "I'm trying to keep you safe, with absolutely no help from you or your family."

"They *are* helping me."

"By taking you back out to the cliff where you nearly died?" He released her abruptly and backed away, the need to shake sense into her so great that he feared he would further injure her arm.

"No! By helping me exorcise the spirit of Catriona."

He rubbed his hands over his face and into his hair, wishing she wouldn't say these things. "Are you insane?"

She threw her hand up into the air as if he was the unreasonable one. "I'm trying to stay alive. You can't protect me because you refuse to see who truly threatens me."

"My dead wife? Bloody Christ, Gillian, stop it!" She tried to speak again, and his temper flared hotter. "Stop it! I can't listen to any more of this rot." He needed a drink before his head exploded. Gillian glared at him, white-lipped, left arm ramrod straight and fisted at her side.

He crossed to his desk, where the cup of whisky he'd poured earlier rested. He lifted it to his lips, then paused, peering into the cup.

"What the hell is this?"

A tiny doll floated on the surface of the whisky. He fished it out and dangled it in front of his face, scowling at it. "What is this? One of your charms?"

Gillian's expression of tight rage faltered, her eyes widening on the doll. "That's why he took the doll."

Nicholas crossed to the fireplace and tossed the whisky in it. The fire blazed up. "Who?"

When Gillian didn't answer, he turned to look at her. She looked tormented, her brows drawn up, white teeth worrying her bottom lip.

"Who?" he repeated, inspecting the wet doll with new interest. It had flax for hair and wore fine velvet clothes, ruined now from the whisky. It must have been part of the dollhouse in the west wing.

Gillian lifted her shoulders and turned away from him. "You wouldn't believe me anyway."

Nicholas closed his eyes, his head dropping forward as the irritation welled up inside. "Oh God. Let me guess. A ghost put it there? Kincreag's ghosts have nothing better to do than drop dolls in my whisky?"

"Malcolm doesn't."

Her soft words hit him like an ax and buried in his chest. His son was condemned to wander endlessly though Kincreag, trying to get Nicholas's attention by dropping dolls in his whisky? It was absurd. And it was cruel. His hand fisted around the tiny doll. He'd been as patient as he could be with all the other ghost nonsense she prattled on about, but this was too much. He flung the horrid thing away from him. It bounced off the wall and skittered beneath a cabinet.

Gillian turned, her gaze darting from the cabinet back to him.

"You've gone too far, Gillian. I don't know what you're trying to prove, or if you really think these things are happening, but I won't listen to another word. Do you understand?"

He expected an argument and prepared himself for it. But she didn't argue. Her large gray eyes regarded him with sadness and resignation. Her shoulders lifted as she took a deep breath. Then she crossed to the door.

"I'm leaving."

"No, you're not. I warned you. You'll be confined to your chambers until you can promise me—"

"No, Nicholas. I'm leaving Kincreag. I'm going to Lochlaire."

Her words brought him up short. "I won't let you."

"My father is dying. You would keep me from him?"

And that easily, she trapped him. A vise closed on his heart as he stared at her. "I'll go with you." The anger drained from his voice, making it sound hollow to his ears.

"I think it best I go alone—with my sisters, of course. Sir Philip and his men will escort and protect me."

Nicholas rubbed a hand over his mouth. "Gillian, wait . . ."

The door closed behind her, shutting him out.

20

In the end, Nicholas let her go. He almost changed his mind when he saw her, sitting wan and frail upon her gray horse. She'd been through a great deal. She should not be moved so soon. She needed rest. But when she refused to look at him as she passed through the gate, he did nothing, just stood there, stone-faced, hands clasped hard behind his back to hide their shaking. Evan rode beside her. She'd tried to refuse the knight's protection, but Nicholas had insisted. He'd made it clear to Evan that if anything happened to her, there would be the devil to pay.

Nicholas toyed with the urge to follow her, but he was still angry, too. He knew Gillian would never purposely be cruel to him, and yet he could not believe his son still roamed the halls of Kincreag, condemned to haunt this place. He'd been so small when he'd died. What God would sentence a baby to endless wandering? He couldn't believe it. He wouldn't.

He paced Gillian's chambers after she was gone. Most of her things were still here; she'd only taken some clothes. How long until she sent for the rest? They'd all pretended it was a temporary visit to Glen Laire, but Nicholas thought she would not be coming back, not unless he allowed her to become the Witch of Kincreag.

He stood at her writing table, fingering the elaborate plume of her quill. She'd left all her writing implements. The parchment was his, but she'd brought a fancy quill and a shiny black stone. He moved it aside and turned over the parchment beneath. He stared down at it for a long time, vaguely disturbed. It was covered with scrawled writing, and the edges were charred, as if she'd rescued it from a fire. He couldn't understand any words except *nave*. Was this about a church or a wheel? He scanned the page again. It was only five words, but they were written over and over again in increasingly frenzied handwriting. There was something familiar about the words, as if he knew them but couldn't understand them.

And then suddenly it made sense. Not nave—Evan. The words were written backward. He'd known a man once who wrote all of his notes backward, as a sort of code. He quickly scanned the words now, understanding them. *Be wary. Sir Evan. Nite.* Not *nite*—but *knight*.

He set the paper down, as if it were hot. Why would she write such a thing? Did she think Evan was in danger? Then why not tell Nicholas? He sighed, a dark cloud weighing him down. He could make no sense of anything Gillian said or did anymore.

He left her chambers feeling worse than he had before. Soon he found himself in the west wing. He trailed his hand over the top of the dollhouse as he circled it. Looking at it now, he was reminded of nothing so much as Gillian. It seemed odd that the sight of it had once troubled him so. He didn't care about any of that anymore. He just wanted his wife back.

He sat on the stool in the open part of the table and wondered what to do next. Again he considered going after her and bringing her home, but as neither of them was prepared to bend, it would be a pointless exercise. Maybe Alan would talk some sense into her.

He should get soused.

He stood, intent on searching out a good bottle of whisky, when he heard a crash. He turned back toward the darkened corridor that led into the bowels of the west wing. He heard nothing for a moment, then a rhythmic slamming. A shutter left open.

He considered sending someone else to find the miscreant shutter and secure it, but everyone except Gillian was afraid to venture into this part of the castle. She feared nothing. Thinking of her and her quiet courage hollowed out his chest, made him question his judgment. And that made him angry again.

He found the flint box and lit a candle. He followed the noise through the dark corridor, pausing when he spotted a candle flickering in a room to his right. The banging stopped abruptly.

He went into the room, heading straight for the windows. The shutters were all tightly secured. He frowned and turned to the candelabra. It held five candles, but only three burned. The candles were freshly lit, the wax hardly melted. He looked sharply around the room, wondering if someone was still here, hiding. It was clean, unlike the other rooms in the west wing, and devoid of the protective sheets that covered everything.

He opened the wardrobe. Women's gowns hung from pegs. He crossed to the chest and flung the top back. Hose, shifts, and an arisaid lay folded within. On the cupboard, the ewer was half full of fresh water. Someone was living here.

He opened the cupboard and found an array of cosmetics, including a white lotion that smelled of sulfur. Women at court artificially whitened their skin, but no one here did. At least no one since Catriona had died. There was a pot of fucus for reddening the lips and kohl for the eyes. When he saw the small brown glass bottle, his heart tripped. When was the last time he'd seen such an array of cosmetics? He unstoppered the bottle and sniffed, smelling the bitter belladonna Catriona had used to make her pupils large and velvety black. He opened a bottle of perfume, and the scent of civet and musk drifted out, gagging him, bringing forth unwanted shades of his late wife.

He shoved the bottle away, looking wildly around the room, his stomach clenched tight. Was this some kind of sick jest? He dug through the cupboard in earnest, coming up with a small wooden box. It was locked, and after a cursory search for the key, Nicholas threw it on the ground until it cracked. Coins spilled out—French and Italian, as well as some English and Scots. He pried the lid off with a splintering crack. Several pieces of jewelry were within: pearl earrings, an amber bracelet, a sparkling purple brooch.

He gazed around the room again, unsettled by the sudden eerie quiet, by the strange events that had brought him here to discover this room. Maybe he'd been too hard on Gillian for believing Kincreag was haunted. Something odd had just occurred. He wasn't quite ready to pin it on the supernatural, but he had no other explanation. Yet.

He replaced everything in the box and took it back to his chambers. He dropped it in the center of his desk and stared down at it. An uncomfortable knot formed in the pit of his stomach. Who the hell was living in his castle—obviously unbeknownst to him? He poured himself a cup of whisky and sat behind the desk, contemplating the box. Some of the jewelry was vaguely familiar. He set the whisky aside and dug out the pearl earrings. He'd given Catriona a pair of pearl earrings once that had looked very much like these.

From the corner of his eye he sensed movement and turned sharply. Nothing. He frowned, his gaze scanning every corner, but he was still alone. He lifted his cup only to find the doll bobbing on the surface of his whisky.

He set it down with a thump, amber liquid sloshing all over the desktop. His heart thundered, the skin all along his scalp and arms tightening. The doll had not been in the cup when he'd poured the whisky. Someone had placed it there in the short time since, and Nicholas was certain he was alone.

Or was he? He scanned the room cautiously, his

muscles tensed as if for flight. Someone didn't want him to drink the whisky. Nicholas stood, cup in hand, and tossed the contents into the fire. What was it? Poison? He set the cup on the desktop and covered his mouth with both hands, eyes constantly searching the room, heart pounding erratically.

The first time this had happened, Gillian had said it was his son.

He dropped his hands and tried to force a swallow past his tight throat. "Malcolm?" It felt ludicrous to call out to his dead son, but Gillian had said . . .

And then he saw him, standing before the door to the bedchamber, wearing his nightshirt. Nicholas grasped the edge of the desk, his eyes burning. He couldn't choke out a single word, could only stare. His son stared back, his dark eyes large and sad. Why was he so sad? Nicholas's heart squeezed just to look upon his small face. His vision blurred, and he scrubbed at his eyes with his sleeve. When he dropped his arm, Malcolm was gone.

Nicholas's heart beat twice into the frozen silence. He ran to the bedchamber door and flung it open. "Malcolm, wait!"

"Malcolm?"

"Jesus God." Nicholas's stomach hit bottom.

Catriona stood in his bedchamber. Golden hair flowed over her shoulders. She gazed back at him with wide, dark eyes. Her skin was white and bloodless, her lips unnaturally red. She wore a fine gown of periwinkle silk. Aquamarines dangled from her ears.

Another ghost, and this one talked. He took a step

toward her, and from the folds of her gown a dag appeared. She leveled it at him.

Why would a ghost need a gun? It hit him then like a fist to the gut. Catriona was not dead. She was living in the west wing of his castle and trying to kill both him and Gillian. He'd never guessed, not even when he'd found the damned room. Gillian was right; he *was* blind.

"Go back into your privy chamber," she said.

He did as she ordered. His mind scrambled, looking for a way out of this. Catriona's gaze flicked from the whisky decanter to the cup on the desk. "Had a drink?" She motioned to it with the barrel of her gun.

"Aye . . ."

She crossed to the cup and peered into it. Finding it empty, she smiled. "Good." She backed up, returning to his bedchamber. "Let's go."

He followed her warily, waiting for her to make some misstep so he could disarm her. The dag was primed and ready, and her finger rested on the trigger.

She jerked the barrel toward the bed. "Lie down."

"I don't want to."

"You will."

He didn't like the sound of that. He crossed to the bed and sat on it. She stood a few feet from him, dag leveled at his face.

"Why did you say Malcolm before?"

"I thought I saw him."

The skin around her painted mouth tightened. "He's dead."

"I know. Did you poison him, Cat?"

She looked him over consideringly, then nodded. "He was sick. He was suffering. I ended the suffering."

Nicholas couldn't speak. Grief choked him, made it difficult to breathe. He heaved a painful breath. *Oh God, Oh God.* She'd killed her own son. *His* son. He might have saved Malcolm if only he'd seen. He was so God damned blind.

"There, there, Nicholas," she murmured, her voice soft and soothing. "It will all be over soon." She thought she'd poisoned him and that his suffering had begun.

He closed his eyes. The tears of anguish and fury squeezed out anyway. He leaned over, his hand over his gut as if in pain, and gasped, "Is that what you did for your servants? Ended their suffering."

She gripped the dag hilt harder. "Aye. We're all suffering in these bodies. I'm helping."

"And who's helping you?"

She didn't answer. Her eyes were fixed on his face, evaluating. He surmised she'd used this poison many times and knew the signs. He must be clever. He groaned loudly and tipped over on the bed, pressing his face into the velvet covers.

"Aye, that's it. Lay down, Nicholas. It will all be over soon."

When he chanced another look, her expression was soft. She drew out a long, sinuous sigh, the tension in her body releasing. She derived great pleasure from this. It was evident in every line of her body, in the darkening of her eyes and the curving of her lips.

"You came back just to poison me?"

"Aye. I've been all over the Continent, but I couldn't forget you."

"How many husbands have you buried?"

"Five—counting the first. But not you. You're the one that got away." She moved closer to the bed.

Nicholas rolled around a bit, holding his stomach and groaning dramatically.

"I know it hurts," she soothed, "but it will be over soon, I promise, and I'll be with you, at the end."

"Someone's been giving you aid," Nicholas said through clenched teeth.

"I've thought about you so much," she said as if she hadn't heard him, her voice soft and urgent. "Nearly every day. It's never been the same."

She was insane. He'd suspected that before she faked her death, but she was completely mad now. She *enjoyed* murder. It excited her.

"What do you want?" he ground out.

"I want to hold you, Nicholas. I want to hold you as the life passes away." Her knee was on the bed, the gun still pointed at his head. "I held Malcolm as he passed away. Did you know that?"

"How could you? I locked you up."

"I had help. Even then."

He turned his face into the bed again, to hide the rage boiling in his gut, rising to swallow his heart. His hands clenched into rigid fists. He would kill her; he would choke her, just like she murdered his son.

"*Who?*"

"Oh, he's dead now."

"Who's helping you now?"

"It doesn't matter."

Nicholas made an anguished sound and brought his knees up. "Why Gillian?"

She touched his leg, trailing her fingers down his thigh. "Do you know how rich I am, Nicholas? I have the fortunes of three husbands. Rich husbands. But not my first husband's wealth and not yours. You have it all. It should be mine. I earned it. After your bride is dead and you've committed suicide, I'll return to claim it all."

"You faked your own death. No one will believe you."

"But they will. I was terrified. Who wouldn't be, married to the Devil Earl, murderer of innocent women and children, and a few not so innocent men? At least that's what everyone believes. And they'll believe me when I tell them I had to run. I had to hide. You would have hunted me down and killed me otherwise."

"Gillian's gone. You can't hurt her anymore."

She made a soft sound, her fingers ruffling his hair. The gun barrel slid down to press just under his chin. "Lover, she's never been safe. Evan is mine. He's probably stringing her from a tree for witchcraft right now."

Nicholas's stomach gripped in earnest. *No. Not Gillian.*

"Oh, dear. I know how fond you are of her. Fash not, you'll soon be together."

Nicholas's arm snapped up, seizing her wrist and twisting the gun away. It discharged. The explosion was deafening. Black smoke engulfed them. He caught her by the throat and pinned her to the bed, squeezing, the rage clouding his mind. She'd murdered his tiny son.

Smoke burned his eyes so that tears streamed down his face. His ears still rang from the shot. She clawed at his hand, her legs kicking. *Gillian.* She might still be alive.

He released Catriona's throat and jerked her off the bed. His chest heaved. "You're going to take me to my wife."

Her hands circled her throat as she swallowed convulsively. Her head bobbed in a terrified nod.

"And you'd better hope she's still alive."

21

By the time they passed through the village at the base of the mountain, Gillian began to have misgivings. He'd not come for her. She'd wanted him to come for her. Prayed for it. Not to lock her up but to tell her he was wrong, to beg her forgiveness for his pigheadedness.

But he did not come. As the day wore on, Gillian began to wonder if she was wrong. He was only trying to protect her, and she had been making that a rather difficult task for him. Uncertainty and frustration warred in her breast, leaving her frustrated and despondent by the time night fell.

She was still tormenting herself when they stopped for the night. Camp was set up, and Rose checked Gillian's arm and hand dressings. They settled down around the fire. Sir Evan disappeared into the darkness to check the perimeter. He hadn't spoken a word to her all day. Not that he was ever especially talkative, but she couldn't help but feel he disapproved of her decision to abandon his master.

Gillian didn't know what to think anymore. There was no right or wrong. It all felt wrong if they weren't together. She lay on the ground, a rolled plaid braced behind her to keep her from rolling onto her right arm in her sleep. In her mind she went over and over everything that had happened, and sorrow settled over her like a blanket. She loved Nicholas. And yet he would imprison her for what she was.

She should have shown him—taken him to the dollhouse so he could see the doll appear and disappear for himself. She should have tried harder. But what good would it have done? The anger sparked again. He thought she was insane. Not merely dotty anymore but a madwoman. Then she thought of his eyes and his dusky skin and his arms around her, his laughter and teasing, and the emptiness yawned wide in her heart. Tears scalded her eyes.

Beside her Rose lifted her head, sharp eyes scanning the darkness.

"What is it?" Gillian whispered.

Before Rose could answer, all hell broke loose.

Gillian was no stranger to raids, having lived on the borders since she was ten. However, they'd always had the tower to run to for protection, where they could light a signal fire and wait for help to arrive. Here they didn't even have a fire. Sir Philip had ordered them doused after they'd eaten, so they would not attract attention.

There was no moon to shed light, and everything

was a dark mass of confusion—screaming and yelling, the clash of metal, the report of guns, gunpowder and smoke flavoring the air, the meaty thwack of fists hitting flesh. Gillian struggled to free herself of her blanket, her heart pumping, her arm hampering her ability to move quickly. Isobel screamed somewhere to her right. Gillian jerked toward the sound. She was grabbed beneath the arms and hauled to her feet.

"Come on." It was Stephen. He led her toward a copse of bushes and boulders. She stumbled, her breath sawing in her lungs. He caught her, trying to help her up, but then he sagged to the ground. Gillian stared dumbly at the dark crumpled shape of him, a horrified scream rising in her throat. Someone yanked her around.

A face was thrust into hers. It stunk of garlic and sour ale. Gillian whimpered and tried to twist away. Another man was behind her. He fingered her braid, pulling roughly on it. Gillian screamed and struggled. A torch was thrust in her face, and the bearded visage of a filthy man peered at her.

"That's her," another said. "He said her arm was broken. Let's go!"

She heard the Gaelic shout for retreat. A horse raced at her, and Gillian was thrust up into someone's arms, wrenching her broken limb. Pain radiated through her. She screamed. A gloved hand clamped over her mouth, muffling her cries of distress. Her stomach pitched queasily from agony and her captor's stench. As they galloped through the darkness, the pain dimmed to a dull throb. Gillian fell silent, trying to determine where they were going. It was dark, but it appeared they headed northeast, back toward Kincreag.

She could see little of her abductors in the darkness, but she was aware of a great many men, outnumbering Gillian's party several times. How many men had died? What of Stephen and Sir Philip? What of her sisters? Sir Evan? She prayed he'd gotten away and returned to Kincreag. Nicholas would come for her. Once Sir Evan told him, nothing would stop him from protecting her. Tears burned tracks down her cheeks. That's all he'd ever wanted to do—protect her.

Dawn lightened the sky, and Gillian was finally able to see. A man at the front of their party was familiar, and as the light grew stronger, she realized with a sinking heart that it was Sir Evan. But the longer she stared, the more she realized something was not quite right. He was not bound, nor had he been disarmed. And when he shouted an order to one of the kidnappers, the air left her all at once. He was not a prisoner. He was the leader. Gillian couldn't believe it. Nicholas trusted him. She'd trusted him.

They rode on, betrayal turning Gillian's fear to bitter anger. Excepting their party, there wasn't a human in sight for miles. The landscape was austere, barren, craggy rocks jutting up from the lichened ground and rough bracken. They topped a rise, and in the distance rose a hill with a tree atop it. An enormous ancient oak, its black branches twisted and gnarled, reaching for the sky. A body dangled from a branch, swaying in the breeze. A woman dressed entirely in black stood on the hill beside the body, waiting.

A hanging tree. Fingers of panic climbed Gillian's throat and held tight. A hanging tree. This was not a mere kidnapping for ransom. Sir Evan meant to hang her.

The thick stink of decay hung like a cloud around the hill. As they neared, the birds feasting on the body scattered. The dull face of the woman in black was suddenly animated, and she ran at them, shrieking, "Go away! Leave this place!"

The horses grew skittish, jerking their heads and rearing, eyes rolling, shying from the tree. No one else paid attention to the woman. They didn't even look at her.

"Cut it down," Evan ordered.

One of the men dismounted and started for the tree—passing right through the woman as she ran about, screeching mournfully.

Gillian gasped. The woman was a ghost. Gillian had not yet grown accustomed to seeing them.

"What's wrong?" her captor asked, his arm tightening around her waist, his other hand hard on the reins to control his frightened horse.

"Nothing."

The body hit the ground with a sickening *thwack*. They kicked it down the hill. A rope was thrown over the thickest branch, and a noose was fashioned.

Gillian was weak with fear, her heart laboring painfully. Her neck craned all around as she looked for some sign of Nicholas or her sisters. But there was no one. Just the ghost woman.

Her captor dismounted, leaving Gillian atop the

horse. Sir Evan rode his horse beside hers. "Are you ready, Mistress MacDonell?"

He said it so normally, just as he always spoke to her. She could only stare at him for a moment, hoping in her heart he was the same Sir Evan. And perhaps he was. His square-jawed face was stone. His pale blue eyes were cold and empty as he regarded her. They'd always been so.

"You pushed me off the cliff," she said.

"Aye."

"Oh my God . . . why did you address me as Mistress MacDonell?"

He grabbed her horse's reins. "Because there can only be one countess, and the first isn't dead."

Sick dread hit her hard. Catriona had been trying to kill her, except she wasn't a ghost at all. And Nicholas was alone with her at Kincreag.

"Nicholas will kill you for this."

His frigid eyes never flickered. "He'll never know. If he's not already dead from poison he'll believe you murdered for witchcraft—just like your mother."

"Why? Why would you do this? Nicholas was good to you! He trusted you!"

"The countess pays better." As they climbed the hill, Sir Evan's eyes lighted on the noose, and a small smile curved his normally granite mouth. "And I like the work."

Gillian's horse shied from the tree, rearing on its back legs. Evan tried leading it to the noose from several angles, but it refused. This caused some consternation among the men, who were trying to decide why the horses didn't seem to like the hill. Gillian could have told them a ghost flew at them every time they came near, screaming at them to go away, but no one asked her.

Finally Evan ordered her off her horse. Her bearded captor dragged her down and led her up the hill, to the noose dangling from the tree limb. Gillian couldn't catch her breath. She dropped her weight back, bending her knees, but he just picked her up. He set her down behind the noose. She stared into his face, her eyes beseeching him to help her. He never met her gaze. He removed the sling that held her right arm immobile and pulled her broken arm around behind her. She screamed out, the world fading as pain ripped through her.

"Dinna fash," someone said. "Soon there will be no more pain."

Gillian sagged against her captor until the pain receded. Then she pushed away, standing rather wobbly but under her own power. The ghost had stopped her mindless shrieking. She stood beside Gillian, peering intently into her face. Her skin was brown and as wrinkled as a walnut, and her graying black hair stood out around her head.

"Dinna fash," she repeated. "Just go to the light, aye, and it will be well."

"Please," Gillian said, her voice hoarse, remembering how Tomas had attempted to aid her. He'd protected her from the ballast and had nearly stopped her from falling off the cliff. "Help me."

The woman nodded comfortingly. "Aye, aye. Go to the light."

Evan had been watching her with a narrow gaze. He made the sign of the horns. "Witch," he hissed.

A noose slipped over her head. Gillian swayed, fighting to keep on her feet, the pain in her arm stabbing through her repeatedly. Despair and hopelessness had her by the throat, leaving her weak and sick. The unthinkable was happening, and there was no rescue. She just wanted it to end quickly.

Evan rode his horse close to Gillian and gazed down at her, a small smile curving his cruel mouth. "You should have listened to Kincreag, Witch. We had a much harder time when he protected you. You made it easy for me."

Gillian spat at him.

The ghost woman's face distorted in sudden fury. She raised her arms, and she ran screaming at Evan's horse. It reared and shrieked, pawing frantically at the air. Evan worked to control the frenzied horse as it fought to bolt. The horse tipped backward, sliding down the hill on its side. Evan managed to jerk his foot from the stirrup and roll away. At the bottom of the hill, the horse struggled to its feet and cantered away, riderless.

Evan stared after his horse, swearing angrily. He crossed himself, then made the sign of the horns at Gillian again and backed away, giving the signal to the men behind Gillian.

The rope pulled taut about her neck, though her feet remained firmly on the ground. Gillian's breath caught, her heart straining in her chest. She closed her eyes and prayed for her soul, prayed for Nicholas to be safe and not too angry with her, prayed that her sisters were still alive and well. The ghost was beside her again, exhorting her not to worry, to go to the light, all would be well.

Gillian's head shot up when she heard a far-off barking, growing steadily nearer. She rose reflexively on her tiptoes, but it did no good. Her body jerked abruptly upward as the noose pulled tight. The air dried up, and the world went red. Two shots rang out and she hit the ground, the acrid scent of gunpowder surrounding her. She lay there, still barely able to pull in air, her lungs struggling.

Swords clashed around her; guns discharged. Her name was shouted several times. Nicholas. Wetness on her cheek, snuffling in her ear. Broc. When Nicholas called her name again, she feared he might get himself killed if she didn't show some sign of life. She rolled onto her left side and pushed herself up, blinking at the world around her.

The man who had stood behind her, pulling the rope to hang her, lay sprawled on the hillside, his blood draining into the dirt. Gillian averted her eyes.

The fighting ended quickly, with the broken men taking to the hills. Nicholas bent over a body sprawled on the rise of the hill. He wiped his sword across the corpse's plaid and sheathed it. Evan.

Nicholas climbed the hill toward her, his gaze scanning the area before settling on her. He dropped to one knee beside her. He smelled of blood and fear and gunmetal. Gillian leaned against him and inhaled. His fingers were on her neck, loosening the noose.

He tossed the noose aside and smoothed his hand over her hair, tilting her chin up with his other. She gazed up into his black eyes and saw what he had gone through, the worry, the fear.

"You're killing me, Gillian."

She smiled and closed her eyes, ready to collapse with fatigue. Her muscles quivered with pain. "I know." He was everything safe and good in her world, and now that he was here, she could finally rest.

He worked the bindings loose from her wrists and gently folded her broken arm onto her lap, apologizing all the while for hurting her. Gillian cried silently and bit her lip until it bled.

He held her against his chest for a long while, rocking, his face pressed into her hair. One of his men addressed him, asking for orders, but Nicholas did not reply. Finally he said, "We have to go now."

Gillian's eyes fluttered open. Nicholas helped her to her feet. The woman in black was still there, smiling at Gillian.

"Why don't you go to the light?" Gillian asked her. Her voice was a rasp, barely audible, but the woman understood her.

Nicholas raised a quizzical brow.

"Oh, I will," the woman said. "Fash not on me. But there's work for me still here." She nodded sagely. "Ye're blessed, ye are. Methinks there's work for you, too." And then she was gone.

Nicholas looked at the empty air where Gillian gazed. "You weren't talking to me, were you?" His voice was resigned.

"No. You're not going to yell at me now, are you? Can't it wait until we get home?"

His lips curved ruefully. "Aye, it can." He found her sling and refashioned it. Gillian saw her then. Catriona. She was on horseback, her hands bound before her, surrounded by guards. She watched Gillian and Nicholas.

Nicholas fussed with the sling, staring at his handiwork with displeasure. "Your sister may have to reset this."

"We're not really married, are we?"

Nicholas looked up quickly and followed her gaze. His jaw hardened. "No."

"What will happen to her?"

"I'll take her to Edinburgh, where she'll answer for her crimes. She will likely be executed. But if for some reason she isn't, I will divorce her. The law is clear in matters of adultery and desertion, not to mention infanticide."

Gillian's eyes widened. "She admitted to it."

He gave a curt nod.

Gillian's heart ached for him, and she wished there were something she could say to make it better. But she knew there was nothing. She leaned against his shoulder. "I'm sorry, Nicholas."

He slid an arm around her and touched her cheek, sliding his fingers down to trace the marks the rope had left on her neck. "You can undo it now, if you wish. If you don't want me. Our marriage never was."

Gillian closed her eyes, turning her face into his plaid. She didn't want to think of this now. She just wanted to sink into his arms and forget this awful day, pretend everything was fine in their world. But that was impossible. The matter lay between them, the wounds still raw.

"What do you want?" she asked softly, afraid of his answer. "A wife or a prisoner?"

"I want a witch. I want you."

She looked up quickly in surprise and disbelief and unbearable happiness.

He smiled at her expression. "Will you marry me again?"

"Aye. And again and again."

22

Castle Kincreag seemed an empty, cavernous labyrinth with Nicholas gone. It had been nearly a fortnight since he'd left for Edinburgh to turn Catriona over to the king's justice. After the raid, Gillian's sisters had returned to Kincreag, relieved to find her safe. Sir Philip had lost some men, but thankfully he and Stephen had sustained only minor injuries. Rose did not stay on, returning to Glen Laire and their father, but Sir Philip and Isobel were to remain at Kincreag until Nicholas returned.

Before leaving, Rose had lectured Gilchrist on how to care for Gillian's arm properly. It was improving, but would be at least another week before she could take it out of the sling.

"Do you remember it now?" Isobel asked one afternoon as they strolled through the garden. "Mother's death?" Isobel watched her, silver-green eyes anxious, fearful of what Gillian would say but unable to curb her curiosity any longer.

Gillian had spent so long avoiding the memory, both consciously and unconsciously, that it hadn't immediately occurred to her to try to recall it. But over the past few days she'd begun to think about it rather cautiously. She cast her mind back to the day her mother had been lynched and burned, and her own frantic flight back up the mountain pass.

She'd fallen and had been lying on the ground crying. She'd seen the smoke, and even at ten years old she'd known what it meant, but her heart had refused to accept it. She'd felt a soft breeze across her cheek, almost a caress, and had looked up. "Mum?"

Her mother had stood beside her, smiling down at her. She'd shimmered and wavered in the sunlight, the mountainside visible through her body.

"I have to go now," she'd said. "They're at the light, calling to me. I'll see you there. But not now."

Gillian had cried for her mother not to leave her, but Lillian had turned away, her face glowing with wonder as she'd looked at something behind her. Then she was gone. Gillian had been hysterical when she'd finally been found, babbling about her mother and ghosts. Alan had taken his men and raced to her rescue. But it had been too late; her mother was dead. He'd not returned for weeks, intent on his fruitless hunt for the culprit. Uncle Roderick had recovered Lillian's ring and given it to Gillian—a remembrance.

Gillian's finger twitched as she looked down at her bare hand. "I lost the ring."

"The ring?"

"Mother's ring, the one I always wore. I removed it on the ledge after I fell."

Isobel took her hand and squeezed it. "It doesn't matter. You have the true gift she gave you, and that's more important than a piece of metal."

"Aye, but it doesn't explain why someone cursed me." After a long moment, Gillian reluctantly gave voice to what truly troubled her. "Rose's counter curse didn't work. I made the connection while I lay on the cliff ledge. When I removed the ring, the pain in my head disappeared and has not returned. It was the ring."

"Someone cursed the ring?" Isobel breathed, eyes wide. "Who could have done that?"

Gillian shook her head. "I don't know. Uncle Roderick brought it back for me . . . but who knows who had it before him?"

"We may never know now. But whoever cursed it thought you might be a threat because of what you see. How were they to know that you saw nothing but Mother moving on to her reward?"

"The light," Gillian murmured. "The boy that dropped the ballast, he came to me after his death, when I'd taken the theriac. He was looking at something just before he disappeared, just as Mother did. They both looked so . . . radiant when they looked at it. And the woman at the tree told me to go to the light. *The light.* Do you think it's heaven?"

"It must be someplace important."

"She said I had work to do."

They walked in silence for a few minutes. Broc rustled around in the bushes, chasing after mice and snapping at dragonflies.

"Maybe," Gillian said thoughtfully, "some ghosts don't know about the light . . . and that's why they're still here?"

"Maybe so," Isobel said. "Maybe that is your work."

Later that day Gillian found Tomas in the west wing, sitting by the window in the solar. She'd seen him when she'd returned to the castle and had told him what had happened. It had upset him, and she'd not seen him since.

"You seem very unhappy, Tomas," Gillian said, and he did. He was a mournful figure, wrapped in his plaid and gazing dolefully out the window. He'd been a handsome man. He'd died young, perhaps Gillian's age. He had startling green eyes and soft auburn hair. And he'd been so kind to her. It saddened her that he was trapped here.

He shrugged. "I'm dead. I dinna think I'm supposed to be happy."

"You said before that you don't know how to move on to heaven, or if you're meant to."

Tomas nodded, looking back out the window morosely.

"Do you see a light?"

He looked at her sharply. "What about it?"

She leaned forward, a jolt of excitement surging through her. "You *do* see it!"

"Aye, but I dinna ken what it is . . . I did some verra bad things when I was alive . . . I . . . I'm afraid to go there."

"You think it's hell?"

He shrugged, then, after a moment, nodded.

"I don't know what you did, Tomas, but I've seen other spirits pass on to the light, and they're happy. I think it's a good place. Their faces when they go are full of rapture."

Tomas's eyes filled with longing. He looked over his shoulder, at something Gillian couldn't see. Then he turned back to her. "I dinna know . . . are ye sure?"

"Aye, I'm sure," Gillian said softly. "My mother was a good woman who never did anyone harm. She went there."

He looked so torn. She could see in his face that he wanted to believe her but was too afraid. "I dinna know," he said again. He seemed less certain now.

"I think this must be your hell, Tomas. A shadow in your old life, one that no one can see or hear. And you've condemned yourself to it. Go on, it's over now."

He stood and gave her a hesitant nod. And then he was gone.

It was another week before Nicholas returned. When Gillian received word that he was sighted climbing the cliff road, she was beside herself with excitement. He seemed larger than she remembered, tall and leanly muscled. He wore black breeks and a dark leather doublet. A plaid mantle was thrown carelessly over his broad shoulders. He seemed a bit hesitant and shy when he dismounted in the courtyard. Gillian ran to him, and he caught her up in his arms.

"I missed you," he whispered into her hair. Then he stepped back. "Your arm is better?" He ran a gentle hand over it.

"It still hurts a bit, but I can use it. Rose showed me exercises that will strengthen it."

"You do them, or I'll tell her."

Gillian grimaced at the thought of how her sister dealt with recalcitrant patients. Nicholas took her hand, gazing down at her warmly, and led her back into the castle. There was a strange bearded man traveling with him, dressed entirely in sober black. Gillian asked about him.

"Och, it's a churchman I brought back to marry us tonight."

Gillian smiled to herself but asked, "So it's done?"

He didn't say anything, and when she glanced up at him, his mouth was grim.

"Nicholas?" Gillian said, worried now.

He stopped and put his hands on her shoulders. "It's done. She was executed. I stayed to make sure she was really dead this time."

A great weight lifted from Gillian's heart, and relief settled over her. "So it really is over."

Nicholas looked around warily. "Unless she returns to haunt me."

Gillian's eyes narrowed. "I thought you didn't believe in ghosts."

He took a deep breath, then put his arm around her and led her through the hall. "That was before."

"Before what?"

"I told you Catriona tried to poison me, but I didn't tell you how I knew the whisky was poisoned."

"Aye, you did. The doll."

He gave her a sideways look. "That's not all."

He led her into his chambers and shut the door. He seemed so uncertain, so unlike himself that Gillian was both bursting with curiosity and uneasy about what he wanted to say.

He licked his lips and took another deep breath, then he faced her and said, "I saw my son."

Gillian sat on the bed. "You *saw* him."

Nicholas nodded. His face was tight, his palms pressed together in front of him, "You were right. He put the doll in the whisky. He knew his mother was trying to kill me. He . . ." Nicholas briefly closed his eyes and swallowed hard. Composed again, he continued, "He's been watching over me all this time. I would dream about him coming to my room at night to watch me sleep, except . . . I think I knew in my heart he wasn't a dream. But to contemplate my own child . . . such a wee lad, haunting Kincreag . . ." He shook his head and stared at the floor. "I suppose it was just too much for me to bear."

Gillian went to him and stroked a hand up his arm. "I don't think he was haunting Kincreag. I think he was waiting."

He looked up at her, confusion and hope marring his brow. "Waiting?"

"Aye, to protect you. And now that the danger is gone, I haven't seen him at all."

"You think he's gone on to heaven?"

"Aye. I looked for him, to help him to the light, but he's nowhere to be found. Even Tomas hasn't seen him."

Nicholas took a shuddering breath, hands braced on his hips, gaze again directed downward. He nodded. "Good," he said, then nodded again, his throat working. "Good."

He crossed to the cabinet against the wall and poured water into the basin. "Who's Tomas?"

"Tomas Campbell . . . he was haunting Kincreag until recently. I meant to ask him how he died. . . . Nicholas? Are you all right?"

He'd been splashing water from the basin over his face while she talked, but had stopped, the water dripping down his dark skin and glistening in ebony whiskers. His eyes were wide with shock. "Did you say Tomas Campbell?"

"Aye. Did you know him?"

Nicholas swiped the water off his face with a towel and sat heavily on the bed. "Aye . . . I knew him."

Gillian joined him. "What is it?"

He let out a loud breath. "Jesus, Gillian . . . Tomas Campbell was the carpenter . . . the one that Catriona brought with her when we wed . . . the one who built the dollhouse. The only one of her men I thought I killed."

Gillian's brows shot up.

"I found them together and beat him . . . he fell onto the dollhouse and crushed the side of it. But the wounds weren't mortal. He was sore beat but alive. Then he just died two days later."

"Catriona," Gillian gasped, hands over her mouth. They sat in silence for a time, thinking about Tomas and Malcolm.

Then Nicholas took her hand and enclosed it in both of his. "There were so many . . . she had so many men ensnared, like a spider with her web. Do you know she poisoned five husbands? Their children, too. No one knows how many lovers and servants."

Gillian shook her head slowly, her throat tight. "But why? Why would she kill them all? I guess I understand the husbands, to get their money, but why children and servants? It makes no sense."

"I know not. Except . . . she enjoyed it. I saw that in her eyes when she thought I was dying. It gave her power, like some angel of death. She was truly evil."

He cast a leery look around the room. "I wonder how many ghosts are here. Will Evan come back, think you? Are they vengeful in death?"

Gillian squeezed his hands. "I don't believe they are. Tomas wasn't vengeful."

He slid her a wry look. "Did you exorcise him?"

"No, I just showed him the light."

He raised a skeptical eyebrow.

"You don't believe me?" she asked tartly and tried to stand.

He caught her about the waist and pulled her back onto the bed, his arms around her. "Oh, I believe you." His mouth covered hers in a soft kiss as he lowered her back onto the bed. "After all, you showed me the light, too."

POCKET BOOKS
PROUDLY PRESENTS

My Shadow Warrior
Jen Holling

**Available in paperback August 2005
from Pocket Books**

**Turn the page for a preview
of *My Shadow Warrior*. . . .**

M y lord? She's still out there. In the rain."

William flicked a disinterested glance at the large, scarred man-at-arms standing in the doorway, wringing his hands. The rather incongruous sight gave him a brief prick of amusement.

When he made no response, Wallace went on, "She'll catch her death, she will. At least let me show her to the stables."

William's brother Drake made a rude noise. He lounged in William's chair before the fire, a leg slung over the carved arm, jet-black hair gleaming in the firelight. "Serves her right if she does catch her death. It's not my lord's fault if she's stupid enough to stand out in the rain like a coof."

"She's not stupid," William said. The carved wooden box on his desk drew his gaze. "She'll get out of the rain eventually." His gaze swept the room. "Leave me."

Drake stood and stretched but didn't leave. When the others were gone, he gave William a keen look. "You're acting strange."

"Rumor has it I *am* strange."

Drake lifted a shoulder and palm to acknowledge that. "Aye, well, more so than usual. You seem preoccupied since the MacDonell lass arrived."

That was true, but William didn't mean to discuss it with Drake. "I'm well enough."

Drake hesitated, as if there was more he wanted to say, but finally left. Alone at last, William crossed the room to his desk. He rested a hand on the wooden box, pensive. Why had he kept that letter? He'd burned all her others. He tapped the lid of the box. The musing question repeated itself with each tap of his fingers against the wood. *Why? Why? Why?*

He removed the letter and held it in his hand, still folded, still bearing the broken red wax and her bold scrawl: *Deliver to Lord William MacKay of Strathwick.*

He had known immediately something was wrong when he'd received this letter. All her letters were full of desperation and pleading—and authority. Her father was dying. He was her only hope. God commanded it of him. Her audacity made him smile. But still, he'd burned all the others. It had never occurred to him to reply.

This letter, however, had been different. His name across the front was uneven, scrawled, lacking the brazen confidence of the others. He strolled to the fireplace, fingers caressing the parchment. He stared down at the folded letter. *Feed it to the flames.*

Instead he sat, leaning back in his chair, and unfolded it for perhaps the hundredth time since receiving it.

My dearest Lord Strathwick,

Why do you ignore me? I know you must be used to such requests. You must receive scores of them with regularity, and I ken I'm just another hopeful petitioner. It is impossible on parchment to convey my earnest need for you. I can only tell you that I, too, am a healer, and every soul I lose is a burden to my conscience. At first, I didn't suppose a man possessing the miracle of healing by touch could understand that, but then recalled that even the Saints endured trials. You are a man with a divine gift, but you are still a man. I know that at times you must feel helpless and alone as I do now. I cannot tell you the circumstances that separated my family for twelve years, but I have only just regained them, and I am now losing my father to a mysterious ailment. The loss of my mother was the catalyst for the events that tore my sisters and I from my father and each other. That is all I can say of that. I cannot bear to lose my father now when there's still so much unfinished. I feel so impotent when it seems as if there must be something I could do. Why would God give me this gift, then make it impossible to help those I loved the most? It vexes me terribly. Surely you can understand this and as a fellow healer will grant me this boon?

My hand has run away with me. I plead like a fool and make little sense. I think to tear this letter to shreds and start anew, but, I fear, you do not read them anyway, so what matter?

> *Your friend eternally,*
> *Rose MacDonell*
> *From the House of Lochlaire on x June*
> *The year of our Lord 1597*

William inhaled deeply, carefully refolding the parchment and tapping it against his thigh. He had replied to this letter. Twice. He'd burned both versions. That was the only reason he'd saved this letter, he told himself, and not very convincingly. Because the rawness of it—as if she'd opened a vein and bled onto the parchment for him alone—deserved an answer. And yet everything he wrote in response was inadequate, mere dressing to cushion the force of his reply. No. He would not help her. And she would not accept that answer.

He lifted the letter so that firelight reflected off the smooth surface of the parchment, smudged now from his many readings. She was here now, outside his walls. Would he really send her away without even talking to her? Without looking upon the face that had written these words? It seemed wrong to invite her in, to give her hope, and yet he needed to see her. It was a physical pull, a hole that somehow wanted filling.

He rubbed the corner of the letter thoughtfully against his chin. Perhaps there was a way.

Rose's clothes were soaked through so that she shivered violently, her teeth chattering, but still she sat in the meager protection of the gatehouse, rainwater pooling about her feet and bottom. She could see faint lights from the village, but the rain and fog obscured the cottages. Logic told her to get to her feet, walk to the village, and seek shelter. Her horse stood over her, head down, the rain beating onto her back.

Rose had told the porter to inform Lord Strathwick that she wasn't leaving until he spoke with her. The porter had warned her she would drown first, but she waited stubbornly. Her mother had always said she was obstinate, that when she got an idea in her head, she refused to let loose of it.

She buried her face in her cold, wet hands as another violent shiver racked her. It had taken a fortnight to get here, and not through easy terrain. It had been long and grueling and she'd done it alone, disguised as a lad. She'd looked forward to company on the return trip, eagerly anticipated long conversations with Strathwick about healing. Perhaps he'd even have been willing to teach her something.

Fool!

And still she sat, stubborn as an ass. She'd said she wouldn't leave until she spoke to him, and by God, she'd drown before she left this spot. Judging by the puddle forming around her, it appeared that might actually occur. Laughter rippled through her unexpectedly.

"Miss? Are you unwell?"

The deep, masculine voice startled her, and a jolt went through her. She dropped her hands and squinted upward, pushing back the sopping brim of her hat. A man towered over her, his plaid pulled over his head, shielding him from the rain and her scrutiny. His face was but a dark shadow, the features indistinct, leaving her only with the impression of great height and breadth.

"Just drowning," she said, then bit back a foolish smile.

He said nothing for a long moment, staring down at her. Though the dark and the plaid hid his expression, she sensed he frowned at her. Probably thought she was mad. Perhaps she was.

"Come," he said, his deep voice kind but impersonal. "You must get out of the rain."

His sudden presence and concern sparked hope. "Inside the castle?"

"No, I know someone in the village who will give you a place before their fire."

Rose sighed. "My thanks, but I'm not moving." She frowned up at him thoughtfully. "Are you from the castle? I didn't see anyone cross the bridge."

He hesitated, then nodded. "Aye, I work in the stables."

"Tell your master he can throw my bloated corpse in the moat when I drown. I'm not moving."

"I doubt he'll want your body floating in his moat, making the place smell, but make no mistake, you will die out here before he'll see you."

Rose's heart sank, and she found herself perilously close to tears for the first time in weeks. She'd held out such hope that Strathwick was the answer to her prayers, had traveled so far, for it to come to this. There was nothing more to do. Her father's cause was lost.

She held out her hand, resigned that she'd lost another battle. He stared at it for a moment, then grasped it. He was solid and warm, and again she felt a wave of despair, along with the urge to sob her story on this nice groom's shoulder. He pulled her to her feet and abruptly dropped her hand.

She turned and gazed up at the tall walls, at the black clouds boiling above.

"Can you tell me why he won't answer my letters? Why he won't even speak to me?"

The man had taken her horse's reins and had already turned Moireach around, ready to lead her across the bridge to the village.

"I know not, miss. I just work in the stables."

Rose turned to get a good look at her new friend. He was very tall, a head taller than her at least. His hair was dark, but that was all she could discern with his plaid covering it. He was a fine-looking man, clean-shaven, with a strong, unsmiling mouth. He had the broad, thick shoulders of someone used to hard work. His trews and boots were faded, though well made.

"What is your name, sir, so I might thank you for your kindness?" She slanted a poisonous glance at the castle. "You are far kinder than your master."

"Dumhnull."

"Well met, Dumhnull. My name is Rose, and you can tell your master that I will be back on the morrow." She looked upward and grimaced. "But for tonight, I think you're right. He cannot speak to a dead woman, can he?"

Dumhnull had yet to smile at her, and though he didn't

now she thought perhaps there was a softening to his stern mouth. His lips parted as if he meant to speak, then shut on an exhalation. Finally he raised his dark brows and said, "No, miss, I suppose he cannot." There was a curious note of forbearance in his voice, but before she could question it, he inclined his head for her to follow him.

She trudged after him, keeping her head down. The brim of her floppy hat bobbed with each step. It had long ceased protecting her from the deluge. Her hair was thoroughly soaked beneath the hat, plastered to her head and streaming in rivulets down the sides of her face and neck. She shivered convulsively, eagerly anticipating dry clothes and a warm fire.

They crossed the bridge and passed several cottages before he stopped near one. Fresh thatching repelled the rain so it flowed down to shower on the ground. Bags of sand pressed up against the base of the dark stones, preventing the rain from seeping underneath.

He nodded at it. "The blacksmith and his wife live there. They'll feed you and give you a place to sleep."

"My thanks, friend." Rose reached for the reins, but when her fingers closed over the leather, he didn't release them. She stood rather close to him. She tilted her head back to meet his eyes. Blue, brilliant as a sapphire and just as startling. She stared for a long moment, and he stared back. His gaze moved over her face in a manner overbold for a mere groom. Rose felt a moment of panic, her sisters' warnings echoing through her mind. He knew she was alone and unprotected. She held his gaze without wavering and tugged on the reins.

He released them and averted his eyes to scan the sky. "You really should be on your way in the morn, if the rain clears."

"I thank you for your warnings, but I cannot." She gave

him a speculative look from beneath her lashes. "Would you be willing to help me, Dumhnull?"

"How?"

"Sneak me in?"

He appeared scandalized at the suggestion. "Nay—you'd not want to do that, miss. Have you not heard the tales? He's a wizard, he's evil."

"Idle gossip spread by ignorant rustics. I pay it no heed."

He glanced around cautiously, then leaned in closer. She resisted the urge to step back. An uncomfortable fluttering had begun in her belly. He was so very large, and she was very much alone. Though he'd shown her nothing but kindness, his proximity unnerved her. But if he had any inappropriate intentions, it did not behoove her to show fear. She knew from experience that to men with mischief in mind, fear was oft an aphrodisiac, whereas courage nearly always discouraged them.

"The villagers have tried to capture him several times. He doesn't dare leave the castle."

Rose's mouth opened on an exhalation as she gazed up at her new friend. "But I mean him no harm. I—I know about that, about persecution. Not myself," she hastened to add when he drew back from her warily. "I— well, someone I knew."

He shook his head firmly. "Your sympathy is wasted, lass. Go home."

She gazed helplessly at him, but he just backed away. "Ask the blacksmith. He knows. He'll tell you true. But do not mention that anyone from the castle sent you. They hate us all."

She frowned at the cozy cottage, beckoning to her as she shivered in the rain. When she turned back, Dumhnull was gone.

* * *

She was welcomed by the blacksmith and his wife. The blacksmith was an enormous redhead named Tadhg, and he was beside himself with excitement when he learned Rose was a healer.

"Ack—my tooth, it aches and throbs. I cannot sleep, I cannot think of aught anymore but the tooth. It's my whole life." He sat, his brawny frame slumped in his chair, his thick-fingered hand cupping his copper-bearded cheek, looking thoroughly pathetic.

His short, stout wife placed a bowl of a thin broth and a chunk of dark bread before Rose, then stopped behind her husband, putting her hands on his shoulder. Her dark hair was caught back in a severe bun and her round face was dour, but she gazed at her husband with affection, kneading his shoulders.

"He moans so terribly at night, I cannot sleep at all, either. Is there aught you can do for him?"

"Do you not have a barber?" Rose asked, gratefully sipping the stew. The goodwife had loaned her a homespun shift that was too large but clean and warm. She sat huddled on the bench under a thick wool plaid while her clothes dried before the fire.

Tadhg shook his head. "Plague got him."

He gazed at Rose with such pained hope, his big hand rubbing his copper-bearded cheek.

She smiled reassuringly. "I'm sure there's something I can do. But tell me, why do you not go to your chief? I've heard he is a great healer."

Tadhg's face darkened. His wife turned away abruptly, returning to the hearth.

"He is not a healer. He is a sorcerer. He doesn't heal people, he gives them to the devil. I'd not let him touch me if he begged."

His wife turned from the cauldron she stirred, her cheeks

ruddy with affronted passion and her eyes dark slits in her doughy face. "Not that my lord would beg. Not him. He'd let us all die afore he'd soil his hands with any real healing, mind you."

Taken aback by their fervor, Rose said, "But the stories I've heard—"

"Och, there's stories all right," the older woman said.

Rose's shoulders slumped. "They're not true then."

"Oh, it's all true." Tadhg nodded sagely. "I've seen him do it myself."

He leaned back in his chair, the pain in his face easing at the prospect of a story. "It was about a year ago. Allister, my apprentice, was out cutting wood. His wee wife came by to bring him some dinner. He didn't know she was there, so he was startled. The ax slipped, and he cut her in the leg. He brought her here. We bound it up, but it festered and she fell into a fever. We knew the end was near. Allister had sent word to Lord Strathwick, but our chief never came. Allister was sore grieving there at the end, and went up to the castle himself, carrying on about how if the chief didn't save his Betty he'd have the MacKay's heart."

Rose leaned across her stew, listening with breathless interest. "Did that work?"

"Aye, it did. He came down, though you could tell just by looking at him he'd rather be any place else. He had a look at Betty's leg, then told her not to fear." Tadhg extended his thick, rough hands in front of him, his expression reverent. "He lay his hands on her leg. It took but a minute. When he lifted his hands, Betty's leg was as smooth as if the accident never happened. She was awake, too, blinking at us like an owl, asking what happened."

Rose sat back on the bench. "So that's it? He touched her leg and the wound disappeared? Did he say anything afterward?"

Tadhg dropped his hands to his knees. "Nay, he never stays after a healing. His brother comes with him, and they leave immediately. Never around long enough for a thank-ee sir."

Rose frowned, confused. "Why do you feel so ill about him? It sounds as if he could heal your tooth better than I could. I have no such magic."

Tadhg's bearded face distorted into a sneer of hatred. "Nay, I'll not let him mark me for the devil."

"What about Betty? He healed her. That is a miracle and you saw it. "

"No miracle—the devil's work. He made her into a witch."

"Really?" Rose said, skeptical. "How do you know? What did she do?"

"She told old Gannon that if the weather turned, his chickens would die. Sure enough, when it got cold last winter, two chickens did die. Allister also said that sometimes he saw her staring at his arm, or his foot, and the next day, he'd have cramps in the limb she'd been staring at. 'She be giving you the evil eye,' I said to him. So he turned her out, and several others drove her into the woods. But did she leave? No, she's with *him* now. A married woman, living in sin with the chief."

Rose raised her brows but didn't respond. Married or not, they'd exiled poor Betty. Rose couldn't blame her for going to her chief for succor. It was a terrible pass they'd come to if a wife could no longer look at her husband without being suspected of witchcraft.

Rose bedded down before the fire with several chickens, a pig, and a large goose. She found she could not sleep, in spite of the comfortable bed and full belly. She was besieged by thoughts of Lord Strathwick and Dumhnull and all Tadhg had said. She remembered Isobel's vision and was more convinced than ever that if she could only speak to the MacKay chief face-to-face she could convince him to aid her. He was not without mercy or kindness, otherwise he'd have left Betty to her fate—both times.

When Tadhg's peaceful snores joined the general snuffling, scratching, and rooting of the animals, Rose slid out from beneath the warmth of her blanket. The rain had stopped. She'd brought a clean shift and gown and had kept them dry by wrapping them in oiled canvas.

She dressed quietly before the fire, putting her boy's boots on and carrying her finer slippers.

She left coins on the blacksmith's table, gathered her things, and left the cottage. Moireach was stabled behind the cottage with the blacksmith's mule and goats. Rose decided to leave her there for now. She was determined to find a way in to Strathwick and it would be easier without a horse in tow.

She hurried along in the dark. She wore a dark plaid wrapped around her to aid in blending into the misty darkness. At the bridge leading to Strathwick she crouched low to the ground. Torches lit the ramparts, and two men-at-arms made a slow circuit of the walls. She tracked their path, and when they disappeared, she sprinted, racing across the bridge and up the path, stopping only when she was in the shelter of the wall. She pressed herself against it, breathing hard, her breath pluming out before her in a cloud. She clapped a plaid-covered hand over her mouth to hide it.

Her heart hammered in her ears as she waited. When she was certain she'd not been sighted, she crept along the berm, staying close to the wall. Dumhnull had left the castle somehow, and not through the gatehouse, as she'd been sitting by it and would have seen him.

She walked for some time, circling the castle and passing two drum towers before arriving at a postern door. There was no porter window on this door, so they'd have to open it if they wanted to see who was there.

She drew her dirk from her boot and set her bundle aside. She took a deep breath, preparing herself, and hid the dirk in the folds of her skirt. She hammered on the door purposefully.

It opened almost immediately, as if someone waited on the other side. She rushed in the open door. A woman stood on the other side, her mouth opened in almost comical surprise.

She came at Rose, frantically trying to push her back out the open doorway. Rose quickly sidestepped, pressing herself against the wall just inside the door.

"Oh, no! You must go!" The woman grabbed Rose's arm and tried dragging her.

The woman was shorter than Rose was, but stouter. Still, when Rose dug in her heels, the woman could not budge her.

"I'm going nowhere until I speak with Lord Strathwick."

The woman ran away, shouting for help. Rose panicked. Men-at-arms would come, prepared to deal with an intruder, and she would be thrown out or worse. Rose sprinted after the woman, fear spurring her to recklessness. The woman was easily caught but not so easily restrained. She fought, arms flailing, screaming and scratching. Rose grappled desperately with her as two men appeared, afraid she might inadvertently stab the woman or herself in the battle.

"Be still, woman, before I cut you," Rose hissed in her ear. Even to her own ears she sounded dangerously unstable.

The woman finally grew still, though she trembled and moaned.

The men stopped in their tracks, hands out in a calming gesture. The other man was younger, a comely man, with thick black hair and dark, angry eyes. He had drawn his sword and looked ready to hack her in two. So much for looking pitiful.

Rose looked from one man to the other, her hand shaking so violently that she feared she would nick the woman inadvertently. She glared at the men. "Take me to Lord Strathwick or I slit her gullet." Rose would never do such a thing, but it sounded sufficiently threatening, and she was desperate.

Apparently some of that desperation showed in her eyes. The men exchanged an alarmed look. The dark man lowered his sword but did not sheath it.

The blond man took a deep breath, his hands still out in a calming gesture. "Put it down, Mistress MacDonell. No need to hurt anyone."

Rose nearly dropped her dirk in astonishment. He knew her name! But there was no time to ask how he knew her. She pulled the woman's hair back, exposing more neck. "Bring me to him, damn it, or she dies!"

The woman whimpered and snuffled, and the men just stood there, watching Rose as if she were a wild animal, which she supposed she was at the moment. She *felt* wild— capable of nearly anything—which was both frightening and exhilarating.

"Now!" she bellowed to emphasize her point. The woman she held flinched and let out a squeak of terror.

But still the men made no move to comply with her demands. Rose was scrambling for her next course of action when she noted the blond man's gaze dart to something behind her.

Rose tried to jerk around, but she wasn't quick enough. Her wrist was seized and her dirk yanked downward, away from the woman's throat. Another arm snaked around her waist and hauled her off her feet. The woman ran, throwing herself into the blond man's arms. Rose fought her captor, frenzied with fear and confusion, legs kicking gracelessly in the air, her free arm flailing. The hand holding her wrist squeezed until she dropped the dirk.

Her captor dropped her abruptly. She fell hard on her posterior, knocking the air from her lungs. She scrambled around, gasping for air and wincing at the pain in her backside.

"Dumhnull!" she gasped, then shut her mouth tightly. She didn't want to cause him trouble, but she feared it was too late. She glanced at the other men. The black-haired one frowned severely at Dumhnull.

The groom leaned over to pick up her dirk, avoiding her gaze. His head was uncovered now, and she saw that he was older than she'd initially thought. Gray streaked his black hair, and though his face was unlined, the set of his jaw was rigid, and his beautiful eyes were hard and flat.

He was angry with her for her brutal entrance after his kindness. She couldn't blame him. She wondered if he would help her still, or even if he could, as a mere groom. She continued to gaze at him, her heart still racing, but he refused to look at her. She was caught now, at their mercy, without a single ally. She closed her eyes, rejecting the urge to capitulate. She was here, in Strathwick. She couldn't give up yet.

She turned her attention to the other men. "I'm here to see Lord Strathwick. I'll not leave until I see him." Her bravado elicited some amused glances and an exclamation of disbelief from the black-haired man, but she rose to her knees and raised her chin.

The comely black-haired man stepped forward, his mouth curved into a sneer of contempt. "*I'm* Lord Strathwick."

A jolt of surprise went through Rose. She closed her eyes

in horror. This was worse than she'd thought. It would have been bad enough having him hear about what she'd done secondhand; she still might have been able to talk her way out of it, charm him. But he'd witnessed her chasing one of his people down and holding a dirk to her throat.

Against her will and pride, she looked back at Dumhnull, unable to hide the blind panic building inside her. He still would not look at her. He tapped her dirk thoughtfully against his thigh, staring at his chief with an odd intensity.

Rose turned back to Strathwick. She spread her hands before her, trying to appear submissive and contrite—not difficult, as she still knelt in the dirt. "I pray you, my lord, just hear me out. If you still refuse me after speaking to me, I vow to leave you in peace."

Lord Strathwick approached her slowly, his slashing black brows lowered over dark blue eyes. He circled her, looking her up and down. Finally he stood before her, his expression scornful, but he said, "Very well, then. Follow me." His gaze jerked behind her. "You, too, *Dumhnull.*" He turned abruptly and stalked toward the castle.

Rose let out an astonished breath, weakness flooding her limbs.

Dumhnull grasped her arm and pulled her to her feet. "Looks as if you've gotten your way, miss."

From his grim expression, she wasn't at all certain that was a good thing.